Alpha Leo
and
The Heart of Fire

Copyright © 2022 Moonlight Muse
Edited by Morrigan Sinclair & Sara A. Gossman
Cover Art by Moorbook Designs
Interior Art by Ced Designs
Typsetted by Sara A. Gossman

ISBN: 978-1-915720-17-7 (ebook)
ISBN: 978-1-915720-18-4 (standard softback)
ISBN: 978-1-915720-20-7 (special edition)

All rights reserved.

www.authormoonlightmuse.com

Alpha Leo and the Heart of Fire

Moonlight Muse

Other Works by Moonlight Muse

The Alpha Series
Book 1 – Her Forbidden Alpha
Book 2 – Her Cold-Hearted Alpha
Book 3 – Her Destined Alpha
Book 4 – Caged between the Beta & Alpha
Book 5 – King Alejandro: The Return of Her Cold-Hearted Alpha

The Power of Bonds Saga
(The Alpha Series Remastered)
Book 1 – My Forbidden Alpha
Book 2 – My Only Luna
Book 3 – My Beloved Alpha
Book 4 – My Dauntless Luna
Book 5 – My Cold-Hearted Alpha
Book 6 – My Blessed Luna
Book 7 – My Destined Alpha
Book 8 – My Hybrid Luna
Book 9 – My Cursed Alpha
Book 10 – My Bite-Sized Luna
Book 11 – The Shadow of Past Sins
Book 12 – Under the Lycan King's Reign

The Rossi Legacies
(Spin-off to The Alpha Series)
Book 1 – Alpha Leo and the Heart of Fire
Book 2 – Leo Rossi: The Rise of a True Alpha
Book 3 – The Lycan Princess and the Temptation of Sin
Book 4 – Skyla Rossi: A Game of Deception and Lies
Book 5 – The Pure-Hearted Princess and the Kiss of Darkness
Book 6 – Kataleya Rossi: A Love to Claim

**The Untold Tales of The Power of Bonds Saga
and The Rossi Legacies Series**
A collection of short novellas
Book 1 – Beautiful Bond
Book 2 – Precious Bond

Magic of Kaeladia Series
Book 1 – My Alpha's Betrayal: Burning in the Flames of his Vengeance
Book 2 – My Alpha's Retribution: Rising from the Ashes of his Vengeance

The Ruthless Kings Trilogy
Book 1 – The Alpha King's Possession
Book 2 – The Dragon King's Seduction
Book 3 – The Fae King's Redemption

Power of Three Series
Book 1 – I Am The Luna
Book 2 – She Is The Alpha
Book 3 – The Alpha In Me
Book 4 – The Luna For Me

Standalones
His Caged Princess
Mr. CEO, Please Marry My Mommy
Till Death Do Us Lie

Daughters of the Moon Series
Book 1 – His Dark Obsession
Book 2 – His Fated Obsessio
Book 3 – His Secret Desire

*To all my readers who love
a tatted bad boy, this one's for you!*

Contents

My Nightmares	1
Kingdom of Sin	6
His Dangerous Temptation	10
Out of Control	15
Devastation	22
My Decision	28
Not the Plan	34
A Compromise	40
A Painful Surprise	47
Struggles	52
My Life	57
The Sangue Pack	65
Cookies and a Voodoo Doll	74
Discussions and Decisions	79
His Return	87
An Outsider	93
His Hope	99
A Memory	106
You'll Never Understand	113
Restlessness	119
Flames of Destruction	124
Shaken	130
An End	137
A Strange Result	143
A Reply	150
Coming Clean	156
A Lie	164
Will You Believe Me	170
Do I Trust Him	176
Was I Not Enough	182
Crepes with Corrado	189
Losing It	196

A Blinding Awakening	202
Refusing to Fail	210
These Emotions	217
Battle of Wills	225
The Path Ahead	230
The Choice to Make	234
A Sizzling Dinner	242
Something I've Never Shared	251
You Don't Know the Pain	257
Passion and Confusion	263
Everything is in Place	271
A Showdown	279
Letting Her Misunderstand	286
Hitting Home	293
Speaking the Truth	300
Family	308
A Call	315
A Devil in Red	320
A Shared Moment of Truth	325
Hitting a Nerve	331
These Choices of Ours	336
A Disappointing Failure	344
A Mama	350
The Beginning of a Haze	355
All I Want	363
Pushing Boundaries	370
Something I Wasn't Expecting	378
The Black Storm Alpha	385
A Mansion Full of Rossis	394
Talk between Four Alphas	402
A Punishment	410
Boys' Night Out	415
Building Bridges	423
Knowing the Answer	430
A Turn of Events	437

My Nightmares
Azura

The laughter rings in my ears, but there is nothing merry about it, filled with malice and jeers.

"Go on!"

"Awe, what's wrong? Too much of a wimp?"

"You're meant to be the boss' woman, can't you do it? Too weak?"

I freeze, standing between my boyfriend and his men. They are torturing someone who I don't even recognise in his wolf form, but what else is new? This is the usual for them. I always try to ignore his ways and stay out of his business, trying to focus on the good in him instead, but today, they expect me to join in with their sick games. I don't want to do this. Staring at the bloody mass on the ground, my stomach churns. This is not meant to happen.

"Just pull the trigger." His voice is devoid of emotions. His cold, murky eyes meet mine as he holds the gun out to me.

"I... I'm not so sure about this. This isn't what you told me," I reply calmly, despite the way my stomach is twisting with nerves.

"Not even for me, my little pet?" He tilts his head, looking at me whilst the rest of his friends spur me on.

I stare at the gun, trying to think of how I got here but I don't know when I fell into this toxic relationship. I'm not someone who needs sympathy. I've never been one who can't sleep at night because of my demons. I'm always carefree, unbothered, and wild. I love to have fun, crush on the good-looking boys in my class or whatever hot alpha crosses my path. But now... I find myself tossing and turning, trying to push away the nightmares my so-called boyfriend has pulled me into.

"Please, come on, let's forget this." I try to shrug it off, wrapping my arms around his neck and hoping he listens.

His scent fills my nose, mixed with the smell of cigarettes and drugs. His hands stroke my waist, and I try to remember the man I fell in love with. Where has he gone?

"Forget what? Oh yeah, forget what he called you? Let me rephrase that, little pet. You don't want to be an outcast, do you? The outsider... the odd one out... the freak?" His tone is a cold sneer as his eyes burn into mine.

Freak.

My heart thumps as I stare at the bloody wolf on the ground.

I'm not a freak. I am Azura Rayne Westwood, daughter of the previous Alpha of the Blood Moon Pack. Even though I'm a child born in a way that played with the very laws of nature, I'm not a freak.

I should be dead, but I'm not.

"Freak. Freak. Freak," his men begin to chant, only making the anger rise within me. He smirks, knowing it's getting to me, making me yank away from his hold. My heart thumps violently as I snatch the weapon from his hand.

I remember when I was a child; I didn't understand why I was disliked. Occasionally there were kids in the pack whispering behind my back, but they didn't dare to do anything to me because I was the daughter of their Alpha. Plus, I was not someone to mess with. I always made anyone who tried to hurt me or those I loved suffer. However, there is one name that never left me – The Freak.

"Do it."

I look at my boyfriend. He knows I hate that term, but he still uses it. It's my fault. I'm the one who was blind enough to tell him my darkest secrets.

"Fine," I spit as I turn, pretending to do his bidding and raise the gun. What should I do?

"Shoot him, baby." His quiet voice, laced with a deadly warning, comes from right behind me.

My hand shakes as I stare at the whimpering wolf on the floor.

His breathing is so shallow...

No amount of logic makes this okay.

I am not going to do this, but the urge to turn around and shoot my so-called boyfriend instead tempts me. I lower my weapon, the laughter fading as a tense silence falls at my act of disobedience.

"I'm not going- "

I gasp when something knocks into me from behind, making me accidentally pull the trigger. The body on the ground shivers before it stills.

"No!" I scream, dropping the gun as I run to the wolf's side. No, no, no!

Laughter follows me as I look at the wolf before me. I can't feel his heartbeat, but he doesn't even shift to his human form. Whatever those bullets contain is deadly. It is so fast that he couldn't even shift back.

"Why, Judah?" I scream.

Silence falls as I glare at the man who stands there, his cold eyes on me. Although he says nothing, the anger in his eyes makes my blood run cold. He hates to be disrespected.

"You do not talk to me like that," he whispers menacingly as he strides over to me. Grabbing a fistful of the wolf's bloody fur, he lifts his body from the ground in one sweep. "You did this."

With those words, he throws the heavy body of the dead wolf on top of me, the weight crushing my legs.

"Do you feel sorry for him? Here, take care of him!" he snarls as I glare back at him. My anger rises as I try to push the body of the wolf off me. "Who said you can get up, my pet?"

"This is not a joke! I'm done with you and your sick ways," I spit resentfully. He's no different from all of the others. In fact, he's worse.

His eyes darken, and he grabs a fistful of my hair.

"Oh, we aren't done until I say we are," he snarls menacingly.

"You don't own me, and I am not your pet!" I hiss, glaring at him in defiance.

He simply laughs loudly, like my childish words amuse him, but I know better. He is beyond angry; I have just disrespected him in front of his men. He won't forgive that.

"You will not disobey me again. Understood, Freak?"

"Yeah, I will. I'm done with you," I spit, my heart pounding with rage.

He tugs my head back violently and, using the hand that he had grabbed the wolf with, he rubs the blood over my face before shoving me roughly onto the ground.

"I think it's time I show you exactly who you belong to," he spits as he hits me across the face, making my vision darken...

I lurch upright in bed. My entire body is soaked with sweat as the memories of that night fill my mind once more. My heart is thumping violently as I look around, and it takes me a few moments to realise I am in my bedroom. Safe.

Taking a shaking breath, I get out of bed and walk to the adjoining bathroom, splashing my face with water.

It has been a year since I walked away from my toxic ex. One year since I thought I was done with him for good, until two days ago when I received a video of that night along with a message.

Unknown caller: Remember that I know what you did.

My stomach knots, feeling sick as the words ring in my head. I turn the tap off and take a deep breath, returning to my bedroom.

I'm safe here... right?

No matter how many times I think it over, I don't know how I got involved with him. The worst part is that if my parents knew, they would be more than disappointed in me, and the one thing I hate the most is letting them down.

Even though my parents are no longer the Alphas, with my brother having taken over, they are still highly respected. Their reputation is known across the country, and Dad is on the Alpha King's Council. He is also one of the Elite Eleven, a title that has been unofficially given to the selection of the most powerful alphas of our time, and here I am making things worse for them.

I wish I never met Judah, and I wish I could turn back time. Glancing at the clock, I realise it's five in the morning. I should try to get some rest. I turn the lamp off just as my phone beeps. Tensing, I frown as I stare at the sleek device. Taking a deep breath, I unlock it and read the message.

> **Unknown caller: Can't sleep? Well, I'll give you something more to think about. Come back to me, or I think your entire family would love to watch all those videos. Do you want them to see exactly how FREAKY their little girl can get?**

I know what other videos he means, and it makes me sick.

I cover my mouth unconsciously, my stomach twisting sickeningly as I glance towards my window. He is watching me. I walk over to the window and peer out. My heart thumps as I scan the darkness outside.

Nothing.

I can't see anything out of the ordinary... is he just messing with me?

My phone beeps again, and I look down at the new message that pops up on the screen, a message that makes my blood run cold.

> **Unknown caller: I see you still sleep in your underwear.**

Kingdom of Sin
Azura

The red and purple lights dance and flash around me, highlighting the bodies of the exotic dancers on the stage. Strippers in expensive lingerie and perfume walk around serving drinks or looking for potential customers. The dark teal booths are half-full, some with men and women enjoying the show, whilst others enjoy a lap dance. A few men in suits are being escorted away by dancers to the private rooms.

Kingdom of Sin is a human strip club in the heart of one of the busiest cities in the country, a place quite far away from my home, and the chance of running into someone I know is unlikely. Not to mention I have used an X2 scent disguiser, a formula which will make me smell like a human to other werewolves.

I don't want Judah to find me here. The fact that he may have been in my town makes my stomach twist, although I keep telling myself he had just guessed what I was wearing.

I need a break from my mind and those messages. The entire day I have been unable to focus on anything. To make matters worse, tonight is the Blood Moon, an occurrence that only happens twice a year.

It's a night when unmated wolves head to one of the Blood Moon Gatherings to see if they can scout out their fated mates. I don't want to go. I'm done with men, and I don't want to be tied down to anyone. After going through a relationship that was a complete failure, I have no expectations of finding my true mate, nor do I think I am mentally up for it. Even though I do want to find my mate, and deep down I want that love that I see those around me have, I'm not sure he would want me. I don't need my heart broken again. Although I won't admit it, I am a little afraid of what he will think of me, how he will hate me when he learns about my past about the skeletons in my closet. Will my mate accept everything about me, or will he simply despise me? Or worse, reject me?

The tasteful music relaxes me a lot. I am tapping my foot to the beat as I sit in a booth, staring at the sexy woman dancing on the stage. Her body sways sensually to the beat.

I down my glass of whisky, wishing there was something stronger here. The liquid burns my throat, my eyes stinging a little as my mind returns to the messages. There is a strict no-phone policy that is enforced in this club, and if I had my phone with me, I know I would be staring at it constantly, thinking about the messages. I need a break from it – from him. Nothing scares me, nothing rocks me, but something about him gets to me.

I pour myself another glass as a gorgeous brunette comes over, ready to entertain me, but I'm not in the mood.

"No thanks." I flash the gorgeous brunette a grin and wink.

I glance around, observing that most of those in this club are affluent businessmen. Grabbing my glass, I gulp it down. I close my eyes for a second before refilling my glass once more.

My mind is a storm of emotions.

Judah has too much on me. Things he is using to blackmail me. I know I can just tell someone, and we can deal with this, but all my life I just cause problems for everyone. There is something about him that just isn't normal. Something that tells me he is more than just a werewolf...

I have drunk a lot, emptying the last drops of my fourth bottle into my glass. I am beginning to feel it is taking a little effect. This is what I need.

I close my eyes, letting the music envelope my senses. Tonight, I just want a break. I'll deal with the messages another day.

I open my eyes, looking through my thick lashes at the women on stage. I love dancing, and something about pole dancing just feels empowering and exhilarating. If done right, it truly is an art.

I had actually applied for a job just over a year ago at a club near home, and I got it, too, but I only managed to do one session before my brother found out. I shudder, remembering the rage in Liam's eyes when he stormed into the club and saw the men with their eyes on me. Although I usually have him wrapped around my finger, on the rare occasions when he does get angry, well, let's just say, yeah. No. Big no! Do not get Liam angry. I prefer him to stick to being an oversized dense puppy, but he's still my favourite.

Maybe I should go dance.

I stand up, making my way over to the dance floor, which is off through a pair of double doors, and running my fingers through my hair when I freeze. A familiar smoky smell hits me, and my heart thuds.

He is here.

Fear that I rarely feel envelopes me, and I scan the area wishing I hadn't worn such high heels.

Keeping my head low, I pray that the scent disguiser works. I need to get out of here. I see a hooded man by the entrance, and a shiver runs down my spine. It's him. He seems to be searching for something.

For me.

Spotting a pair of doors leading to the VIP area open, a woman in a tiny skirt and revealing blouse steps out with a keycard in her hand, giving me an idea. She struts towards the bar, and I head towards her, accidentally-on-purpose bumping into her. I mumble an apology as I swipe the card from her pocket.

My heart is pounding. The fear that he will find me makes me sick. Why can't he just let me go?

I scan the card, take a discreet glance around, and slip through the doors that click open. I just need a place to wait around until he leaves. If he had entered our pack, then he must know that is my bike out there.

"Did you hear that?"

I freeze. Werewolves? I can smell them. What on earth is going on? This is a human club, right?

"I don't recognise that scent. Did someone sneak in?"

Oh, shit.

I look around, frowning. Three corridors lead off from here. Silently, I hurry down the left one and up the flight of steps, thanking the Goddess for the carpeted halls to muffle my footsteps. To my relief, I see a pair of glass doors that are standing open. I rush inside, closing them behind me and let out a breath of relief.

I am in a large room that looks down upon the club. From here, I can see everything. I am sure from down below this is just part of the mirrored design of the ceiling, or what I had thought was the ceiling. I look around the room; the floor is a glittering black marble, with two blue velvet sofas and a glass table at the centre. A bar with drinks stands to the side, but no matter where you look, this room gives the perfect view of the show put on below, without the smell of sweat or arousal hanging in the air.

Should I wait around here? What should I do? Goddess, what have I gotten myself into? My phone is in the locker, too.

Suddenly the sound of footsteps and talking reaches my ears. They are approaching fast. Looking around, I see the bar, my heart thumping as I quickly hide underneath it. I peep out from the side, spotting several men coming closer. Two men get to the door first, holding them open for the rest. My heart sinks when I realise there are a few werewolves present as well. From their suits and their dangerous appearances, each man clearly means business, but it is the one in the centre that stands out, pulling my attention to him entirely.

Not only is he an alpha, but the power and dominance that roll off him are so intense I almost forget to breathe. Everyone else seems to fade away as I stare at the man in the middle. He wears a fitted black shirt, his sleeves rolled up, with black pants and boots. He holds his jacket over his shoulder on one finger, and despite the darkness in the club, he wears a pair of shades. His chocolate-coloured hair is styled sexily. From what I can tell, his entire neck, arms, and hands are covered in tattoos. Then, my heart lurches when the most intoxicating, orgasm-inducing scent hits me: woody and dangerously seductive, with a hint of blood mandarin, warm cinnamon, and patchouli. The scent is coming from none other than the alpha male in the centre.

He pauses, tensing as he turns his head slightly. He has smelt me.

The restlessness of my wolf and the pounding of my heart is no longer under my control. Every cell in my body is going haywire as I stare at none other than the god before me. My mate.

His Dangerous Temptation
Azura

I move back, my heart thumping. He must have heard me. He must have smelt me.

What the hell do I do? Judah is dangerous, but the man standing a few metres from me screams of power and danger of a far higher calibre. I need to get out of here before he sees me, but how do I do that?

"We can continue this another day. Reschedule," his deep, velvety voice that sends shivers of desire through me orders.

Oh, fuck, that voice is hot. Come on, Azura, breathe steadily and focus.

"Ah, of course."

"Absolutely."

I don't dare move as I hear the rest recede, but my mate remains. The doors shut, and I close my eyes in defeat. He's still here.

"Why don't you step out from your hiding spot?" His voice suggests.

I close my eyes. Any dream I have that I would be able to escape from him is gone. Slowly I stand up and turn, staring at the man before me. If I had thought he was the epitome of sexiness and dominance before, he is a thousand times hotter when you see him properly. His scent intoxicates me. I feel lightheaded as he slowly removes his shades, and I look into a pair of the coldest ice-blue eyes I have ever seen; eyes that trail over me but give away nothing.

He is tall, maybe around six-foot-six. His muscular arms strain with his bulging biceps. I notice that he has three piercings in his right ear and one in his left.

"Who would have thought I'd be given a human…" he mutters so quietly I almost don't hear him.

"I'm not human," I reply coldly. He looks into my eyes with a glimmer of interest in his cold ones.

"Then join me for a drink."

It isn't an offer but a command.

The very temptation to turn and run away from him consumes me, but I can't. As much as I hadn't wanted to find my mate, the curiosity to know what kind of person the Goddess has made for me wins, and I find myself nodding.

He comes over to the bar. I have to admit that his posture and attitude speak volumes. This is a man who knows what he wants, and he gets it. The temptation to tell him about Judah and why I am up here almost overcomes me, but I can't. This is not his fight, and he hasn't asked why I am up here. Something tells me I have walked straight into the wolf's den.

"Do you like your drink strong or light?" he asks after dropping his jacket onto the sofa.

"Strong, although I don't think there's anything you have to offer that could work on me," I muse, staring at the window that looks down upon the club.

"Don't be so sure," he replies arrogantly. I turn to him as he pours a green liquid into two glasses before he holds one out to me.

"What is this?" I ask, looking at it curiously.

"Absinthe," he replies with a small, cold smirk before he raises the glass. I clink mine against his, looking surprised. Absinthe…

"Isn't this illegal here?" I ask, unable to stop the curiosity that seeps into my mind.

"Being up here without permission is illegal, too. This is the only drink that can really take the edge away. Clearly, four bottles of whiskey didn't work for you," he remarks mockingly. My heart skips a beat. Had he seen me? I look down below, only to see the booth I was sitting at is in plain sight.

"So you were watching me?"

"You may have caught my eye. Not many women do." I don't miss the 'many' in that sentence.

He steps closer, and I find myself looking into those dangerous eyes of his.

"You wanted to run when you realised that we are mates."

He knows.

I take a sip of the alcohol. Oh, this is strong... the taste is intense, but I like it.

"I think you would actually be happy if I run. I'm a nightmare you do not want in your life."

"Funny that you should refer to yourself as a nightmare. You look far from one, but even I know not everything that looks like a dream is one."

I can't deny the fluttering in my stomach at his words. As he downs his glass of absinthe, my eyes dip to his Adam's apple. Damn, the boy is sizzling. I feel a clench in my core and avert my gaze.

Deep down, something tells me not to do this. I don't know anything about him, but he seems to be the boss of this club, and he is definitely an alpha. Who though? I have seen many alphas. Okay, not really. Damn, I wish I had paid more attention, but I don't care for them. I'm always too busy in my own world.

"You don't want to find your mate? Good. Neither do I."

"Then, why didn't you just walk away?" I ask.

"I wanted to see exactly what the Goddess created for me."

"And?" I find myself asking, my stomach fluttering.

His icy-blue eyes trail over me, and I see them flash a stunning steel blue as they fall on my breasts. If his gaze alone can have such an effect on me, then what will his touch feel like? He steps closer, and I find myself backing away until my ass touches the glass behind me.

"If we're going on looks alone, better than expected."

My core throbs at his words. How does someone I have just met have such an intense effect on me?

"You're an alpha, that's undeniable, but what pack- "

He cuts me off by placing the back of the hand that holds his glass against my lips. The crazy fireworks that erupt from his touch are dizzying, sending a dangerous jolt to my core. It makes sense... all of it. The way the mated couples around me are so love-crazed. All they want is to be next to their mates. Just a single touch from someone I don't even know is driving me nuts, and I am unable to stop myself from softly kissing the fingers that are pressing against my lips. His eyes flash a steely blue as our eyes meet, and the moment he removes his hands, I slowly lick my lips before taking another sip of the strong alcohol.

Turning my back to him, I stare down at the club below. My core is throbbing, and I know if I drink this entire glass, I will be pretty high. I see him pour himself another glass and down it in one go before he places it on the bar counter and walks back over to me. I look at him once again, turning towards him as he steps closer. This time the gap between us is almost non-existent. I can smell his addictive scent, feel the heat from his body, and hear the steady beating of his heart. All of it consumes me.

"Two glasses, and you seem perfectly sober. I'm impressed," I whisper, trying to break the intense sexual tension that is ripping me apart with desire. He rests his arm against the glass above my head, forcing me to back up against it.

"I didn't think you would be that easily impressed." His eyes stare down at me, and I notice his thick lashes. I could picture waking up to this hunk every day...

"I do have pretty high standards in some departments," I reply haughtily, staring into his eyes.

The faintest smirk crosses his lips as he runs the knuckles of his free hand down my waist, making my heart thump in anticipation. His body is barely inches from mine, and the urge to press my thighs together is incredibly strong.

"Good. Let's just hope you can handle me," he replies seductively. We are chest to chest, and he parts my legs with his knee, making my core clench.

"Shall we try and see?" I ask, a challenging glint in my eyes.

He may be an alpha, but I'm not just anyone. Still holding my glass, I lock my arm around his neck, pressing myself against him and placing my free hand on his abs.

"Confident," he muses, running his fingers up the side of my waist, still so tantalisingly slowly that the urge to moan overwhelms me, but I keep it in.

"Incredibly. I am not a submissive little good girl."

"See, the thing is..." he trails off, smirking as he presses his body against me. "Good girls get fucked, and bad girls... bad girls get punished. Which is it going to be?" His tone makes me bite my lip, my arousal scenting the air, and I know he can smell it.

"Then you're going to have to punish me, Alpha," I whisper, hooking my fingers into his belt and pulling him against me just as he grabs my hair.

His lips meet mine in one incredibly mind-blowing, hungry kiss that sends pleasure erupting through my body. Tingles and sparks ripple through me wave after wave as his lips dominate mine, fuelled by power, hunger, and desire, a kiss that is out of this world and one that I know has ruined all men for me.

I hear my glass shatter as it hits the floor behind him, but neither of us cares.

His plush lips are heaven and sin all at once, and I find myself fighting for dominance. Our tongues dance against one another as our hands travel over the other's bodies, feeling and groping every inch that we can get our hands on. His tongue is pierced, and the sensation of it feels so damn good. My body is on fire, my pussy clenching at his touch. It is rough yet sensual, turning me on so strongly that I am unable to hold back the sounds of pleasure that leave my lips. I moan, feeling his huge, hard cock press against my stomach. Oh, fuck.

I want to pull his pants down and take his cock in my mouth, but before I can even begin to undo his belt, he pulls back, his eyes a dazzling steel blue.

"Let's get the fuck out of here," he growls huskily, breathing hard as he looks me over. I nod, not needing to be told twice. I want him here and now.

Oh, Goddess, I'm done for.

Out of Control
Azura

We take a back exit where a sleek black car is waiting for us. I don't see the driver; my focus is on the man before me. The moment we are in the car, he pulls me on top of him. I straddle him, welcoming the feeling of intoxication he brings. I don't need ten bottles of whiskey or several glasses of absinthe to forget everything. This works.

He pulls my jacket off me, and I help, reaching behind and pulling it down from my wrists before tossing it to the ground. His eyes are on my breasts, his hands running down my arms. I lock them around his neck, tangling one hand through his delicious chocolate locks.

Oh, fuck, he is so handsome.

Our lips meet once more in a sinful kiss. I gyrate my hips against his crotch, his grip tightening on my waist, the other squeezing my ass.

"Fuck," he growls, sucking on my neck.

I tilt my head back, my eyes fluttering shut as rivers of pleasure rock through me. His hand twists in my hair as his lips trail down my collarbone, kissing, sucking, and nipping at my smooth skin. He grabs my breast, making me swear in pleasure. I don't want any items of clothing between us, but just when I think he'll yank my top down, the car comes to a stop.

The door is opened for us, and I realise we are in an underground car park. His hands never leave me, and I am not bothered that the suited man who has opened the door is right there. Instead, he carries on kissing my shoulders and neck roughly as he guides me to the lift. The moment his thumbprint is scanned, the doors open, and he pushes me up against the wall of the lift, pressing a button before he has my wrists pinned against the wall, his lips meeting mine once more. I moan into his mouth, feeling his hard shaft against me.

Oh, fuck.

When the doors open, we carry on making out passionately as he guides us down the hall and through to a bedroom. The feeling of his hands on me is like a slice of heaven itself. Any logic or sense of self is gone. All I want is him. It is all I crave.

The bedroom door opens, and the cool air-conditioning touches our heated skin. I pull open the buttons of his shirt, wanting him naked.

This place smells of him, and I love it.

For a moment, I pull away, staring down at the fully tatted body of the god before me. Oh, fuck, he is totally drool-worthy. The type of guy my girls and I would strip for any day. Every ridge and curve of his body is chiselled to perfection. His Adonis belt dips into his belt, and my hands instantly go there, raking down his abs. With the other, I pull his shirt off completely just as he grabs my neck, pulling me closer and kissing me more whilst I begin working to take his belt off.

His hands reach for the hooks on my top and undo them swiftly. Someone is an expert.

His eyes rake over me as he grabs my breasts, squeezing them as he kisses me harder. The moment I have his zip down, I pull away from his perfect lips. As much as I want to keep kissing him, I want something else between my lips…

I crouch down sexily, keeping my eyes locked with his steely blue ones and undo his pants, yanking them down. My long black nails graze his hips, my core throbbing when I look at the sight before me. Ink covers his V-cut and thighs, spreading over his hips. There are words and quotes alongside the images that I am curious to learn about, but not as much as I want to see the monster of a cock that he is packing. I pull his boxers down his muscular thighs. He is perfectly groomed, just the way I like it, with just a sprinkle of trimmed hair. His balls are hard, and as for his cock... not only is it fucking huge, putting any that I have seen to shame, but there is also a ladder of piercings running along the entire underside of the shaft right up to the mushroom tip. Ten perfect parallel bars.

Oh, Goddess.

"What's the matter? Never see a Jacob's Ladder before?"

"No," I find myself saying as I wrap my hands around it and begin stroking it. His head tilts back slightly, but his eyes still hold mine as I stick my tongue out, licking the tip where a pearly white drop of pre-cum sits, begging to be sucked off.

"Fuck," he swears the moment I wrap my lips around him and begin sucking him harder.

I have never seen a man look hotter while in the throes of pleasure than the one above me. His hair isn't as slick as it had been when I first saw him, thanks to me running my fingers through it on the way here. It is now a hot, smoking mess, one that only makes me want to yank it even more.

His eyes find mine, his hand pulling my hair as he begins thrusting faster into my mouth. I almost gag, breathing through my nose and relaxing as his dick hits the back of my throat. My lips are fully stretched around him, burning at the friction. He is huge, and this feels so good. His body tenses as he begins thrusting harder, shoving his dick fully down my throat roughly. I choke as he pulls out, making me gasp for air, only for him to ram it down my throat again. I moan against him, my pussy aching for more. He swears, pulling out, and, with a few swift strokes, comes all over my breasts. I stick my tongue out, making it obvious what I want, and he taps his cock on it, making me whimper as I taste his salted caramel-like cum. Oh, I wouldn't mind making this my favourite dessert.

A sexy smirk crosses his lips, and he yanks me up, kissing my neck as he quickly unzips my pants, pulling them down in one swift movement. Crouching down, he peels my panties off, taking a moment to admire me before his tongue flicks between my pussy lips.

"Oh, fuck!" My head hits the wall behind me, and my entire body shakes with electrifying bolts of pleasure as his tongue flicks my clit, his ball piercing only adding to the sensation. Oh, Goddess, this is...

He lifts my leg, and unashamedly, I drape it over his shoulder, threading my fingers through his hair as I become lost in the pleasure of his touch. I wish I didn't come this fast. I want to revel in this pleasure for so much longer.

The moment my release hits me, he pulls away, standing and yanking me into his arms as he shoves his tongue into my mouth, allowing me to taste myself as my body convulses in pleasure. I can barely focus, the aftermath of that sizzling orgasm rocking me. I gasp for air as I cling to him.

His hands cup my ass, squeezing hard as he lifts me up. I lock my legs around his waist, feeling his cock brush against my pussy, sending a dangerous jolt through me. He pushes me up against the wall just as he thrusts into me. I gasp, feeling the pressure of having something so fucking big in me. *Damn, my dildo does not compare.*

"Fuck," I groan, burying my head into his neck.

"Good thing you're not a virgin," he whispers huskily as he begins fucking me hard and fast.

He kisses and nibbles on my neck, sucking hard and adding to the euphoria I am feeling. I can't respond, even when we somehow end up on the bed, his hands all over me as he fucks me senseless. I can't focus on anything but the sheer bliss of the moment. This is heaven.

"Fuck," he growls.

Is he trying to pull away? I'm not sure, but I don't want him to move away.

My hand intertwines in his hair as I meet his powerful, brutal thrusts with my own, each time burying him deep within me. His piercings only heighten the pleasure that he is inflicting me with.

"Harder. I can take it. Don't hold back," I moan, feeling the pressure reach a biting point.

He obliges, fucking me harder and faster than I thought possible. I scream in pleasure, unable to stop myself. A moan of pure ecstasy escapes me, and I feel something pierce my neck, sending another bolt of pleasure and pain through me. He is... marking me...

I don't care. This pleasure... another moan leaves my lips as I arch my neck, allowing him better access. He growls as he fucks me roughly, his teeth sinking into me completely, triggering my release, and I cry out hornily, my back arching off the bed. My eyes roll, and my vision darkens as the most intense, mind-blowing orgasm consumes me. The bond strengthens, and it feels like I am about to faint.

I hear his grunt as he finishes with a few rough thrusts, our juices mixing, and our bodies coming down from their highs.

"Fuck."

Is that anger?

I am too light-headed to focus, but I turn my head to look at him. He is looking at my neck, and the sudden realisation that I am marked hits me.

Goddess, I am marked.

"It's fine," I murmur breathlessly, wondering if it is the fact that he has marked me without even telling me that is making him react like that.

His ice-blue eyes seem to hold some conflict, but I am too tired. Letting the darkness welcome me, I feel him pull out, and I think I feel his lips brush the mark on my neck, sending a shiver through me before getting off the bed, but I'm not sure. I just want to sleep.

I'm not out for long; I open my eyes, feeling refreshed despite the ache that now remains between my legs. I look around, realising he is still in the bathroom. I can hear the shower on. I need to get his name.

Goddess, that had been… perfect. I had forgotten all about Judah, and now it all returns, but somehow it doesn't take away from the sex I had just had.

I sit up, pulling the bed sheet to my chest as I look around for something to put on, although my body just wants to succumb to the darkness once more. The bathroom door opens, and I see the inked god step out, wearing nothing but a pair of pants, with a cigarette between two fingers, as he takes a drag on it. For a moment, he reminds me of Alejandro Rossi, the Lycan King, who is also my brother-in-law. *Weird.*

I shake my head, pushing the thought away. Why the hell did he even come to my mind?

"Are you just going to stare?" he asks, tossing the towel he has been holding onto the bed.

"Well, I was thinking we just fucked, but I still don't know your name," I remark, about to get off the bed, but the moment my feet hit the floor, I realise they feel like lead, and I am forced to sit there. Okay, I need to stay put for a bit.

"You still don't know who I am?" he asks, taking out a grey T-shirt. I look at him curiously, only for those icy blue eyes to meet mine.

"No. I just know you're an alpha." His aura seems to change, and I can feel his anger through the bond.

"Soon to be Alpha." His voice is filled with venom, and I look at him in complete shock. His aura is impressive; how the hell is he not an alpha yet?

"Soon to be?" I ask curiously.

"What's your name?" he asks instead, bringing me out of my thoughts.

"I still didn't get yours…"

"Leo. Leo Rossi," he replies coldly, making me freeze.

My eyes widen in shock as my head snaps to the man before me.

No fucking way…

"Leo Rossi?" I jump off the bed, almost falling to the floor. Grabbing the towel and wrapping it around myself, I stumble over to him. "How did I not see it?" He frowns, stepping back just as I cup his face, feeling his stubble graze my fingertips. "Oh, Dante is never going to let me live this down! Oh my god, a Rossi? What will Dad think?"

My head is spinning, but I can't deny the sliver of excitement that rushes through me at the thought of being mated to him. Kiara and I will be mated into the same family! I am mated to Sky's cousin! Oh, Goddess, she definitely won't be jealous, yup, definitely not. And Dad! What will Dad think, realising that both of his daughters are mated to tatted, pierced Rossis? My poor dad! And then-

"Who are you?" His voice is quiet yet deadly, and I freeze mid-thought, glancing back at him.

"You don't recognise me?"

"Should I?" My smile falters at the hostility in his tone.

I know Leo has distanced himself from the Rossis to the point that he is never around. Marcel, his father, still holds the Alpha title, although Leo runs the pack, refusing to allow Leo to take over. The feud between Leo and the rest of the Rossis is from years ago, and it is obvious it still remains.

"Azura. Azura Rayne Westwood," I state, no longer smiling as I look at him seriously. His eyes flash dangerously as they run over me. His heart is thudding, and when his eyes return to mine, I only see the blinding rage in them.

"Westwood. Is Selene for fucking real?" he almost spits, "I knew it was too fucking ideal."

"What's wrong with be-"

"Being a Westwood? Sure, one of the Elite packs, right? Entitled bastards who are free to do whatever the fuck they want." He steps back. Eyes that had held desire and interest now hold nothing more than hatred.

"Hey, that's not fair-"

"I, Leo Rossi, future Alpha of the Sangue Pack, reject you, Azura Rayne Westwood, as my mate and Luna."

I freeze as the violent ripping pain tears through me, and a scream leaves my lips. Burning pain grips my neck, and I fall to my knees. He mated with me, marked me, and then rejected me, causing the pain to be even worse than an instant rejection...

I can't breathe, the intensity of the pain in my neck killing me. I claw at my neck, my heart beating harshly.

"I will never accept the daughter of an Elite as my mate." His cruel words are faint and far, and my vision darkens slightly. I look ahead, seeing him walk away. Only one truth screams in my head, leaving me completely devastated.

Rejected.

He rejected me.

Devastation
Azura

Four weeks have passed since his rejection. That night has shaken me far more than anything Judah has ever done to me. I still remember grabbing my clothes before I stumbled out of the penthouse. I had nothing, not my phone, not my bike. I had managed to beg someone for a phone, and I rang Liam as the rain began falling, washing away the scent of my so-called mate, but it couldn't wash away what he did to me. My mark burned with agony, the healing slowing due to the rejection.

When Liam showed up, I had been silent. When he saw the state I was in, the anger in his eyes made me succumb to tears. I had never seen him so enraged, and if I didn't grab onto him and reassure him that it was consensual, he was ready to kill. I had managed to tell him that my mate had marked and rejected me. If it was anyone else but Leo, I wouldn't have cared, but I couldn't tell anyone because it would ruin things. Alejandro would lose it, and Marcel, Leo's dad, would feel guilty over it. This involved my entire family, not just me. I just couldn't. I now clutch at my neck, where his mark stains it. It had taken a full week for it to heal.

Frustration and anger fill me as I stare at the message on my phone. Judah. He is a problem that still won't go away, and he, like the rest of my pack, had found out I had been marked and rejected. His anger had been clear in his messages, and he had begun to ring me, too, calls I refuse to answer, which only makes his threats worsen.

The Blood Moon and its sister pack, the Blue Moon, combined are over four thousand members. We literally share the same territory, although the residency homes are separate. Years ago, we were like this pack of people living in the woods. Weird, right? Yeah, tell me about it, but now, we have a mini town here. There are shops, a restaurant, cafés, even a school, and, of course, a huge hospital. Somehow, word of me being marked had still travelled like wildfire, even though I had tried to keep it a secret.

My mark... a shimmering midnight blue crescent moon, with stars and a lotus, set against a background of blue flames. A beautiful mark with an opposing ugly story. A reminder of the painful memories I want to forget.

I still remember the look on Dad's face when Liam had brought me home, the way he had hugged me, the way his heart was thumping... Mama's pain and the worry and anger in her blazing eyes. I had to stay quiet for everyone's benefit, but they only got angry at me for refusing to share his name. I still haven't said the words to accept his rejection... I know we don't need to be face-to-face to do so, but still, it is daunting.

Two nights after what had happened, Liam had reinitiated me back into the pack. Only Mama and Raven had been there for it. When Leo had marked me, being of alpha blood, his mark had the power to break my pack-link to the Blood Moon, by default tying me to a prospective new pack, yet I was pretty much pack-less now and rejected, and so had rejoined the Blood Moon.

Everything has made me sick; I have lost my appetite, and I am unable to focus on anything. I need a break from it all. I want to run away... and although Liam told me it wasn't the answer, I still want to.

A light knock on my bedroom door makes my head jerk up.

"Hey, Zu," Liam's voice calls, concern clear in his magnetic blue eyes.

"Hey," I reply, picking up my jacket and slipping it on.

"Are you going out?" he asks.

Devastation | 23

I nod as he steps into the room, wrapping his arms around me tightly. I close my eyes, hugging him back, his familiar scent reminding me of home. I want to cry and throw a tantrum for him to fix, but I'm not a child anymore, and this isn't his problem to deal with. He has enough to handle with six kids and a pack to take care of.

"Talk to me, Zu," he whispers, kissing the top of my head. I don't reply, simply hugging him tighter.

"Am I your favourite sister, Liam?" I ask, looking up at him and using my best doe eyes on him, trying to sound cute. He smirks, amused, and cups my face, kissing my forehead.

"Without a doubt." He gives me a wink, and I smile.

"You're my favourite, too," I say quietly, taking a deep breath as I step back. "Do you know where my old collection of voodoo dolls is that I didn't want to throw away?" He looks at me worriedly.

"Umm, are you really going down that path?"

"I am tempted to learn some dark magic… I think I wouldn't mind causing a few people some pain." I'm sure I have a Leo Voodoo doll somewhere.

Leo Rossi. A man who is known to be ruthless, cutthroat, and dangerous. A man whose heart is frozen in ice. A man who cares for no one… I have heard the stories, but what he did just makes them all seem very real.

"I'm going to head out for a bit," I tell Liam before I grab my bike keys and leave the house.

I ride through the streets of our small town. Maybe some pastries from Granny June's will cheer me up. Luckily for me, today is her day off. She hates me, and I dislike going there if she is around. I park my bike, ignoring the looks that a group of girls who are sitting at the outside table give me, and enter the bakery. All five of those Barbie dolls had gone to school with me, and, well, I can't deny that I did prank them once. Okay, maybe twice? Let's just say we no longer get on. It was a harmless prank, I swear.

"We're closed," a grumpy voice comes.

Just my luck. Granny June is here.

I look around the bakery. It is definitely not closed. Three of the old crones who hate me are here, too. Perfect. I wish I had checked with Justin before coming here.

"Leave. You're dirtying my floors," she growls.

"Aw, come on, Granny June, my shoes are clean. I'm only here for a few pecan pies, and then I'm out."

"Leave."

"You know... the faster you give me those pastries, the faster I'm out of here?" I slip my hand into my jacket pocket and pull out my wallet.

"No, I've run out. I don't serve fr..." She purses her lips, looking me over with barely disguised contempt, knowing if she says those words, it would be direct disobedience of her Alpha.

Freaks of nature.

That is what she always likes to mumble. We may be in a time where we live in peace amongst witches, although most of the pack are absolutely fine with witches and the way I was born, there is still the handful who won't change and don't approve of how I was born. Usually I would snap back at them with everything I have, but lately, I have just had enough.

"Well, then, I will wait here until someone shows up to serve me." I cross my arms.

The smell of the various baked goods suddenly makes me sick. Maybe I should just leave.

She tenses, and I see her eyes dart to the window as if checking if anyone who may support me is around.

"I have nothing to give you," she says suddenly, picking up the tray of freshly baked croissants she has brought out and walking into the back kitchen, slamming the door behind her.

"I don't understand why we have to tolerate her," one of the hags mutters from behind me. I don't bother to look in their direction.

I sigh, my smile fading before I turn away, pushing open the bakery door. The urge to find some bugs to infest the bakery tempts me, but I don't have the time nor the will to do so.

Note to self—make a Granny June voodoo doll.

I step out into the fresh air, my stomach lurching nauseatingly, about to get on my bike.

"No wonder she was rejected. No one would want her. She's a psychotic freak." I hear an old woman sitting at the table outside mutter to her mate.

I swear, if it wasn't for how good Granny June's bakes are, I would avoid this place. All the same types of people gather here.

Don't do this now.

My anger is rising, and I know I am on the brink of losing control.

Don't.

I get onto my bike, trying to ignore them.

"Yeah, definitely a freak," the old man grumbles.

I freeze, my head snapping towards the couple who had spoken.

"Want to say that again?" I growl menacingly.

"I said nothing, pup. Move along," he growls, standing up.

"Don't lie. Say it again."

"I said I said nothing."

"I said say it again!" I scream, not caring that two passersby have stopped and are staring at me.

"Azura, come-"

"No! If you want to call me a freak, then say it to my fucking face!" I scream, cutting off whoever had tried to stop me. The older man's face turns an angry shade of red as he glares at me.

"There's no such thing as respect around here! I said nothing!" he lies as everyone shakes their heads in disapproval.

My chest heaves, my emotions in turmoil as I look around. These people knew me growing up, and although they were silenced, recently, since my rejection, they are becoming vocal once more. June and one of the other hags come to the door, watching me with contempt, disapproval, and irritation.

"She's so dramatic," one of the girls from the Academy mutters.

"I'm not dramatic."

"You shouldn't lie, dear," the elderly woman at the table scolds gently with fake sympathy in her eyes as she stands up, taking her mate's arm. "It doesn't look good on your parents."

Yeah, I get it. I'm a failure and a disappointment to them too.

"I didn't lie," I retort defensively; my emotions are getting out of control as I stare at the man whose face holds the tiniest of smirks. "You know exactly what he said."

"I said nothing. Stop trying to get me in trouble," he scoffs, walking off.

"Hey!" I shout, getting off my bike. I storm over to the old penis. I am about to grab him when a hand grabs hold of my wrist and stops me. I am ready to lash out when I look into the eyes of one of my thirteen-year-old nephews, Renji.

"Come on, Azura. Let's go home," he coaxes gently.

"I don't want to go home; I have things to do," I growl.

"Dad won't let this slide. Don't worry; no one will get away with this," he says clearly. I'm about to pull free from his hold, but the look of concern in his soft blue eyes makes me close mine and nod in agreement.

"It's no big deal. This bunch of wrinkles will never change. Don't tell Liam," I say quietly, not wanting to cause him more work. They are already concerned over my mark and rejection. He nods hesitantly, and I give him a small smile. "I'm just going out of the town for a bit. I promise."

Renji, the sweetest angel of the quintuplets. I know if it was anyone else, I wouldn't have listened. He believes me and nods.

Don't let them get to you, one of the two passersby says through the link.

I never do.

I get back on the bike as the woman gives me a warm smile, and I flash her a grin. I cast a deathly glare at the old, wrinkled vaginas before feeling super nauseous. Revving the engine, I suddenly freeze. For the last week or so, I have been feeling like this. As a werewolf, I should have healed from any cold by now...

My heart thunders as I quickly ride out of the pack territory. A sudden and terrifying thought occurs to me, and the fear of the possibility of it envelops me. *Please, no.*

Thirty minutes later, I am in a public stall at the drugstore. I hold a stick in one hand, my eyes shut as I count the seconds before taking a deep breath and looking at it. My stomach sinks when I see the two clear lines that stain the test.

I am pregnant.

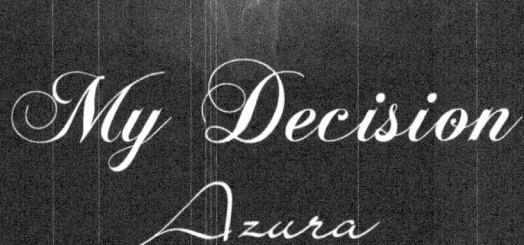

My Decision
Azura

Pregnant. I slide to the floor against the stall wall, not caring about the germs that probably fill this place, and stare unblinkingly at the stick, my mind blank.

Pregnant.

With his child.

"I'm fine," I say, taking a shuddering breath.

I am not fine.

I'm pregnant. I'm only nineteen, and I'm pregnant.

Pregnant with the child of someone who wants nothing to do with me.

I know I will have to tell my parents, but the thought makes my stomach sink. The hurt in Dad's eyes when I told him I had been rejected... I don't know if I'll be able to handle telling them I am pregnant, too. What do I do?

My mind is reeling, and the pain in my chest is suffocating me. As much as I want to crush Leo for what he has done, I can't, not without making this hard for Alejandro. I can't do that to them. I've already caused problems for my family without meaning to.

There was a time I dreamt of a love like my parents, but who am I kidding? My mate ripped that from me when he marked me, only to reject me. A true mate's mark... it can only be removed if he marks another or if he dies and someone else marks me... but unless that happens, I am stuck with this. I clutch my neck, letting my nails dig into it as I slowly look down at my stomach. I drop the stick, placing my hand over my stomach.

It is not this baby's fault... it is not at fault.

I was meant to die before I was born... there is no chance on earth that I would do anything to this baby. I close my eyes, taking deep, steadying breaths.

I'm fine.

I guess it is time to tell Mama and Dad about the pregnancy. I just hope they don't try to push for a name. Standing up, I gather the rubbish, binning the pregnancy test before I wash my hands and leave the washroom. Time to tell them and get this over with.

Night has fallen, and I am sitting in the lounge with Mama and Dad. I am curled up between them. Mama has her head resting on my shoulder whilst Dad is running his fingers through Mama's hair. His head is resting on top of mine. We are watching a movie, and although I have a lot of chances to drop the bomb, I am unable to tell them.

"What's wrong, baby? You're really quiet," Mama asks, lifting her head and looking at me with concern in her gorgeous sage-green eyes.

"I'm fine."

"Is this about the run-in with Olson earlier?" Dad asks. So they know about my run-in with that old penis.

"You heard about that? Were you just going to pretend it never happened?" I ask, feeling upset for no reason. Are they going to just walk around on eggshells now because I have been rejected?

"It's not like that. Liam will deal with him. Gemma Kingston told us what happened. Rest assured, they will all be questioned about it and dealt with. There is no tolerance in these packs for that behaviour," Dad's icy reply comes. It is obvious he is pretty pissed.

I get up from the sofa, running my fingers through my hair, only for it to fall back in my face again.

"I don't need anyone to be dealt with. I just want to be left alone! I can handle my own battles," I say, feeling frustrated. I can feel my emotions rising, knowing I'm going to lose it soon.

"Azura, this isn't just about you, it's about everything, and their attitude is not right. What's wrong, baby? Tell me," Mama asks, coming over to me as she places her hands on my arms. She is a lot shorter than me, and I am wearing heels whilst she is barefooted, making her look even smaller.

Do I tell them? How, when I know they already want to kill him for rejecting me? I don't want to see that pain in Dad's eyes again.

"It's nothing," I say, trying to pull away, but Mama refuses to let me go.

"Azura. Something is wrong. What is it?" she asks, her eyes flashing silver and her voice holding a quiet warning, a tone that tells me she is not going to back down.

"I said it's nothing! Leave me alone, for the love of the Goddess!" I shout in frustration, my eyes flashing the very same colour as hers. I see the flash of hurt in her eyes, but along with it is the determination that she never lost.

"Now, Azura," she growls.

"Please," Liam's quiet voice comes.

I look up to see him standing with his Bite-Sized Luna by his side. Her long black hair with blue tips is pulled into a high ponytail as she looks at me with concern in her unique eyes. One blue, one green.

I close my eyes, my head pounding as I gather the courage to speak up.

"I'm pregnant. There," I declare before I push past Liam and Raven, leaving all four of them stunned.

"Zu!" Liam's voice comes, and I hear him on the steps.

Fuck, he is fast.

I speed up, reaching my bedroom and slamming the door shut behind me just as he catches up. I hear him swear as he taps lightly on it.

"Come on, Azura, talk to us," his voice calls.

I stay silent, pushing myself away from the door, walking over to the bed, and dropping onto it on my stomach. I just want the ground to split open and swallow me whole.

My phone beeps, and I stare at the glow from it as it sits on my bedside table. I dread every incoming message these days.

"Azura, open up, come on."

"I'm tired, Liam," I reply.

"Please?" Dad's voice makes me close my eyes in frustration. How do I say no to him?

I get to my feet and unlock the door, only for Dad to envelope me in his warm embrace. My heart squeezes, feeling guilty for causing him to worry. I look up at him.

Dad may be sixty, but he looks as if he is in his mid-forties. Werewolf genes at its finest, and on top of that, he is one of the most handsome men I have seen. Even if not by blood, he *is* my dad.

"Why did you run?" he asks, raising an eyebrow. I look away, wondering where Mama and Raven are. Is Mama angry?

"I messed up," I say, turning my back to him and dropping onto my bed.

"He was your mate, and things happened... besides, it kind of reminds me of Kiara and Alejandro." He gives me a small smirk, although it doesn't take away the concern in his eyes, and my heart thuds at the mention of them. I have heard their story... but this is different.

Liam comes over and drops onto my bed, wrapping his arms around my shoulders.

"Trust me, you are definitely getting off easier," he whispers, making me smile.

Of course I am. Everyone knows I am spoiled in comparison to Kia and Liam.

"Scooch over. Make some space for me," Dad says. Liam and I shuffle over, allowing him enough space to sit down on the bed. He runs his fingers through my hair. "I don't know why, but I feel like there's a reason you aren't sharing his identity." I tense, but with Liam holding me in a tight bear hug, I am unable to escape.

"Do we know him?" Mama asks as she enters along with Raven, holding a tray of hot drinks for the four of them and a glass of milk for me. She places it down on my cabinet near my bed, right next to my phone, which sits silently for now.

"You guys know everyone," I reply smoothly as Raven sits down cross-legged on the end of the bed, giving me a vibrant smile.

My Decision

"How are you feeling?" she asks as Mama sits next to her.

How do I feel? A mess.

"I don't know."

"Whatever you decide to do, we are here. As for that bastard, if I ever find out his name..." Dad leaves his threat hanging, his eyes flashing a cobalt blue. *And that's exactly why I will never tell you.*

"So, where's Katara? With the boys?" I ask, referring to Raven and Liam's youngest child. She is seven years old and their only daughter after five boys.

"Yes. Jayce isn't happy, but they have no choice," Raven replies.

Their house is not far from ours. From my bedroom window, I can see the side of their house. They begin talking, and although I know they are just here for moral support, I am unable to join in with the conversation. Even when Dad passes me my glass of milk, I am unable to think of anything but my own turmoil. No one mentions the pregnancy until everyone finally leaves my room after I tell them I want to rest. Mama looks at me as she picks up the tray of empty cups.

"We'll go to the doctor tomorrow, or would you prefer Kiara to come down?" she asks quietly.

"I don't want anyone to know yet... just... for a little while. I just want to process it all," I mutter, trying to sound nonchalant. Mama nods before she kisses my cheek and leaves the room.

I lock the door after them and drop onto my bed once more, staring at the ceiling, my mind a storm.

I awake with a start, looking around my room. The light is still on, and I realise I fell asleep without even showering or changing.

What has awoken me? I rub my head as my phone screen lights up once again. I reach for it and unlock it, seeing the message from an unrecognised number. That same sickening feeling settles into the pit of my stomach as I look at the message.

Unknown caller: Congratulations on the new addition. We both know we can't have you carrying anyone else's pup but mine.

Fear envelops me, and my hand goes to my stomach. I may not have heard a heartbeat or seen the tiny blimp on a sonography screen, but there is a life within me. I look over at the window, wondering how he found out.

I need to keep this baby safe.

For the first time, I decide to reply. I take a deep shuddering breath and type a message.

Me: What do you want?

Unknown caller: You know what I want. Let's speak in person.

His response comes almost instantly.

Me: Yeah, let's meet and get this over with once and for all.

I feel my anger rising. I want to kill him.

Unknown caller: Now that's more like it... I miss you. Meet me at our favourite place tomorrow at midnight.

Me: No. Let's meet somewhere more public.

I am not going to risk this pup's life.

Unknown caller: Scared?

I frown, about to text when another message comes.

Unknown caller: We meet where I say, my pet.

I am not his fucking pet.

Me: Fine.

I grit my teeth, feeling so damn pissed.

I toss my phone down and stand up. Going to my wardrobe, I take a small suitcase out from the top shelf and begin filling it with clothes. I need to leave, at least until I have this baby. I am not going to stick around, nor am I going to risk its life. I am getting out of here.

Not the Plan
Azura

"A holiday?" Dad asks, concerned.

It is the following day, and we are over at Liam's. Katara is playing on the floor, her blonde hair pulled into two pigtails whilst her cerulean blue eyes watch me curiously. She may be seven, but she is quite small for her age. Despite her strength and determination, she is a minuscule-sized princess.

"I don't think you should be going alone," Jayce adds. I frown, planting my hands on my hips.

"Says who?" I ask.

"Says logic and the situation," he shoots back.

Moody little git. I wonder what he'd say if he knew I'm pregnant, but I am not going to listen to a thirteen-year-old, who is meant to be my subordinate, telling me what I should and shouldn't be doing.

"He ain't wrong," Theo adds with a cocky grin. "Besides, you just get in trouble every damn time."

"Boys, go outside. Now," Raven orders, frowning at her sons.

"We are only saying it because we care for her," Carter adds, making me sigh.

"I am going somewhere so I can just have a break from everything... I need this," I persist, looking at Mama and Dad.

"She's right," Mama replies to my relief. "But I'm not sure I want you going alone. Maybe Dante could- "

"I am not taking Dante. I don't need my nephew babysitting me," I reply, rather offended. That pup is a day younger than me!

"He's stronger than you," Theo adds, oh so very helpfully.

"Oi! I helped change your diapers, show some respect!" I growl, grabbing a cushion and hitting him over the head with it. He just catches it, smirking as Ares shakes his head, and Liam sighs, running a hand down his face.

"Be careful, Theo!" Raven warns. I know she's worried for my baby. My baby... it still feels weird to say that. Leo's baby...

It hasn't really hit what this would mean... my dreams... my plans.

Well, they were all kind of gone the moment Judah fucked me over anyway.

"I just need a break, just a few months to be alone and away from everything," I promise, dropping onto the sofa next to Theo.

My family knows I had a boyfriend back when I was at the Academy but they don't know much about Judah, and I really don't want them to find out either.

"Where will you go?" Dad asks.

Somewhere beautiful and peaceful.

"Sweden."

Night has fallen, and I have packed. Dad wanted to book my ticket, but I told him I already had. I had booked two to make sure that they think I'm on the first flight, but I intend to get on the second. Liam wants to drop me at the airport, but I tell them I'm meeting up with some friends first, and I'll let them know when I'm on the flight.

The flight I plan to take is tomorrow morning, which is fine. It will give me enough time to meet Judah and get this crap over with. It takes me over an hour to reach the location he picked, a place not too far from Midnight Academy, one of the four academies for supernatural species.

I get out of the car I rented for the drive, making sure that the weapon I brought is tucked into my jacket pocket. I am wearing an oversized jumper with jeans and a knee-length puffer jacket on top. I have several weapons on me, just in case. I don't trust Judah at all.

I walk through the woods to the cavern where we often met, stopping several feet away from it.

"I'm here," I call, the smell of cocaine reaching my nose. I clench my jaw. There was a time he wore the perfect mask. Sure, he was a bad boy... but his twisted dark side had only become clear once I was far too deep into it all.

"Ah, my little pet." His voice, which I now hate, comes, and he steps out of the cavern, smoking a joint. His gaze travels over me, making my skin crawl. Funny how that works; someone whose touch you once desired now makes you sick.

"What do you want, Judah?" I ask icily.

The urge to rip him apart is pretty strong, but killing without reason would mean I'd be trialled at the Supernatural Court of Selene, a court which would bring everything to light, including everything he has on me. Maybe I have reason to pull the trigger or rip his heart out, but I don't want to kill anyone else.

"You. You promised to be mine, but you let another mark you. How about I carve that thing out of your neck?" His voice holds barely controlled rage as he steps closer.

"Stay back. We are through. It's been a year, Judah, and what you did, I won't ever forgive. You're a sick bastard, and I don't want you in my life." I don't bother hiding the resentment in my tone.

"The thing is, babe, you don't get to decide."

I shake my head as I laugh, "You're fucking stupid if you think I'm going to actually bend or fear a bastard like you. You may have forgotten who I am, but allow me to remind you. Piss me off, and not only will I rip your dick off, soak it in vinegar and spice, and then force-feed it to you, but I won't hesitate to go to the King himself. I'm sure he won't mind dealing with you." He comes closer, and I am ready to reach for my gun if I need to.

"No, I haven't forgotten. I have forgotten nothing. If you go to him, yeah, he will manage to kill me. Of course. But will he be able to stop me from spreading the images I have of you and your precious little friends?

Ah, shit, the twins, they're his girls, right? Damn, imagine nude images of his precious little princesses plastered all over the net? And the blonde, damn, she has curves to fucking die for."

Anger flares through me. I lunge at him, punching him across the face. The joint he is smoking falls to the floor, and the smell of blood tells me I had hit him hard. Good.

"Don't you ever fucking try to blackmail me with them! Your issue is with me, right? Then fucking focus on me!" I spit as he grabs me by my neck.

I twist out of his hold, about to punch him, when he shoves me back, pulling out a gun just as I grab mine. My chest is heaving as I glare at him with pure hatred.

Not Kataleya. Skyla and Song would probably be able to deal with it, but not our Angel. No fucking way. Fear for her envelopes me, just imagining something like that happening to Kataleya. She and Skyla are the twin daughters of Kiara and Alejandro. Kataleya suffered far too much as a child. She still never got over what happened to her back then.

"They are seventeen, how sick are you?" He cocks his gun, aiming it at my stomach.

"Want me to show you?"

"What the fuck do you want, Judah? You can't have me back, I'm never going to be yours. Do you want money? Anything. Tell me how much, and then just let's end this. Please." I am tired of this. He sneers at me, wiping the blood from his mouth.

"I want you... but I guess if you do me a few favours, I can let you go."

"And the videos and images you have of us will be returned to me," I clarify. I can't trust him, but I don't really have a choice. This is just too risky, but I need to buy some time.

"Hmm, that can work, but I expect you to obey me, Azura. I'll be watching."

I will look for a way to get everything he has on us back, I just... I need to figure something out. I have tried. The only problem is I don't even have anything belonging to him to see if I can have a witch do a locator spell. I'm so screwed.

"Now how about the first favour?" He smirks, and I frown at him.

"If you think I'll get with you then- "

A menacing growl reaches my ears, and I spin around just as a huge wolf launches itself at me.

"Oh, I'll sleep with you if I want but right now, I want to see you get rid of one rabid wolf. Shit, I hope the pup doesn't die so soon." His voice is getting fainter, and I hear him snicker.

I stare at the beast that launches itself at me, saliva dripping from his mouth as he tries to attack me. I realise what Judah's aim is, his words ringing in my mind. I feel sick. He is risking my baby's life. Bastard.

Do I shift? Can I shift?

I pull the trigger, aiming for the wolf's leg. I don't know who this is or what has happened to him. I just need to injure it enough for me to get away. The wolf growls as it claws me across my back. The pain is accompanied by intense burning, and I flinch, spinning around and kicking him off me, throwing him to the floor violently.

"Judah! What the fuck is this?"

"Entertainment, my beautiful freak," his sick voice answers. I have never hated anyone more. "Oh, and I'd be careful of his claws... they're poisoned."

I can feel it spreading through my back, the pain heightening. I need to end this now. I cock my gun, shooting several rounds at his legs. The wolf howls and falls to his knees, shifting back into a rather weak-looking boy who writhes in pain. Guilt instantly fills me just as I hear footsteps approaching. I run to the young man. He is about my age or a bit younger.

"Who is he?" I shout, looking up at Judah and the two men who have just come out of the cavern.

"Just some entertainment," Judah sneers, raising his gun and shooting the writhing boy. To my horror, the boy's heart stops beating. I freeze as I look at the boy, whose eyes are still wide in shock. He died instantly.

"What did you use?" I ask, staring at his gun.

"Some new bullets," he smirks before tensing. I hear it, too, the sound of a car approaching. "I'll be in touch. Don't try to leave the country, Azura, because I'm watching you."

He seems to hesitate, pointing the gun at me before he turns and leaves swiftly, leaving me with the lifeless boy next to me. Fuck, I messed up. Again.

I try to get to my feet, but the poison is too much. I stumble, falling to the ground again as several scents fill my nose, and my heart begins thumping. Is that Leo? My stomach flutters as his scent becomes stronger.

I look at the blinding light I can see through the trees as my vision begins to darken, and all I see are the boots of the man approaching. He crouches down, and two tattooed fingers tilt my head up. I find myself staring into icy-blue eyes that hold no emotions.

"What happened?"

I try to speak, but I can't, the poison in my back numbing my senses, and then everything goes black.

A Compromise
Azura

I awake to a dull ache in my back. I'm in a comfortable bed, and I can smell a citrusy fresh scent. I frown, opening my eyes and looking around what appears to be a hospital room. The walls are pale green, with the far wall being covered in forest scenery. I am hooked up to some drips. Sitting up, I yank them off and slide out of the bed. Sunlight is streaming through the window that is open a crack, and I can hear the faint sounds of laughter and chatter from outside.

I look down, realising I am wearing a pale green hospital gown. My clothes. Where are they? I scan the room, my heart leaping when I spot my luggage and coat on the couch in the corner. I rush over to it, wincing as a pang of pain rushes through my back. Oh, fuck.

What time is it? Or worse, what day is it, and where am I? Where is my phone?

I am about to grab some clothes when one of the two doors leading off the room opens, and a woman in a white coat with her brown hair pulled into a ponytail enters. Her grey eyes are full of concern when she spots the empty bed before she turns to me.

"Oh, you're awake. Thank the Goddess!" She places the file she is holding down and comes over. I stand up from where I am rummaging in my clothes, looking at the woman who is a few inches shorter than me warily.

"Where am I?"

"You are at the Sangue Pack, our Alpha, Leo, found you injured and brought you here. I'm Doctor Demiko," she explains.

Her words make my heart thump violently. Leo... the Sangue Pack. I almost clutch my stomach in panic. He can't know. I have to keep this a secret.

"How long was I out?"

"Just for the night. It's not even noon yet."

"I need to make a call. Where's my phone?"

"I'm sorry, there was no phone on you, but you can use mine," she offers. I nod, and she takes the sleek black device from the pocket of her white coat. Activating No Caller ID, my heart thumping, I quickly dial Mama's number.

"Hello?" I let out a silent breath, hearing her voice.

"Hey, Mama, don't kill me, but I lost my phone."

"Seriously, Azura! We were worried."

"I know, but you know me and phones."

For once, I'm glad I'm a bit of a scatter-brained person with phones because I'm sure if I didn't reply straight away, they would have been worried. Mama sighs in relief.

"Are you in Sweden?"

"Yes, Mama, I'm just calling from someone's phone to let you know. I was so tired after the flight that I just crashed. When I'm rested and settled in, I will call you all, okay?"

"Okay, baby. Thank the Goddess, you are okay. Get some rest."

"I love you."

"I love you, too," Mama replies. I hang up and look at the doctor, who is filling in some forms, passing the phone back to her.

"Thanks," I say as she takes it with a small smile.

"I hope you trust that we mean no harm." She raises her hand in surrender, smiling warmly, clearly sensing my discontent. "I'm Jackie, and I'm the doctor who attended to you. The injury you had contained WB12. Luckily, it was a very small amount."

One of the deadliest forms of wolfsbane out there. My baby. My heart thumps as I look at her.

"Did you do a blood test?" I ask. I'm in turmoil. I want to know if my baby is okay, but I also don't want Leo to learn about it. I need to get out of here.

"No, we didn't need to. The green pus is enough to let us know what it was, and we were able to treat you quickly." She smiles before motioning to the bed. "Please sit down so I can check your vitals." The baby...

"I... I need to leave," I say quietly.

"Miss... you can't leave yet. You're not in any condition to leave the hospital. Besides, the Alpha said you are not to leave yet," she mumbles. Leo.

"He isn't the Alpha of this pack yet, correct? Where is the real Alph... fuck." Marcel. Marcel can't see me here!

"Alpha Marcel is on holiday, and although he may not have passed the official title down to his son, I assure you Alpha Leo is still very much in charge," she whispers, glancing furtively towards the door. "Please, don't say that again."

"I... shit." I run my hand through my hair.

I need to see if my baby is okay, and I can't get that done here without Leo's knowledge. It still feels weird to think this child is his, too... would he even care? I'm sure he'd just cast it aside, too. My heart squeezes, but I refuse to let my thoughts go down that path.

"Calm down, it's going to be okay. You will be allowed to go soon," she whispers, guiding me to the bed. How can I calm down when I am scared for my baby's life?

"Is there any poison left in my body?" I ask quietly.

"No, we have treated it. You will soon be back to your normal self."

I nod hesitantly. I need to get out of here, and I don't care if it is risky. I need to go to Kia and make sure my baby is safe. I can fuck up my own life, not this unborn pup's life.

"Okay, so when can I leave?"

"I've told the Alpha you are awake. I'm sure he will let you go when he deems fit."

"I'm not his property. I will pay for the medical expenses and offer my gratitude, but I need to leave," I insist, my eyes flashing. I know it's not her fault, and it isn't fair for me to take it all out on her, but I need to get checked and there is no one else here. I run a frustrated hand through my hair.

"He'll be here soon," she replies politely.

She leaves the room, and I go over to my bag. I don't want to face him. Sure he had saved me, but...

I'm getting out of here.

I pull on some black jeans and a bra before grabbing the first top I find. Once I had put the tank top on, I look around. *Okay, let's go.*

I rummage around in my bag with one hand, looking for my essentials as I pull on some black sneakers with my other hand. I look for my wallet, but I can't find either my wallet or passport. They aren't here.

Fuck. No... shit, come on!

I empty my bag onto the floor, desperation filling me, and, in my panic, I don't realise the door has opened until it clicks shut, and a familiar seductive scent fills my nose.

"Why are you always where you shouldn't be?" His cold, deep voice asks, making my stomach flutter, and that familiar pang of pain squeeze around my heart.

"Where are my passport and wallet?" I ask, standing up. I don't want to see him. He made a mockery of me and left me in pain that night.

"Wherever I want them to be. You're in my kingdom now, and only my rules go."

I force myself to turn around and face him. There he stands, his piercing icy blue eyes bearing into me. He looks as handsome as he did that night, and although I have tried to distort the image of how handsome he was, seeing him before me reminds me that he is too fucking handsome. Why did the Goddess make these men so fucking good-looking and, at the same time, total assholes? There is only one Alpha who I know who is equally sexy and charming. Rayhan Rossi, this fuckboy's cousin.

His plump, shaped lips are slightly parted in that arrogant pout that I am sure he doesn't even realise he has, and his hair is a sexy, tousled mess. He is wearing all black, in jeans, a tee, and a jacket. Casual, but he still oozes power, danger, and dominance. I roll my eyes, cross my arms and try not to show how he affects me by just being in the same room as me.

"You can be the king of the toilet or the entire world for all I care. I don't abide by anyone's rules. Give me my passport and wallet, I need to leave."

"I will." His eyes bear into mine, and something tells me he wants to say more. He steps closer, but I stand my ground as his gaze falls on my neck. "You haven't accepted it."

His rejection. I guess he really wants me gone. I never thought anyone could brutally reject someone after marking them.

"Why should I make things easier for you? You marked me, then you fucking rejected me, and I should just accept it because it's what you want?" I ask quietly, trying to control the rage that is ready to unleash hell upon him. Our eyes meet, and I can hear his heart thudding as he tries to control whatever he is feeling. Does he want to kill me?

"Have you told anyone?" he asks dangerously, stepping closer.

I scoff. *Don't come closer.* I'm not sure what I want to do if he does; slap him? Knee him? Rip his dick off? *Tempting...*

I don't let my wolf's pain or the other thoughts that swim in the deepest corners of my mind surface. Leo Rossi is nothing to me.

"Why? Don't want to be humiliated if everyone finds out you're mated to me?"

He takes hold of my chin, and I feel the sparks of our wounded bond. His eyes flash, and he glares at me.

"I don't care what anyone thinks, but I want to know how they all felt, knowing I'm the one who rejected you. Did it hurt them?" A cold smirk crosses his lips, and I shove him back, my eyes flashing as the pain returns once again.

"No. I didn't tell them because they don't deserve to worry over trash like you," I spit, pulling free and grabbing my bag. "I'm leaving."

"Go right ahead, this pack is impenetrable. No one comes in or goes out without my knowledge."

I freeze.

Safe. What if...

My heart thumps, and I remember the little I have heard about the Sangue Pack, one of the most feared and most powerful packs in the country. Judah won't come for me here... if... if I pretend Leo has kidnapped me, it might make Judah think I can't do anything to help him. Leo's reputation is vast.

Everyone knows who he is. My mind is running a thousand miles per hour as I quickly weigh the pros and cons. I just need a bit of time.

"Do you really not want anyone to know we are mated?" I ask slyly.

"I'm not bothered," he says carelessly, and I tilt my head. *Don't try to pull reverse psychology on me, Blue-Eyes.*

"Oh... you do. You don't want anyone to know..." I tut as I approach him. The tense clench in his jaw tells me I am right as his eyes flash dangerously. I am onto something. "And you want me to accept your rejection. How about a deal?" His murderous gaze meets mine, and I smirk.

"What do you want in return?" His icy reply comes.

"I need a little time to heal and lay low. I just... need a break from stuff. So if you allow me to stay in this pack for a month, I'll accept your rejection. I'll be gone from your life forever. No one will ever know about us. I just need some space away from everyone," I say, trying to pick my words carefully. He frowns.

"No. Fucking no. I want you gone. Immediately."

I sigh before I stare at him, unblinking. Moments earlier, I would have been happy to hear those words, but now...

"Then I think I'll scream and shout from the rooftops that I'm your Luna, and this mark will grant me that title. I wonder what Marcel will think when he realises what you did. Damn, he's still the Alpha, isn't he? Shame you're twenty-eight and still not. Does it hurt?" I taunt. I know I am hitting a sore spot, but I know the rumours. When his eyes blaze a steel blue, his aura surges around us, and he grabs hold of my neck, I know I have hit a very dangerous nerve.

"Cross me, and there's not a corner on this earth where you can hide from me. I will find you, and I will fucking destroy you."

"Then accept my deal. Allow me to stay here for one month, and I will keep our secret forever. I will reject you in secret, and Azura Westwood will be nothing more than a shadow of your past. One month is all I'm asking."

"No." His eyes flash, and I frown slightly.

"Then I think it's time everyone learns the truth."

"Don't try me. Heed my fucking words: run, little she-wolf, as far as you can, because if I ever catch you, your worst fucking nightmare will become your reality," he whispers dangerously, his grip on me painfully tight. A smile

A Compromise

curls the corner of my lips, and I raise an eyebrow, running the tip of my nail down his chiselled jaw challengingly.

"Oh, but you're wrong, Blue-Eyes, because I am the stuff of nightmares, and I'm here to create hell in your life. Not scared, are we?" Icy blue eyes meet my unblinking, bright blue ones.

"I'm warning you. Don't mess with me," he growls.

"Oh? But the thing is, I always do what I'm not supposed to."

"Then you will regret it."

A Painful Surprise
Azura

"One month. It's all I'm asking for, and then I'll be a good little she-wolf and walk away without unleashing hell," I reply, trying not to let the mockery in my voice show. I grip his wrist, forcing him to let go of me. He releases me, taking out a cigarette and lighting it.

An image of Judah smoking his joint comes to my mind, and the vast difference between the both of them hits me hard. Leo oozes power and danger, yet, despite the pain, I don't know if it is the mate bond, but I feel better around him. Sure, the pain he has caused me still hurts, and that emptiness that has grown inside of me is still there, but... I know I will be safe here until I find a way to deal with Judah.

"You will behave, and you will not tell anyone why you're here. Marcel won't be back for a few weeks, and I want you gone before then. Deal?" Marcel? Something about him using his dad's first name tells me things aren't great between them.

"Fine, I will be gone before your dad is back."

Our eyes meet before he turns and walks out, slamming the door behind him. I let out a breath, not realising how overwhelming it was to have him here. I place a hand on my stomach. With Leo agreeing, it's bought me enough time to think of a plan, and maybe I can ask the doctor to do a check. But will she be trustworthy enough not to tell Leo? Her Alpha?

The door opens and the doctor re-enters, holding a tray of food. Her gaze instantly goes to my neck.

"Are you okay?" she asks, coming over with fear in her eyes.

"I'm fine, relax." I give her a wink, walking over to the small sink basin where a mirror hangs above it. Fucker. He left a mark on my neck. "He just has a shitty attitude, but it's fine. My family knows him, so I'm staying here for a bit." I shrug. I should have asked Leo what we were going to say, but staying any longer than necessary in his presence is hard, too.

"Oh, I'm glad everything is okay. Please get some rest. I'll ask the Alpha and have an apartment arranged for you. I have got some food for you to eat for now." She is so adorable.

"Doctor Demiko, right?"

"Yes, you can call me Jackie. What's your name?"

"Azura." I wink, flashing her a small smile. "There's something you could help me with, but I don't want Alpha Leo finding out because I don't want my family to know." Her smile falters.

"I'm sorry, but if it is something that can compromise-"

"It's nothing that could possibly affect the Alpha. It's something personal," I say with the best dramatic sigh I can muster as I shake my head and sit down on the bed, trying to look pitiful and turn my big eyes on her. She hesitates, then sighs and nods. *Thank you, Goddess, for these eyes. They always work.*

"Oh, of course. If it's something I can help with, I will do my best to do so," she offers gently.

"It's because you're a doctor that I'm asking for your help," I answer quietly, keeping my eyes sorrowful. The moment she places her hand on my shoulder, concern filling her eyes, I know she has bought it, hook, line, and sinker. Oh, this poor angel. But, honestly, I do need help. I am nineteen, pregnant, and injured. Surely, she'd feel for me.

"I'm pregnant, but I don't want anyone to know... I just... I just need to know if my baby is okay since I've been poisoned," I explain, hoping she understands. Her face drains of all colour as she jumps to her feet.

"I'll run some additional tests. We didn't realise-"

"Is there a chance the poison harmed my baby?" I whisper, real fear filling me. Her heart is thumping as she struggles to calm herself down.

"I... I can't say. I will run some further tests, and we will do a scan. I will check-"

"But I need you to promise you won't tell anyone," I cut in. She nods as she looks at me and tilts her head.

"What about your mate?" She looks at my neck, and I place my hand over my mark. What do I say? I need her to understand that this has to be a secret. Feeling horrible, I decide to weave a story.

"My ex... he isn't a good person. If he finds out... things won't be good." It isn't an entire lie, Judah is a psychotic dick. Even if the baby isn't his, he would harm it. She seems to understand and nods.

"I will have everything set up. I will return soon," she says before she hurries to the door. "Your secret is safe with me."

Her words are like a wave of relief, and something tells me she will keep her promise. She just has that vibe about her.

Three hours later, I feel entirely at ease. The baby is fine. Strong and growing perfectly. I am now just waiting for someone to come show me to a place to stay. Jackie said no one would learn of my pregnancy, and she would be here to take care of me. Now all I need to do is find a way to deal with Judah and leave as soon as it is safe to do so.

A knock on the door makes me look up, and Jackie steps inside. She is no longer in her white coat. She looks more carefree and younger in jeans and a powder pink top. With her is a gorgeous woman with black hair, wearing a lace bodysuit and black flared pants.

"Hi. Azura, isn't it?" She smiles slightly.

"Yeah, hey."

"I'm Nikki, Jackie's sister, and Leo told me you need a place to stay. I've got a great apartment all ready for you, stocked with snacks, streaming services, and everything else you will need. Come on, leave your luggage. One of the boys will come to get it soon."

"Thanks, that will be great," I say, standing up. My injuries are getting better. The pain has eased as time passes, but I'm still not one hundred percent.

The three of us leave the room and walk down the halls, which are very modern, clean, and stylish for a hospital. If it wasn't for the occasional doctor or patient, I would have thought we were in a hotel. We leave the building and step out onto the paved streets.

"Where is she being housed?"

"Floor below mine," Nikki replies. Their eyes meet, and I know they are mind-linking.

"Lucky! We will be neighbours," Jackie smiles.

I don't really care where it is going to be as long as I have a place to stay for a bit without Judah getting through to me. I know I don't have long because he will lose his shit fast, and in about two weeks, unless I find a way to hide my pregnancy, Leo may hear the heartbeat if I am near him. Although I plan to stay far away from him, I know it would be unrealistic to think we will never cross paths.

After five minutes of walking, we finally reached a luxurious block of apartments. The mirrored walls of the entire building stand out, and it is the largest building around. We enter, and Nikki leads the way to the lift, keying in a code, and the lift doors shut. She isn't mated, unlike her sister; her neck is bare from any mark.

"So, what pack are you from?" she asks me.

"That's a secret."

"Oh, please, tell me, I can keep a secret." She rolls her eyes.

"Hmm, but if I tell you, I'll have to silence you," I joke, crossing my arms.

"Whatever. It's just that we don't really have visitors from other packs. Like ever."

"Yeah, I know. Sorry, I just can't say," I respond, but I don't engage her, not wanting her to pry any further.

The doors open, and we step out into a lavish hall. Four doors go off from here, and a curved staircase to the side leads to a higher floor.

"That one is mine and my mate's." Jackie smiles, "If you ever need anything, you are welcome to call me."

"Emmet won't like that," Nikki murmurs in a sing-song voice, walking off towards a door next to the stairs.

"He'll be fine," Jackie replies with a small smile.

We have just reached the door when I hear the sound of footsteps and laughter, turning just in time to see a little boy running down the stairs.

"I won! I won!"

"Careful," Leo's deep voice calls just as a young boy, no older than six, comes into view, looking over his shoulder as he runs dangerously fast. He is obviously not paying attention to the fact that he has already reached the bottom step, stumbling and falling face forward. I rush over, catching him before his face hits the marble.

"Easy there, kiddo," I say, finding myself staring into a pair of hazel eyes. He smiles up at me sheepishly.

"Thank you!"

"Corrado, I have told you to be careful countless times," Leo's cold voice makes me look up, my heart thumping when our eyes meet. He looks away first, coming down the rest of the steps.

"Don't worry, Daddy, she saved me," the young boy says, pointing at me as he rushes over to Leo.

Daddy.

I stare in shock as Leo lifts the boy into his arms. Our eyes meet, and despite the fact that we are nothing to one another, I can't deny that the one word burns in my mind. My heart thunders as I try to make sense of it. I look away, ready to escape into the apartment, when Nikki steps out into the hall again.

"Oh, hey, babe. I was showing Azura the apartment," she says, walking over to Leo. Reaching up, she kisses his cheek before turning and smiling at me.

Leo doesn't speak, and neither do I, but the crushing pain in my chest makes me simply stare blankly at them. He has a family, and he had slept with me...

I hate people who cheat, and somehow, I have become the other woman in this sick situation. Things just can't get fucking worse; he has rejected me and had a family before me.

So, why does it hurt so much?

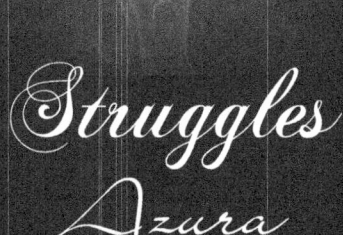

Struggles
Azura

He has a family...

I stare at the marble tiles of the shower walls, letting the water pour down my body.

Nikki is his woman, and the boy...

I close my eyes, resting my forehead against the cool wall.

He has a son...

Why don't I know this? Sure, I never cared about the latest news, but it was never something that was mentioned. Sky or Kat would have mentioned it but then again, Leo has moved away from his family entirely.

Nikki seems damn nice, and I have gone and slept with her man.

He was your mate, Azura.

Would he have broken up with her if I wasn't a Westwood? I don't know... why did he mark me then?

Does he love her? Probably...

What he felt for me was just because of the bond...

I am the other woman.

My heart squeezes, remembering the story of my biological mother. Her mate cheated on her. In fact, thanks to his infidelity I even have a brother; a brother who has been desperately trying to get to know me, but it's been me who just hasn't wanted to. I'm not ready. I feel bitter. He is the reason Indigo ended up giving up the will to live. I know the story from Mama and Dad from the first time when they told me that I wasn't their biological child, like Kia and Liam...

OVER NINE YEARS AGO

I stared at Mama and Dad, feeling worried. They were on either side of me in my bed, but they wanted to talk to me about something. Did they find out I cut the squares in Liam's underwear because he refused to allow me to taste whiskey? But... I made sure I had an alibi... hmm. Something wasn't right.

No, wait, oh my god, they must have realised I emptied the pot of worms on that dumb boy's head! But he was calling me names! No, wait... what if they realised I'm the one who made Jayce and Theo flood the bathrooms? Or wait, what if it-

"Hey, stop overthinking it, Wildfire," Dad said, tapping my nose.

"I just want to say, whatever it is, I didn't do it. I've done nothing at all."

"We haven't said anything yet," Mama added, looking amused.

"I know, but it might be a trick, so whatever you think I've done, I haven't done what you think I've done."

"You usually have done what we think you have done, but it's nothing of the sort. There's something we want to tell you," Mama replied, wrapping her arms around me tightly as she smiled. I snuggled into her, letting out a breath of relief, wondering what it was. "You know Mama Indy, right?"

"Yes, Mama. You always go on about her because I look like her, right? Are you missing her tonight?" I asked softly, looking up at her. Her eyes filled with sadness, and she kissed my forehead.

"We always are," she responded softly, looking at Dad, who put his arms around us.

"Yeah..." Dad agreed.

Dad always got sad when he looked at her picture, too. I knew Mama and Dad's parents were married, although Mama and Dad had never really mentioned it directly. I had heard things. They turned out to be mates, too, so everyone had to accept that their love was meant to be, even if it was very shocking to imagine it... naughty Dad and Mama having a secret love affair.

"What we are going to tell you, Angel, is only because you deserve to know the truth. It doesn't change anything," Dad said, kissing my head.

I frowned but nodded. This is weird...

"When the battle that took Indigo's life occurred, she was pregnant, but she wanted to help us against the evil. It cost Indy her life."

I frowned. "Wow, but what about her baby then? Didn't she care about it?" Mama tensed, and then I saw her and Dad exchange looks. Dad gave her hand a squeeze and continued.

"She did, but she had been through a lot in life, and she wanted to do something to protect everyone because, without us winning, things would have been terrible for us. When she was killed... Marcel and Mama took her to Grandma Amelia. You know her, right?"

"Yes, I do. Grandma Amy, how can I not? You all make sure I remember her all the time," I said with a roll of my eyes. "I think I would have loved her. So then, what happened?"

"Well, Grandma Amy had some magic that we never knew she possessed, and, using it, she placed the baby that was still fighting for life into me instead," Mama explained. I furrowed my brows, staring at Mama's tummy.

"Then the baby lived?"

"She did, and she became a beautiful little soul with lots of spark," Mama added, her eyes glistening with tears. *Mama's tummy...*

"Then, where is she now..." I asked. *That battle happened before I was born. Wait... did they mean...*

"Right here," Dad said softly, hugging me tightly.

My heart thudded loudly in my chest as I realised what they meant. *I was Mama Indy's baby...*

My mind felt funny. It felt like it was being squeezed.

No, I can't be... but I don't look like Mama and Dad...

I knew it was the truth...

Mama Indy didn't care enough about me. She didn't care if she died. What if I had died? I don't care if she's my mama! I don't want her to be!

"Baby..." Mama calls, but I didn't know what to say.

"I'm still your favourite, right?" I asked, looking at them intently.

"Always," they said in unison.

"Then, I don't understand why you had to tell me. You two are my parents, the ones who take care of me and raise me. I don't care if... she was meant to be my mama because she didn't care if I died anyway." I shrugged lightly. I didn't want to know anymore. I saw the flicker of hurt in Mama's expression, but I didn't care... I was only *their* daughter.

"We always have and always will love you, but you have the right to know about Indy, too."

"Okay." I shrug.

That night they had slept by my side... although I know they loved Indigo... I didn't feel that same way. I was horrible, maybe... I didn't dare tell Mama or Dad how I felt, but she didn't care if I died. Maybe I'm not a nice person...

Especially as I grew up, I learned more about her abusive mate who destroyed her mentally. I know not everyone can escape an abusive relationship, but I thought a mother's love was greater than anything. She didn't care if I lived or died. My parents are Elijah and Scarlett Westwood, and I will never be like her.

Even if I want to go into combat and become a pack warrior, this baby is my world now. I have taken classes in every fighting and weapon class the Academy offers, along with Herbology, doing the higher level and learning about poisons and antidotes. I am ready to go onto the battlefield if the need arises. I may have messed up, been a prankster and every teacher's worst nightmare, but in the lessons I liked, I did my best. That dream isn't forgotten, but right now, my priority is my pup, and I had almost risked its life by thinking Judah wouldn't try something stupid. I have to be more careful.

And what Mama Indigo had been through at the hands of her cheating mate... I never want to ruin another person's relationship.

I switch the shower off and step out, towelling myself dry before I enter the bedroom and pull on a black sports bra with matching Brazilian briefs. The image of Leo, Nikki, and Corrado returns to my mind once again. I begin blow-drying my hair, mulling over everything. Is Nikki Corrado's mother? She isn't an omega, so how...

Why do I care? Leo and I are nothing. He rejected me, remember?

I sit on the bed once my hair is done, applying some moisturiser to my arms and legs. Spotting the tablet and laptop that sits on one of the shelves that surround the huge headboard, I am tempted to use them. Should I try getting in touch with the girls? Just share what's going on? I need to tell someone...

I pick up the tablet and switch it on. It's fully charged, and it looks brand new. Do I trust it?

No. I can't talk about my pregnancy on a device and internet that Leo might be watching. Isn't he said to be tech-savvy? Yeah, definitely not.

I stand up, walking out into the lounge and over to the double doors that lead out onto the balcony. Opening the doors, I step out, inhaling as I lean over the balcony wall and look down at the pack. It is beautiful... more modern than our area, yet it looks stunning.

I sigh, staring out. As much as I would want my child to have a father, it doesn't need to be my fated mate, or anyone for that matter. I have my family and friends who love me. I don't need someone who doesn't want us.

Is the fact that I am a Westwood that bad? I want to ask him, but what's the point? He has his life set.

I think I see something on the ground below and lean down, spotting a burly-looking man petting two dogs. Cute things. I always wanted a pet, but seriously, I wouldn't be able to take care of it or give it time. I am having a baby which means I will have to pay attention to it and give it time. I will be a mama...

For a moment, as a cool breeze passes through my hair, I feel the weight of reality hit me, and I close my eyes. Responsibilities...

I turn around, leaning back against the rail and stare up at the night sky as I tilt my head back, closing my eyes.

You've got this, Azura. You're known as the Westwood Devil. You can handle anything.

It is then that I sense someone is watching me. This feeling...

I know who it is as my eyes snap open, and I stare at the balcony far above. His scent is faint, but it is definitely him.

"Stop perving, you old man. I can sense you."

My Life
Leo

Night has fallen, and I can't sleep. Something about seeing her again is fucking with my mind...

It is one of the rare fucking days I'm able to get home before midnight and just crash, but yeah, that isn't going to happen. I frown, pushing the thought away as I look down at the Sangue territory from my apartment window. The glittering lights in the windows of the building are a reminder of how far we have come from the caverns we once resided in. The mini-town is not only a sign of our prosperity, but it is proof of advancement. Not to mention it is pretty easy on the eyes, with modern buildings, high-tech security, and packed with everything my people need to thrive in this world.

The Sangue Pack... one would not think that we were once a pack of rogues who had been raised and forced to serve one of the most psychotic evil monsters of all time. Living in torment, fear, and abuse left its mark on us all, marks that don't just vanish overnight. We have the highest number of people suffering from PTSD. Memories of torture and terror don't just leave us. Even the few who agreed to have their memories removed didn't feel as settled as they had had hoped. Some things just don't go away...

The dreams that haunt my nights still remain; the abuse, the torture, the fear... they don't just go away. I grew up thinking maybe I was fucking weak to not be able to deal with it but then I realised it is part of who I am, what helped shape me into the man I am today, even if people can't fucking stand me. I don't care. My pack is my priority, and although we are one family, I still make sure that each one of them is able to fend for themselves and would be able to live alone if the need ever comes. We need no one else.

A pack that I run, yet I do not hold the official title... a title that Marcel, my father, holds. In fear of my views, he refuses to hand it over to me, instead taking the side of his family, staying true to his vow that until I yield to the Council and find my mate, only then will he deem me worthy as the Alpha. I will never bow down to the King's Council like a coward. I won't lie. That title will be mine. The last time we talked before he went on holiday, I had told him he needed to let me take over, but still, he refused. He wants me to find my mate, saying only she can guide me and get rid of the hatred within me.

Hatred... I don't really know if I feel it anymore. I feel numb to it all. There are only a few things that make me feel anything. But soon... I am planning to force his hand until he passes that title to me. I have proven my fucking worth. I'm not a child who will obey his dictatorship.

As for a mate... fuck, I do not want to become a fucking slave to a woman, but when I saw her in that club... I had lost control. She had been so fucking appealing. I was in a meeting when I noticed her from one of the rooms. I was dating Nikki, and I hadn't planned on having fun. Didn't mean I couldn't enjoy the view but then that same sexy doll had turned out to be my fucking mate, and the sex... well, if the mark isn't proof of how fucking good she felt and tasted, then I don't know what is. At that moment, I wanted to make her mine forever. Meant to be mine fucking forever but she turned out to be none other than a Westwood. Fuck that.

Her father is one of the Elite Eleven, a title that is unofficially given to the strongest alphas in the country, and then they act like they aren't fucking elite. Pricks.

When I found her last night, it was a fucking coincidence. We were heading home from a certain trade I had to take care of when I saw a wolf running through the trees, but it didn't look normal, so we followed it. No matter how much I hate the elite, it doesn't mean I will let someone die. Even if she isn't my mate... I hate the odd pull of our broken bond. The fear for her wellbeing as I carried her to my car, driving as fast as I fucking could to get her back here, unnerved me. I hate the feeling.

She shouldn't be here. I don't need her to fuck anything up. I agreed to a few weeks, and I need her fucking gone fast, and whilst she is here, I will ignore her but I still want to know exactly how she had ended up with that rabid wolf. Only she has the answers, and although I fucking don't care, I still want to know. I am certain there was someone else there. I smelt no one but there had been footprints, my men confirmed that. I even tried to get the data from her broken phone to see what she was up to out there, but the entire thing had been damaged in the fight. I'll still get something out of it; it will just take a while longer since the acid from the WB12 has damaged the circuit board.

It didn't happen on my territory, and I know it shouldn't bother me, that I should just let it go, but the poison bothers me. A flare of anger and irritation rushes through me at the storm of emotions that run through me, and I light a cigarette, taking a long drag.

Just then, the sound of soft footsteps padding on the marble floors reaches me, and Nikki's scent fills my nose, a smell that has always appealed to me, yet it doesn't compare to hers.

"Hey, you have been working for three days straight. Today you're home. Come on, let's get to bed." She wraps her arms around my waist, her hand caressing my abs as it dips down to the band of my pants. "Come on, Leo." She kisses my neck as I smoke my cigarette, slipping her hand into my pants and massaging my cock.

"I'm not tired," I reply quietly. Despite the pleasure that rushes through me at her touch, I am far too preoccupied.

"Then how about some fun?" She kisses my neck sensually.

"Not in the mood."

She sighs and lets go of me. "Leo." She has my attention, but she doesn't speak. Instead, she sighs in frustration. "Leo!"

"What?"

"Can you look at me when I'm talking to you? What is going on? You've been so distracted for the last few weeks; it's getting to me. Don't tell me it's

My Life | 59

that same woman you cheated on me with!" Her brown eyes fill with irritation and accusation. Pain is clear in her voice.

My eyes flash dangerously, and I glare coldly at her. I had showered that night, washing away every memory of Azura, but it didn't take away the marks that she had left on my body. Marks she had seen.

"Do not fucking question me! What I do has nothing to do with you. As for your petty worries, I haven't seen her again, nor is she on my mind. It was one fucking mistake. I won't see her again. She's fucking no one." My anger is rising, and I glare out of the window.

"You better be telling the truth. Since then, I feel we don't even have sex as often as before!"

"We fucked yesterday," I growl.

"Three days ago. Not yesterday," she corrects me.

"I'm not fucking counting," I reply dangerously, turning and grabbing her throat. Her eyes flash gold, but her heart is pounding as she stares at me with a flicker of fear and desire.

"I just mean it's not the same. It hurt knowing you cheated on me, Leo. I'm trying my best to keep us together. To get over this..." she whispers, her gaze turning to my lips. I take a drag on my cigarette, letting go of her.

"I've been busy. If you want to walk, Nikki, walk. I won't hold it against you."

"We've been together for over two years, Leo. This change is scaring me," she exclaims in frustration and desperation. "I forgave you for cheating on me-"

"Forgave me?" My eyes flash dangerously as I glare at her.

Dressed in nothing but a red satin gown, she looks perfect, and I know exactly what hides behind that tiny piece of fabric. With black hair, light brown eyes, sexy curves, and slightly on the petite side, Nikki is a piece of candy that only a fool would deny. She is only three years younger than me, the ideal age gap. She is smart, level-headed, and she is fucking good in bed, or so I thought until I had the taste of something I should never have had.

If Nikki is good, the fucking psycho on the floor beneath us is fucking euphoric. I hate her, from her large dazzling blue eyes, those plump lips that are so fuckable, and glossy black hair which looks unreal. She is-

"Leo! You're doing it again. Can you even hear what I'm saying?" Nikki yells, cutting off the train of thought that I fucking hate. "Leo, I am so fucking-"

The sounds of a door opening and small feet reach my ears. I clamp my hand over Nikki's mouth, warning her to stay silent. I turn just as Corrado comes into view, removing my hand. His brown hair is a tousled mess, and his hazel eyes are full of sleep.

"Daddy?" He rubs his eyes. "Why are you shouting?"

I warned you, do not give me fucking shit when he's around. Get the fuck out of my sight.

She looks at me before nodding tersely and walking back towards my bedroom, and I stride over to my five-year-old.

"What's wrong with Nikki?" he asks me innocently. I crouch down, ruffling his hair.

"Women. They are pretty crazy. We were just having a debate over football. You know, she's a Man U fan," I reply quietly. I don't want his life to ever have problems. He chuckles before hugging me.

"Oh, no, wrong team! So when did Daddy come home?" he asks. I wrap my arms around him.

"Not long ago. You were asleep, so I didn't disturb you," I reply, standing up and lifting him onto my shoulder. He grins, holding on tight. I pause to stub out my cigarette before heading to his room.

"I tried to stay awake, but Jackie said I should sleep. I want Grandad to come home. I get bored. Will you have a day off soon?"

I have something I need to take care of that doesn't involve pack work, and I have been swamped for the last few months with it, but after tonight, I'll have a bit more time. Revenge sure is fucking sweet.

"I can't promise that, kid, but I'll try," I reply quietly, frowning as I push the door to his bedroom open wider and crouch down as we enter so as not to bump his head. I place him on his bed, and the look of disappointment in his eyes makes me feel the need to explain myself. "I have a lot going on, Corrado. Things I need to take care of."

"But you always have things going on... I want you to be here with me."

He is fighting back tears, and I stroke his hair. He needs someone who can take care of him. The only problem is although Nikki treats him well, he doesn't warm up to her. Plus, he is mine. I can't expect it of her. What the fuck do I do?

"Well, how about I sleep with you tonight?" I suggest, looking at the tiny car bed.

"Yes!" His excitement lights up his eyes, and I give him the tiniest of smiles as he moves right to the edge. This pup would sacrifice his own space and everything for me. I get onto the tiny bed, my legs dangling off just as they always do, and I hold my arm out to him, allowing him to pounce back into my arms. "Now I'm happy," he declares, staring up at me with pure happiness in his eyes.

"Yeah? Now sleep."

"Will you please take a day off, Daddy?" I look into his eyes. This pup is the thing I really fucking care for. Sure, Nikki and the pack are close seconds, but nothing beats him.

"I'll try," I reply after a moment, making his heart skip a beat.

"Yes! Thank you!"

"Now, sleep," I order seriously.

He nods, and, despite his excitement, he soon becomes drowsy. His breathing becomes steady, and shortly after, he is fast asleep. I pull my phone from my back pocket, looking at the time. I'm sure the news will have reached him by now...

I turn on a news channel, keeping the volume low as I stare at the short clip of a plane that had exploded mid-flight.

"... currently debating if the explosion was due to a technical issue or if this was a targeted attack. On board was twenty-seven-year-old..." I smirk coldly.

"That's what happens when you mess with me," I mutter, switching it off.

I take out a small burner phone from my back pocket and dial a number. I wait for someone to pick it up. The moment it is answered, I don't wait for anyone to speak.

"I hope you enjoyed your gift. Courtesy of The Heimtückische Wölfe Cartel." My voice is low, but the power that is in it shows I mean business. A roar of pure rage rings through the phone.

"How dare you kill my son?! I made the mistake, not him! I asked for forgiveness!" My smirk fades, and I stare at the phone.

"There is no space for mistakes in this business, Web. Take it as a warning. Try to double-cross me again, and I will fucking kill each and every person that you love. Schurke Wolf forgives no one."

Another roar of anger follows, and I cut the call. My message has reached him loud and clear. No one messes with me and gets away with it. I dial another number and sit up, slowly easing Corrado off my arm. *Sorry, kid. I got some work to handle, but I'll be back before you wake up.*

I leave the apartment, stepping out into the hall. Only the lift and a flight of stairs lead off from here, with the entire top floor being mine.

Is she asleep? Not that I fucking care.

I crush the burner phone and take out my usual one, calling Eric.

"Hi, Alpha."

"Any updates?" I ask.

"No, there was no scent to catch onto. Whoever was with her, they just vanished. I'm back now, but the team is still out there."

"Good. Keep looking. I want to know exactly who else was there."

I hang up, frowning as my mind wanders to Azura. There is definitely a reason she wants to stay here. She had tickets to Sweden, which means she was leaving. Is it the rejection that is making her want to run? I know the emptiness inside doesn't go away... is it that, or is there more? No. There is definitely more. Her staying here is the biggest sign of that. I had seen her cogs working before she suddenly wanted to stay. She is up to something...

I step back inside the apartment, walking through to the huge balcony and staring down at the pack. My gaze dips to the room to the left on the lower floor. The lights are on, and the balcony doors are open. I rein in my aura, my eyes fixed on the balcony, and that's when I see her, clad in nothing but a sports bra and a tiny pair of briefs, running her fingers through her hair as she steps out.

I lick my lips, my gaze raking over her ass as she leans on the rail for a moment. Her silky hair slides over her shoulder, and I can see her injuries are almost gone. Good.

My gaze falls on her ass. Thinking back, it is fucking crazy that she is that psycho kid who I had once made cry before we went to fight that Djinn. She sure has grown up fucking fine.

I'm so lost in checking out that ass that I don't realise she is leaning pretty far out, and, for a second, I think she'll fall. Moving forward, I am ready to jump, but then she moves back, turning and bracing her hands on the rail as she dips her head back, staring at the sky. What the fuck was I about to do?

Her breasts are pushed together, the perfect fucking size that fits nicely in my hand. Not tiny, not huge. Enough to wrap around my dick perfectly whilst she sucked me off.

Fuck, Leo, focus.

I move back slightly, making sure she can't see me, when her eyes suddenly snap toward me. I know she can't see me. Had she sensed me watching? But it is her words that fucking grate on my nerves.

"Stop perving, you old man. I can sense you."

The Sangue Pack
Azura

He steps forward, raising his eyebrow as he takes a drag on the cigarette. Why does that look so damn fine? Something about a man smoking always looks sexy. My mind is messed up…

He is shirtless, that drool-worthy body of his making my stomach flutter like crazy. His black jeans sit low on his hips, and from this angle, I can see the curve of that sexy ass of his, too.

"Keep wishing for that. You ain't all that," he replies, his sharp blue eyes meeting mine.

"Oh, yeah, right, it's my dream to have you drooling over me. How can I forget? I'm head over heels," I shoot back mockingly, not missing the way his eyes trail over me smoothly before he looks back into my eyes.

Although I want to ask about his son, I'm not sure if I should. To hell with it, I'm asking.

"I never knew you had a son. Like, no one has ever mentioned it."

"Why should they? My business is no one else's."

"He's cute, unlike you."

I shrug, turning my back to him. I don't want him to look at me with those eyes that are so intense that I feel that he is peering into my soul. He has already done so, took it all, and then tossed me aside.

"He's a good kid."

At least you treat him well.

"Definitely not like you," I say, turning back to him.

His eyes meet mine, and, to my surprise, he jumps down, landing a foot away from me. My heart skips, and I almost smile. Now that is something I would do. I am about to speak when his gaze flickers over me, and I suddenly realise what I am wearing.

"I have some questions regarding that dead wolf," he says, hooking the thumb of his free hand into his jeans as he smokes his cigarette. My stomach sinks. How did I think that would never come up?

"I was just… there's nothing to say."

What was I doing in the middle of nowhere…

"You weren't alone. Care to share exactly who you were there with?"

"I don't know who that wolf was. He came out of nowhere and attacked me," I reply defensively, suddenly feeling as if I am being interrogated. Leo steps closer, his eyes on me as he blows out a string of smoke.

"You weren't alone. There were others who vanished. So, let's do this again. Who were you meeting out there? Because as far as I'm concerned, your parents think you are in Sweden. What are you running from?" My stomach sinks, but I look at him emotionlessly.

"You."

His eyes flash, and he grabs hold of my hair, twisting his hand into my locks as he yanks me closer, tilting my head up. My breath hitches as his scent invades my senses.

"I know when I'm being lied to, little she-wolf, so don't test me," he growls.

My heart is thumping, and I hear his speed up slightly. Chest to chest, the bond between us sparks… an emotion I don't want… a pull I don't need… pain I don't deserve… but the moment I feel his package brush my stomach, reality hits me with a slap. I place my hands on his chest and force him away.

"First of all, I don't owe you any answers. Secondly, be a bit respectful to the woman in your life and stay the fuck away from me," I say coldly. "Damn Rossi."

I don't wait for a reply. Pushing past him, I enter the apartment and lock the door. His eyes meet mine for a moment through the glass, glowing steely blue, before I pull the curtains shut and close my eyes.

I need to stay away from him, physically, at least. The moment he got in my personal space, it became hard. I will not let him play with my emotions.

I press my legs together, hating how he has fixed himself in my mind, the image of him in just those black jeans... even if I am never going to approach him, it is definitely okay to masturbate to him. Yup, I'll assault him in my thoughts. I chuckle at the thought, dropping onto the bed and rolling onto my stomach, imagining Leo in hot pink boxers. I cackle at that image. Aww, he would look cute! No, wait, imagine those plush lips covered in hot pink lipstick. So adorable!

I wish I could speak to Sky about this, she would have fun mocking him with me, but I can't tell anyone anything. Especially not who my mate is.

I grab the tablet and open one of the two chat apps I use. I sign in and text Mama and the others, not wanting them to worry about me, before going to sleep.

The sound of someone knocking on the door wakes me, and I sit up.

"What time is it?"

Another knock. I drag myself out of bed and grab my discarded pants from the night before. I slip them on as I walk through to the main room and open the door.

Oh, it is a good thing I put some pants on. There stands Nikki, carrying some breakfast. The girl is fine. I don't blame Leo for choosing her. Plus, those breasts are sexy. Some women are just blessed with cantaloupe melons, then there are some who have big honeydew melons, and then there is me with my mango-sized ones. Shame.

"Good morning. Did you sleep well?" she asks.

"Morning. Yes, I did, thank you." I smile at her, ignoring the pang inside of me as the image of her kissing Leo returns. He's hers.

"Great." She saunters past me and places the bag on the kitchen counter. "I brought breakfast. You are welcome to cook if you want, but I know you have nothing for today."

"I can't cook, trust me, but thanks, and don't worry about me. I'll find something to eat, I always do. You guys got mice or rats running around here? I could just grab one of them."

Her smile vanishes, and she looks disgusted. I guess my humour doesn't go down well with her.

"Kidding," I add.

"Oh, yeah, of course!" She tosses her hair back and shakes her head. "So, anyway, breakfast is here. You are free to roam around town, permission from Leo." She emphasises his name, leaning on the counter.

"That's nice of him," I reply, opening the bag.

"Yeah, it's not like Leo to even allow anyone from another pack here, especially if they aren't mated to someone from our pack... so, how did you get into his good graces?"

Thanks to Selene's weird humour, I guess?

"You should ask him; it's a mystery to me, too. He isn't very likeable, is he? I mean, apart from being handsome, he's quite mean. Don't tell him I said that! But if it helps, he let me come here because he knows my mate," I say, placing my fingers on my neck as I give her a playful wink. It isn't a lie.

"Oh, yeah, sorry. I forgot you're mated," she says, her gaze dipping to my neck, and she frowns.

"Is something worrying you?" I ask, taking out the sandwich. Ah, tuna crunch! Nice.

"I just, I don't want to sound like I'm possessive or anything, but I'd appreciate it if you didn't hang around my boyfriend in nothing but your underwear." She purses her lips, looking at me defiantly. Last night... she must have seen Leo and me from one of the windows. I look at her and raise my eyebrow.

"Are you actually worried? Seriously, Leo hates my guts. Besides, I'm a little psycho and am not as sexy as you, my girl, so don't worry. You're the one Leo wants." I place the best grin I can summon onto my face, despite the crushing pain inside of me.

Yeah, I don't compare. She is sexy, polite, with no loose screws, and she is calm. Leo and I would just knock heads constantly. We are a match the Goddess made whilst she was drunk on moon wine or something weird like that. Do they have wine up there? Hmm, I'm sure they probably do. Damn, she should stop working when she's so damn drunk. Are you listening, Selene?

"Yeah, I guess it is just me being possessive." She forces a smile. Guess she no longer likes me.

"He kind of intruded on my balcony. You need to whip his ass into behaving." I shrug, biting into the sandwich. She lets out a laugh.

"Oh, I miss the days I was a careless teenager. You'll grow up, and you'll realise nothing is so easy," she replies in her sweet tone. "Well, have fun." Nice dig. She waves her fingers at me before she struts out, and I sigh.

"I will definitely have fun."

That fucker. Damn Rossi.

Once I pull on some ripped denim skinnies, a black crossover halter top, and a pair of sneakers, I leave the apartment. I will go to the shops, get some groceries, order a sim card, and grab a phone.

I walk through the streets, feeling so many eyes on me, but no one says anything until I am busy looking at a window display.

"Whose mate is she?"

"She is marked..."

"She's hot."

I look over at the two men who are talking quietly and give them a withering look.

"I burn, too," I reply sweetly, turning towards them. "You do know it's rude to talk about someone when they're within hearing distance?"

The two blond men exchange looks, and I realise the big, muscular one is the one I had seen with the dogs last night. He has a beard and dark blue eyes, whilst the other has quite a lean build and grey eyes.

"Emmet, Delta of this pack," the leaner one says, walking over to me and holding his hand out.

"Azura," I reply, taking his hand. Jackie's mate?

"Ah, Azura. Now it makes sense. Jackie, the pretty little doctor who treated you, is-"

"Your mate. Nice to meet you." He smirks and nods.

"Eric, Emmett's older brother," the bearded bear replies, his eyes wrinkling as he smiles.

"I like you," I reply, shaking his hand. Emmet cocks a brow as Eric grins.

"I like you, too."

"Don't let his words get to you. He's just a thirty-four-year-old who hasn't found his mate," Emmet mocks.

"Jealous that he is living the single life?" I reply, automatically going into defensive mode. Emmet's smirk vanishes as Eric lets out a loud laugh. He raises his hand for a fist bump.

"I'm being real now, I like you." I wink at him, fist-bumping him.

"So, care to point me in the direction where I can buy some sewing stuff?" The boys exchange looks.

"Yeah, no one really has that kind of shop here."

"Hmm, shame," I sigh. I really want to make a voodoo doll to pass my time.

"If you write me a list, I'll be going out to the city later. I could maybe grab what you want?" Eric offers. I think I definitely like him.

"Oh, yes, please, that would be great!" I exclaim.

Eric takes his phone out of his pocket before unlocking it and holding it out to me. He has opened the note app, and I begin writing my list quickly. I skim it over and type in the last item. Ice blue buttons at least 1 cm in size.

"Thanks so much," I say, taking my wallet out of my pocket and passing him forty pounds.

"That won't be necessary, it's just a few-"

"I'm paying," I cut in firmly, ending the conversation with one glare.

"So, how are your injuries now?" Emmet asks, watching me keenly. He seems too sharp for my liking, and I give him a thumbs-up casually.

"They're healed. I can't even tell anymore," I reply, turning so they can see my back, where all that is left is some slight bruising which should hopefully be gone soon enough.

"Cool. Welcome to the Sangue Pack, home to the most fearless wolves in the country. I'm sure your pack doesn't compare," Emmet smirks. Is it just me being paranoid, or is he trying to find out where I'm from?

"Nice, well it's great to stop by here... I'll be on my way, bye."

I walk off, slipping my hands into my back pockets as I walk away, feeling their eyes on me. Why is everyone so curious to find out where I am from?

Two hours later, I have walked around the entire town, and I have even done some shopping. The pack is impressive and of a good size, but it is the training section that is to die for. Not only do they have the latest state-of-the-art gym hall, but the training facility, which is a computerised hall with built-in automated firearms and machinery that will attack the training wolves, is something right out of a movie. I am in awe. Sure, the Academy and even our packs have similar things, but this... this is at an entirely new level. The entire ground in the room moves, giving the effect of an earthquake. The illusions created by the computers make real-life situations appear in the room down below. Right now, they are in a forest setting, being attacked by some kind of monster. This shit is right out of a zombie apocalypse movie! A few men and women are watching.

"It's impressive, isn't it?"

I turn away from the indestructible display window and look at a man who seems to be in his thirties. He is in a suit, well built, tall, with black hair and hazel eyes.

"Raj Kapoor, the Sangue Pack Beta," he introduces himself.

"Azura," I reply with a small smile as we shake hands. "And yes, very impressive; the technology is so advanced. We have rooms with firearms and stuff, but the life-like illusion without any eyewear? Plus the fact that they are actually using their sense of smell, although it's all machinery?"

"The younger Alpha is impressive with anything to do with technology. He actually came up with this when he was abroad at the tender age of twenty. He had the blueprints and a vision. His father is the one who put the idea forth to the Council, and... well, everyone started something similar, but it is our young Alpha who is the mastermind behind it. You have to admit, even with all the impressive magic and technology of the Academies for the Gifted, none will be as fine as this."

I stare at the screen above the glass, a view that shows us exactly what those below are seeing, and shake my head.

"No, we see a metal room, one that will often be filled with magic, but this… it's a game changer… Alpha Leo is smart. I'm impressed."

"He is a good man, too," Raj says with a nod before he points at a woman who has been thrown to the ground. "There's a system that also assesses teamwork and strategy."

"No wonder no one from this pack even needs to go to the Academy," I murmur. Raj smiles slightly.

"Well, that's another story. I haven't seen you before. I thought all the new mates had arrived a few weeks ago."

"Oh, no, I'm not mated to anyone here, I'm just visiting. The Little Alpha knows my mate," I reply, internally smug at my newfound name for Leo.

"Ah, I see." Raj nods and after chatting for a bit, I take my leave. It is obvious, unlike my pack, anyone who enters this one is strictly watched. Did the Beta talk to me to evaluate me?

I enter the block of apartments, and the first thing I notice is Corrado sitting forlornly on the floor whilst a woman is crouched over him, trying to cheer him.

"Would you like to go play outside, Corrado?" she asks.

"No."

"Ice cream?"

"No."

I head to the lift, looking at the boy who now turns, watching me curiously.

"Hey, kiddo." I flash him a smile. "You alright?"

"I'm… bored," he says after a moment. That wasn't the word he was going to use. He had changed his mind mid-sentence.

"Now you shouldn't be bored. Kids your age should be up to some mischief! Want to come to my place? I'm going to cook," I offer before I can stop myself.

"I don't know if Alpha Leo will be okay with that," the woman says hesitantly.

"He's bored, and besides, you will be there with him," I reassure her, pressing the lift button.

"Ah, of course. That can work," she smiles, obviously relieved.

We enter the lift, and Corrado hurries in excitedly. Are there no other children around for him to play with?

"What are we going to cook?" he asks.

We?

"Well... I'm thinking, sandwiches."

"Oh, I love sandwiches!"

"Perfect. When will his dad be back again?" I ask the woman.

"Late, I'm afraid," she replies.

That works. I do not want Leo showing up and giving me shit. I guess I will be having company for dinner tonight.

Cookies and a Voodoo Doll

Azura

This kid is a little devil in disguise, and I like it. With Katara having no interest in mischief and the quintuplets too big to obey, I miss them at this age.

"So, you can't cook?" I look at the tomato and cucumber sandwiches that he is gawking at disdainfully.

"Yes, I can. I made these." I push the plate towards him, proud of my accomplishment. No, I can't cook. All I can make is nachos, and that's in the microwave.

"Oh. We don't call this cooking," he adds.

"Well, can you cook?"

"I'm five."

"And?"

"I'm too young to cook." I smile, reaching over and tugging his cheek.

"Yeah, sure, but you are old enough to judge. Let me tell you something, making a sandwich is an art. Look, I had to margarine the bread slices perfectly, then spread the cucumbers that were cut into equally sized thin slices, we then added some sliced cheese before finishing with perfect thin slices of tomato."

"The tomato is thick, and the cucumber slices aren't equal sizes," Corrado mumbles, looking at the sandwich sadly. "I thought I'd have a home-cooked meal today." My heart squeezes at his pitiful tone.

"I will have Rosaline prepare you your favourite meal, Corrado," Winona, the woman who has been minding him, offers.

"No, thank you. I will have the lumpy sandwich."

"You really are your father's son," I grumble. Prudish Rossis.

I smile despite myself, watching the child bite into the sandwich. See? I can do this. In a few years, it will be me and my pup, and I will make them sandwiches. My smile fades as I wonder if I'll be enough, but then I shake the thought away. I have Mama, Dad, Liam, and Raven. I'll be okay. I have to be.

"Are you alright?" Winona asks. I smile and nod.

"After we eat, what will we do next?" Corrado asks.

"I can take him to his room if you like," Winona offers.

"No, he can keep me company, I don't mind."

When I return to my apartment, the bag of sewing supplies I had asked for was outside. I guess I will create a voodoo doll tonight, and this little cutie can help me.

"His dad isn't back, right?" I ask once we have eaten, and I sent Corrado to set the stuff up on the table.

"No. Is there a problem?"

"No, not at all. I just don't want him to worry or anything." I am a little uneasy. Have I done the wrong thing by inviting him like this?

"I mind him on the nights he is out. He will be back after midnight. It's nice to see Corrado having fun." Winona smiles, watching Corrado take the things out of the bag and put them on the table. She is a pretty woman, probably in her mid-twenties, with blonde hair and brown eyes. "Don't worry. The Alpha may be an intimidating man, but I will tell him Corrado wanted to spend time with you. I'm sure he'll appreciate it."

I'm sure he won't.

"Well, if he doesn't ask, then we don't need to mention it," I suggest lightly, pouring two glasses of milk for Corrado and me. "I'm sorry, I don't have any tea bags or anything. I don't drink hot drinks."

"Oh, it's fine, I'm not thirsty. The sandwich was rather nice. I will wash up whilst you and Corrado... knit?"

"Not exactly knitting..." I smile, winking at her as I walk over to the table, placing the tray of milk and biscuits down before plopping down. A wave of nausea washes over me, and I take a steady breath before I pick up the stack of fabric squares.

"Okay, so we are going to make dolls, all right?"

"Dolls? I don't want to make a doll." He scrunches up his nose, and I chuckle.

"We are going to make cool dolls," I say, taking up a light blue fabric. "So, we will sew this like this and stuff it with wool, then we will create two legs, feet... Look, we even have dark colours; we can make a pirate doll?" I suggest, offering him a cookie.

"Oh, I see! Can we have a robber doll!?"

"Perfect, and I even have black and white striped fabric for the torso!" I wave the fabric square, and he smiles, now a lot more excited.

An hour and many pricked fingers for me later, we are done. There on the table lie two round-bellied cloth dolls. One has a striped body with black legs and feet and a strip across the eyes where we had attached two black buttons. The other has a creamy peach fabric face and arms, with a black body and grey bottoms. I am now drawing some black doodles onto the arms.

"What are you doing, Azura?" he asks, leaning over curiously.

"Oh, I'm giving him tattoos," I tell him as we both munch on the chocolate chip cookies.

"Oh, like Daddy! He even has blue eyes like Daddy!"

"No, no, it's not your daddy. It's just someone I know," I say, putting the doll aside. I will finish it later.

"Corrado, shall we head to bed now? It's late." Winona asks him.

"No, Winnie, five more minutes?"

"It's bedtime," she persists gently.

"Six more minutes... okay, then, seven more minutes?" he barters as she continues to shake her head.

"Well, I'm going to sleep now, too, so how about you go to bed?" I offer gently. "We can hang out tomorrow if you are a good boy and go straight to bed?" He seems to ponder it over before nodding.

"Promise?"

"I promise." It isn't like I have anything to do whilst I am here.

He stands up, giving me a hug before he runs off, taking hold of Winona's hand, his robber doll in the other. I smile, getting up and walking them to the door.

"It was nice to meet you, Azura. Thank you for spending some time with him."

"You, too, Winnie. Nice meeting you."

She smiles and waves as Corrado gives me a smile. I close the door and go back to finishing off my Leo doll. Now all I need is something that belongs to him, then when it is done, I will staple gun his ass, or better yet, his dick. It will look just like his precious Jacob's Ladder.

I begin cleaning up the sewing stuff. It is a relief that Winona had cleaned the kitchen for me. Although I had just made sandwiches, I had created quite a mess. I am now gathering up the needles, trying to find the lid of the thread picker.

Earlier, Corrado had referred to Nikki by her name... which means she isn't his mom. So, who is? My stomach churns at the scary déjà vu the entire situation is giving me. Two children from two different women... one a mate... a mate that he doesn't want...

Stop it, Azura. You are not Indigo.

"Where have you gone?" I murmur, bending down to look under the table for the lid when the doorbell rings. I frown, glancing over at it and stand up. I wonder who that could be.

I pull the door open, only to see Leo standing there, dressed in a suit, his eyes blazing steely blue as he grabs me by my neck, making me gasp.

"Stay away from my son," he growls threateningly, his hand around my neck painfully tight. "If you think that you can use a child to weave your way into my life, you're fucking wrong."

My eyes flash, and I ram the thread picker that I hold in my hand straight into his arm, making him let go of me, his eyes flashing. Taking advantage of his disbelief at what I have just done, I raise my hand and punch him hard, aiming for that pretty fuckboy face, but he is fast, dodging it, and I only manage to graze his jaw. Works for me.

"Don't you *ever* manhandle me again," I growl, my own eyes blazing silver and my heart thumping.

A cold smirk crosses his face, and in a flash, he has grabbed my arms, twisting them painfully behind my back before he spins me around and pushes me up against the wall. My first thought is for my baby, and I shift positions, letting my shoulder take the impact.

"Then don't come near my son," he whispers menacingly in my ear. His scent and his touch send my heart into a frenzy, but it does nothing to soften the pain that squeezes my heart at what he is insinuating.

"I wouldn't use a child to get something I want," I shoot back quietly. *If that was the case, I'm carrying your child in me... that alone would have given me leverage if I wanted.*

"Your actions say otherwise," he says, shoving me away. I turn back to him, my own anger blinding me.

"I don't want you in my fucking life, Leo. As for the boy, he was lonely. If you were a decent parent, you would at least try to be around for him," I growl, "and next time you fucking touch me, I will claw your eyes out. Do not test me."

"I'd like to see you try," he spits. I step closer, my heart beating.

"Don't push me, Leo, because I do as I say, and I'm sure you don't want this entire pack to know who I am," I hiss. His eyes darken, and he clenches his jaw, fighting his anger.

"Stay away from him. He's mine, and I don't want a Westwood anywhere near him. You don't belong here. The sooner you're fucking gone, the better." His words hurt, but I just stare at him challengingly, unblinkingly matching his glare.

"I can't wait either," I spit resentfully.

"At least we agree on one thing," Leo's icy reply comes. Grabbing the thread picker and ripping it from his arm, he tosses it onto the ground, our eyes meeting once. "You are a fucking psycho." With that, he turns and storms off.

My heart is raging. I grab the bloody object from the ground before slamming the door shut. I toss it in the kitchen sink, trying to calm the intense storm inside of me. Staying here isn't helping... maybe I should just leave. This baby's safety worries me... what do I do? This is a bad idea.

Maybe I should just come clean to someone about everything, including what happened last year. I wonder if Judah will try to contact me soon; hopefully, he thinks I'm still wounded or dying somewhere. A girl can hope, right?

I run my hand through my hair. An evening that had started off pleasant and happy had been ruined by just a few words.

Dickface.

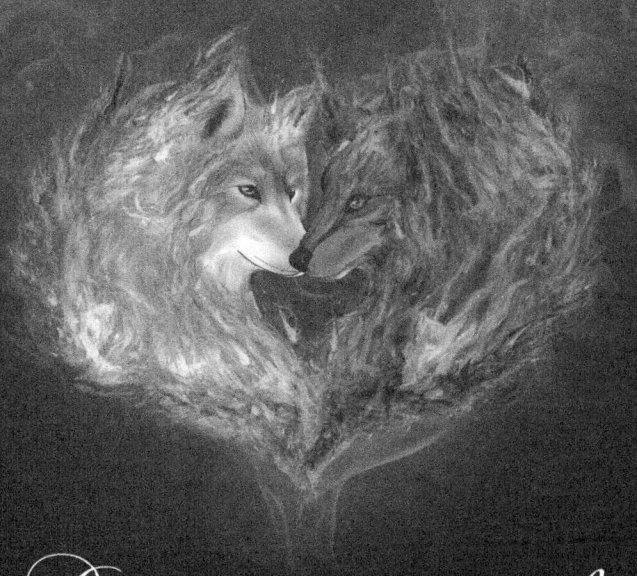

Discussions and Decisions

Leo

I switch the coffee machine on, smoking a cigarette as I lean against the worktop, looking down at my arm. The wound is long gone, but the memory remains. She is a fucking psycho. Who the fuck goes around stabbing people with whatever shit they have at hand?

I overreacted. I know I fucking did, but the moment Corrado started to show off his doll…

I want her out of my life. I need her gone, but I also know she has reasons that are forcing her to stay, none that involve me. There is something that she is running from, and I am certain it is linked to whatever the fuck happened that night. If I am able to find out, I can have it dealt with and then tell her she is safe to leave early.

Her phone. I need to get to work on that shit.

"Good morning, Daddy," Corrado says as he comes out of his bedroom with Winona.

"Good morning. You sleep okay?" I ask, crouching down and ruffling his hair. He smiles at me and nods, giving me a hug.

"I slept the best, and Simon the robber slept with me! I want to go to Azura's again today, okay? She said I can!" I resist frowning, hiding my irritation as I ruffle his hair.

"Don't you want to hang with Jackie or Nikki instead? Or Winona? I'm sure she takes good care of you."

"But Azura is so fun."

Yeah, she is fun, and a complete psycho! You never know what shit she's going to pull next.

"She even made a doll that looks like you, Daddy!" I raise an eyebrow.

"Did she now?"

"Yeah, she said it's not you, but it does look like you." He grins as Winona begins taking things out for breakfast. I stand up, lifting Corrado onto the worktop.

"I'll make breakfast for us today," I tell her. She has already dressed him. I have a bit of time before Emmet shows up anyway, and I need to explain to this kid that he is not to see her again.

"Are you sure, Alpha?" I nod, and just as she is about to leave, I speak to her through the mind-link.

He is not to meet Azura. She is a guest here, nothing more. I don't trust her entirely. Be more careful next time, Winona. Not everyone who appears to be good is good.

Sorry, Alpha, I will keep that in mind.

It's fine.

Thank you. I'll be back at noon.

Perfect.

She lowers her head to me before closing the door behind her.

"So, what do you want to eat, kid?"

"Pancakes," he replies without even thinking.

"Pancakes it is. Nutella?"

"Yes, and fruit!"

Flipping the kettle switch on, I take the ready-made mix out, adding water before getting the pan. He watches me, smiling happily, and I ruffle his hair before I begin on the pancakes.

"Thank you for spending time with me, Daddy." This kid can induce so many fucking emotions in me, I don't even know how. I give him a one-armed hug, squeezing him.

"You don't need to thank me for anything. I told you that," I remind him, pouring some boiling water into a large bowl.

"Yes, but I want to." He smiles as I flip the pancakes, adding some Nutella to a small bowl and placing it in the boiling water to soften. He sighs heavily, and I glance at him as I take the three pancakes off and add some more.

"What's up?" I ask him, waiting for the second batch to be done.

"You know Azura? She can't cook. She said making sandwiches is cooking."

My heart fucking does some weird shit. I hate when I learn new shit about her because I hate how it fucking catches my attention. *She is a Westwood, remember that, Leo.*

"Yeah?"

"Yes."

I drizzle the Nutella on top before slicing some strawberries and raspberries, scattering them over the pancakes. I grab a knife and fork and then pick up the plate.

"You should teach her," he adds as I lift him down from the worktop and carry his breakfast to the table.

"She's only visiting, Corrado. She isn't a friend, so you need to stay away from her," I remind him quietly as he happily climbs into his chair. Stubbing my cigarette out, I walk to the fridge and take out a bottle of milk. I pour him a glass before picking up my coffee, and I carry both to the table and sit down.

"But I really get bored. I don't have anyone to play with."

"Corrado, we have an entire pack here. What about Amanda and Jake?" He scrunches his face at the mention of his friends at school. He has just started, but he is already a grade ahead of the rest of his age group. I made sure he focused on learning the moment he showed signs of being ready.

"I don't like Jake anymore, and Amanda cries all the time."

Corrado is a mature kid in many ways, he doesn't really get on with the other kids his age, and those a little older don't really mix with him due to the age gap. He also isn't interested in playing ball as much as he likes watching it, preferring to colour and paint in his free time.

"What about the other one, what's her name... Anita? Didn't you say you are going to marry her?" He puts down his fork and rolls his eyes as if I have just asked a dumb question.

"Daddy? Did you marry the first girl you liked?" I raise an eyebrow. The kid has a point.

The first girl I liked... I don't remember her name but I remember she was killed back in the caverns because her father refused to obey Endora. I remember those days still... seeing the blank look in Dad's eyes as he obeyed her blindly... the scary reminder that I was on my own... even though he doesn't remember half of what he was forced to do, I do. I remember it all. The horrors of life without even an ounce of daylight. Every night I fell asleep, not knowing who would be dead the following morning.

"Daddy!" I glance at him, picking up my coffee as he pulls me from my thoughts.

"Yeah?"

"Will you marry Nikki?" he whispers, glancing towards my bedroom door.

She is probably still asleep. I know I have been avoiding her because I just can't get intimate with her lately. Seeing Azura here has made it fucking weird. Sure, I ended it with her, but try fucking someone when the woman you're fucking distracted by is in the same building.

"Probably not, kid. I'm not considering marrying her. Now, drink up."

I run my fingers through my hair, thinking back to that night. I was ready to come home and tell Nikki I had found my mate and it was over. I never wanted a mate, nor did I ever try to look for her, but when I ended up marking her, I knew I needed her. I craved her, and so did my wolf. I didn't even know her name, but I was ready to make this shit work, but then I learned her identity... I couldn't accept her. Fuck, how do you accept someone who would never share the same views as you? I know she isn't biologically a Westwood by blood, but she is by birth and upbringing.

"Nikki said you will." Corrado's words make me look at him sharply.

"What do you mean?"

"She was on the phone to the birds, and they were saying that because you made a mistake, she should ask you," he continues, eating his food contently, chocolate covering his lips. Birds. He means her screechy nasal-voiced friends who I can't fucking stand.

Marriage... why can't anyone just take life a day at a fucking time?

"Hmm," I reply, grabbing a tissue and wiping his face. He gives me a grin as he eats a strawberry.

"These are the best pancakes. Ever."

"I'm glad, kid."

Leo, I'm outside.

Come on in, I reply, unlocking the door via my smartwatch.

"Good morning, champ! Damn, pancakes without me?"

"Sorry, Daddy made them, and you know Daddy only cooks for me," Corrado replies, making me smirk slightly. This kid knows the fact that he is my number one perfectly well.

"Damn, Leo. I'm sure a few more won't make a difference?" Emmet says, dropping into the chair opposite me.

Is the shipment here yet? I question through the link.

No, tomorrow night. It's a big one, Leo. Risky as fuck, and I don't even want to think about the consequences if we're caught.

No one will get caught. I've rewired security long enough for our shipment to get past the radar. This shipment alone will give us the money to set us ahead. Every child here will have funding in their bank to fall back on.

I love you, Leo, and I love how much you care for our pack... but risking it all just to make sure every child is financially set? This one was fucking risky. Come on, man, people can fend for themselves. You ain't their fucking godfather to have to deal with everyone.

I know what I'm doing.

I look at Corrado, who is scrutinising us sharply.

"I'll go play in my room, Daddy," he suggests, knowing we are talking business through the link. Smart pup.

"Sure." I ruffle his hair as he gulps his milk down.

I stand up, turning the TV in his room on from my watch, and head to my study with Emmet behind me.

"Leo, your father, the Alpha, is coming back. Where are you going to keep such a big amount of drugs?"

"Right here. Like I said, Emmet, I know what I'm doing. I already have buyers from the entire continent ready to get their hands on some. When

I'm done, I will become one of the wealthiest men in the world," I say coldly, sitting down in my chair.

"At a very dangerous risk... I heard Web is not going to sit back, Leo."

"Let him come. The next time he crosses my path, I will kill him," I say carelessly. He sighs and sits down opposite my desk.

"I'm the Delta, Leo, if your dad so much as questions me-"

"I put you in that position, Emmet, we both know the truth. You work for me, not Marcel," I warn icily, lighting another cigarette. He sighs but nods.

"I know, man, but the Alpha said if you settle down and shit, he'll pass the title to you. Are you going to mark Nikki soon? Do it. She's hot, and I'm sure she's good for you. You haven't been in any relationship longer than a year before her."

"Yeah, but I have a plan."

"Marcel will be back soon, right? What is your plan?" Marcel... yeah, he will be.

"I'm sure he'll visit his precious brother before returning home," I reply, ignoring his comment about Nikki. "My plan is of no concern to you. I've got a shitload to do." He understands the dismissal and stands up.

"Well, I hope he doesn't come back here and act like you owe those Elite anything. All they fucking did was ruin our lives," Emmet says coldly, his eyes filled with hatred. I nod.

"Yeah. He can try. Nothing can change me."

"Good man. You know they're all manipulative and fake. Oh, yeah, all okay with you and the visitor? I heard shouting last night."

"Did you? Then why are you asking me?" He simply shrugs and nods.

"Well, I don't know what the deal is between you two, but if you need someone to talk to, that's what friends are for, right, mate?"

"Right," I say, standing up, thinking, *She hasn't left her apartment today.*

Emmet leaves, and I lock the door after him with the touch of a button before I walk over to the wall behind me. Placing my hand on the small square panel on the wall, it instantly lights up, and my hand is scanned by a blue light. A keypad shows up, and I thumb in the twelve-digit code before the wall opens, and I step into a lift. Closing it after me, I key in a third code before it zooms downwards towards one of my favourite places. One final code and a handprint opens the metal door that covers the entrance to my cave.

The room is dark. Only the lights from the screens and the blue LED lights fill the dark room. My main desk is a curved one, which contains three screens hooked up to the main monitor. A touch screen with maps is on the far wall whilst the wall opposite has twenty screens, each displaying different things, connected to a tower computer block. I have a few tables covered with things I am working on, including one of the latest weapon designs. In the wrong hands, these would be dangerous, but they are made only for the Sangue Pack. A screen near the lift looks into my office up in my apartment, so I know if anyone knocks. Two doors lead off from here, one to the underground car park, my secret passage away from the pack, and the second to a bedroom.

I walk over to the far table where I have been working on the psycho's phone, picking up the decoder just as my watch beeps. Will you look at that…

I press a button, making one of the screens flicker on, and I turn to see none other than Azura sitting on the bed. She leans down as she keys something into the laptop I had left in her room. Her breasts catch my attention in just her blue sports bra. She is fucking fine, I can't deny that.

So, she has finally decided to use the laptop I have given her. Who is she about to contact?

I walk over to my desk and sit down, turning the volume up and splitting the screen, bringing up the screen that Azura is looking at. She is video-calling two people. It takes me less than ten seconds to check the IP addresses. One is from down towards London, and the other is from Midnight Academy.

She sighs, and I look into her blue eyes as she waits for her call to be answered. I can tell from her eyes that she hasn't slept well, and she almost looks upset. She tilts her head, and my attention falls to her neck. My mark is fucking beautiful and it sits perfectly on her smooth skin.

She looks into the webcam, and for a moment, she seems to be staring right at me. She doesn't look away until I hear a sound as her call is answered.

"Hey, hey, Zu!"

The green-eyed girl on the screen is none other than Alejandro's daughter, Skyla. Next to her is her twin, Kataleya. The two are opposites, with Skyla having black hair and several piercings, while Kataleya has sandy blonde hair and is by far the gentler one. She waves at Azura as a fourth girl joins their conversation. She has short, dyed hair. I know her, too, from when I did a background check on Azura. Song Daquin. She is Azura's age and one of her friends from the Academy, a witch.

Feeling like a creepy online stalker, I mute the images from the screen so the only one I can see is Azura's, and sit back, still able to hear them perfectly. I know even watching her is fucking wrong, but I need to see her facial expressions. See what exactly she is planning to tell them. I light a cigarette as I wait for them to finish their mundane conversation. I want to see if I learn anything interesting from this conversation.

"Where are you, Azura?" Kataleya asks softly, obviously concerned for Azura.

"Yeah, we all know that you are not in Sweden," Skyla adds.

"I'm... at his pack," Azura replies quietly. I raise an eyebrow, my gaze flicking back to her gorgeous face.

"Shut the fucking front door!" Skyla snaps, and I hear a thud.

"But he... rejected you, right?" Song asks quietly.

"He did... but I don't have a choice."

"What do you mean?" Skyla asks sharply. Azura frowns and stares at her nails. I had never seen her so serious.

"He contacted-"

My phone beeps, and I take it out. It is from Emmet, a fucking image that makes my heart thud. An image of none other than Marcel below my apartment block.

The Alpha's back. His voice fills my head.

Oh, shit, no, he isn't meant to be back for a few fucking weeks. I need to get Azura out of here ASAP. I hit close on the window and head back up. I have to get her out before Marcel sees her.

His Return
Azura

"He contacted me, wanting to meet me. I just need a break." I shrug, trying to fight my nausea. I am lucky it only comes now and then and that I'm not vomiting buckets, unlike Raven with Katara.

The girls know a lot of what happened with Judah since Kataleya and Song both had not wanted me to get involved with him to begin with. I wish I had listened, but I never really ever do, do I?

"Fuck, Azura, you need to tell someone," Skyla says, her eyes flashing a deep plum purple that turns darker the closer it gets to the pupil. Her anger is clear within them. "He needs to die."

"Skyla," Kataleya murmurs soothingly, placing her hand on her sister's shoulder.

Skyla closes her eyes, exhaling deeply as she fights her emotions. Malevolent, her cat, meows, brushing her shoulder, and Skyla's eyes open as she smiles down at her little fur ball. Those two have been together for years. Alejandro had gotten it for her when she was little; ten years on, they are still the dangerous green-eyed duo.

I am the eldest of us four and it is my job to take care of them and be there for them, but instead I am giving them more stress. Skyla has her own troubles to deal with.

"I do agree, you need to tell someone about him. What's holding you back?" Song asks, raising an eyebrow.

"There's a lot... I just wanted to let you guys know I'm okay, and if anyone asks, you spoke to me, and I'm perfectly fine. Song, can you get me some images of Sweden and email them over to me in case Mama or anyone asks me about it?" I can't really tell them much when there is a chance that he has something in this room recording me. "Look, I got a new number, adding it to this chat right now. Save it and miscall me with yours. I may not have much data, but I have downloaded the chat app for emergencies, but for the life of me, I couldn't remember your numbers."

Besides, I have no idea if Judah is watching my social media accounts. I don't want him to know I have access to anything.

"Oh, perfect," Song says as Sky miscalls me straight away. My phone rings, and I smile.

"Okay, great, now we're in touch again." I also need something from Dante... but how do I ask him? I look at his sisters, and an idea comes to me. "There's something I need from you, Kat." She raises her eyebrows innocently and nods.

"Of course, anything. What is it?" I smile at her. They are only seventeen, but she is so mature. Probably the most mature of the four of us.

"Dante, I need you to ask him for something since he will trust you." I hesitate, wondering if they'll question me if I ask for it. Her face falls, and she looks at me worriedly.

"Azura, Dante's not in England. He flew to Italy three days ago and won't be back for a month."

"Shit."

"What is it?"

"I need to ask if I can borrow something from-"

I hear the apartment door open and frown. I am only in my lingerie. Who would just come in here like that? How the fuck did they get in? And then he appears, Leo – in nothing but pants, his sexy tattooed body on full display, making my core automatically clench with desire. He is looking at me, but the look on his face tells me something is very wrong. Even when his eyes flickered as they lingered on my breasts, it was only for a second.

"Got to go," I say, snapping the laptop shut.

"We have got to go," Leo says, his voice dangerous. His eyes run over me before he looks around the messy bedroom and grabs my pants. "Put them on. You need to leave. Right now." My heart thunders as his words echo in my mind.

"Why?" I find myself asking as I slip my jeans on, my hands shaking slightly as the urgency in his voice gets to me. I don't have a plan. What if Judah finds me? No, I just need to focus, I'll find-

"Azura, are you listening?" he asks coldly, yanking me up from the bed. I gasp when I'm slammed into his chest. Flickers of sparks rush through us, his scent invading my nose. I freeze when he pulls my pants up over my ass, making my heart skip a beat as he looks down, zipping them up.

"Why do I have to go? I can't go yet, I haven't made a plan where to go." He frowns, grabbing my bag and shoes super-fast.

"I don't care. I need you out." His words sting. Then, he grabs my arm, pulling me to the door.

I try to tell myself it is fine. Go home, and just tell someone. I don't have any other option. After last night's drama, I need to leave anyway. Maybe it is for the best, but he needs to at least let me grab my stuff!

"Leo, listen to me!"

"Fuck, keep your voice down," he growls, trying to pull me out of the apartment.

"No. Do not fucking manhandle me, I told you that already! What the fuck is going on?" I need time, and I need to know why he is acting like this!

"Listen to me, little she-wolf, either you come quietly, or I will force you," he growls menacingly, grabbing my upper arm as he pulls me from the room.

Fuck, he is strong. He almost has me at the stairs when we hear footsteps and Corrado comes into view, instantly making Leo let go of me.

"What are you doing with Azura, Daddy?"

"You should never have told him your name," Leo mutters quietly. "Corrado, go back up."

"No, Daddy! Grandad is coming!"

Marcel is here? Now his behaviour makes sense. It is obvious he doesn't want Marcel to see me, and I don't either.

"I can just stay in the apartment and away from your dad, then just leave when the coast is clear?" I suggest quietly as Leo looks around, assessing the best way out. Corrado runs to one of the windows, excitedly looking out of it. It would buy me some time if he listens and lets me wait in my apartment! Why is he so fucking stubborn?

"No. I don't want to risk it. Here's your passport, Eric will drop you at the edge of the territory. Go wherever you want. Sweden, home, I don't really care. Just stay the fuck out of my life," he says, making me freeze.

Our eyes meet, and that crushing pain returns with a vengeance, my heart thumping violently. It is stupid of me to feel like this, but I suddenly feel alone and so damn lost. *I'm not fucking alone. I have a family,* I remind myself.

He frowns, his gaze sharp as he scrutinises me as if wondering what is on my mind.

We hear the ding of the lift coming up, and Leo swears,

"Fuck."

"That's what happens when you have only one damn lift," I mutter.

He doesn't reply, glancing towards the lift before he pulls me back to my apartment and enters, kicking the door shut behind us. I close my eyes, pulling out of his hold.

"Stop pulling me around like I'm a damn doll!" I hiss.

He ignores me, instead advancing on me until I am pushed against the wall. I don't dare shout, not wanting to be heard. I can hear Corrado's faint shout and Marcel's laugh. Shit, I am in a pickle. And, to make it worse, Leo is invading my personal space. I hate how he makes me feel, the way his scent intoxicates me, the way those icy blue eyes seem to look through me.

He has Nikki. I would never do that to anyone but then why am I not rejecting him?

I gasp when he places one of his hands on the wall, caging me between himself and the wall, the other finger placed to his lips, warning me to keep my voice down.

"What are you running from? This time don't lie because my patience is already thin," he asks quietly. Leaning closer now, he places his other hand on the other side of the wall, trapping me completely. Do I tell him?

"You don't care, so why should I tell you?" I whisper breathlessly, trying not to focus on the heat radiating off his body.

"If you don't tell me, it's your fucking loss, but you're right. I don't care. I just want you gone from my life," he says coldly. "Last chance. Who are you running from?" I close my eyes.

Do I tell him? No, I can't tell him. Why though? Because I'm scared he won't care? I know he won't care but to hear it after I tell him my troubles. I don't know if I can handle it.

"It's... no one really... I can handle it." He raises an eyebrow coldly.

"Fine, whatever the fuck you want-"

"Leo?" He clenches his jaw, his eyes blazing a steely blue.

"Fuck. Stay here and stay the fuck quiet. Eric will get you out of here the first chance he gets," he warns, his eyes telling me not to mess with him right now. I nod, about to move away, but he doesn't remove his hand.

"Leo!"

"Daddy's in there!"

"Leo, you need to go," I whisper, shoving him back and taking a deep breath. He frowns, looking at me.

"Are you certain you don't want to tell me what is going on?" he asks one final time, rubbing his hand down his face.

"No. You don't care, and I'm just a Westwood who you resent, remember?" I'm not able to stop myself, the words escaping before I can stop them.

The one question that burns within me is if he found out about this child, would he hate it, too?

He looks at me, his gaze cold.

"I guess that's a no," he says quietly, turning and walking to the door. He pauses, looking over his shoulder at me, and jerks his head towards the bedroom. Is this the last I'll see of him? I quickly move away, my heart thumping as I slip in. I hear the door open, listening quietly.

"Son. I missed you." Marcel's voice comes.

"Why are you back early?" Leo's cold reply follows.

"Why? Because I decided to. Raj actually told me some interesting news. He said we had an outsider welcomed into our pack by your selflessness and was staying as a guest. I just wanted to know who it was."

"That is none of your business. So you came home to check up on me? I am not a child." Leo's voice is cold and dangerous, but I have a feeling he's holding back. His voice drips poison. He's trying to rein it in, but what worries me is what Marcel just said. Did Raj tell him anything else about me? I hope not.

"It's Azura! That's her room!" Corrado exclaims, making me close my eyes.

"Azura?" Marcel asks, his voice sharp. "Who is she?"

"Does it fucking matter?" Leo growls.

"Babe, why aren't you dressed yet?" Nikki's voice comes. "Alpha Marcel, welcome home."

"Thank you, Nikki. Now, tell me, do you know anything about this Azura?"

"It's none of anyone's business. Let's go downstairs," Leo cuts in.

"Leo, it's only your dad," Nikki murmurs.

"Azura!" Corrado calls. "My grandad is here! Daddy, let me go in!"

What do I do? Fuck, what do I do? Shall I shift and stay in wolf form? No, don't be stupid, Azura, you can't do that.

"Leo, who is in that room?"

"Babe, I'm sure Azura won't mind meeting the Alpha." Nikki's voice comes.

"Azura!" I hear Corrado, and his voice is close.

I take a deep breath, knowing Leo is going to be pissed, but I have no other option than to step out of my bedroom just as Corrado comes to a stop in front of the bedroom door.

"Hey, kiddo." I smile.

I look up to see Marcel, Nikki, and Leo enter. Leo is frowning deeply whilst Nikki is looking me over. Then I remember I am just in pants and my bra. Well, hey, I wear this look often enough. Deal with it, girl.

"Azura?" Marcel looks shocked and confused.

Well, I think it is time I divert the topic away from why I am here, and so, plastering a huge smile on my face, I give him a big wink.

"Yup. None other than the Westwood Devil herself."

An Outsider
Azura

And with those words, I walk over to him confidently and give him a big bear hug, praying that this works. I feel Leo's aura rolling off him in waves, but just when I think he is going to slit my throat in anger, Marcel lets out a hearty laugh.

"It's a true honour! I need to hear what is going on, but how about I let you finish getting dressed…" he trails off as his eyes fall on my mark, frowning deeply. "I didn't know you are mated?"

"Oh, I am. Kinda." I wink.

"Azura is really cool, but she can't cook," Corrado adds helpfully. I pout as I look at Mini-Leo. Did he really need to add that part?

Marcel chuckles, "Well, we won't need Azura to cook. We have plenty of people who can cook! But I'm happy to see you here. Surprised but happy." He places his hand on my head, and I can see the happiness in his eyes. I smile back, seeing Nikki turn and walk off. Leo glances at me but doesn't say anything.

I have a feeling he knows I won't say anything before he follows her, and I hear their footsteps receding. I hate how that hurts.

"Well, I will let you get dressed. Come down to mine when you are ready! Come, Corrado, I have brought you some gifts."

He picks up his grandson, and the moment I shut the door after them, I let out a breath of relief and run a hand through my hair. Oh, for fuck's sake, I am so screwed. My heart thuds when a sudden thought comes to me. What if Marcel mentions to someone that I am here? *Goddess, help me.*

I need some air. Entering my bedroom, I push open one of the windows, taking a few deep breaths to calm myself, not to mention the nausea that is getting to me. After a few minutes, I begin looking through my things for something decent to wear.

"For fuck's sake, Nikki, stop it!" I freeze when I hear Leo's voice through the window, my heart thundering.

"Why were you in her room? Why is she here? Something isn't right, and you're hiding it from me! Who the fuck is she?"

"I'm not fucking doing this with you! She's no one."

Thanks, dickface. But what did I expect? Him to tell her I'm his mate?

"Is she? Then why were you in her room? She was in her bra!"

"Oh, for real, Nikki? We're fucking werewolves. I've seen hundreds of she-wolves in their bras or without."

Wow, that's one way for you to make a point, Leo, fucking perv.

"In her room, Leo? With the door shut? I'm not fucking stupid! I want to know who she is."

"You heard her, she's a fucking Westwood. Happy?"

"Exactly! Why would you allow someone from a family you dislike here? There's something going on!" she shouts.

I feel a wave of guilt wash over me. I am becoming the cause of problems in their relationship. I will go to this lunch, and then I'll figure something out. Maybe I need to go to Alejandro and Kiara. Plan or not, I have to go.

"Leo!"

"I'm not having this fucking conversation with you." His voice is fainter, and I hear the distant sound of a door shutting.

I look at the beige top in my hand, feeling disappointed in myself. I have wasted enough time mulling over things and coming up with zero solutions. I walk over to the bed and sit down, taking a moment to collect my thoughts.

Going to Alejandro would fuck up a lot. Dante would have been my next option, but he isn't here. What do I even tell Alejandro and Kiara? *"Hey, so I've got some pretty wild sex tapes that my ex secretly made last year that he is threatening to release on the net. Oh, and the same fucker has something on my girls, two of whom are your underage daughters? Oh, and I accidentally killed someone, and then I was forced to help get rid of the evidence?"*

Yeah, shit is going to go down. This could get Dad pushed off the Council, too.

I run my hand through my hair before I stand up and begin gathering my things. The sooner I get out of here, the better. I shove all my things into my bag, gathering my phone and stuff and putting it into my shoulder bag. I'll ask Leo to let Eric get me out of here. I am causing problems by being here, not only for Leo, but for everyone.

I place my hand on my stomach, feeling the crushing pain in my chest once more. I need to reject him before I leave. Face-to-face if I can because I want to see the pain in his eyes when I destroy the bond completely. Anger rushes through me, and for a second, I want to unleash hell, but I simply take a deep breath.

My phone beeps, and I pick it up, my stomach lurching at the unknown number. My heart thunders as I unlock the device. Is it Judah? But after looking at the text, I close my eyes in relief.

Leo: Make sure you do not tell Marcel anything. I will handle it.

Leo. It is Leo. Thank the Goddess. The phone beeps again with a second message with the story I am to tell Marcel.

An hour later, I am at Marcel's mansion after pulling on a baggy pair of jeans that I hold up with a belt, a beige cropped long-sleeved top, and twisting my hair into a messy knot on top of my head. I know it looks silly as my hair is very silky and straight, making strands of hair stick up in all directions refusing to bend, but, hey, I'm not trying to please anyone.

Leo and Nikki are here, and if they had argued before, there is no sign of it now. He looks effortlessly handsome as ever in black jeans and a dark grey short-sleeved shirt, leaving his muscular tattooed arms on display. He is wearing shades and has a cigarette between those lips of his. He leans against the wall of the mansion as Marcel puts slices of meat on the barbeque.

"Azura, look what Grandad made!" Corrado calls, hurrying over to me the moment I step into the garden. I know Leo told me to stay away from him, but the boy approached me, and I don't plan to ignore him.

"What has he made?" I ask.

"Milkshakes with fresh strawberries and bananas."

"Oh, damn, really? I love anything with milk!"

"Me, too!" Corrado says, grabbing my hand and tugging me towards Marcel.

"Ah, Azura, come. I wasn't sure what you would like, so I have made a variety," Marcel says with a grin. He may be sixty, but he looks much younger, with his long brown hair pulled into a messy bun. His skin is tanned, and he has a very rugged look about him. Typical Rossi genes.

"Thanks, it all looks really yummy, but aren't you tired after your journey? You really didn't need to do this."

"Azura doesn't know how to cook this." I look at Corrado. Does this kid really find it so weird that I can't cook? It seems he will keep on mentioning it until all of England knows I can't cook.

"Tell me, kiddo, does everyone you know know how to cook?" He looks over at Leo and Nikki. Nikki is at the table, texting away on her phone.

"Yes. Daddy can cook the best, and Nikki makes healthy food. It doesn't taste that good because it is healthy food, but it looks really good," he whispers loudly. I'm not sure he knows werewolf hearing is a thing. I smile, tugging his chubby cheek.

"And then there's your grandad, who seems to be a pro," I add, and he nods.

"Yes."

"Here, have a milkshake," Marcel passes us both a glass. "Leo, Nikki?"

"No thanks," Nikki says with a small smile that looks a bit forced, with Leo simply ignoring him. How rude.

I look between the father and son. From what I remember, Leo wasn't like this towards his dad. I mean, it's just the rest of the Rossis he has a problem with, right?

"Thank you, it's yummy," I compliment, taking a big gulp.

"You have a moustache, Azura!"

"I rock the look, right?" Corrado laughs, and I can feel Leo's glare burning into my back.

"So, tell me, Azura, what brings you here?" Marcel asks, flipping the lamb chops over. I see Nikki raise her head slightly, paying attention.

I remember the message Leo had sent earlier, and although he has decided on the story, I don't like it. If I really want to mess this up, I know I could, and there is fuck all he can do about it, but I need him not to lose his shit. So, I sigh heavily, clutching my glass with both hands as I lick my lips. *Okay, girl, work those eyes.* I blink slowly, looking down at the milkshake before I look at Marcel.

"My mate," I say sadly, making the corners of my lips dip downwards. Only one person is immune to this façade of mine, and that is Mama.

"Your mate?" Marcel asks sharply. I nod, taking a small sip of my milkshake. Damn, this is so yummy. If Nikki doesn't want any, perfect, more for me!

"Yes. He marked me, and then he left me, and since he's from this pack, Leo is trying to make him come around and accept me," I say quietly. The lie leaves a bitter taste in my mouth. I don't know if Leo is trying to earn brownie points in his dad's book, but I hate it. Not to mention that it hurts. For a moment, I let my real emotions show on my face as I look up at Marcel. "Please, don't tell anyone I'm here. My parents think I've gone to Sweden, and I don't want trouble." Marcel is frowning, his chest heaving as he turns to Leo.

"Who is it?" he asks dangerously. Leo raises an eyebrow, but it is the words he speaks that cut like a knife.

"I'm handling it. We can't force anyone to do anything. Remember, Marcel? Or is the daughter of an Elite so precious that she just can't be rejected?" His icy reply comes.

"Leo," Marcel warns.

"I'm handling it. I'm trying, despite that little fact," Leo replies coldly.

Like hell, you are fucking handling it.

An Outsider | 97

"You better handle it, and swiftly."

"Excuse me." I smile, placing my glass down and wiping my mouth on a tissue as I walk towards the mansion. I need a minute.

Entering the mansion, I open a few doors before I find the bathroom. Stepping inside, I shut the door behind me, closing my eyes as I lean against it.

The daughter of an Elite. It is funny how differently he thinks of me. If only he knew who I really am.

The daughter of an Elite? No. I am just a freak who should have died. But either way, it is the same thing, right?

Some dislike me for my birth, others dislike me because of my personality, and then there is Leo, who hates me for being the daughter of two amazing people. My parents have done nothing to him. They don't deserve his hatred. And if they are the reason he doesn't want me, then it's his loss because they are fucking amazing.

I look into the mirror, trying to calm the storm within me. I know Marcel won't tell anyone, but I really need to get out of here. I leave the bathroom after splashing my face and head back to the garden.

"I look so cool."

I stop in my tracks, spotting Leo crouching down by Corrado as he slips his sunglasses onto his face. A small, proud grin crosses Corrado's cute little face as he turns to Nikki.

"Nikki, do I look cool?"

"Awe baby, you do! Super cute!" She smiles at him, and I simply stand there, feeling so out of place.

You're leaving tonight, Azura. End of story.

Placing a blank expression on my face, I saunter into the garden just as Nikki walks over to Leo, locking her arms around his neck. I don't know why it stings when he grabs hold of her hips.

"I'm sorry, babe," she whispers, and if I thought the day just couldn't get any worse, she kisses him straight on those plump lips of his.

I turn away, doing my best to control the pain in my chest, my eyes stinging as I take silent, steadying breaths. Shit, it hurts. A whole fucking lot.

His Hope
Azura

"Later." Leo's quiet, cold voice comes as I walk over to Marcel. "Babe..."

Conceal how you feel. You got this, girl.

"It smells so good," I say, smiling as I look at the flames.

"Be careful, Azura, it's very hot," Marcel warns. The heat of the grill is nothing compared to the burning pain in my chest.

"I don't mind getting burned," I reply quietly before giving him a smile. "So, where did you go on holiday?"

"Well, I was in Scotland for the most part, and then I stopped at a few places before my visit to Alejandro was cut short." I can feel Leo's irritation, but I don't bother paying him any attention.

"I'm sorry about that," I reply as I pick up the platter of cooked meat and carry it to the round table, where everything is already set up. I don't want to sit at the table with him, but I have no choice.

When Corrado jumps into the seat between Marcel and me, I expect Leo to take the seat next to his father, but instead, he takes the seat on my left. I clench my jaw but don't even spare him a glance as I begin filling my plate. Nikki sits down last, placing her hand on Leo's bulging bicep before she moves back, a small smile on her face.

"It's tasty!" Corrado declares, and I smile as I carry on building my tower burger.

"That's so big!"

"Well, she's got a big gob," Leo remarks.

I clench my jaw. Yeah, I fucking do, or I wouldn't have been able to take your damn dick! I should have bitten it off when I had the fucking chance.

"Leo, be nice," Nikki says, despite the small, amused smile on her face.

"Oh, it's okay. I get a lot of people jealous of my big mouth. Are you jealous, Little Alpha?" I ask sweetly, turning my attention to Leo. He raises his eyebrow as he looks at me.

"No. How about you? Jealous?"

We aren't talking about my lips anymore.

"Keep talking," I challenge him with a dangerous smirk, satisfied when his confidence falters. "Oh, yes, Marcel, what is the law against marking someone without permission?" Leo's hand shoots out under the table, grabbing my thigh as he gives it a squeeze in a warning. Marcel frowns as he stares at my neck before his eyes meet mine.

"It's a serious crime, one that would be taken to the Court of Selene."

Leo scoffs, "No one from this pack is going to ever be trialled at the Court."

"Why not, Daddy?" Corrado asks. I discreetly try to push Leo's hand off me. His fingers on my inner thigh are driving me nuts, with equal desire and anger.

"Because-"

"We follow the Council, Leo. We are part of this country and its rules."

"I follow no rules."

Right. If he's not going to remove his fucking hand then I'm just going to have to remove it for him. *One last chance, fucker.*

I glare at him, but he simply gives me another one of his cold, emotionless glares that ooze power and dominance. Nope? Okay.

I pick up the knife and cut my burger down the middle before slipping my hand under the table, knife in hand. Everyone is too busy eating, or, in

Marcel's case, trying to get Leo to acknowledge the Court. Leo is arrogantly ignoring him, drinking some Coca-Cola, so I take the chance, slamming the knife into his hand that grips my thigh and clench my teeth as I feel the blade dig into my leg.

Good. It means I went right through his fucking hand.

"The fuck!" Leo growls, his knee hitting the table and jolting the entire thing as he almost spills his coke. Sitting up straight, he turns sharply, glaring at me with steely blue eyes. That's what you get for fucking touching me! His murderous aura swirls around him, but I am not going to be fucking intimidated by him.

"What?" I snap, yanking the knife from his hand and my leg before quickly wiping the blade clean on my pants.

"What happened?" Nikki exclaims.

"I can smell blood," Marcel says, getting up as Leo smoothly shoves his hand into his pocket, his eyes flashing.

"Sorry, I just accidentally cut myself. I didn't realise how sharp the knife was," I reassure him, blinking at him innocently before waving my hand. "It's nothing at all."

"Oh, do you need a band-aid?" Nikki asks, concerned.

"No, not at all." The dickface might. Oh, wait, a band-aid won't cover that. I almost snicker.

"Babe, what happened to you? Why did you swear?" Nikki asks, confused as she now turns to Leo. Leo clenches his jaw, turning his cold glare toward me.

"She's just fucking crazy. She almost cut me," he hisses icily, suddenly standing up.

Almost? LOL Blue-Eyes, I fucking impaled you, and next time it will be your dick.

"Daddy isn't scared of a knife..." Corrado mumbles, but he looks scared, too, and remains silent. I feel bad for that, but Leo had pissed me off.

Without a glance back, Leo storms off. Nikki stands up, but after a moment she sits down, frowning deeply, and I'm sure Leo had told her not to follow.

"He just needs space, dear," Marcel sighs. I place the knife down.

Poor little Alpha has no fucking idea who he's messing with. I pick my burger up, and I see Nikki watching me as I bite into my triple stack with ease. Yeah, this big mouth comes in damn good use.

After lunch, I play with Corrado for a bit before thanking Marcel for the food and telling him I'll be heading back. He asks me once more if I'm sure I don't want my parents to know, how he feels bad for me and he can talk to them himself, but I don't want them to know and make that clear. Time to get out of here.

I'll get a taxi once I'm in the nearest city, then, from there, I'll go straight to Kiara's pack. I don't have any other option. Surely they won't put me forward to the Court of Selene.

"Daughter of an Elite."

Leo's words return to me, and I sigh. Trying to hide my crimes... wanting to be pardoned by those in power... aren't I proving to him that it is exactly what I am?

I pick up my phone, staring at it. Kataleya had texted, asking to let her know what I need from Dante. She had also attached his number, telling me that they would always be there for me. She really is a gem.

What have I gotten myself into?

I look at the number Leo had texted me from. Would he even agree to get me out of here when I had stabbed him just hours ago? I have nothing to lose.

'I'm going to be leaving. With Marcel here, I don't think it's smart for me to linger.' I pause, wondering how to word the next part. See me out? Let me out? Can I get a ride?

I put my phone down, musing over what to write, and grab the voodoo doll from the bedside table. I had placed the bloody thread picker inside of it and stitched it up. Now it contains the perfect part of Leo to make this shit work. I had stuck two pins in it earlier, but I think I'm the only one doing any damage to the real dude. Maybe if had a staple gun or maybe I should soak him in boiling water...

I smirk at my thoughts before picking up my phone to finish my text.

> Me: I'm going to be leaving. With Marcel here, I don't think it's smart for me to linger. Arrange me a car, or at least let your security know to let me out.

I hit send, thinking I should stop at Marcel's and tell him it isn't working, so I would reject my mate and leave. If I leave like this, it isn't going to help anyone's case. Marcel would be suspicious.

It is at least five minutes later when his reply comes.

> Leo: Fine. I will come get you shortly. Stay in your apartment until then.

> Me: Give me an hour.

> Leo: Fine.

I know he's probably pissed, but at least he replied. Time to get this over with.

I stand up, grabbing the voodoo doll. I fill a bowl with water and place the doll's head downwards in it. *Suffocate and drown.* I don't know why I feel gloomy but something about the entire atmosphere feels dark.

It doesn't take long to get back to Marcel's, and when I ring the door, a member of staff opens it, giving me a smile.

"The Alpha saw you arrive. He's right through here."

"Thanks," I say, flashing the man a smile before entering the living room. Marcel is standing by the window, and he turns, giving me a smile.

"I had a feeling you might come back," he says, making my heart race a little. Why did he think that? Is he on to something?

"Oh, great, I just came to let you know that I'm leaving soon. Me and my... mate just won't work, so I'm going to end it and leave," I say, feeling a wave of pain wash through me. How the fuck is this hurting me? Marcel smiles slightly, but his eyes hold emotions I can't read.

"I see."

Not what I was expecting but okay.

"Well, goodbye. I know my visit was super short, but I did get a look around the pack, and it's incredible. I think as a member of the Blood Moon Alpha family, I am lucky to even have a chance to see this place. Thank you for the delicious barbeque." I don't know what else to say, and turn to leave.

"Is it selfish of me to wish that you tried harder?" His voice is quiet, but the words scream an alarm within my head. My heart thuds, and I freeze, turning back sharply to the man that stands by the window, a few strands of my hair fall in front of my face. A wave of panic washes through me.

Calm down, he doesn't know.

"He has a good heart. He has simply let it harden with bitterness and hatred. When he loves, he loves deeply."

Leo, He is talking about Leo.

Shit.

He sighs, and looks at the sky.

"My brother, Rafael, once told me the story of Alejandro in his younger days. He was consumed by his own demons, and no matter what Rafael did, nothing brought him out from that darkness until Kiara Westwood stepped into his life. She pulled him from the darkness and became his light. Without her, the Lycan King would not be the man he is today. There is only so much that a father or brother can do but a mate... it's a mate who is given that power and connection to guide their other halves." Marcel now looks at me as I stand there, my chest heaving as I stare at him.

He knows the truth. I don't know how, but he does. His words get to me. I know the story of Kiara and Alejandro. They are an epic couple, and their story will never be forgotten, but it is his next words that really hit home.

"When you were transferred into Scarlett's womb, I was there. I saw Amelia perform that spell, and I knew from that day that you were destined for great things. You were destined to live because you were a survivor, you were strong enough to hold on after your mother's heartbeat faded. Perhaps it is only a Westwood woman who can tame a Rossi, who is so far gone that even I have lost faith."

It isn't just a statement. It is a silent plea for me to not leave. I look out into the hallway and step inside, closing the door silently behind me. I turn and look at him.

"He has a family already. He has Nikki. I am not going to take anyone's man from them. I'm sorry, but if he was single, it would have been an entirely different story, but he isn't," I say, trying my best not to let my emotions show.

"But he marked you."

"In a momentary lapse of judgement. A mistake. I'm sorry, Marcel, but that ship has sailed." I open the door, pausing, my hand lingering on the oak door. "How did you figure it out?" He lets out a small chuckle, and I look at him.

"The boy can't keep his eyes off you. He may have thought I'd buy it but putting you in the closest apartment to him was the first red flag, and the rest all fell into place. However, I knew for certain when I saw your mark. A lotus before a crescent moon... so similar to my mark that once adorned his mother's neck." His voice is deep, yet the emotions in it are powerful, and I realise for him that I am the hope he has waited for, to bring change to Leo.

But the thing is, Leo is not Alejandro, and I am not Kia.

"I'm sorry but I will never be the cause of a relationship being destroyed. Goodbye, Alpha Marcel."

He doesn't reply, and as I close the door behind me, I realise that me being pregnant with Marcel's second grandchild means I will never truly be free from Leo... free from this connection.

That's why you will reject him, Azura. Before you leave.

A Memory
Leo

I look at my phone. The message is crystal clear, but even then, I have to fucking read it a few times.

> **Azura: I'm going to be leaving. With Marcel here, I don't think it's smart for me to linger. Arrange me a car, or at least let your security know to let me out.**

She is leaving. Just like I fucking wanted…

There is no relief, nor fucking excitement at the fact that she is because once she's gone, Marcel will have a shit-ton of questions for me to answer about why didn't I fix stuff with her 'mate', and then Corrado will do my fucking head in about why I let her go.

Stop fucking with yourself Leo, you know that isn't the reason.

I light a cigarette, taking a drag on it as I stare at the phone, slowly letting out a string of smoke. It is for the best that she leaves. Her being here is fucking with me. I text her back that I'll come to get her, but she asks for an hour in return.

Me: Fine. I will come get you shortly. Stay in your apartment until then.

I toss the phone onto the desk and place my feet on it, resting back in my chair. Is it really Marcel that is pushing her to leave, or is it because of the kiss between Nikki and me? She hadn't reacted. Did I want a reaction? Yeah, I fucking did, and she didn't seem to care, or so I fucking thought until she fucking stabbed me. She had gotten pissed, and I was sure the kiss had been the fucking trigger.

Azura Rayne Westwood...

JUST OVER A DECADE AGO

I walked into the garden of Alejandro Rossi's mansion, not wanting to see Rayhan the Bastard again. I was damn bored. I wanted to get to the battle to see exactly how strong I was. A chance to unleash it all and not have to fucking hold back.

This lot takes so fucking long to say goodbye.

Alejandro's twins were out there playing with the Westwood pup.

"I got the ball, Sky! You are slow!" she teased, sticking her tongue out. Skyla frowned as she ran over, knocking the ball from her hand.

"Not that slow."

Crazy kids. I glanced over at Kataleya, who was standing there lost in thought. I knew what she had been through. I fucking hated it when people did shit like that to kids. I scanned the area, making sure we were alone, before I walked over and crouched down by her side.

"You know, if you keep on making that face, your lips are going to forever stay fucking down. You might end up looking like your dad, and that's not a pretty look," I teased, lightly prodding the corner of her lips. She blinked, coming out of her reverie, and forced a smile as she nodded.

"I'm okay," she said quickly, almost as if it was an automatic mechanism.

I'm okay. Something I always said to Dad when I was child... the times when he was himself and he worried. I'm fine, I'm okay, I'm great... lies to keep him from feeling burdened.

"It's alright not to be okay all the fucking time, you know?" I said quietly, like the fucking hypocrite I am. I never took my own fucking advice, always acting like fuck all bothered me.

"Oi, boy!"

I turned to see the Westwood pup standing behind me with her hands on her hips. She was a cute kid with big blue eyes, but I swear she gave me a vibe that told me she was not to be trusted.

"What?" She leaned closer and shielded her mouth with her hand, as if not wanting anyone to hear.

"I can see your smelly knickers," she whispered loudly, making Skyla laugh manically. I raised an eyebrow. What the fuck are these kids fucking bred on?

"First of all, they ain't knickers. Second, what the actual fuck?" I asked, standing up and glaring at the pup. She simply shrugged.

"Well, I was only trying to help you," she retorted, about to pick up the ball when I grabbed it and walked over to the steps, spinning it on a finger. "Give our ball back."

"Ask nicely."

"Give it back, knicker boy!"

"I ain't fucking giving it back now," I growled, tossing the ball lightly against her forehead. I saw Liam step out into the garden, ready to intervene as I caught the ball with ease.

"That didn't hurt. Try again," she challenged, catching the ball and tossing it back at me. Doe she mean it, or is it a threat?

I resisted a smirk, bouncing the ball off her forehead again as lightly as I could. Liam stopped a few feet away, clearly fucking worried for his sister, but to my surprise, he didn't intervene.

"Zuz-"

"Not now, Liam. I said – again."

"You sure, pup?"

"I. Said. Again," she challenged, her chest heaving as she threw the ball back at me. Yup, she was fucking pissed. I wondered what'd happen if I carried on. Would she end up crying?

I kept bouncing the ball lightly off her head, but it was beginning to look a little red. Is no one going to stop me? I didn't want to stop by myself, that would make me look like a fucking wuss.

"Azura, enough. Come on, let's go inside," Liam tried again. Why the fuck is he listening to a kid?

"No, I said again," she said firmly, her large eyes glaring at me. The little psycho.

I saw Alejandro step out from inside from the corner of my eye as I raised my eyebrow at the determined kid in front of me.

"Again." I frowned.

"You're fucking weird," I stated coldly, tossing the ball at her head again.

"Again," she commanded, and this time, I realised she wasn't even blinking. The first sign of a serial killer.

"This kid's fucking psychotic," I remarked.

"Again," she repeated, making me frown. Okay, no. Her fucking head was red, it was going to bruise if I carried on.

"Nah, I'm bored," I said carelessly, tossing the ball to the ground and letting it roll away.

"Cut that shit out," Alejandro growled.

She stared at me for a moment, and for a split second I felt fucking bad. She was going to cry. I hated making kids cry. We stared at one another before she quickly ran after the rolling ball. Maybe not.

"Leo started it," Skyla chimed in, frowning at me. That little shit.

"Yeah, once. She's the one who told me to hit her again," I shot back, taking my lighter from my pocket.

Liam sighed, "Azura is just..."

"A weirdo," I finished helpfully, pulling out a cigarette.

"I thought you weren't going to come here?" Alejandro asked me, crossing his arms as Azura returned with the ball. Damn, she was totally okay. Maybe I didn't need to worry. She walked off, and I shrugged as I looked at Alejandro.

"I changed my mind; I was bored as fuck waiting around," I replied, placing the cigarette between my lips. I was about to light it, when something hits the back of my head hard, knocking the cigarette from my lips.

I growled menacingly, turning in a flash. Kataleya gasped, and it was the only thing that held me fucking back. As for the little psycho, she simply stared at me, anger clear in her eyes.

"What the fuck was that?" I hissed. Alejandro was next to me in fucking seconds. He doesn't trust me.

A Memory | 109

"What the, was what?" the psycho pup shot back, stopping herself from swearing.

My eyes flashed and I felt angry, but more so because of the fact that Alejandro had jumped to my fucking side. Yeah, he'd never trust me, no matter how much he fucking pretended to care, but it was half my fault I guess. I did make Rayhan the Bastard's pup cry not that long ago, although he was the one I was trying to scare. I turned my attention to the pup, glaring at her.

"The actual fuck? You psychotic-"

"Stupid person!"

"Leo did that to Azura first, Daddy!" Skyla added defensively. Liam picked the deranged pup up protectively, as if she was not a fucking psycho but a precious little shit.

"Put me down!" she screamed.

See?

"Come on, Zuzu, calm down," Liam tried to soothe her.

"No! He hit me first!"

"But weren't you saying 'again, again'?" Liam asked gently, trying to calm his sister, who was struggling to get free.

"I don't care! Give me the ball!" she shouted.

I stood up, ready to get the fuck out of there. I was done. Alejandro placed a hand on my shoulder as if he thought I was going to attack her or some shit.

"She's a kid. Are you seriously going to start a fucking fight? Why the fuck were you using her as a target?" he asked, frowning. Once again, he had me fucking wrong. Nothing new there. My eyes blazed a steely blue as I shrugged him off.

"She's a fucking maniac," I growled.

"You're the maniac!" Azura shouted, glaring at me murderously. "Get out of my sight, or I will poke your eyes out and cook them!"

Haha, kid. I wouldn't mind picking on you a little longer, but I think I've fucking overstayed my welcome.

"Azura!" Her brother tried to calm her, unsuccessfully.

"Oh, yeah?" I growled.

"Yeah!"

One thing I learned from back then, and what happened over lunch, was not to trust that fucking calm of hers. The calmer she appears to be, the higher the chance that she isn't okay. I wish I had the power to read her mind. Does Nikki really bother her to that extent? Or is she just fucking pissed at me for some other shit? Either way, she wants to get out of here, and I am going to show her out. I could have Eric or Emmet show her out, but I just need to see her one last fucking time.

She hasn't accepted my rejection yet. The pull of the mate bond is so powerful, and I need it fucking gone. I'll tell her to reject me. I'll make sure this thing between us is destroyed. Just the thought of it unnerves me for some fucking reason. I run my hand through my spiky hair, trying not to let my thoughts divert elsewhere. Azura and I are never going to work.

An hour passes faster than I anticipate, even though I have done nothing but sit here. I have to go get her. I stand up, feeling the weight of reality sitting on my shoulders.

My phone beeps, and I look at the reminder that crosses the screen. Fuck, has a month passed already?

Slipping my phone into my pocket, I leave my office, only for Nikki to jump up from the sofa. She never disturbs me when I am in my office, my rules that she obeys, but sometimes it just let the dark thoughts consume me freely without a distraction. If it was Azura in her place, she would fucking throw out all the rules I had in place. It would make for one crazy life. How the fuck did the Goddess pair us?

"Leo, are you going out already? You changed?" She looks me over, and I frown.

Obviously, I fucking changed. The psycho fucking stabbed me, and I had blood everywhere.

"Azura is leaving." *Azura...* I rolled her name on my tongue. I like how it sounded, even if she is a fucking maniac.

"She's leaving?" Nikki looks surprised, and maybe a tad fucking happy.

"Yeah. Things didn't work between her and her mate, so I'll be showing her out."

"Thank, Goddess." She crosses her arms, and I raise an eyebrow.

"Do you have an issue with her?" I ask, taking a drag on my cigarette.

"Not really, she's a little weird." Her words irritate me, and I raise an eyebrow.

"Not following the fucking stereotype doesn't make a person weird." *Fuck, Leo, keep your mouth shut.* Nikki looks surprised at my comment as she walks over to me.

"So, are you saying you don't find her weird?"

"I don't really have an opinion about her." I shrug coldly. She nods slowly.

"Okay, whatever. I'll come with you to bid her farewell."

I need to talk to Azura alone. I'll send Nikki off once she has said her goodbye. We have just left the apartment when Corrado and Winona appear at the top of the stairs. Corrado is near tears as Winona struggles to calm him.

"What's going on?" I ask sharply.

"I want to go to Azura's!" Corrado frowns. I guess me telling him he couldn't see her went out the fucking window. They had played together at Marcel's, and I know he fucking likes her.

"Azura is leaving today. Want to go say goodbye?" Nikki asks him.

"I don't want her to go," he whispers, stilling suddenly. Something stirs inside of me as I stare at my son. He has never taken to anyone as he has to her. *Why does she have to be one of them?*

"Leo, you coming?" Nikki's voice brings me out of my reverie.

"Yeah."

"Alpha." I turn to look at Winona.

"What is it?" I ask.

"Can I bid her farewell, too?"

"Sure. I don't get why an entire fucking entourage is needed to get rid of one woman, but fine." A smile crosses her face as she thanks me, waiting for me to go down the stairs first. I reach the bottom only to see Corrado with his arms around Azura's neck as she crouches on the floor in front of him, hugging him tightly.

"Please don't leave, Azura."

"I'm sorry, kiddo. I got to go," she replies. Her black hair, which had been put up into a sexy bun, is half out, and my fingers itch to brush it back.

"Please."

As if sensing me watching her, her large blue eyes snap up to meet mine, eyes that are filled with so much fucking emotion that if Corrado's voice wasn't enough, the pain and sadness in her eyes are enough to tug at something deep inside of me. I force myself to look away and turn, smoking my cigarette.

"If you've packed, let's fucking leave."

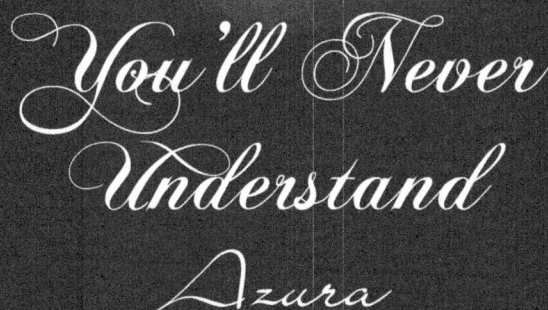

You'll Never Understand
Azura

"Let him say goodbye," Nikki says, placing her hand on Leo's arm. He doesn't reply, and I hate how he has an effect on me. Why that single touch of Nikki's squeezes my heart. *Fuck, Azura. This isn't you.*

"Please don't go yet. How about staying for five more weeks?" Corrado pleads, drawing my attention back to his gorgeous hazel eyes.

"I can't. I'm sorry," I apologise softly. Oh, why is this kid making my heart break just like Marcel almost did?

When he loves, he loves deeply.

I push the memory away and smile apologetically at the boy before me.

"Then why not six more weeks?" I let out a breathy laugh.

"You know you're adding days on top?" I ask, ruffling his hair.

"But I had fun. I want to make a police doll, too…"

My heart clenches, but I can sense Leo's anger rising and know he is getting impatient or simply annoyed that Corrado is talking to me, but I'm at least glad he let him say goodbye. Maybe the Ice Prince has a soft spot for his son at least.

"I'll have one sent to you, okay?"

"What is this?" Nikki's voice, which is full of disgust, asks.

I turn to see her lift the Leo doll from the bowl of water. It looks a mess with the ink having run all over the fabric.

"Oh, Daddy! That's the doll that looks like you!" Corrado exclaims, making Leo's eyes snap to the doll as Nikki looks at it with a look of obvious disgust.

"Eww, why do you have it in water? You're so weird," she says, dropping the doll onto the worktop. My eyes flash, and I do my best to remain calm as I stand up and walk over to her. *Just because I've been nice you, don't go around calling me weird. I hate the damn word.*

"It's a voodoo doll, made to be tortured," I explain in an extremely sweet voice that drips with venom before picking it up from the worktop and dunking it back into the water, not caring that water splatters over her. She jumps back, staring at me as if I lost my mind. I hate how I suddenly feel upset.

I know I am different. I fucking get it, and if voodoo dolls make me happy, then I'll make them. I don't need anyone to judge me.

"A voodoo doll," Corrado says in awe. "Daddy, what is a voodoo doll?" I smile, his words lifting my spirits a little. This is why I like kids best, because they don't judge you.

Leo comes over. Just the way he walks makes my stomach flutter infuriatingly. One hand in his pocket the other holding his cigarette. His sharp blue eyes are as cold as ice, but they still seem to ignite a fire inside of me. I look away from him as he reaches for the doll, and I brush past him to grab my bag.

"I'm ready to leave," I declare. I do not want him to examine the doll. I'm sure he'll realise it is meant to be him.

"Yeah, let's go. Nikki take Corrado home."

Home. Their home.

"Azura, please don't go," Corrado whispers, running over to me as Nikki holds her hand out to him.

"Corrado, she has to leave. Winona take him," he commands icily when Winona enters.

"Yes, Alpha." She looks at me and gives me a small smile. "It was nice meeting you, Azura. Thank you for spending the evening with Corrado."

"It was great getting to know you, too, Winnie," I reply, when suddenly an idea comes to me, and I hurry over to my suitcase. Crouching down, I unzip it and take out the rest of the swatches, wool, and stuff I had to make my dolls. I stand up and pass them to Winona. "If you could make a doll with Corrado?" I ask quietly. I think I hear Nikki mutter something, but I'm not sure what it is.

"But making dolls with Azura was more fun," Corrado protests, staring at the supplies.

"I know. Come on, Corrado, let's go," Winona says gently yet firmly as she leads him away. He looks over his shoulder at me, looking disappointed, before he vanishes from view, and I quickly crouch down and zip my case back up before picking it up.

"Shall we?"

I was hoping to get him alone but that's not going to happen as Nikki follows me out of the room. I walk to the lift seeing Leo and Nikki looking at each other. I step into the lift, placing my foot between the doors so it doesn't shut. Nikki is frowning, and Leo looks as indifferent as ever, but I can tell they are mind-linking. Leo turns to her, his face as arrogant and sexy as ever, and I don't know what he says, but it makes her look away.

"Bye," Nikki says after a moment, glancing between Leo and myself before she walks off towards Jackie's apartment, running her fingers through her hair.

Leo's attention turns to me as he strides over, oozing with power, and steps into the lift. Once the door shuts, he presses a button and scans his thumb. This is my chance.

"I-"

"I don't want to hear it," he says, making me frown.

"I haven't even said anything, and trust me, you will love to hear this," I retort. "By the way... Marcel knows." His heart rate speeds up as he looks at me sharply, his eyes turning a steely blue before he calms himself.

"Fuck. What else did he say?" he asks coldly, his eyes look dangerous.

"Not much, but he loves you," I reply, Marcel's words still burning in my mind. He simply scoffs in obvious contempt.

I know that many would say fight for my mate... and maybe if there was no Nikki in the picture, maybe, just maybe, I might have. I want to see the Leo that his dad said existed inside. Don't get me wrong, if he pissed me off, I'd still unleash hell upon him, but seeing him with Corrado shows he is a good dad.

Fuck! I need to stop thinking like that.

"Sure, he'd want the perfect fucking woman to be the Luna. You're a Westwood. I'm sure that made him feel fucking proud."

The lift doors open, and I realise we are in what looks like a dark underground car park. The walls are fully made of steel with dim lighting and more cars than I can count. There are a few doors leading off from here, too.

"I'm far from perfect, and your dad knows that. You don't know anything about my life, Leo, so stop fucking pretending you do," I shoot back.

"Oh, yeah? So you're not just a pampered princess who has been given the entire fucking world at her feet." He stops in his tracks and turns towards me. I almost knock into him, stepping forward just as the lift door shuts behind me.

"I'm not doing this with you. Don't judge when you don't know anything about my life. Everyone has their trials, Leo. No one's life is just fun and games," I reply, shaking my head in irritation. I'm about to shove past him when I pause and look up at him, trying not to pay attention to the heat of his body.

"Wow, you don't even see what you have. Tell me, little she-wolf, what exactly have you faced in life?" he asks coldly, his tone laced with mockery. It fucking hurts, and he is only making me angrier. I had heard how his life had been, how the rogues had lived, but his behaviour is unfair. I have done nothing to hurt him.

"My life may not have been as bad as yours, but I refuse to let it shape me. I refuse to let it become my present and future. I will always look for the positivity and happiness in life. You can hold on to your past, Leo, I don't really care. I'm done with you," I say, glaring up at him before I make to step around him, only for him to grab hold of my arm, stopping me. My heart thumps at his touch as I try to focus on our conversation and not his touch. I am already fucking stressed out about what Judah is capable of once I am out of here. I am sure he will find me and try to do something again.

"Do enlighten me," he says coldly. I shake my head, ready to push past him when he blocks my path once more, caging me between the lift door and his body. "I asked for an answer." His voice is dangerous, menacing even, but what annoys me the most is the way it makes my core throb.

"You won't get it because in your eyes we are just entitled, but have you ever considered that if it wasn't for those so-called Elites that you fucking hate, you would still be in those caverns! We helped save you all! We freed you! My grandfather and biological mother fought in that battle that gave you your freedom! So many members of those so-called Elite packs died for us all! Alejandro almost died! Fuck, he did die! Even though Kia was pregnant, she knew she had to fight that battle! And Rayhan, who you fucking hate so much, it was his mate who travelled to the veil to the other world to make sure Endora had no way back here! I'm fucking tired of you throwing a bitch fit! I get it, Leo. What Rayhan did was wrong! I feel that! But what have my parents ever fucking done to you? Those Elite you hate so much helped you and your people!"

I shove him back, but he doesn't even budge. He tosses his cigarette onto the floor, his eyes flashing steely blue as he sneers coldly.

"So, there it is, the part of you who feels like you did us a fucking favour."

"No! I'm just saying I get it! Rayhan fucking messed up, but he admitted it! He gets it! But don't you see how many fought Endora? If those Elites, as you called them, didn't, this world wouldn't be what it is today!" I shout in exasperation, grabbing his shirt as I shake him, but even then, he is unmoving. White-hot rage is clear in his eyes as he steps closer, his body pressing against mine.

"Spoken like a true entitled princess. You will never get it because you only see it from your point of view. No one ever fucking gets it." I try to push him away only for him to grab hold of my hips sending a violent jolt to my core.

"Then try to make me get it! I want to know!" I shout, my chest heaving in anger. He swallows, his eyes searching mine, and I know they are blazing silver. Our anger and whatever this is between us rages around us like a hurricane. "Tell me!" I scream, my eyes stinging with tears of frustration. "I want to know!"

"Shut up."

My eyes widen in shock and confusion before another wave of anger flashes through me. I try to knee him in the balls, only for him to knock my leg aside with his foot and trap my leg between his. My heart thunders as a jolt of pleasure rushes through me when his thigh presses against my core. Oh, fuck.

"Don't tell me to shut up!" I growl, trying not to focus on his body. "You have an argument, then throw it at me. Give me a good fucking excuse for you to be so-"

"I said shut the fuck up," he growls huskily.

"You can't make me-"

I am cut off when his lips suddenly press against mine in a rough, blinding kiss that sends my body into a frenzy of pure bliss. A thousand tingles course through me, and I feel every pore of my body react. My heart pounds, and I find myself kissing him back with passion fuelled by my anger and frustration. His hand slides up to my bare waist, pulling me closer as he deepens the kiss, my stomach knotting as he devours me.

Oh, fuck, he definitely can make me shut up.

The moment I feel him throb against me, and a moan leaves my lips, I freeze. One word screams in my head.

Nikki.

I push him away, and this time he staggers slightly, his eyes flashing as he stares at me, our hearts thumping violently as we both realise what we have just done.

Restlessness
Azura

"We shouldn't have done that," I say quietly.

He shouldn't have done that.

"Yeah, but don't go fucking taking it the wrong way. It was to shut you up," he says, his voice sounding thicker as he looks away. It had gotten to him, too.

This is it, the moment to reject him. I look up at him, trying to force myself to say the words.

"I..."

Do it, Azura.

Leo frowns as he searches my face for something.

Reject him. Fuck, why is it so hard? It fucking hurts.

How had he had the strength to do so? And after marking me, too. He raises an eyebrow, waiting, but I can't do it. His scent is overpowering me.

I am looking for an excuse... asking myself what I should do. When I thought of what I wanted in a mate, I always imagined someone who found me funny, someone who would be okay with me being crazy. The type to laugh at the shit I get up to. Not everyone finds their fated mate, and not everyone has it easy. But is rejection the answer, without even fighting for him? Am I just going to walk away?

Nikki, remember Nikki.

"I..."

"Yeah, I got the 'you' part, what's next?" he asks me in a husky voice. "What's wrong? Are you so distracted you can't even string two fucking words together?"

I frown, splaying my hands on his hard chest and shoving him back. The tingles of the bond ripple through us, and I think I hear his heart race.

"There's nothing about you that distracts me. I just was thinking about something," I scoff.

"Oh?"

"Aren't you short on time? Let's go." He frowns as if suddenly remembering, and he turns away, taking out some keys from his pocket.

"Yeah, let's go."

He presses a button on his keys, and a sleek, matte black Mercedes Benz SUV' lights flash. Damn, that is one sexy car.

"Wait, what do you mean let's go? Aren't you just showing me out? Or are you driving me to the pack border?"

"I'm dropping you wherever the fuck you want to go."

My heart skips a beat. Three hours in the car with Leo? After that kiss? No. That is a bad idea.

But it'll give you more time to reject him, or try to reject him...

No, just no.

"I can..." I trail off. It is safer if Judah doesn't see me leave, he won't realise where I am.

"Get in," he commands, watching me keenly as he pops open the trunk and takes my suitcase, which I had dropped on the ground at some point. Oh, fuck. His gaze flickers to my lips before he looks away, tossing the suitcase into the trunk and shutting it. "Are you getting in, or do you need me to get the fucking door for you?" He is composed once more, and I am trying my best not to savour how he had felt and tasted.

He's Nikki's.

I walk around to the passenger side and get in, admiring the luxurious, spacious interior. *Now, this is the perfect car to have sex in. Fuck, don't think of sex right now. Wait, did he and Nikki fuck in this car? Urgh, yup, probably.* The thought of it stings, but I refuse to ponder on it. Right now, I feel like shit. Sure, as werewolves, if you meet and mark your mate, or fuck them, it is fine, as then any other relationship becomes meaningless, but Leo... he should have broken up with Nikki for it to be okay, but he didn't, making me the side piece.

Reject him, Azura.

"Where to?" Leo asks as he starts the car up, and R&B music comes on.

"You might change your mind about dropping me off, but I'm going to Alejandro's pack." His hand tightens on the steering wheel, and my attention falls to the two rings he is wearing.

"Right," he says coldly.

"You're still taking me?" I ask, unable to hide my surprise.

"I already said I would. I don't go back on my word."

"But you can go back on your marking." I am unable to stop myself. The jolt of pain in my chest is powerful. Our eyes meet, and I wish I knew what he is thinking. I look away first. I'm not going to act like I care.

"Yeah, well, shit happens."

His words cut worse than a knife, and for some crazy reason, they hurt far worse than anything Judah has ever said. Is it because of the bond?

I turn my attention out the window and cross my legs, not wanting to look at him. He drives in silence, but from the corner of my eyes, I can see his tatted hand on the steering wheel. His knuckles are white.

The Sangue Pack has an underground road, one that runs for miles, and I can't deny that it intrigues me. A secret tunnel is something very ideal in many scenarios. It takes us a good ten minutes before we are out in the open. The sun is low in the sky, and the trees cast shadows on the road.

I sigh heavily, hoping that I have the courage to tell Alejandro and Kiara my entire fucked up mess. If they can just get the images of the other three, I'll be happy. I'm ready to take the fall if I have to. I need to confess to my crimes.... I kick off my shoes and place my feet on my seat, wrapping my arms around myself and resting my chin on my knees.

Will Judah come for me? Will Marcel tell everyone that Leo is my mate? Will everyone find out about the baby?

Back in the Sangue Pack, I felt safe, even though I knew I was fucking running from my problems. My baby's safety is the topmost priority for me. The Sangue Pack gave me that. Would Alejandro's pack do the same? I'm not sure. I know for a fact that Judah will find out I am there. Only Leo's pack is unreachable. Plus, he is there; my brother... I don't want to see him. I don't know what to say or what to do. I know his mom is alive. Is it wrong that I feel bitter that she even fucked my sperm donor when she knew he was mated? Urgh, I'm the same by kissing Leo back.

I hate myself for it. Does Leo really not have that much respect for Nikki? Will he be the type of mate to cheat on his mate, fated or chosen? My stomach churns, and I sigh heavily.

Reaching onto the ground, I grab my bag and take my phone out. First, I send Mama some pictures that Song had sent to me, saying I'm enjoying Sweden. Fuck, I hate lying to her, and if she knew I went to Kia's pack... well, she'll find out soon, and she will be so damn pissed. I run my hand through my hair, yanking it by accident. I had forgotten that I had pinned it up. It is a fucking mess.

I skim through the girls' messages, but I'm unable to focus enough to reply.

I begin removing my pins, letting my hair cascade down. I run my fingers through it, shaking my head to get the kinks out. The Goddess gave me hair that barely ever needs combing, probably because she knew I would forget to comb it half the time. I sit back, feeling restless, and turn in my seat a little before crossing and uncrossing my legs.

"Can you not sit in one fucking position?" His husky, deep voice that seems to vibrate within me comes. I raise an eyebrow and cast him a scathing glare.

"I'm bored," I growl.

"It's not even been an hour."

I look at him, thinking he hadn't driven himself from the club, yet here he is sending me off. I'm sure if he wanted, he could have had his driver bring me. Ignoring his annoying remark, I observe him intently.

"So, why did you come to drop me off yourself?" I ask, wanting a distraction from my mind. He doesn't reply for a few moments, as if pondering what to say as he licks his lips, his jaw clenching before he glances at me.

"You were on my pack grounds, so I will make sure you get to your destination safely." I am about to give a snarky reply when his next words stop me. "We both know you're running from something, right?" He looks at me. His eyes are sharp, and my stomach twists.

I look away, and this time I know there is no way out if he pushes me. I am stuck in this car with him, and although it felt spacious before, it suddenly feels too damn tight.

"Azura."

Azura... like always, it catches my attention. He says it differently, emphasising the "U".

"What?" I say, realising he is waiting for a reply.

"I'm waiting for a denial or an excuse," he remarks coldly.

My phone beeps, and I thank the Goddess for an excuse. I quickly unlock it, and my stomach twists sickeningly as I stare at the message that glares back at me.

> **Unknown caller: It's been a while. For a moment, I thought you were dead. By the way, nice ride. The question is, who is the driver? Or more like, how much do you care if he dies? You're mine, and it's time you come back to me like a good little pet or your new friend dies.**

This nightmare is far from over.

Flames of Destruction
Azura

Shit.

No.

Do I tell Leo?

I am trying to calm my racing heart. What do I do?

The first thing that comes to my mind is to ask him to stop at the service station and get away from him, but I have to think about my baby. Doing that would not only be a risk to me but the baby, too.

"Who is the message from?" Leo's voice snaps me from my thoughts, making my breath hitch at his question. He is watching me intensely. His piercing eyes seem to be peering into my soul.

"One of my girls." I find myself lying as I gaze out of the side mirror, trying to see behind us. Only the glaring headlights of a car can be seen. Is that him? Is he close? Will he try something? I am putting Leo at risk as well if I don't tell him. What should I do?

"Oh, yeah? Stop lying, Azura. Are you going to keep hiding it from me?"

"I'm not hiding anything…" I'm struggling.

Why should I tell him? I know why I don't want to because I'm not ready for him to tell me he doesn't care. Maybe the mate bond will make him feel something? Yet I'm still not convinced.

"My patience is fucking wearing thin. Tell me the truth because for the last fifteen minutes, we've been followed, and I fucking assure you, it's not one of my enemies."

Followed.

"Have we?" I ask, my heart thudding as I do my all not to press my hand against my stomach protectively.

"You've been too distracted to even notice, but I've taken several detours, yet that black McLaren has continued to fucking follow us. So, either you tell me the fucking truth now, or I will fucking stop this car and deal with this shit my way, no questions asked," he almost growls, his eyes flashing a steely blue.

"No," I say, grabbing hold of his arm.

Judah has weapons that kill instantly. If he uses something on Leo… just the thought of him getting hurt terrifies me. Although he pisses me off, I can't let anyone else get hurt because of me, especially when he has Corrado waiting for him at home.

"Then start talking," he threatens icily.

Our eyes meet before I look away, not wanting to appear as vulnerable as I feel, and I run my other hand through my hair, trying to form a sentence.

"It was from my ex," I begin hesitantly, not daring to look at him, but I feel his aura fill the car. "He-"

"Is he the one who was there the day I found you?" he cuts in. His voice is menacing, although I can tell he is trying to control his anger. My stomach twists. Fuck, why is he so pissed?

"Yeah," I murmur, now daring to look at Leo, realising I am still holding his arm. I am about to remove it, but the look in his eyes tells me that pissed is an understatement. Doesn't the touch of a mate calm a person? Well, I don't want him to fucking blow, and even if I'm not sure how well our broken bond will work, I keep my hand on him, praying it calms him even a little. I shouldn't have lied to him. Fuck, now he is pissed at me, and I have nowhere to run to.

"And he's the one you're running from."

It is a statement, not a question, so I stay quiet.

Flames of Destruction

"When I asked you to tell me, you fucking should have," he says dangerously, and I can see he is driving faster, way too fast. The cars around us are a blur, and when he turns, taking a side road, darkness falls over us. I know we are no longer on the right track. He has taken a detour on purpose.

"Leo, he's dangerous. This has nothing to do with you, I will deal with him. Just drop me at Alejandro's pack and walk away. He's not someone to mess with," I warn, not liking the speed we are driving at. One wrong move, and we'll crash. He turns those piercing blue eyes on me, and my head is screaming at me to tell him to watch the road ahead.

"Leo, keep your eyes-"

"Here's a news flash, little she-wolf, if you think that he isn't someone to be messed with, then you really have no fucking idea who I am. He just fucked with the wrong fucking wolf."

Fuck, why does that sound so sexy and comforting? Wrong time, Azura.

"Leo, I get that you are the big bad wolf, but there's something weird about Judah... fuck, it's complicated. "

"Why haven't you told anyone? Aren't you a goddamn Westwood?"

Our eyes meet for a second, and then his gaze flickers to my hand on his arm. I quickly remove it, feeling an odd hollowness inside at the loss of contact. It is weird.

"I don't need others to fight my battles. Plus, I've done stuff, and if they find out, shit's going to hit the fan. Besides, Judah has some stuff on me," I explain quietly. It feels oddly good telling someone about it, although I never thought Leo would be that person. Speaking it out loud makes the weight that burdens me lift a little, and my chest feels lighter.

"What kind of stuff?" he asks icily.

I can see that the car behind us is literally tailgating us. It is too fucking close, and Leo's anger is rising with each passing second. I'm not sure if it is because of me or the car behind us, but it is almost suffocating in this car.

"I killed someone. I didn't mean to, but I did, and then he forced me to help get rid of the body after I came to," I reply quietly, remembering after he had – I swallow hard, pushing the painful memories away and focusing on the present. "He also..." It is hard to talk about it. I meant to tell Alejandro and prepare myself for the words, but here I am, spilling it all to Leo when he will just drop me off and leave. So why am I even telling him?

"Continue"

The videos. I need to tell him about those.

I take a deep breath. Just the memory of fucking Judah makes me sick. How did I ever fall for such a sicko?

"He has explicit videos of me that he's threatening to release on the net if I don't do as he wishes."

Suddenly Leo turns the steering wheel violently to the left, and I am thrown into him, unable to stop the scream that leaves my lips as I hear something being fired outside, hitting the side mirror. His eyes are blazing steel blue as the car spins violently at his move, just as I see an explosion go off through the window, one that I know was meant for us.

I cling to his arm as the spinning motion of the car makes me sick. I feel his arm reach over, pressing against my chest and holding me against my seat as the car careens in circles. The smell of something burning and the intense screeching overwhelm me, and sparks fill the sky outside.

"Bastard," Leo growls, letting go of me. He reaches for the glove compartment, taking out a gun and switching the steering wheel to his left hand as he lowers the window and shoots a round of bullets at something behind us. The sound of shattering glass, fire and screeching metal echoes in my mind.

The sound triggers me, and memories of long ago flash through my mind. I hear the sound of something crashing. I have no idea what is going on, and when the car finally comes to a stop, he loads his gun once again. My heart thunders as I realise he is about to get out.

"Don't," I say, still feeling nauseous, my heart still pounding and my hands shaking. I can't let him die. He has a son. "This is my battle."

"He fucking just made it mine, too. Stay in the car." He gets out of the car, and I am about to follow him, only for the doors to lock.

"Leo! He's dangerous!" I shout.

I know Leo isn't weak, but still I look around, searching for the unlock button. My heart thumps in relief when I spot it and frantically press it, clambering out of the car just in time to see Leo rip the door of the McLaren off its hinges.

"Fuck!" he growls, kicking the flaming wreck, making it fly a few feet into the air before it hits the ground with a loud crash as it explodes into smithereens. I shield my face as flying pieces of debris fill the air, looking at Leo through squinted eyes. With the flames creating a backdrop behind him, he walks towards me, gun in hand. He looks around, scanning the area before his cold eyes meet mine.

"I locked the doors for a reason." He grabs hold of my elbow and opens the door, pushing me into my seat before swiftly walking around to the other side, getting in. "Phone."

"Why do you-"

"For fuck's sake, do what you're told!"

"News flash! I don't do-" I am cut off when he leans over and grabs my phone from the floor.

"Password." I clench my jaw, but I know better than to argue when Judah might be lurking close by.

"Six sixes."

He raises an eyebrow, unlocking the device and going to the last text. His eyes flash as he reads the message before he texts something back, tossing the phone onto the floor.

"We're going back to my pack."

"What?" I ask, my heart skipping a beat.

"You heard me. I'm taking you back to the Sangue Pack."

"Leo, no."

I can't go there. Being around him is fucking with me. I am constantly fighting my emotions, but it hurts seeing him with Nikki knowing that he isn't mine. I can't stay there any longer than I already have.

"You don't have a fucking choice. Plus, this is why you were going to Alejandro, right? To ask for his help? I can do a better job. I'm far more experienced in hacking than he is. I will retrieve those videos he has, and I'll kill the fucking bastard. Who cares about consequences?"

"No. Drop me at Alejandro's pack. I can't go back with you!" I argue, my heart pounding. I feel so sick, and his words are messing me up. He begins driving back the way we came, my mind reeling with what had just happened. "Leo, please!"

"No."

"Leo! I don't want to go back with you! Let me the fuck out! I will handle this! This isn't your issue." He ignores me, only making my anger rise. *"Leo!"*

The car screeches to a stop on the narrow country road, and he turns his blazing eyes on me. Reaching over, he grabs hold of my neck and leans closer to me. My own eyes burn silver as we stare into each other's eyes. Our hearts are racing, and I try not to let his scent get to me. Doesn't he fucking get that it is this exact connection that I am fucking scared of?

"I'm not giving you a fucking choice. End of discussion. We are returning to the Sangue Pack."

His gaze trails over me for a split second, but then he pulls away, hitting the gas and zooming into the darkness. Consequences... deep down, I am scared for the truth to come out. I know Leo will deal with him without caring for the laws of the King and the Court of Selene, but going back to his pack is so hard. It is getting tougher to be around him without the bond playing up, and I know I won't be able to reject him. Even fuelled by anger, I hadn't managed to when I tried. The words seem to get stuck in my throat.

I run my fingers through my hair before reaching down and picking up my phone. Unlocking it, I stare at the message Leo had texted back.

Me: You just made this fucking personal, and Schurke Wolf forgives no one. Let the countdown to your end begin.

Shaken
Leo

I knew something was fucking up, but I wasn't expecting this and the fact that the bastard somehow managed to get away... I didn't see him leave the fucking car. I don't know how, but he seems to have just fucking vanished. Unless... he wasn't in the car to start with.

Blackmailing her with sex tapes. That fucking triggers me. I don't care if she is a fucking princess or not, right now, she is someone who needs help. Why the fuck is she dealing with this shit alone? On top of that, somehow, the bastard had even managed to track us down. Does he have some sort of tracer on her?

Her luggage.

I pull up to the side of the road, making her grab the edge of her seat and glare at me with those large, gorgeous eyes of hers.

"What are you doing?"

I don't reply. Getting out of the car, I walk to the trunk and grab her luggage, flipping her suitcase open just as she comes out of the car.

"What are you doing?"

"I want to know how the fuck he found us," I reply, trying not to notice her tiny thongs in the suitcase, and toss the entire thing into the hedges.

"What the fuck? How the hell would he have something tracing me?" she growls. I look her over, my gaze falling to her shoes.

"Take your shoes off, too," I command.

"No. Seriously, when would he have had time to-"

I don't have fucking time for this. I grab her by the arm, pulling her close, and lift her up onto the edge of the open trunk before I pull her shoes off myself. Fucking stubborn woman.

"You are fucking crazy," she growls, clearly agitated, but I can also sense her unease and worry.

"Makes two of us then," I reply icily.

I look at her pants. They don't have anything metal, they should be fine. She sure has sexy fucking legs. I look her over before I point to her earrings.

"Remove them."

She glares at me but obeys, tossing them into the bushes. I pull her down and slam the trunk shut before I walk over to the passenger seat, grabbing her bag.

"Leo, he didn't have a chance to touch my things!"

"You can't be so fucking sure. There's some way he's tracing you." I frown as I spill the contents onto the seat. I take out my lighter, setting her passport alight.

"Hey!"

"Sorry, little she-wolf, but I'm not fucking risking it. You've been in this guy's company, so you can't trust any of this shit."

"You're being extreme," she growls, trying to snatch it from me, but I hold it out of reach with ease.

"I know how small chips can be." I watch until her face and the details on the passport melt away, toss it aside and then destroy her bank cards before emptying her entire bag out. I switch her phone off but keep it with me. I'll do some tracing later.

The last thought I have is if she has a chip inside of her, extreme but not fucking unheard of. I had all the pups in my pack chipped in case something happened to them. I'll check when we get back not that it would work in my pack anyway, but I want to be sure either way.

She now stands there seething. Her heart is pounding loudly as she stares at her things.

"Get in."

"I have no money, no clothes, no passport!" she shouts suddenly, her eyes flashing. I clamp a hand over her mouth, pushing her up against the car.

"No fucking big deal! You'll get clothes and cash, now get your little ass into the car," I growl. She shoves me back, and I step away, letting her get in, my gaze dropping to her ass. Sexy.

I look away and slam the door shut, going around to get into the driver's seat. I am about to start the car back up when she quickly tries to open the door.

"I'm not letting you out. I already told-"

She waves her hand, retching as she points at her mouth. Fuck, she is going to be sick. I unlock the door, and she stumbles out, running to the bushes and throwing up. I get out, swiftly scanning the surroundings before I walk over to her. Guess she got motion sickness.

I stand by her side as she clutches her stomach with one hand, the other struggling to hold back her silky locks. I reach over, gathering her hair up and holding it back as she empties her stomach.

"Urgh," she groans once she has finished emptying the contents of her stomach.

"Guess you're not as strong as one would think," I remark, letting go of her glossy hair. I grab one of her discarded items of clothes and pass it to her. She wipes her mouth and tosses it onto the floor again, then looks at me. I have half a mind to make another comment, but she looks fucking pale.

"Thanks," she says with an expression in her eyes that I can't read.

"We'll stop at the next service station and grab something to drink," I suggest.

She doesn't argue, instead walking to the passenger side and getting in, resting her head back against the headrest. I get in, locking the doors before I start driving. She keeps her eyes closed as we continue. It is already late, and it has gotten dark outside. I turn the volume up a little on the music, enjoying the peace that gives me the space to think things over.

The pull of the bond is still hanging between us. Even though I have weakened it by rejecting her, it doesn't stop me from thinking about her. Her arguing with me earlier had fucking made me lose my self-control, the way her eyes were flashing, her chest heaving with rage that she wasn't afraid to express, it was a fucking turn-on and I wanted to fuck her senseless, but I can't. Accepting her means me swallowing my words when I have stood against the Elite for so fucking long. *Why the fuck am I even considering it?*

If I take her back, everyone is going to question it; although Marcel and Corrado would be fucking happy. She is fucking crazy, and with her, you never know what she'll do next, but it is pretty fucking amusing. Like that doll that I sure as fuck know was meant to be me when she said it was a voodoo doll.

And now I have to fucking decide where to put her. Should I place her in my penthouse in the city? Nah, it is too far if shit happens. Maybe I should keep her in my underground bedroom? Yeah, like a fucking prisoner. That would be fucking weird.

What should I do? I know I don't need to answer to anyone, but things are already fucking rocky between Nikki and me and with Marcel saying he'll hand me the title if I settle down and take a Luna? I don't want him to think I am choosing Azura, and neither do I want her to be the reason I attain that title. *A title I fucking deserve anyway.*

I glance over at her. She is staring blankly out the window. I can see her expression in the glass, blank and emotionless, but one thing I have learned is when she wears that expression, her mind and emotions are working in overdrive.

I should be preparing for my shipment tomorrow, but instead, I'm here with her, my mind consumed with other things.

We have stopped at a service station and, having no fucking clue what she likes, I just grabbed some snacks and drinks before we finish heading back home. She has barely said a word for the entire journey, and even though the car is fucking big, I am very aware of her every move. Her scent is still as appealing as it was the when I had found out she was my mate, a temptation that doesn't just go away.

I have kept an eye out, but after that, we haven't been followed, making the rest of the journey pass without a hitch. We finally reach home, and I have just parked up in my underground car park again. Only I have access to this place.

A chill has fallen, and when we step out of the car, I see her curl her toes as they touch the cold ground. I'm still not sure what to do with her, so I decide to take her to the bedroom that leads off my cave.

Yeah, keep her like a fucking creep in the basement.

"Where are we going?" she asks as I lead her away from the lift.

"You're staying down here until I get some stuff sorted."

"Oh, so you force me to come back and then want to keep me hidden? Geez, I wonder why?" she remarks icily. I don't know what her fucking issue is, but being back here reminds me of the kiss we shared earlier.

"Think whatever the fuck you want, you're staying here until I say."

"I am not your prisoner," she growls.

Alpha? Leo? I frown when Jackie's voice comes into my head.

What is it? I ask coldly as I unlock the entrance and lead the way in, not missing the way she looks around. Despite her irritation, she still follows as I lead her to the bedroom. The room is pretty private, even though the main wall is frosted and looks out into the main room.

Sorry… but we had a time set. I made sure Emmet wouldn't know.

I frown. Yeah, I forgot with all this shit going on.

I'll meet you later, around midnight, just tell Emmet the hospital needs you.

Of course, got it. Same place?

Yeah. I cut the link. I don't need anyone fucking seeing us together.

I look over at Azura, who is scanning the room. It is a modern room with a dark interior, a huge tv, and surround sound. A king-sized bed is on the far wall with a panelled backdrop. There is a black fitted wardrobe and chest of drawers containing my clothes to one side. She won't get bored with plenty to watch, or at least not entirely fucking bored.

"There's a bathroom right through there. Grab something of mine to wear for now. I'll get Winona to get some stuff for you. Or there's a tablet, just choose whatever the fuck you want. Here's my card." I place the card on the bedside table. "There's a fridge there next to the bed in that cabinet, and there's a collection of alcoholic drinks out in the main room. Help yourself, just don't touch anything else."

"And my phone?" she asks, completely ignoring everything I said.

"This is a new number, right? He still got a hold of it somehow. I need to check a few things out before I can give it back to you." She lets out an irritated exhale.

"Look, I feel like you've taken me prisoner. I get that you have taken this personally, but why? I am nothing to you, remember? I don't want to be here, Leo!" She snaps, running her fingers through her hair. Yeah, obviously.

"Do you want him fucking caught or not?"

"I don't have the time to stay here! Yes, I want him caught. Goddess! He has pictures of Kat, Sky, and my other friend, Song! What if he releases them on the net? Fuck, I don't know if this is a good idea. Leo, this could fucking break Kataleya. She's so damn innocent and sweet. I know you hate the Elite, but this will really affect her. She has done nothing to you, think of her."

I clench my jaw. Yeah, I fucking do hate the Elite but that doesn't mean I hate the kids.

Then why not accept Azura? Being okay with someone and making them my Luna are two fucking different things.

I take out a cigarette and light it, taking a drag on it.

"I have a better chance at doing something about this shit than Alejandro does. Unless it comes down to not trusting me-"

"Oh, for fuck's sake, can you stop stressing me the fuck out? This isn't about me not trusting you! Goddess! I know you're fucking smart! Everyone has mentioned how you're fucking tech savvy! But me being here is messed up. I need to get away from you! Don't you get it, Leo? Being around you is hard!" she shouts, her eyes glittering with tears of frustration. "I don't want to see your fucking face!"

My eyes flash as anger flares through me. I close the gap between us and grab hold of her elbow, pulling her close.

"If I'm so fucking repulsive, reject me. Get rid of the fucking bond that is keeping us both trapped in fucking limbo," I hiss menacingly. I am fucking trying to help, and here she is acting like I am the fucking issue.

A flash of hurt flickers in her eyes before she shoves me violently. She is strong, but not fucking strong enough.

"Fine. You want it, I'll give it to you."

My heart races as I stare at her. She is going to do it. I can see it in her eyes, the pain, the fear, and, above all, that fire of determination. Will she really be able to do it?

It had been fucking hard to say those words. I'd had to give it my fucking all. I had reminded myself of everything I hated, and only then had I been able to do it. Is she strong enough to do the same? But her next words hit hard.

"I, Azura Rayne Westwood..." *She is doing it, fuck, this is it.* A few stray tears splash down her cheeks, and my heart is thundering. Why now that she is ready to accept it, is it fucking messing me up? "Accept your-"

"Not yet," I cut her off, my voice hoarse as I clamp my hand over her mouth and stare into her beautiful blue eyes. Our hearts are thudding as we both stare into each other's eyes. Two shades of blue yet so fucking different from one another. "You can accept it when you leave." It is a fucking poor excuse. I turn away, feeling shaken. "I have a lot going on right now and need to be at the top of my game..."

Why had that fucking unnerved me? Isn't her rejection what I wanted, so these emotions could fucking go away?

I leave the room swiftly, knowing if she wanted, she could reject me at any time and I knew her enough to know that she'd do it, too.

An End

Leo

I leave the cave and step out into the car park, trying to clear my head. Locking the door behind me, I slide to the ground, resting my head against the cold metal of the wall behind me as I take a drag on my cigarette.

Winona? I call through the link.

Yes, Alpha?

Winona, she is one of the few I have taken in. She wasn't born in the Sangue Pack, but she is still someone I trust, one of the rare few I trust completely around my son.

What's Rosaline cooked tonight? Rosaline is my cook. She lives two floors down from me, and she makes the best food for Corrado and me. When I had put out the notice for the position, I remember choosing the one whose food Corrado loved the best after tasting it all. I still remember his smile of happiness.

She made chicken pasta and stuffed taco cups.

Perfect, bring a tray down to my garage. I'll let you down when you're outside.

Of course. She doesn't question me. She never does, and I am grateful.
Oh, and Winona?
Yes, Alpha?
Bring a woman's toiletry pack or some shit with basic supplies.
A pause follows before she replies,
Is the dinner for one or two?
One.
Understood. Anything else, Alpha?
No, I think that's it.

I stare at the fleet of supercars that I own. I have it all; power, money, cars, a son, and a girlfriend but even then, something is missing, something that is starting to poison my mind, just as I had heard the bond would do, making even the most powerful of men succumb to the will of their females. I never wanted to become a slave to this shit. Besides it is fucking cruel to give false hope of something I could never offer to anyone. It is the reason I never wanted to mark anyone, but then I already fucked that shit up and marked her.

Alpha, I'm at the lift.

I get up, walk to the lift, and key in the passcode. After a few moments, the lift opens to reveal Winona holding a large tray containing Rosaline's delicious pasta and two stuffed taco cups with minced meat, cheese, and jalapenos. There are also two cold bottles of juice and a trifle bowl.

"Thanks, I'll take it," I say, taking the tray from her.

"And the supplies," Winona adds with a small smile, holding the bag out to me.

"Thanks."

"Anytime, Alpha," she replies. I give her a small nod, about to close the lift when I look back at her.

"How's Corrado been?" Her smile vanishes and she shakes her head.

"He didn't eat and has been in a strop since Azura left." I nod. "Would you like any food for yourself, Alpha?" She sure isn't dumb.

"No," I say before turning away and closing the lift.

Even my son is fucking attached to her. She isn't mother material. She is wild and crazy more than anything, but she is good with him.

I quickly slip inside and open the bedroom door, then see she is in the bathroom. I silently place the tray next to the bed and drop the bag onto the mattress before I exit the room, shutting the door behind me.

I glance around, picking up the weapon I am working on and a few other items, locking them away. I pick up her damaged phone and drop it into one of the lockable drawers that won't open without my thumbprint and code. Satisfied that I have gotten rid of anything that I don't want her to see, I leave the room and head up to my office from the lift. I have a few hours before I need to go see Jackie; I'll shower and see if Corrado is still awake.

I enter Corrado's bedroom, only to see he is fast asleep, but I can tell he had fallen asleep upset. His lips are dry, and there are tear stains on his face. I frown, crouching down and wiping his cheek. *Sorry, kid.*

I sigh, lean over and kiss his forehead before I stand up and leave the room. I grab a bottle of water from the fridge and enter my own bedroom. The smell of Nikki's seductive fragrance fills the room. The lights are dimmed, and Nikki is sitting on the bed in red lingerie and a black silk gown that is fully open, showing off her curves, while she scrolls through her phone.

"Babe, you're back, finally. Did you not get my texts?" She gets up from the bed, but once again, I don't want to do this. As sexy as I know she is, she doesn't appeal to me anymore. It is fucking weird how it works.

"I was driving. Didn't get time to check my phone."

She wraps her arms around my neck, her expression darkening, and I know she can smell Azura on me. She instantly lets go of me and steps back, ruffling her hair.

"So, you took her?"

"Yeah, I took her." And it was fucking hot.

"Leo, who is she?"

"Azura," I reply unhelpfully as I take off my jacket and head through the open arch to the dressing room area.

"I know her name, who is she to you?" Her voice is accusatory. She crosses her arms, looking at me sharply. I don't want to do this shit right now.

"What are you trying to say?" I ask, raising an eyebrow as I grab a pair of grey sweatpants and a white t-shirt.

"I..." She purses her lips as she looks at me, trying to control her emotions. "You don't drive strangers. You don't look at other women. Leo...

An End | 139

you and Azura... why do I feel like there's more to it?" Her voice is low but clearly irritated.

"I've had a long day, Nikki. I don't want to do this now."

"Then when? You're always fucking busy or avoiding it! Tell me, Leo, do you love me? Do you still care for me, or is someone else in your eyes now?"

Did I ever love Nikki? Yeah, somewhat. I cared for her, and she became a daily part of my life, a partial distraction from the shit that consumes my mind, but is there someone else now? Yeah, obviously, the bond fucked that all up.

"Leo!" She blocks my path, looking up at me with tears in her eyes, tears that fill me with guilt. I am hurting her, too. "Azura, is she important to you?" she whispers, clutching my shirt. My eyes flash, and I look down at her, not sure what I should fucking say. "Leo, you cheated on me, which meant I wasn't enough, right? And since then, it's like you're done with me."

"I didn't exactly cheat," I mutter coldly, brushing past her.

"Fucking someone is cheating. You didn't even check me out today! I'm wearing lace!"

Yeah, because you're not the one on my mind. I stub out the cigarette and am about to enter the bathroom when she grabs my arm.

"Leo, what is going on? We'd been friends for years before we began dating. I'm begging you, just tell me what's going on with you. How many secrets will you keep from me?" I know what I have to do.

"That night... tell me, what day was it?" I ask quietly. She frowns, thinking for a moment.

"The Blood Moon. I'll never forget," she says bitterly. I nod.

"Yeah, me neither. She is my mate, Nikki. That night, I found my mate." She gasps. Her heart is thundering as she lets go of me, backing away. Tears begin streaming down her cheeks as she covers her mouth.

"You... slept with your mate," she whispers, dropping onto the bed. "Goddess..." I stay silent, running my hand through my hair.

"Yeah." She looks up at me sharply, her eyes flashing.

"Azura. Is she your mate?" I don't reply as she jumps up from the bed, her eyes flashing again. "You brought her here... her mark... oh, fucking hell, tell me it's not true! Did neither of you have shame that I was right here? Were you hooking up with her behind my back? What a skank she is!"

"Hey," I growl warningly, grabbing hold of her arm. My eyes flash as anger rushes through me. "I was the one who fucking cheated on you. She didn't even fucking know you existed or what you were to me until she saw us together," I growl, my grip on her tight. "I rejected her, and it was by fucking chance that I found her injured and brought her here, and although it's none of your business, I haven't fucking slept with her since she's been here." Her heart is thumping, and I can see the fear in her eyes.

"But you said you didn't want your mate... then why is she here?" she asks, her voice softer as if scared I am going to snap, and I fucking am.

"That's none of your fucking concern, and I think it's for the fucking better if we end this. We're through." Her eyes widen in shock as she grabs hold of my biceps.

"Leo, look at me. No, you can't end it. You said you rejected her, you've kicked her out. Let her go, we can-"

"You have until the end of the week to move out. Take any apartment you want."

"Leo, no, no, don't do this. She's weird, and you rejected her, which means you obviously don't want her. You said you never wanted to find your mate." Her voice is full of pain as she holds on to me tightly, and as much as her insult to Azura pisses me off, I know she is hurting, too. Our eyes meet, and I realise we are already over. From the day I laid eyes on Azura in that club...

"We're over, Nikki."

Her heart is pounding as she locks her arms around my neck and pulls me down. She is about to kiss me, but I turn my head away, unable to allow her one final kiss. Her lips meet the corner of my lips as she whimpers in pain. I don't know why I did it. It is just one kiss but I don't want the feel of Azura's lips to leave mine.

A sob escapes her as I look down at her.

"It gets easier," I say quietly. I reach up, brushing a few tears from her cheek, but even then, it is Azura's tear-filled eyes from earlier that come to mind. "And one more thing... no one is to know Azura is my mate."

I turn away and enter the bathroom to shower. I see her break into tears as she drops onto the floor, so I shut the door, blocking her out. I ended it, and although it was the end of a two-year relationship, I feel lighter.

I know that the day will come when Azura will leave but regardless, I feel better. There is no point in staying in another relationship when she has already ruined the taste of all others for me.

I look at Jackie just as she is about to speak, but I don't bother replying, putting my shirt back on.

"I'll see you around." She nods, biting her lip.

"Leo, where did Azura go?" I tense, wondering if Nikki has already told her.

"That's none of your concern." She nods, looking down.

"Is she safe?" Odd question. I turn back to her slowly, looking at her sharply.

"Why do you ask?" She swallows and shakes her head, her heart thumping.

"She said her ex wasn't a good person." Interesting.

"Oh? What else?" I ask, looking at her keenly. Her heart is racing far too fast, and she steps back in fear.

"Nothing else. She just didn't want him finding her," she mumbles. Hmm. I frown deeply.

"Next time, if anyone tells you anything, you are to fucking report to me. Understood?"

"Y-yes, Alpha," she says, fidgeting.

I don't wait for a reply as I leave the room, making sure no one sees me as I slip away. Jackie's words from earlier fill my mind, but I push them away. I won't think about them for tonight. All I want to do is shift and go for a run, but I can't. I have things to do. It is time I fucking found this ex of Azura's and show him exactly what happens when you mess with me.

A Strange Result
Azura

I don't want to be back here. It is hard being here and feeling this pain. I still don't know how to feel about him wanting to help. Sure, it feels great having someone as smart, powerful, and ruthless as Leo on my side, but I also know that Judah is twisted, dark, and manipulative. Will Leo be able to fix this? It is a game of risk.

I stay in the shower for a while before I wrap a towel around myself, then dry my hair with a second towel. I walk into the bedroom, spotting the tray of food on the bed. My stomach rumbles, and I can't wait to dig in. Goddess, I am starved.

I pull on my panties and walk over to the wardrobe, taking out a white shirt. I look at it before putting it on. I sigh heavily as I plop onto the bed, reminiscing on the moment he had held my hair back when I vomited. *And he should, this is his kid, too!* But he doesn't know I am pregnant.

Well, it seems he has some humanity in him.

This baby... I am beginning to realise I may not be able to keep it from him. If he wants to see his child, can I really be a bitch and refuse him? I pickup the tray, place it on the bed, and begin eating.

Since I am going to be staying here, I need to get Dante's necklace somehow without Leo realising why, and I think it is time I told Mama and them who my mate is. And the fact that I am here at the Sangue Pack.

I play with the pasta. Despite how hungry I am, I'm suddenly not really in the mood to eat. I notice the bag on the bed and pull it closer, emptying its contents. Shampoo, conditioner, body wash, a body sponge, toothpaste, a toothbrush, a pack of tampons, a hairbrush, and moisturiser. Wow, seems like he can be a little considerate. Shame for him I used his toothbrush and products already. I shrug as I pick up the box of tampons and toss them in the air. I smack it, letting it fly across the room. It hits the wall and drops to the floor. *Now that is something I don't need, thanks to the dumb Rossi and his sperm.*

I begin eating again, my gaze flitting to the tablet, musing over my options. I could contact Dante via email. Yeah, I know, old-school, but at least he'll get it and hopefully check it soon... Kat even gave me his number, but oh well. I pick up the tablet and switch it on. The screen goes blank for a second before it turns on. Logging into my email, I find Dante's address and begin typing a message.

> Hey Nephew!
>
> Hope you are enjoying your time in Italy. Eat my share of pizza and pasta, and send me pictures.
>
> So, the reason I am messaging you, and I really hope you see this message... I need to borrow a certain amulet of yours. You can probably guess what I'm talking about and why. I know you wear it but is there a chance I can borrow it for a bit? Please? I'll stop nagging you about calling me Aunty? And don't ignore me. I am very sorry for putting the scorpion down your swimming trunks a few years ago and for adding super glue to your hair last year. I swear I was just jealous. You know I have to hold the title of the best hair, right? I mean, aside from Rayhan.
>
> Anyway, since I apologised, can I borrow it?'
>
> Lots and lots of love, your simple, poor, innocent, misguided Aunty – sorry, I mean Azura, not Aunty.
>
> I love you lots, remember that, okay? Even your annoying face. Okay, bye.

I look at my messages, thinking I have pranked him a lot over the years, with the help of Sky, of course. The guy needed to lighten up a little. Broody Rossis.

I place the tablet aside and eat some more pasta. Through the frosty wall of the bedroom, I notice the outside room light up a little. Is Leo back down here?

Today has been strange. I sigh as I finish eating, placing the tray to the side, and lay down on the bed, pondering over everything that has happened. I sigh heavily once again as I place my hand on my belly.

I'm sorry, little one. I hope I'm not stressing you out.

I feel exhausted, and I hope tomorrow is a better day.

The following day, I'm awoken by Leo knocking on the door, leaving breakfast and a few bags of clothes outside before I see him disappear through another door.

His weird behaviour has surprised me, but I don't ponder over it much before helping myself to breakfast and getting ready for the day, although I'm not sure I'm going to see anything outside of this room.

I have checked the tablet several times, but there is no message from Dante yet.

It is now past one in the afternoon when a knock on the door makes me look up. Leo opens it before I even say enter.

"You should knock and wait," I remark.

Our eyes meet, but he is as emotionless as ever. Something has changed, though. I can't be sure, but since the last time we talked, there is something off about him. He doesn't reply to my comment and instead frowns seriously.

"I need you to give me all the information you can on your ex: full name, age, height, anything, including any images you may have of him. I also need certain dates and locations that might help me. So, when you have a moment, come outside."

"Okay," I reply, equally as emotionless.

Neither of us looks away, staring at one another for a moment longer before Leo looks away, his eyes falling to the discarded tampon box I had thrown last night. I feel my cheeks heat up slightly, and I frown.

"I'm a devil, and devils don't bleed," I state, although he didn't ask me anything.

I want to smack myself. That sure was dumb, I admit, but yeah, right now, I don't bleed from down there.

He simply raises an eyebrow before closing the door after him with a small snap. Weird. He is behaving fucking weird and I had just said the weirdest shit to him. Oh, well, what is there to lose? He already rejected me, so I'll be as strange as I want to be.

I get up and place all the dishes in a pile. I'll take them outside with me. I pick up the tampon box and shove it into the bag before making the bed and checking my email once more. Nothing. I wonder if Leo can access everything. The way he talked unnerved me a little, like he could hack into anything.

Once the room looks presentable, I look in the mirror. I am wearing a black satin cami that is tucked into torn skinny jeans. I pull on some heeled boots, ready to leave my room. There are a few sports bras and briefs in the bags, too. Whoever had gotten them had definitely had an idea of my size, but what annoys me the most is this stuff is all branded. I don't want to owe him anything.

I run my fingers through my hair and leave the room with the dishes.

"Where shall I put these?" I ask when my eyes fall on Leo, sitting back in his seat, his long legs sprawled in front of him with a hand resting under his chin. In black jeans and a black tee, he looks beyond handsome. The entire room smells of him, a scent that I can't help but find very appealing.

"Put them near the door." He jerks his head towards the door we had entered through last night. I do as he said, feeling his eyes on me. I turn and walk over to him. There is no other chair in here, so he motions to me to sit on the edge of the desk.

"I'm okay standing," I reply, trying not to look at the belt he is wearing with a statement buckle. He doesn't reply, instead turning to the screen next to me.

"From your call records, the unknown numbers you received calls from have all been different, most likely from burner phones. But from what I've observed, he has been rerouting messages sent to and from your phone to himself. Meaning from Scarlett's, Liam's, Elijah's, all of their numbers. The only ones that seem to be safe from this are Alejandro's and his family's numbers," he explains seriously, looking at the screen.

I want to ask how on earth he got into my old phone data, but I decide not to ask him irrelevant questions. There is an odd tension radiating off him, and after my ridiculous breakdown last night with him stopping me from rejecting him, things are already odd. I clear my head, paying attention to him.

"So does that mean he's wary of Alejandro finding out?"

"Most likely. I don't think he will release any images of Kataleya or Skyla. I think that's definitely something he said to scare you with. He probably knew it would fuck you up. They are Alejandro's daughters, that is not an enemy he wants to make," Leo's deep seductive voice murmurs.

"Judah is sick. He would do anything. I wouldn't put it past him," I reply, a cold shiver running down my spine.

"I don't know. We'll see."

He is like an entirely different man right now, mature, serious, and calm. He takes a cigarette out of his pocket, and I watch him light it, my stomach fluttering. His eyebrow shoots up questioningly as he catches me staring.

"Want one?"

"No, thanks," I say, turning and staring at the screen.

"You said his name is Judah, Judah, what?"

"Gallahan."

"Gallahan… why does that name sound so fucking familiar?" Leo sits forward, pulls up another window and begins typing something. A string of numbers appears before several windows pop up. Goddess, this is gibberish to me.

"Gallahan… there was a Gallahan family in the Shadow Wolves Pack, but didn't they die?" He frowns as I look at him sharply.

"Meaning?" I really have no idea, nor have I heard of it. "I just know although he didn't reside in his pack, he wasn't a rogue. Just a lone wolf."

"Hmm, well, let's see if they're linked, or if I can identify him. There's a chance he may have used a fake identity." My heart skips a beat at just the thought that I may not even know Judah's real identity. "Relax, it's just an assumption."

"You're being pretty nice today. Why?" I ask, unable to stop myself as I watch him suspiciously. He raises an eyebrow, his eyes cold as he looks me over.

"I plan to make you lower your guard, and then, when you least suspect it, I intend to devour you," he shoots back sarcastically.

We both freeze, and I realise although he hadn't meant it to come out like that, that sentence could be taken two ways. The image that flashes through my mind makes my pussy clench in anticipation.

"Yeah, and I mean like Red Riding Hood and the Wolf," he mutters, and I smirk. He had thought the very same thing.

"Oh? Sure didn't sound like that," I taunt, glad he is looking at the screen. His eyes snap to me, and I wish I hadn't jinxed it.

"The fact that you thought it meant that's where your mind went, too. What's wrong? Thinking about a certain night?" he taunts slowly, his eyes flickering a steely blue.

"I can say the same about you then, and no, I was not thinking about anything because if I had the opportunity to redo that night, I'd have bitten your dick off when I had the chance," I reply, smirking confidently at the flash of surprise that flickers in his eyes at my words.

"Don't poke a wolf if you aren't ready for the consequences." His voice is low and dangerous, making my core clench. The temptation to push him further entices me, but, remembering Nikki, I force myself to focus on the topic at hand.

His computer beeps before I can reply, and there on the screen are several profiles, most of which contain images alongside the information. I shift from where I am now perched against the edge of the desk and move closer to see better just as Leo leans closer, too.

Jeremiah Gallahan, Lydia Gallahan... I skim through. Most of these are from a century ago. My heart skips a beat just as Leo clicks on one profile that contains no image. Judah Gallahan. An eerie, ominous chill surrounds me as memories of his torment return.

"Judah Gallahan... as I thought," Leo murmured. "I was right. This family died out years ago."

"No, that says Judah-"

"Look at the date," Leo cuts in, grabbing hold of my chin and turning my face back to the computer. I frown, about to snap at him, when my eyes fall on the date beneath Judah's name. My heart thumps as I grab hold of Leo's wrist.

"How is that..."

There written right under Judah's name is a date of death. A date that is over fifty years ago.

My heart thuds as fear encases me, a fear like none before. What on earth is happening? Who is Judah? And why has he taken the name of someone who is long dead?

A Reply
Azura

"As I presumed, it seems you know far less than you thought about your ex," Leo murmurs, frowning. His eyes are cold as he stares at the screen.

"I don't get it, how is this even possible? Are you sure that file isn't corrupt or false or something?" I ask.

"No. Years ago, I began to gather all possible data on the werewolves in this country, just for my own knowledge, and I remember this particular family's story intrigued me." He sits back, smoking his cigarette.

"Are you sure it's not wrong? Maybe a glitch-"

"I have an excellent memory. Don't question my intelligence," he growls.

"Okay, fine, Mr. I'm-So-Damn-Smart," I mutter.

"Good. At least you're learning to listen," he replies, his voice almost antagonising. My eyes flash, and I look him square in the eye.

"Don't try me. I don't listen unless I want to." Neither of us look away, a clash of wills, with both of us refusing to bend.

"Maybe that's what got you into this mess to start with. Your lack of logic and your rash temper are enough to land you in this kind of shit," he says icily.

I hate how he has a point. I don't want to admit it, and I won't, but I don't like the way he seems to see right through me.

"These files are from just under a decade ago. I'm curious to see what the current Shadow Wolves database says." He presses some buttons on his keyboard, and I narrow my eyes.

"Are you hacking into their database?"

"Do you want to know or not?"

"I do... but-"

"So this is on both of us."

"No, it's not. Why not go to the Shadow Wolves Pack and ask them?" I frown. He looks at me with a cold, arrogant expression.

"So, instead of doing something I can do right here within a few hours, you expect me to travel to the Shadow Wolves Pack and waste an entire fucking day?"

"It's called doing things the right way?" Yeah, I'm one to talk, especially after everything I have done. He sits forward, taking a drag on his cigarette, his eyes locked with mine.

"Here's a news flash, little she-wolf. I don't follow rules." I hate how my stomach knots in pleasure at his deep, sexy voice. Why do I have a thing for bad boys?

No, I don't like Leo. Nope. Never. It doesn't matter if he has those sexy lips, or those eyes that are so damn sexy or-

Stop, Azura! I frown, trying to rearrange my thoughts when he speaks.

"Do you have any pictures of him?" he asks.

"No. I deleted what I had when I broke up with him, but he hated pictures so the ones I had were very rare." I shrug.

"Great," he mutters, sounding very sarcastic. "I need to check if he's chipped you."

"How?" I ask, narrowing my eyes.

"An X-ray. It's pretty simple."

X-ray. My heart begins thudding. Although the radiation can't damage my baby due to our healing, it would show up on the X-ray, and I do not want Leo to know about this baby. Not yet. Deep down I know at some point I will have to because even though he didn't want me, he would be a good father.

"No," I reply, firmly pushing the thoughts away before that sadness comes over me once more. He raises an eyebrow.

"Why not?"

"He didn't know I was here, so obviously whatever you've got in place stops any unwanted-"

"It's one fucking X-ray. My jammers hold off any unwanted signals, but unless you never plan to venture out of this pack, we need to make sure he hasn't chipped you."

My heart is thudding, and I don't know what to say. *Think quick, Azura...* He is watching me intently and he sure isn't dumb.

"I dated him for a while and I can assure you that he was not tech savvy."

"Yet you don't seem to know enough about him to convince me. It's one fucking X-ray. What's the issue?" he asks sharply.

Fuck, fuck, fuck!

"Let's do that at another time," I suggest, not wanting to discuss this further.

"What are you hiding?" My heart thuds and I try to calm myself, but I know he is watching me intently.

"Nothing," I lie, swallowing hard and looking back at the screen.

"Oh, yeah? It doesn't seem like it."

"I don't need to explain myself to you," I growl, standing up, ready to storm off. I need time to hatch a plan to get out of this.

"You're not going anywhere." His voice is cold as he grabs my arm, yanking me back to the desk and pushing me down onto it.

I gasp as I glare up at him, bracing my hands behind me to stop myself from falling on my back. Leo towers over me, smoking his cigarette as he looks down at me and grabs hold of my chin. My stomach flutters, sending a jolt of pleasure to my core. Fuck, why is he so damn sexy?

"Let's try this again. What are you hiding from me? And it's in your fucking best interest to tell me the truth so I can fucking help you, Azura," he says menacingly, his long legs on either side of mine. *Help me.*

This has nothing to do with Judah but I can't tell him.

"Like I said, it's nothing," I retort, pulling out of his grip and trying to stand up. I push him, trying to put enough space between us so I can regain my balance, but I almost fall back onto the table and grab hold of his shirt to stop myself, yanking him down with me.

I hear it.

The increase in his heart rate, the way his gaze dips to my lips as he braces his hand on the table next to me.

"Don't tempt me to punish you, little she-wolf," he whispers huskily.

We are too close; his scent is getting to me. No matter how much he says he hates me and my pack, I can see the raw hunger in his eyes that he thinks he is doing a good job of masking. Oh, this boy wants me bad.

My heart thumps, and a sinful thought comes into my mind. What if I distract him with a kiss and then run away?

Nikki.

Yeah, I can't do that. Think, Azura, think!

"I need to pee!" I say suddenly.

Leo raises an eyebrow, clearly not expecting that, but it works, breaking the moment between us, and I push him away and rush back to the bedroom. I slam the door behind me and hurry to the bathroom, locking the door behind me. *Wow, Azura, you really are so charming.*

I groan as I slide down the wall and rest my head against the door behind me. What should I do? Goddess... even if I get the necklace, it will only hide the heartbeat, it will still show in the X-ray. Oh, fuck, I'm screwed in more damn ways than one.

"Grab your stuff. I'm taking you back to your previous apartment." Leo's voice comes from the other side of the door, making me jump. Fuck, he is so silent.

"Okay," I reply, rushing to the toilet and flushing it before I wash my hands.

Back to that apartment... I'm not sure if it is a good idea, but I really don't want to be stuck down here with only Leo for company.

He leads me through another door and up via a lift until we are in a private office. I realise when he leads me out that this is his apartment. It smells of him, Nikki, and Corrado... a family I really don't want to wreck.

He makes his way out of the apartment and down the stairs to the apartment I had just left yesterday. It is spotless, and the voodoo doll is nowhere in sight. Leo places the bags of clothing down on the coffee table and looks at me.

"I have some shit to deal with tonight, but tomorrow, first thing, you will get that X-ray done."

I guess it gives me a little time to hatch a plan. I nod but say nothing as we both look at one another, a tense silence falling between us. He is obviously waiting for me to say something.

"Okay," I say, picking up the tablet I had brought along with me from his underground room. His eyes fall on it, and he looks up at me.

"I'll have a phone set up for you by tomorrow. I'll have your contacts all encrypted as well, so there's no way he'll realise if you're contacting them or vice versa." My heart skips a beat just imagining being able to use my phone without some creepy incoming texts.

"Really? Oh, I could kiss you! I hate-" I freeze, realising what I have just said. "I mean, like, thank you. It's a figure of speech, I didn't mean that I could actually..." *Why do you always do this, Azura? Why the hell do you go put your foot in your mouth every goddamn time?*

He is simply watching me make a fool of myself with that hard, emotionless expression of his, with an eyebrow raised arrogantly.

"Okay, yeah, Azura shutting up now." *So smart of you, Azura.*

"Winona will bring you food; try to not cause trouble?" I simply pout at that, nodding like the good girl I sure as heck am not. My cheeks heat from my ridiculous comment. "Good. I will probably be back really late, so if you do need to contact me, tell Winona." I nod, and he turns away, about to leave when I call him.

"Oi, Blue Eyes!" He stops and looks at me over his shoulder. "Thank you. For helping me out." Our eyes meet, that intense spark simmering between us before he nods and turns away.

"Anytime."

His one word ignites a storm of emotions inside of me before the door shuts with a small thud.

Anytime. Even if he doesn't want me as a mate, he is still helping me, and I don't feel so alone. I feel protected. I have family, but right now, there is so much I just don't want them to know.

I walk over to the sofa and drop onto it, turning the tablet on. I log onto my email, and my heart skips a beat when I see the email from 'The D Rossi'. Dante has replied! My heart thumps as I quickly click on the message.

> Hey,
>
> I don't think one apology covers everything you did, but I'll take it since I now have proof in writing of what you have attempted.
>
> We haven't talked in a while, and I guess you've got some stuff going on, but you're not alone. Always remember, no matter what crap comes your way, that the first person who comes to your mind will always be there for you. Ok those are my words of wisdom lol... moving on...
>
> As for that necklace, you don't need it. I mean, I could send it to you, but there won't be any use for it. However, if you still want it, let me know.
>
> Pictures of Italy? I'm here due to work. There's nothing pretty to look at, trust me, but I'm attaching one below of the best thing I've seen around here.
>
> Love, your current favourite Rossi male.

I pout as I stare at his email. I don't need it? Why don't I need it? Does it mean Leo figures this out? Please, no...

Right below the message is a picture of none other than himself. Cocky much? He has the angular jaw famous in the Rossi men, plump lips like his mama, and those glossy curls that I hate because, of course, I am jealous of them. I stick my tongue out at the picture before placing the tablet down as I mull over Dante's message. Current favourite Rossi? Is that a hint at Leo or my baby? Urgh, I love this guy, but the way he talks messes with my head. It can't be Leo besides who said I'll give my baby the Rossi name?

I suddenly sit bolt upright, placing my hand on my stomach as the sudden realisation that I am carrying a Rossi hits me like a freight train.

An actual goddamn Rossi.

Imagining an arrogant little snarky mini-Leo, I shudder. Oh, I'm really screwed.

Coming Clean
Azura

I stay in the apartment, not wanting to run into anyone else, and it is so boring with nothing to do. Winona had come with lunch and then again for dinner. It is obvious from the way she is looking around that no one knows I am here. Guess dickface wants no one to know. I am tempted to ask her if I can see Corrado but after last time I'm not sure Leo would appreciate it.

So here I am wondering what I should do. Marcel knows who my mate is, and it has come to a point where I know I can't keep lying to my family.

I stare at the tablet that sits on the bed, then glance at the time. Just past ten. Katara would be put to bed by now... should I video-call? My fingers itch before I take a deep breath, thinking, *Just go ahead with it.* Marcel knows, and Leo doesn't want anyone here knowing, but that doesn't mean my parents can't know. If he pushes for the X-ray, then he'll find out about the baby, too.

Before I end up changing my mind, I quickly set up a video call between Kiara, Raven, and Mama, knowing their mates will be there, too. *Goddess... here goes nothing.* Kiara is the first to accept the call.

"Hey, Azura! It's been a while. How are you?" she asks with a smile on her face.

Kia, my sister, is the younger twin, with Liam being older. She has shoulder-length sandy blond hair, with gorgeous eyes that are sage green with a blue ring around them. Plump lips and a gorgeous curvy figure complete her goddess-like looks. She is a blessed wolf with healing abilities, as well as being the Queen.

"I'm okay, how are you guys?" I ask as a shirtless Alejandro comes into view. Even though he is now in his fifties, he is still as hot as ever, if not getting hotter with age. Alejandro Rossi, the tattooed Lycan King, is also Leo's uncle. *This is going to be fun.*

"Good until you decided to fucking interrupt," Alejandro remarks, sitting behind Kiara with ease, his legs on each side of her and wrapping his arms around her tightly.

"I swear, Alejandro, with age, you are getting crankier by the second. Poor Kia, stuck with a grumpy old man," I taunt.

"Ignore him. He may be acting like this, but when he saw the call was from you, he came over rather quickly," Kiara says, smiling slightly. Just then, Mama and Raven join the call.

"Hmm, of course, everyone loves the Westwood Devil," I declare with a flick of my hair.

"Or I'm here to see the drama unfold. There's no fucking chance you ain't been up to something," Alejandro replies, smirking. Urgh, if only he knew. Would he be smirking if he realised it was his damn nephew who screwed me over?

"Hey, guys," Liam says, and I smirk at them. From Raven's messy hair, I have a feeling she and my brother have just done the dirty.

"Hey, Zu!" Raven says as everyone exchanges greetings.

"You know, I'm glad you video-called. We've been worried," Dad says quietly. I know he is upset with me. I nod, giving him an apologetic smile and one of my best doe-eyed looks.

"Not to mention, we can't even get through to you. Azura, what are you doing out there?" Mama asks, frowning slightly.

"Okay, so I wanted to talk to you all together. Please hear me out before any of you unleash hell," I say, sitting forward. My heart is racing as I see Dad's eyes flash, and Liam and Alejandro are watching me intently. Mama is frowning, and Raven and Kiara look concerned. *Come on, Azura, tell them.*

"Okay, first of all, I didn't go to Sweden. I planned to, but I didn't make it," I begin.

"What?" Dad asks, "Where are you?"

"I…" I almost lie, *I had car trouble*, but no, I can't lie anymore to them. "I'm at my mate's pack." There it is. The hurt in Dad's eyes, the concern in Mama's, the anger in Liam's, and that sharp, calculating look in Alejandro's.

"The mate who rejected you?" Liam growls. Raven grabs hold of his arm, looking back at him as she shakes her head gently, and I know she is trying to calm him down via the mind-link.

"Yes, and he doesn't know about…" I point at my stomach. "Anyway, moving on, I thought I should tell you. I had every intention of going to Sweden, but then stuff happened, and here I am."

"Are you two trying to make it work?" Mama asks quietly.

"He doesn't deserve you," Dad says coldly.

"Dad," Kiara says softly, "Look if Zu wants to do this, we should support her. Tell me, Azura, is there good in him?" I nod slowly. Although he is an ass, there is good… even if it's very little.

"He loves his pack, his family, well, some of his family. He's a stuck-up arrogant jerk, but he is an okay human. Kinda… a bit of a dick… or a real big dick," I mumble. Kiara smiles knowingly.

"Then, we all should support her. I remember how hard Alejandro was to deal with to the point he almost marked someone in front of me," Kiara says, placing a hand on her man's jaw and tilting her head up as he leans down and kisses her.

"Kia is right, maybe there are other factors," Raven muses.

I nod. There definitely are…

"What pack?" Alejandro asks, frowning. "I want to know what fucker rejected you."

"Why is his pack important?" I ask.

"You said he cares for his pack, so he's someone ranked then?" Dad asks. I sigh. Should I tell them? I examine my nails before Mama calls me.

"Azura." I look at her, seeing the concern and the pain in her green eyes. "No more secrets." *Oh, there are so many more secrets. I'm sorry, Mama.*

"Okay, if I tell you, no one loses their shit. Okay? What we do is our decision to make. Please," I say, looking at them all.

"He's fucking dead," Liam mutters, but I tilt my head.

"Liam."

"I'm not going to stand by and let people constantly hurt you," he threatens, his eyes full of hurt and anger. I know how much he hated how the rare few of the pack treated me. He hates that no matter what he did, there were always a few old vaginas and penises that would never change.

"So, let's have the fucker's name," Alejandro says, taking out a cigarette and lighting it. A smile crosses my lips as I watch.

"He reminds me a bit of you, which is gross," I say, making a gagging face. Alejandro narrows his eyes.

"There's only one Alejandro Rossi. No one can fucking be me."

"Yeah, there's only one Alejandro, but there isn't only one Rossi, now is there?" Alejandro raises an eyebrow, and I take a deep breath.

"My mate is Leo, Marcel's son," I confess, staring at them, waiting for their reactions.

Alejandro freezes as Kiara's eyes widen in shock. Raven's mouth drops open as Liam takes a second to comprehend what I said. Whilst Dad looks pale, Mama is staring at me in shock.

"That fucker..." Alejandro is the first to speak as he sits forward, his arm still around Kiara, but he is frowning deeply. "He..."

"Another Alejandro." Liam doesn't sound happy; his usual smile is gone. "So now the mark makes sense. He marked you, and then when he found out you're a Westwood, he rejected you for that very reason, correct?" His voice is cold, and for someone who can be pretty dense, I wish he hadn't picked up on it so fast, but when it came to serious matters, Liam is not to be messed with.

I don't say anything, trying to hide the pain I feel at the memory of that night. Liam had seen me, the way he had broken me.

Everyone is quiet, my silence screaming my response. It is too silent, and then anger appears on Dad's and Alejandro's faces, matching Liam's. Kiara looks... guilty. I don't want them to blame themselves. Goddess!

"Look, whatever the reason, it doesn't matter. Marcel returned yesterday, and he found out, so I'm not alone here. If things don't work out, I'll come straight home." It isn't exactly a lie. I will go home when all this is over, even if the thought of leaving him makes my heart ache. I hate this.

"Marking you and rejecting you, that ain't fucking tolerable," Alejandro growls. "I'm going to-"

"Let Azura handle it," Kiara cuts in firmly. "Dad, Alejandro, Liam, look... I know that not every mate is worth fighting for, but Leo does have a good heart. Deep down, I feel if he just let it go, he would be the best mate for Azura... if he knew-" I place a finger on my lips, not putting it past him to have maybe bugged the place. "I'm sure he'd take care of her," Kiara continues.

"Also, Alejandro was horrible until Kiara made him into her big puppy! I'm sure Azura can do the same with Leo! Only a Westwood woman can tame a Rossi!" Raven exclaims.

I don't know what to say, knowing Nikki is there in his bed. I won't fight for him when he doesn't want me, well, aside from physically. I also don't want to burst her poor bubble. I look at Dad and Mama. Dad looks pissed, his jaw clenched and his eyes hard.

"I don't get why both my girls are mated to Rossis. Isn't the pain that one of them went through enough?" Alejandro frowns, but he says nothing, a glimmer of guilt in his eyes, clearly knowing what Dad said is true. Kia gives his arm a gentle squeeze, leaning into him. She has forgiven him, and they are one of the best couples around.

"I want to fucking punch him a few times myself. Call me selfish, but is it wrong that I think perhaps it is Azura who can make him let go of the bitterness and hatred from within him? That she'll be the one to melt his heart of ice that he's let harden with all the anger that has consumed him? Just the way Amore Mio did to me. I'm not saying you shouldn't fucking be pissed, Elijah, but the fact that another of your daughters is mated to a Rossi just shows they are fucking strong enough to deal with us," Alejandro says, smoking his cigarette. "She's also right. Leo is similar to me, and although she and Kiara are opposites, both are strong women."

"So, you're saying she should stay there when Goddess knows how he's treating her?" Liam asks with concern and irritation in his eyes.

"You made mistakes too, Liam," Elijah reminds him, rubbing his temples. "If he hurts her, I won't care who he is…" His threat remains open, the anger in his eyes as they burn bright, cobalt blue. Indigo… I know he will still never forgive himself for what she went through.

Liam doesn't reply, obviously remembering what he had done in his past. Their story was complicated, and although it was a long time ago, it just shows that no one is perfect. These men before me love their mates with their entire souls and beings, yet they have made mistakes.

"I won't let anyone hurt me, I'm not weak. I will come home if I realise it's not worth staying here," I promise. Mama nods slowly.

"Okay, and I expect at least a call or message every day," she says firmly. I nod.

"Okay, promise," I reply.

"I know you'll be able to get through to him," Alejandro says quietly. "No fucking pressure. It's something I never managed to do, but I hope you can." Kiara looks at him gently, sympathy in her eyes as she leans into him.

"And it's not your duty to. If he doesn't treat you right, come home, angel," Dad says firmly. Mama simply gives me a faint smile.

"Whatever you do, we are here for you. You are a woman who can make her own choices. Just do what you feel is right and think before you act." Yeah, I never do think…

I nod. I feel awful. Both Marcel and Alejandro have faith in me…

I bid farewell to them before ending the call and slumping back against the sofa, staring at the ceiling. Even if he doesn't show it, it is obvious he has hope that I can get through to Leo. I don't know how they expected me to do that. The guy is so damn stubborn! Telling them has made it all the more real. So goddamn real.

I don't see Leo and I having a serious conversation at all. Ever. But wait, wasn't that a serious conversation earlier?

I run my fingers through my hair, sighing heavily as I stare at the ceiling. How could I try when he has Nikki?

I sigh, standing up and walking over to the window. I open it, relishing the fresh air. I prefer it over air conditioning. I rest my arms on the windowsill with my chin on top of my arms, gazing down at the glittering lights of the mini-city. Leo's pack — it sure is beautiful.

I hear a faint bang, and I freeze, looking at the wall next to me. Isn't that Jackie's apartment? I walk closer to the wall, but I don't hear anything.

Hmm. I'm so bored! What shall I do? Maybe I-

Another thud makes me freeze, and I stare at the wall. It doesn't sound normal. The first thing that comes to my mind is that they are having sex, but the random bangs don't add up. Should I just go and ask if everything is okay? I'm sure it isn't someone breaking in.

Being as bored as I am and wanting to get out of here, I decide to just check up for my own piece of mind. Leo never really said I can't leave, did he? I can't remember. Oh, well, who cares? He wants me here.

I leave my apartment silently, and I haven't even shut my door when across the hall Jackie's door opens and Emmet storms out. He is angry. Scratch that, he is fucking fuming. He doesn't even see me as he storms to the lift swearing under his breath. I guess he was throwing things in anger. Men...

Once the lift starts descending, I walk over to Jackie's door and ring the bell. She is nice, and I bet she is feeling down. Maybe I can cheer her up and I won't feel so bored either. The door opens to reveal a distraught Jackie.

"Emmet, ple-" She stops in her tracks as she stares up at me in fear as she realises I am not Emmet.

I'm seeing red. She has a bruise on her jaw, and I can see the finger marks and blood around her neck where it is obvious she has been grabbed by a clawed hand. Oh, hell no.

Both our hearts are thumping for very different reasons.

"This isn't what it looks like," she whispers, but the way she is shaking, trying to cover her neck and the way her heart is thumping.

Lies.

He hurt her. He fucking hurt her.

"What the hell happened?" I ask quietly, trying to control the rage within me.

"Azura, this is nothing. Please just don't tell anyone. I haven't told anyone your secret." She is blackmailing me, but the thing is, I would rather sacrifice my own secrets and so much more than let something like this go. "Go back to your apartment," she says softly, fear and confusion clear on her face at my silence. I nod slowly, and she looks at me. "Promise me you won't tell the Alpha."

"Promise," I say quietly. She searches my face which is expressionless, before nodding in relief.

"Thanks, he was just a little angry," she whispers.

Yeah, and he's fucking dead.

I nod, and she closes the door. I count to ten, my eyes flashing silver before I turn and run to the lift. I may not tell Leo, but I am going to deal with him myself. How dare he? He is supposed to be the Delta and he fucking hurt his own mate? Not on my fucking watch.

I hit the lift to the ground floor ready to unleash hell on the fucking bastard.

A Lie
Azura

I leave the lift, and he is nowhere in sight, but that isn't going to deter me. I follow his scent, my eyes blazing as the image of Jackie's bruises flashes in my mind. I look around, sniffing the air and following my nose around the side of the apartment before breaking into a jog, just in time to see him disappear behind another building. I look back at the streetlights and wonder where he is going.

"Emmet!" I shout as I rush to catch up. I turn the corner and see him about to enter the dark building, but he stops when I call him.

"Azura?" He looks surprised to see me. "Didn't you leave?" I guess he really didn't see me upstairs.

"Oh, I came back," I reply, walking over to him. *And I'm fucking glad I did.* His eyes narrow as if suddenly suspicious of why I am here, his expression darkens, and he looks me over.

"Why are you following me?"

"Because I was right there when you stormed out of your apartment, right before I saw the marks on Jackie's neck," I reply, looking him square in the eye.

"Look here, I don't know what the fuck you want, but what I do is none of your goddamned business. Stay out of this. Remember you and your kind are not fucking welcome here," he spits.

"My kind? We are all fucking werewolves, you dumb dick. We are fucking one, and even if it wasn't, there shouldn't be fucking discrimination." *Okay, Azura, you are going off-topic.*

"You know, I checked, and there's only one fucking Azura, and she's a Westwood. I wonder if Leo even realised or was he so busy with work he didn't even know who he was helping?"

"Oh, whatever, that shit won't work. Leo knows I'm a Westwood. This isn't about who I am, but what you fucking did. Do Leo or Marcel know that their Delta is an abuser?" I shout, my anger rising at his lack of care. He scoffs stepping closer to me threateningly.

"Only thing is, it's your word against mine and Jackie's. Trust me, she won't rat me out. So you think Leo will ever listen to an Elit-"

I punch him across his irritating-as-fuck face, cutting him off. His eyes flash menacingly as he cups his jaw, glaring at me with pure hatred.

"I don't care who listens and who doesn't, but if you think you can just abuse your mate and get away with-"

He raises his hand, but before he can even grab or do whatever the fuck he planned to do, I knock his hand away.

"Then you're wrong," I finish, "and I am not Jackie, who will fucking sit by and allow you to touch me."

"What you going to do, run to your big brother?" Emmet growls mockingly.

"No, I'll just break your fucking arms myself," I hiss as he grabs hold of my arm, shoving me against the wall, but I'm ready. I kick him on the shin and try to push him back, but he is fucking strong. But guess what, so am I.

He swears as he manages to grab hold of my arm, twisting it behind my back, and is about to do the very fucking same move that Leo had almost done on me. I raise my feet, jamming them against the wall. Jarring pain rushes through my legs before I use all my force and push back while, at the same time, slamming my head back against Emmet's nose as hard as I can before I flip up and over behind him and kick him square in the centre of his back. Bet that hurt like a bitch in heat.

He swears as he stumbles, spinning around and recovering pretty fast.

"You may be the Delta of an impressive pack, but I'm the daughter of two of the best alphas out there. You are no match for me."

"Daughter, yeah, right. We all know you aren't their real daughter," he scoffs, wiping blood from his nose. He did not just go there.

"Blood alone doesn't make you family. I don't care who conceived me, I am their daughter. Take it back," I threaten quietly. He smirks, realising he has hit a nerve.

"Then stay the fuck out of my business bitch!"

It takes my fucking all not to do worse. Jackie said not to tell the Alpha. Marcel is Alpha, not Leo... right?

"The moment you hurt her, you made it my business. I don't know what the hell this pack is, or their rules, but I don't believe that Alpha Marcel would allow abuse here."

I turn ready to storm off when he is suddenly behind me, grabbing my hair and twisting me around to face him. I hiss at the pain in my head, reaching out and digging my claws into his face in defence. He lets out a blinding roar, slamming me with full force into the far wall, but I don't let go, digging my claws further into his face and pulling him with me.

Yup, here are two facts. I'm a psychotic bitch, and he may need stitches considering I just ripped his face up, but I sure as fuck don't care.

His fist connects with my jaw, and I am forced to let go of him, my head snapping sideways. Something cricks, and I bite my lip, fighting back a groan of pain as I elbow him in the neck just as he shoves me to the ground. I land on my ass, bringing my legs up and shieling my stomach, just in time to block his vicious kick. Is he aiming to hurt but not to make me bleed? If he is, then he is smart but not fucking smart enough. When he aims another kick, I block with my arm, his boot scraping the skin and I feel something crack.

He is attacking blindly. Clearly, he isn't used to being hit back. I knock his feet out from under him, making him fall to the ground. Bastard. I take the chance, jumping on top of him as I straddle him, grabbing his shirt in my fist, ready to punch him.

"Oi! What's going on?" We both turn sharply to see none other than Emmet's older brother, Eric. He looks between us, worry and confusion on his face as he runs and pulls me off Emmet. He looks us over, clearly unsure what to make of it, frowning deeply.

I'm sure Emmet looks worse off. I had dug my nails into his cheeks, and I had messed them up bad, not to mention the bloody nose.

"What on earth is this?" Eric growls again. Gone is the cute teddy bear. Shame, I liked him better happy, but I guess we can all become psychos when we need to.

"She attacked me out of nowhere," Emmet growls.

"Oh?" I challenge.

"You're in our pack, if I were you I'd be fucking careful," he hisses.

"Is that a threat? Because I know how to make those, too," I spit back. Oh, I want to fucking rip his damn eyes out. Eric swears as he pushes Emmet back trying to diffuse the situation. He then turns to me.

"Leo isn't here, Azura. He doesn't allow people into this pack as it is… you're his guest and doing something like-"

"I'm not his goddamn guest, and I will attack someone if they fuck-"

"Leo will kick you out if you cause trouble," Emmet snaps, ripping his shirt off and wiping his bloody face. Even though he is pretty lean, he is well-built. Well, the kicks are proof of that.

"Oh? Even if he knows the truth? Then how about we take this to Alpha Marcel?" I challenge. His eyes flash, and he clenches his fist.

"He just got back from his trip. Let's not make things harder for him," he says, and Eric frowns, nodding.

"Hmm. Sure," I say, gripping my forearm and rolling my wrist.

"You both need to go get seen over. Damn, Emmet, you're literally going to need to get that glued," Eric mutters, poking a bit of skin that is actually hanging. I sure did a number on him, but he fucking deserved it. I examine my nails.

"Oh, look, I think I have bits of skin under my nails. Do you want it back?" I ask, blinking innocently as I flick whatever crap of his was under my nails at him. His eyes flash murderously, but he says nothing, simply shaking his head.

"I guess this is what the Elite think. That they can just walk into any pack and do whatever the fuck they want," he mutters quietly. I don't bother replying. I have no idea what he may be telling Eric through the link, but this isn't over.

"I'm going back to my apartment," I state when we round the building.

"You may need to be seen, Azura," Eric says, although he no longer sounds so friendly.

"No, I don't. It's a few bruises, they'll heal," I reply coldly.

"Me too. I'm going to return home. Jackie can fix this up." His cold eyes meet mine, and I feel my anger rise at just the mention of Jackie.

"Alright. I will be mentioning this to Alpha Leo," Eric states, looking between the two of us.

"Sure, so will I," I reply as Eric continues to lead us inside the building as if he doesn't trust us alone. Well, heck, neither do I.

"Like he'd take the word of an Elite princess over his best friend," Emmet mutters.

"I truly pity him for having such a best friend, then," I reply as we enter the lift.

Those words of his sting but I wonder if Leo would take my word or his. It is something that I am unable to push away. Like, why should I care if he doesn't believe me? Sure, I will make sure Jackie's issue is made known to at least one person who can help her. Eric may not believe me, and if Leo, who technically isn't the Alpha yet doesn't believe me, then I will break my promise to Jackie and tell Marcel. But I know the reason I want to see if Leo will believe me or not is personal. Almost like a test. A test for what? I have no idea.

"Right, the both of you, go to your own apartments. Now," Eric orders, sounding like that annoying older brother.

"Sure, or we can go see if Jackie will just have a quick check over of me, too. What do you think, Eric, would that be okay?" I ask innocently, giving him the best innocent expression that I can put on despite feeling completely pissed off. The brothers exchange looks, but Emmet shakes his head.

"No," he says coldly.

"Why not?" I ask, sauntering over to their door. *Sorry, Jackie, you kept my trust, but I won't be doing the same.*

"Eric, I'm trying to be calm. As Delta, I'm commanding you to get her to her apartment, she's not entering mine."

"Emmet, it won't take long for Jackie to have a look at her."

"Maybe he's simply just scared that someone will see why this entire fight even began," I remark, ringing Jackie's door.

"What do you mean?" Eric asks sharply.

"Want to tell him, or shall I?" I challenge Emmet. He just looks confused as he raises an eyebrow.

"You attack me after looking down on our pack, and mock the fact that Leo isn't Alpha. What do you mean?" he asks just as the door opens to reveal Jackie.

She is wearing a different top now that covers her neck, but apart from that, she looks absolutely fine, with slightly heavier makeup on than before, covering the bruise on her face entirely. My stomach sinks at the smile on her face realising she is going to play along. She is going to hide Emmet's truth, just the way Indigo hid Fred's. I swallow, looking at her intently as her smile fades, looking between me and Emmet.

"Oh my... Emmet." She rushes to his side, touching his face gingerly.

"I'm okay, doll, it's nothing," he says.

Say it, Azura. Eric is standing there, and I realise I need to. Even if no one believes me, I'd speak the truth.

"You hurt Jackie. I saw the marks. Jackie, you don't need to deal with this," I say, looking between the three. She exchanges looks with the men before turning to me with a look of confusion on her face.

"I have no idea what you mean, Azura. You must have misunderstood. Emmet left in anger because the TV wasn't working." She gives me a small smile and shakes her head. Eric sighs as he looks at me in disappointment.

"I'm sorry, Azura, you seemed like a nice girl. I didn't think you'd try to cause issues like this. Maybe they're right. Good night, guys." He walks off, and I feel awful as I turn to Jackie, who is guiding Emmet inside.

"Good night, Azura," she says, and that's when I see it, the tiny glimmer of guilt in her eyes before she shuts the door in my face.

Will You Believe Me
Leo

Schurke Wolf, my alias, is the name the cartel world knows me by. I rule the United Kingdom from the underground, with ties and allies in Italy, Germany, and most European countries. Power and money, I have it all. The humans look to their king and prime minister, and the supernatural species looks to Alejandro, but from the shadows, England is mine.

Humans work for me, and although they don't know who I am exactly, they sense the power that I hold. They can feel it when in my presence and know I am not to be trifled with. I am feared by all, and there are not many who can look me in the eye.

My most trusted men from my pack are also part of my cartel, but I always made it clear that if they want to step back from the front lines, they are welcome to because in this world, death is always hanging over you. Luckily, being a werewolf makes us pretty much invincible when it comes to dealing with humans. But even then, the risk of the unknown is always there, and I do not want my people to be left without their mates because of my own ambitions. Nothing happens without my knowledge and if someone ever tries to double cross me, then I fucking take care of them.

I now wear a dark grey suit, a black shirt, and smart boots as I head to one of my underground warehouses. The drugs have finally arrived, and I am here to take a look at them myself. I am flanked by my most trusted; The Six as they are referred to. Ace, Shane, Dan, Jin, Li, and Jax. I don't trust easily, but these six, I grew up with them, and I know they are ideal for this job. They go by aliases here, just like most of us. Within the pack, we don't really show that we talk much. I prefer not to mix the two identities. Only Ace and Jax live at the pack, whilst the other four live in the city.

I slow down as I look at the crates in front of me. The LSD has been separated from the fruit they had been hidden with, and I look at the endless packets in the assorted crates, letting out a low whistle. We did it. One huge, risky, shipment, but with the correctly planned journey that I had mapped, they got into the UK without being discovered by border control. I crouch down by one of the crates, opening one of the clear packs and take a pinch in my fingers. I sniff it; it is clean. The very best that money can buy.

"Check every individual packet and get it to Seven X. Open the market for our buyers a week from now," I command, turning around. Those who that was directed at know the location of that site. The less who know where I am keeping it, the better.

"Understood. We've already begun getting everything in place," Snider, one of my human Lieutenants, speaks.

"Perfect," I reply, about to say something else when I suddenly feel a wave of unease wash through me. Something is wrong. I look up sharply scanning the place, but it is completely secure. Only a few I trust are in here and it is heavy with security.

Check if this place is secure, I command through the link. A few minutes later, they tell me all is fine. What is this feeling?

"Everything okay, boss?" Snider asks.

"Get them to Seven X now via separate routes as planned," I say, pocketing the packet I had opened.

"Understood!" He moves away, and I take my phone out. No phones work in here and I'm not about to lower my defences. Is something wrong at home? Azura comes to my mind and that unease grows.

Noir, call Emmet, I command one of the men who is standing guard outside.

Yes, boss. After a moment, he says, **He isn't answering, Alpha.**

Fine.

I frown. That feeling isn't going away, and I wonder if something has happened to her. Has that bastard found a way into the pack?

"I'm leaving. Take care of the rest," I tell The Six before I walk past them.

As much as I want to oversee this myself, I have to go back. I need to make sure she is fucking okay. Stepping out into the underground carpark, I get into my car, commanding my driver to get moving and close the screen between us so he can't overhear before ringing Eric.

"Hey, Alpha."

"Where are you?" I ask coldly.

"I, uh, was just at Emmet's floor and am heading down now. Everything okay?" He sounds tense.

"How about you answer that?"

He sighs, "Emmet told you?"

"Emmet didn't even answer my call. What the fuck is going on?"

"He and Azura, the visitor, got into a physical fight."

Fight. A flash of anger ripples through me, and my eyes blaze steel blue.

Drive faster, I growl to the driver through the link.

"Details." My voice is calm, but anger is pulsating through me.

"I don't know the details, but Emmet said she insulted you and this pack. It got physical, and she did a number on his face whilst he also landed a few on her. They are both pretty bruised up... but he shouldn't have hit her." His voice is quiet in that last sentence. No, he fucking shouldn't have.

My eyes blaze, my heart is thundering, and the anger that is raging through me is blinding. *Bruised up.*

"Alpha?" I swallow hard, ending the call.

"Stop the car." He instantly brakes, and I get out just as he opens his door quickly.

"Boss, is everything okay?"

I don't reply, getting into the driver's seat and slamming the door shut behind me, I start the car, hitting the gas as I pick up speed.

He shouldn't have touched her. I don't give a fuck what she said, she is there under my fucking protection. My head is fucking pounding with uncontrollable rage that I am trying to control so I don't end up fucking ripping the steering wheel right off, trying to comprehend what Eric had said.

Azura isn't the type to insult our pack. She's never looked down on us or me for that matter. Sure, she's lost her temper, but that was if she was triggered, which means Emmet must have said something. His hatred for the Elite is not something I am fucking blind to. He is one of the few who understands my hatred but if that is the case, it means he must have found out exactly who Azura is.

I am driving this thing as fast as it will fucking go, a blur in comparison to everything around me.

Tell me exactly what happened, I command Eric the moment I am in range.

Sure, I found them around the side of the apartment block when Azura was on top of him ready to punch him and I broke them apart, he begins to explain.

It takes me less than half an hour to get back, half the time it should have fucking taken. Getting out, I head upstairs and into my office, pulling my jacket off.

She...

She what? I ask coldly.

She then said he hurt Jackie and wanted her to tell me the truth. He sounds tense and his words surprise me, too. Emmet hurting Jackie? Sure, he has a temper, but he wouldn't hurt her.

Continue.

I know he doesn't want to speak up as he and Emmet have enough issues between them, never seeing eye-to-eye. Although both had tried for the Delta position, I gave it to Emmet but even then, I found myself asking Eric to deal with a lot more. It should have been Eric. He had been more Delta material, but it was Emmet I ultimately wanted closer to Marcel, and when he had needed a new Delta when his last one retired, I suggested Emmet.

Well, Jackie denied it, and when I was leaving, I just saw Jackie take Emmet inside and say goodbye to Azura before shutting the door, he briefs me as I head out of the office, tossing my jacket onto the sofa. I pause, furrowing my brows.

She just took Emmet inside?

Yeah.

Yet Azura had bruises and grazes?

Yes.

But Jackie as a doctor didn't check her. Even if someone went against her Alpha or mate, Jackie is the type of person who would still tend to the sick or injured, no matter who they are.

Get the CCTV footage sent to me from the fight, I say before ending the link.

I stop for a second outside Corrado's bedroom, opening the door slightly to see he is fast asleep with Winona sitting on the bed, leaning against the headboard asleep, too. He is safe. I close the door silently and leave the apartment, heading straight for Azura's as I undo my shirt cuffs, rolling the sleeves of my black shirt up. I raise my hand and knock hard.

Nothing.

I knock again. Nothing.

Fuck, I don't care, I'm going in.

I enter a code on my smart watch before I hold it against the scanner and hear the lock click open. I step into the apartment, shutting the door behind me. Her scent fills my senses and I head to her bedroom. Why didn't she fucking answer?

I knock on the door trying to control the anger and restlessness that is now not only mine. I feel my wolf prowling in my mind, his urgency and concern for the mate that I deprived the both of us of. I knock again, frowning.

"Azura. Fuck, open the door."

She is here. I can fucking smell her. Is she in the bathroom?

I push the door open, just as the bathroom door opens, and I come face-to-face with none other than the she-devil herself. Oh, and right now she is the image of pure sin in nothing but a black lace bra and a tiny pair of underwear. She freezes in surprise, staring at me for a moment, her heart thundering. Pleasure fucking rushes south, and I feel myself harden as my eyes rake over her. At least she is fucking here.

I let my gaze trail over her once again but this time I see past those gorgeous curves of hers, taking in the bruises on her legs, arm, shoulder, and even her cheek. My eyes flash with anger at the same time reality seems to hit her. She quickly grabs a discarded towel and wraps it clumsily around her shoulders, although it barely covers her panties. She then gives me a scathing glare.

"Have you ever heard of knocking?" she growls. She sure didn't lose her spark.

"I did. Several fucking times. You didn't answer," I reply arrogantly.

"For a reason," she retorts as she slowly eases the towel off her shoulders and frees her arms. Wrapping it around her chest, she walks over to the wardrobe and grabs an oversized shirt. My eyes are on her back. I can see the curve of her ass from under the towel and the painful scrape that is slightly bloody on her left cheek. It only makes my anger grow; this hadn't been a small fucking scuffle. Emmet had aimed to hurt her. She pulls the grey t-shirt over her head, and lets the towel fall as she turns back to me. "Why are you here?" she asks, sounding almost accusing.

"You know why," I reply coldly, walking over to her. Her eyes flash defensively as I approach. The urge to fuck her is intense, but instead, I cage her between my arms, her back pressed against the wardrobe behind her. My eyes scan her face. She has another bruise under her jaw and on her neck.

I clench my teeth, masking my emotions. Raising my hand, I run my fingers down her cheek, making her tense. These tingles rushing through us both... I had weakened them, but they are still here. Her heart is racing as I continue to run my hand down her neck.

I am beyond fuming and what fucking gets to me the most is she is supposed to be safe here with me.

"Want to share what exactly happened, little she-wolf?" I ask, dangerously quiet. I look into those fucking beautiful eyes of hers and see she is hesitating as if she doesn't think she should tell me. There is no anger in them, so despite the fight, she is calm. Then again, she might just be hiding her emotions but it is her words that fucking surprise me.

"Will you believe me?"

I frown. What does she even mean by that?

She is serious. Gone is the woman who is not afraid to unleash hell. Whatever had happened had shaken her. There is a vulnerability in her eyes that is throwing me off, reminding me of that night that I rejected her and forced myself to fucking turn away from her.

"Try me."

Do I Trust Him
Azura

"**Try me.**" His words ring in my head, and I want to. Somehow, I want to blurt it all out and have him fix it. It is weird, the way he makes me feel like I can rely on him. It confuses the heck out of me because I always handle everything myself.

He looks so yummy in that black shirt and grey pants. His toned thighs, narrow waist and those delicious muscular biceps… this guy was born with incredible genes, and those blue eyes… Goddess, never have I liked the colour more. But the way he is behaving is unnerving me.

I can feel his anger. I'm just not sure if it is because I left the room, or fucked up his Delta's face, or because maybe seeing me injured pisses him off?

Stop kidding yourself, Azura. He marked you, rejected you, and watched you collapse before walking away. The memory feels like a harsh slap in the face, and I break our eye contact, moving away from his touch. I push the painful thought away, and take a deep breath.

"I was in here when I heard two loud bangs, and they sounded a bit weird, so I thought I'd go see if Jackie was okay. I barely got out the door when I saw Emmet storm out their door." I nudge him away with my shoulder and slide out from where he has me trapped. "He entered the lift, and I hurried to their door. Jackie opened it, thinking it was Emmet. That's when I saw that she had a bruise on her cheek and around her neck. It wasn't even just finger marks. He had dug his claws into her skin. And then... she just asked me not to tell the Alpha." I turn and look at him. He is standing there, one hand to his chin, the other in his pocket, and he is frowning deeply, obviously wanting me to continue. So I look him square in the eye and carry on, "When I went down there, he was around the side of the building about to go through some door, and I called him. When I confronted him, he told me to mind my own business. He got pissed and threatened me. Then I defended myself by losing my shit and attacking him like the psycho I am," I finish with a shrug.

No reaction. That frown remains as his eyes dip to my forearm, where I am bleeding a little, although it is already healing up pretty well. It isn't a big deal. If he sees Emmet...

"So, although he's your Delta, he could use some work," I mumble as he advances on me but despite the fact that he is oozing dominance and power, it isn't threatening, even if my heart is racing. I know that is because of something entirely different.

He takes my wrist in his hand before raising it to his mouth, and, to my surprise, he runs his tongue along the graze, sending a riveting jolt of pleasure straight to my core. I know alpha saliva helps heal faster, but the way he is looking at me is anything but innocent. I yank my arm away, frowning at him, despite feeling my cheeks heat up.

"What are you doing?" I growl. He cocks a brow, taking out a cigarette and lighting it.

"Alpha saliva heals, or don't you know that?"

"I do, but just because I have a graze doesn't mean you are going to go around licking it." I frown, although it left a cooling touch in its wake.

"I saw a cut, and I licked it. End of fucking story," he growls, smoking his cigarette.

"I have a graze on my ass, are you going to lick that, too?" I shoot back before freezing as his eyes meet mine. *You really are the classiest woman in the world, Azura. Is there ever a time I don't put my foot in my damn mouth?*

"Do you want me to?" he replies mockingly.

Leo's pierced tongue on my ass? *Hmm, yes, please. Wait, no.* I glare at him.

"No thanks," I mutter, stalking out of the bedroom. I do not want to be in there when everything that is coming into my head is far from decent. I know I am frustrated, and I always get carried away when I'm overwhelmed. I hear him follow me silently before I turn to him. "So, uh, do you believe me?"

"I can tell when someone lies," he says simply. "I'll have someone come to check up on your injuries. Get some rest." He didn't answer me. Will he do nothing?

"I'm not lying," I try, unable to hide the frustration in my voice. He pauses, his hand on the door handle, before turning and looking at me, and I know this is my last chance. "I've heard of stories where people hide abuse, where even the best of alphas don't notice it happening beneath their noses. Women or even men, who keep it a secret because they love their mates too much to let them go." He turns back to me, watching me with that sharp, calculating look in his eyes.

"Seems like you know someone who has been through that."

I'm not going to hide it because of my own pride, because if this gets him to see that Jackie needs him, then I am ready to tell him.

"Indigo, my biological mother... she let her mate treat her like shit just so he stayed by her side. She was so blinded that without him, she lost the will to live." *And she didn't care if I died or lived...* I look away from those ice-cold eyes, hating how vulnerable I sound. "I'm just... Jackie is a good person. I don't want her to go down that path." I look down at my nails.

He approaches, but I don't look up, trying to compose my emotions. When he places two fingers under my chin, forcing my face up, our eyes meet.

"Friend, brother, or pack member, if someone is abusing their mate, I will deal with them. Rest assured, little she-wolf. I know you're not lying. You've told me what you saw. Now I'll handle the rest. Get some sleep once you're checked over." He cares for others, but it kind of hurt that he had also hurt me.

This isn't about you, Azura, but Jackie. I don't want another woman to become Indigo.

178 | *Do I Trust Him*

I give a small nod, trying to pull away from his touch that is making my heart pound and head feel light. He refuses to let go, curling his fingers under my chin and forcing me to look at him. He searches my eyes for something before I pull away and turn my back on him. He doesn't say anything, and I sense him moving away. I can only breathe when I hear the door click shut.

Leo

I leave the room, taking my phone out.

Becky, can you come to the 7th floor of my apartment block? There's an important guest in the apartment across from Emmet's. Check her over. She was in a fight and may have a few fractures.

Of course, Alpha Leo. I will be there in ten.

Thanks.

I end the link, looking at the video Eric had sent. From their body language it is clear they were arguing. Then, Emmet grabs her, and my eyes blaze. The urge to cross the floor and rip that door off its hinges and-

Stop. I am thinking like a deranged beast. One that reminds me of someone I hate to the fucking core. Emmet will get what's coming to him, but it's too late. I will handle this in the morning.

I hook up her door to my phone, every time she leaves, I'll know. I think I will pay Marcel a visit. I'm certain he has answers I can use.

Jax, are you there?

Yeah, Alpha, I just got back. Any issue?

I want you to keep an eye on Azura Westwood. She's on the 7th floor across from Emmet's place. A slight silence follows as I enter the lift and head down.

Yeah, of course.

No one aside from Winona is to go to her room. Make sure no one sees you, especially Emmet.

Understood, Alpha.

I leave the apartment building, smoking a cigarette as I make my way to Marcel's, a place I hate going to. I hate the fact that he will always choose them over me. I ring the doorbell, although I know the code. I refuse to walk into a place that I do not consider mine. The door is opened by a shirtless Marcel, a towel around his shoulders. It is obvious he has just showered after his workout.

"Leo." A smile crosses his face as if he is happy to see me, and I simply brush past him.

"I have a few questions," I reply coldly, looking at him. He closes the door and nods.

"Ask away," he says, crossing his arms.

"What's the story behind Azura Westwood's biological mother?" I ask. He raises an eyebrow, smirking slightly.

"Why would you be interested in Azura's life?"

"I'm not, and don't antagonise me. You already know that she was my mate."

"Is your mate." Our eyes meet, and I hold his cold gaze.

"I rejected her." He looks almost sympathetic before nodding and jerking his head towards the lounge.

"Come on in." I follow, refusing to take a seat and instead walk over to the window overlooking the front garden as I smoke my cigarette. "I thought Azura left, but I heard not long ago that she's back?"

"Plans changed. She'll be leaving soon, don't worry," I reply, looking at him indifferently. He nods, sitting down and observing me with a tilt of his head.

"She's a strong woman with a good heart, albeit a little adventurous. Leo, she's perfect for you."

"Yeah, of course. A Westwood can't be anything but perfect in your eyes. I don't really fucking care. I asked about Indigo Malone, not if Azura is perfect for me or not." Marcel sighs before looking at his hands.

"Fine. She had a mate who abused her and cheated on her. In fact, she even miscarried a few times because of his abuse." So, is that why this situation with Jackie triggered her? Because it reminded her of Indigo? "It was terrible, and when it came to light, Alejandro lost it. Fred was one of his most trusted men, and the fact that this was happening under his nose made him lose it. He made the hard decision to send him on a suicide mission and he died. Just like everyone knew he would. Alejandro felt the pack-link break and Indigo felt the loss of a mate." I didn't know that.

"So, Alejandro punished him by killing him off. So ultimately, isn't he responsible for Indigo's death? Because everyone knows that not many can survive the loss of their fucking mate." I smoke my cigarette, raising an eyebrow. Marcel frowns.

"It's not like that," he says sharply, but he looks a bit unnerved.

"It fucking is. He ended two lives that day, fuck almost three. A logical person would have put him in prison, not for his sake but for his mate's. So, the way I see it, this brother of yours has made a lot of fucking mistakes."

"Everyone makes mistakes, Leo, but Alejandro did it for Indigo, hoping she'd find someone-"

"Did he know she was pregnant?"

"Yes, but that's-"

"So he still fucking risked her and Azura's lives? Because everyone knows the loss of a mate can fucking break you. She went into that battle wanting to die, right?" He is frowning as he looks at me, almost as if he doesn't know what to say.

"Can I assume you are worried or angry for Azura?" He is watching me intently.

"Why would I be?" I deny.

This entire conversation leaves a bitter taste in my mouth. There is more to Azura Westwood than meets the eye, and the urge to learn and figure her out is growing. I like puzzles, and she brings a few, the topmost being her fucking ex. I actually want to see exactly what this fucker has that made her fucking date him.

"I'll be leaving." I stride to the door when he speaks,

"Leo, take her as your Luna. I assure you she will make you happy, and Corrado loves her already," he says quietly. I don't bother turning back or answering. Shutting the door behind me, I leave.

I replay the video once again as I make my way home, not wanting to think about what Marcel said. I watch the clip, seeing her brace her feet on the wall before flipping over and landing behind him. Damn, there is nothing hotter than seeing a woman kick ass. I am unable to stop the smirk on my face as she knocked Emmet to the ground. He is a cocky shit, so this is fun to see. I should ask her for a sparring match, I'm sure that would be pretty interesting.

Pocketing my phone, I head back. Emmet will meet me in the morning regarding the shipment anyway, and I don't want him to be on alert when I question him. I want to know his fucking side, and then I'll be the judge.

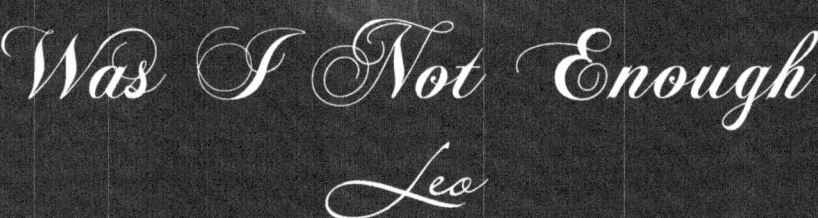

Was I Not Enough
Leo

I am ready to hit the gym with Emmet once I have Corrado fed. I am already dressed in grey sweatpants, a white tank top, and sneakers. He is still giving me those sad looks, and I wonder if he is just being stubborn or actually missing Azura. What's to miss anyway?

An image of her, comes to my mind.

Pretty much a lot.

Fuck that.

"Want to have breakfast with Azura today?" I ask as I flip the crepes over in the pan. His eyes widen in excitement, and he nods.

"Is she back? Yes! Let's go!" he says, jumping off the worktop.

"Hold up, fast guy, we need to get your breakfast made."

"Oh, yes, Azura can't cook. We must make her breakfast too, Daddy." I frown.

"She must have food at her place."

"But you said I'll have breakfast with her..."

"I only cook for you," I mutter, glancing down at him, only to see the sadness in his eyes.

"But this is for me." Fuck, this kid is good at emotional blackmail.

"Fine." I frown, and he smiles happily, as if he hadn't just been near tears a few seconds ago.

"Yes! Azura will love your crepes, Daddy!"

"You get crepes for her on one condition. You don't tell her that I made them, deal?"

"Deal!" he says very fast as he runs to get a tray.

Great. Now I am cooking for her.

Once the two plates of crepes are done, complete with Nutella and strawberries, I place two glasses on the tray and am about to take the milk carton and a juice bottle out when Corrado grabs the milk carton from me.

"Daddy, no juice; Azura likes milk," he says this while hurrying to the tray and placing the milk on it. *I'm sure she fucking does.*

I grab the tray, frowning down at it. They sure look fucking good. Guess I'm a better cook than her. Not that I've eaten anything she's made, but then again, it would be better not to because who knows what she'd put into it. At least she tasted fucking good.

Reaching Azura's door, I knock and pass the tray to Corrado; I don't want to be seen carrying it. I hope she gets here quickly before he drops it, too. I watch him. Seeing the excited smile on his face as he watches the door with avid anticipation makes me smile slightly. I'd do anything for him.

The door opens to a sleepy Azura. Her hair is as smooth as ever, but you can tell she has just woken up from the strands that fall in front of her face. Her eyes are half open, her plump lips set in a pout. The oversize shirt she had pulled on last night is hanging off her shoulder, barely covering those thighs of hers... totally fuckable. Her eyes widen when she looks us both over before she smiles brightly at Corrado.

"Hi, Azura! Daddy said I could have breakfast with you today."

"Corrado! Oh, that would be amazing! And pancakes with Nutella. Yummy!" She crouches down slightly and takes the tray from him. My gaze dips to her ass as she turns and takes the tray to the table, Corrado following her excitedly. I realise the shirt is inside out, meaning she had pulled it on before getting the door. An image of her in nothing but her lingerie returns to me, and I have to force myself to look away from her ass.

"No, Azura, we call these crepes! Daddy made them, but he said I can't tell you," he declares, and I raise my eyebrow. Well, he sure doesn't know how to keep a damn secret.

"Oh…" Azura for once seems to not know what to say. She turns to look at me, and I raise an eyebrow.

"I'll pick him up in an hour and a half after training," I say emotionlessly, trying to keep my eyes locked on hers and not over that body of hers.

"Sure," she replies with a nod. Her gaze rakes over me, and I feel something inside when her eyes linger on the front of my pants before she bites her lip and turns her back on me smoothly. Fuck. We shouldn't be in a room together.

I cross the room to Corrado, who is already waiting with his fork and knife in hand, and ruffle his hair.

"I'll see you soon, kid."

"Take your time, Daddy. I'm okay with Azura," he says, giving me another bright smile. I look into his hazel eyes. Someone he can live with, without me…

I push the thought away and turn. My eyes meet hers as I walk past her, brushing my arm against hers. Tingles of pleasure spread through my arm at the slight contact.

I leave her apartment, mind-linking Emmet to come out. The door to his place opens, and I see him, Jackie, and Nikki. Our eyes meet, and hers fill with hurt before I look away. Jackie gives her a gentle smile. I guess she knows, which means so does Emmet.

"Morning, bro," Emmet says, fist-bumping me. I entertain him, but the urge to crush his fist is tempting. I glance over at the women, smoothly observing Jackie's face. She is wearing a shirt with her collar buttoned, so I can't see her neck, but if it happened last night, those bruises would be gone just like Azura's had.

"Hey, Leo," Nikki says softly. Is it bad that not once has she crossed my mind since we broke up? Sure, she's messaged a few times, but I haven't bothered with them. We are done.

"Hey," I reply before glancing at Emmet. "Shall we get going?" He nods, and we both leave, leaving the women behind.

It is twenty minutes later, and we are now sparring after warming up and an intense twenty minutes of cardio. Both of us are exchanging blows, and I know Emmet will bring it up any minute now.

"So, that chick Azura, when is she going back, man? She's fucking trouble," he says shaking his head.

"Yeah?" I ask, blocking and aiming a punch at his shoulder. He steps back before aiming another punch.

"Yeah. Last night we had a bit of a run-in, and she was acting like she was above the rest of us." He shakes his head as he throws a punch, and I block, throwing an uppercut at him. Weird. Emmet is acting completely normal.

Acting. It is almost as if I have already made up my mind that Azura is telling the truth, and Emmet is probably hiding a lot of shit from me.

"Is she? She doesn't really seem the type to get into other's business," I reply.

Emmet is a friend, one I trust with almost everything. The only thing I have kept from him is Azura being my mate and what is between Jackie and me. I know the reason I didn't tell him about Azura being my mate is because, just like me, he hates the Elite. Emmet and Eric's father was killed by Rayhan Rossi for the crimes committed against Delsanra under Endora's reign. In turn, their mother passed away less than six months later, leaving two more orphans in a pack that was created from broken families.

Rogues. Although we are all just rogues gathered together, there are many different reasons we had become rogues. Some of our ancestors were thrown from their packs for different reasons. Some were for disrespect or betraying their alphas, and there were many who didn't deserve to be thrown out. Then, there were some who left for their own safety from abusive leaders. I remember there was one old man back in the cavern who was kicked out of his pack because his mate was the woman the Alpha wanted and saw him as a threat. He was killed when I was around eight.

Emmet's hatred runs as deep as mine, and what we often hoped would become a better place never did. We were the happiest duo when we learnt we were going to be a real pack... until that was all taken away, and the fear that we would never truly be safe if we opened up became embedded deep within us. Deep down, I wish there was a misunderstanding about all of this but I can't see how.

"Nah, she was getting a bit iffy. It's obvious her mate doesn't want her, bro. Send her packing."

"You seem in a rush to get her out of the picture. I heard what went down from Eric. Really curious why would she fucking accuse you of hurting Jackie though," I remark, knocking his fist aside and catching his jaw. He swears and frowns, stepping back.

"You played dirty."

"Hm, did I?" I ask, running my fingers through my sweat-soaked hair. Our eyes meet, and he shakes his head.

"You know I don't hide anything from you, man. I lost my cool over some shit, and she was trying to calm me down. In my anger, I grabbed her neck. I left the apartment to calm down," he says, looking disappointed in himself.

I am good at reading people, but right now, I don't know if he is telling the truth or lying. Although I'm not officially Alpha, I could still use my Alpha command, but I hate using it, pushing people to do something by force. If I end up being wrong, I'm the one who will have fucked up and it would only create hostility within my people. However, I also know Emmet knows me well, and he knows how my brain works. He would have been ready for this style of questioning.

I'll ask Jackie, she is far easier to read.

"So you hurt her," I say instead. He looks disgusted with himself as he nods.

"Yeah... I messed up, but you know how it can get sometimes, right? When you lose control?"

I frown, feeling a sliver of guilt wash through me. I had hurt Azura when I lost it over Corrado. Shit, now I feel like a fucking hypocrite.

"Make sure it never fucking happens again," I warn him seriously. My eyes flash. "And never hurt her again. You're meant to be her protector, not her fucking abuser." He looks surprised at the aura that is raging around me, but that anger is half directed towards myself. I had hurt Azura, too.

"Got it," he says curtly. I nod, and we continue sparring in silence until Emmet speaks up, "You dumped Nikki."

"Yeah." He lets out a whistle.

"That's some crazy shit. She's hot. Come on, she got you. Plus, she's smart, mature, and a good match for you. Why, man?"

"She just doesn't do it for me anymore. Did she tell you herself, or did Jackie?" I ask, wondering what Nikki had said. I was certain she wouldn't mention Azura, but still if she had, I'm sure Emmet would have mentioned it.

"Nah, Jackie told me. She said she was really upset. Jackie felt super bad for her, too. She gave you her all, you know?"

"It was over weeks before I ended it," I reply with finality, and he doesn't push it.

I couldn't get into it after meeting Azura, no matter how much I had fucking tried. Sure, we fucked, but it was to get Azura out of my system, and it began to leave a bitter taste in my mouth after it was over with.

We end our training session. Usually, we head back to shower and stuff, but I planned to stop to see Jackie at the hospital so I told him I'd be going for a jog.

I have just knocked on Jackie's office door when she calls me in. I step inside, shutting the door behind me. That distinct hospital smell lingers, despite the lavender air freshener.

"Leo." She sounds surprised as she stands up, looking nervous. That's new. Jackie never gets nervous if I show up. "You just finished your training session with Emmet."

"I do hope you aren't mind-linking him right now, Jackie," I reply, walking over to the desk. She shakes her head, her heart racing as I look her square in the eyes.

"No, of course not. Why would I?"

"Good. I have a question or two, and I do hope you answer them correctly." She nods.

"Emmet told me what happened last night. So did Eric. I want you to answer my questions with a simple yes or no. Did Emmet hurt you last night?" Her heart is thumping, and she nods hesitantly.

"Yes, but it wasn't-"

I raise my finger in warning, and she falls silent. That is a truth. I brace my hands on her desk, leaning closer. My eyes meet hers that now hold fear.

Was I Not Enough | 187

What's to be afraid of if you have nothing to hide? Emmet must have told her our conversation, and they should stick to the same story.

"Is this the first time it has happened?"

"Yes."

That was a lie. She is nowhere as good at lying as Emmet which means Emmet *is* abusing her. I nod.

"L-Leo, he just, it was just a one-off, he didn't mean to hurt me."

"If it happens again, you are to tell me immediately," I state, my voice overlayed with my wolf's, my Alpha command resonating through my words. Fear fills her eyes, and it fucking irritates me that this is someone I thought could share anything with me. "I'm still the Leo you grew up with, Jackie. You can share your problems with me. I may not be the official Alpha but I will always have your back," I reply quietly. She nods, looking away, and I turn and leave the office.

The moment I leave the hospital, I break into a run, my mind a storm of emotions and thoughts. Emmet will be removed from his position as Delta until I see how things go. Even if he said it was a one-time thing, that would have been enough to remove him from a position of power.

The wind rushes through my hair as I speed up, pushing myself to my limits, moving faster and faster. The urge to shift is intense, but I refuse.

I thought I was doing a good job, and I had always remained approachable to the pack members. Is this it? Does no one see me as someone they can confide in? Why has it taken someone who has only been here for a mere few days to point this out to me? Had Nikki never seen the signs? Had I never seen them? Will this pack continue to support one another when I am no longer around?

Sharp pains rip through my stomach, and I grit my teeth, pushing onwards. I see black spots blur my vision, but I'm not going to let it get to me. I can taste blood in my mouth and swear internally.

What will happen to this pack when I'm gone?

What about Corrado?

I keep going, hearing my heart pounding, the rush of my blood loud in my ears as my body screams with the flaring pain that now rushes through it. Endora's torture has left me with unhealable internal damage and it is catching up to me.

I know I don't have much time left.

Crepes with Corrado
Azura

The door shuts behind Leo, and I let out the breath I was holding. It's weird. I don't know if I prefer him in the suit that he was wearing last night, his leather jacket, or in those sweatpants. *Fuck, this guy is far sexier than he should even be allowed to be.*

I miss my own workouts, but being pregnant and with everything going on, I have fallen behind. I know that training during pregnancy is fine as long as you don't have any frontal impact on the stomach.

"Let's eat, Azura. Daddy makes the best food," Corrado declares, drawing me out of my thoughts. Leo made these…

I don't even know what to think as I sit down, my heart still racing from the way he had brushed my arm on purpose. What does he want from me?

I look at the plate in front of me, crepes folded into triangles drizzled with Nutella, a dusting of icing sugar, and strawberries on top. So aesthetically pleasing. This plate looks almost as good as Leo. Almost.

"Oh, it looks very yummy!" I exclaim, smiling at the gorgeous little devil sitting there, smiling sweetly.

"It is, and Daddy even made it look nicer today. I think for you," he adds thoughtfully, making my heart skip another beat.

"Hmm, he was probably worried that I can make better crepes than he can," I tease.

"Oh no, Daddy knows Azura can't cook." *Thanks, kid.*

"And you like to make that clear, huh," I tease as I take my first bite. He grins and nods. "Oh, these are good." I have to admit it because they are perfect. Damn, I could get used to this. *No, I can't because he's not mine.* I won't lie, the way he had spoken to me last night remained in my mind. He isn't a bad person. Well, aside from being a dick.

"You're very lucky, Azura. Daddy only cooks for me, but he cooked for you, too," Corrado says, watching me eat. I pour us both a glass of milk, placing his next to him.

"I sure am lucky, so what else can your daddy do?" I ask, resting my chin on my knuckles. *Aside from being deadly sexy, incredible in bed, an- stop it, Azura.*

"He is good at everything! He is the best daddy in the world! He always takes care of everyone; he is my hero!" His eyes sparkle with light and hope. It is obvious that Leo isn't lacking when it comes to being a father. I wonder where Corrado's mama is... does Leo let him see her? Or is he keeping him away from her? Or did something happen to her? I push the thoughts away, placing a hand on my stomach slowly.

"Oh, I'm sure he is an incredible daddy," I reply, giving him a small smile. The fact that he even left me alone with him, from the point he didn't even allow me to be with him around Winona is a big change.

"Yes, and I think he's very sad now," he adds, sighing.

"Sad?" I ask curiously. He nods as I pick up my glass.

"He broke up with Nikki, so he's all alone now."

My heart thunders as I freeze. He broke up with Nikki? I don't want to be one of those people who asks kids for answers, but...

"Oh, how do you know?" I ask, feeling a tad guilty. He looks at me as if I am asking a silly question.

"I know everything. She and Jackie were packing her stuff. She was crying and saying Daddy broke up with her." He finishes off his pancakes and licks his lips. I grab a tissue and wipe his face.

"Oh. Are you okay?" I don't know what to say. How do I react to that? Were they not in a committed relationship? What caused him to break up with her? Is it because of me? Who am I kidding? Leo wouldn't choose me over her. But this does mean Leo is now single...

Don't go there, Azura.

"Yes, I'm okay. Nikki didn't really spend time with me, so it's okay! I'm just sad for Daddy, so sad," Corrado sighs, watching me pointedly. "Will you be Daddy's girlfriend, please?" I blink as I stare at him, taking a few seconds to comprehend what he just said.

"I don't think that's for us to decide. Besides your daddy and me... we..." I shake my head, unable to explain myself, and he simply looks disappointed. "Ooh, let's have a race! Who can eat faster?"

I am able to distract him quickly. After we devour our crepes, I wash up before putting the TV on for him, telling him I am going to quickly get ready. He nods, and I get dressed super-fast in a white vest top with leather pants, not sure if he is safe to be in a room alone. I don't trust kids; if they are alone for even a minute, they can wreak havoc. Trust me, I've been there. Surprisingly, when I come back, he is sitting where I left him, and everything is in order.

After that, we play tag in the apartment before having a pillow fight. I love kids, and Corrado is a pretty well-behaved kid, but I know if taught well, he'd be up to lots of mischief! We have a lot of fun. He is just adorable. By the time we are done, the apartment looks like it has been hit by a tornado, but it is worth it. Corrado's laughter is contagious, and it takes my mind off everything I am feeling.

A knock on the door makes us finally get up from the pile of cushions that we have been lying on as he tries to tickle me. I go to the door, pulling it open to reveal none other than Leo, who is glistening with sweat, pouring water into his mouth from a water bottle. For a moment, time seems to stand still as I simply stare at his gorgeous brown locks that are falling in front of his forehead. From his broad shoulders, his lats and traps are as defined as ever, and his shirt clings to his narrow waist and deliciously defined abs. Then there is the front of those sexy sweatpants that-

He clears his throat, and I feel my cheeks heat up when he snaps his fingers in front of my face.

"I'm here for Corrado. If you aren't too busy enjoying the view, how about you call him?" he mocks arrogantly.

"Nah, I was just wondering how you aren't even blessed with one good feature. I'll call him," I lie, hoping I am convincing enough. The reminder that he has broken up with Nikki returns to my mind, and I force it away.

He steps closer, raising an eyebrow when he places a finger under my chin. My heart thunders, and I can't ignore the tingles that rush through me.

"What the fuck is wrong with you?"

"Nothing," I manage to say, realising I have spaced again. He narrows his eyes, searching my eyes for an answer he won't get.

"Corrado?" he calls, looking away from me.

"Corrado isn't here," Corrado's voice calls, and I can't help but smile. This kid is damn cute.

"Well, I was planning to take Corrado out for dinner and a movie tonight. It seems like he doesn't want-"

"I'm here! I'm here!" Corrado comes running. His eyes are shining with excitement. "You mean you'll spend the full evening with me?" he asks with barely contained anticipation.

"Yeah, I am. If, of course, you want to?" Leo raises an eyebrow, and Corrado nods.

"Oh, yes, please, Daddy, I always like spending time with you!" He grabs Leo's hand and smiles at me. "Thank you, Azura. I had lots of fun today." I smile at him, crouching down and plant a kiss on his forehead.

"I had lots of fun, too," I reply, poking his little dimple, only to be rewarded with a bigger smile. I suddenly feel overwhelmed with emotions. This is my pup's sibling...

I look up at Leo only to realise I am pretty much level with his dick and smoothly stand up, trying not to think of anything explicit.

"The crepes were pretty nice," I find myself saying.

"They were pretty basic," comes Leo's cold reply before he leads Corrado away.

Once they are gone, I close the door, looking around my apartment. Well, I guess I should clean up.

A few hours later, Winona comes with lunch, and I'm not going to complain, considering everything she brought is delicious. I am falling asleep on the sofa when I hear a knock at the door. Who is it now?

I walk to the door, fixing the strap of my bra as I open the door, only to be hit by none other than Leo's intoxicating scent. Our eyes meet, and he brushes past me, not even waiting for an invitation.

"Sure, why not just come in without an invitation," I remark, shutting the door. Leo turns towards me, totally unbothered by my remark. He is dressed semi-formal, in black jeans with a smart white shirt that has its sleeves pushed up and a few buttons showing the necklaces that hang around his neck.

"I already did," he shoots back arrogantly. I frown, about to respond, when he holds out a phone. I raise my eyebrow as I take it slowly. "You can call your friends and family. That bastard will not be able to contact you. To make sure he doesn't even trace this back to you, the only numbers that can contact you are those on the phone already," he says as I stare down at the device. "The password is the same as your last phone."

"I'll be changing it," I state. Like hell, will I allow him to know my password... although I have a feeling a password isn't enough to keep him out of it.

"Go ahead." Our eyes meet, and an intense silence falls over us. Fuck, there is no Corrado here to distract me, either.

"So I-"

"I wanted to-" he starts at the same time. We stare at each other before he looks away for a second.

"Uh, you can go first," I say, running my fingers through my hair.

"No, it's okay, what did you want to say?" he asks. *What did I want to say?*

"I've forgotten." He raises an eyebrow as he closes the gap between us, and I slowly step back, trying not to focus on how good he looks.

"You really are crazy."

"Yeah, I am, and proud to be," I shoot back, giving him a withering glare.

"Do you always have your claws raised to attack?" he asks mockingly.

Crepes with Corrado

"Oh, yeah. I'm ready to bite if I have to. So, back off. Ever hear of personal space?" I frown as my ass touches the counter. His eyebrow seems to go up higher as he looks down between us, and I realise he has stopped two feet away.

"I think this is pretty sufficient... it would be a different story if I was closer." His voice is low and dangerous, and when he steps closer, I feel like I can't breathe. My heart thumps when he places his hands on either side of the countertop, his arms brushing my waist. Oh, Goddess, what is he doing?

"What did you want to say?" I ask, staring at him defiantly and trying not to focus on the fact that he has me trapped once more and the way I can feel his body heat. *Focus, Azura.*

My words seem to bring him back to reality, and he frowns. Despite not moving back, his eyes are sharp as they look directly into mine.

"I spoke to Emmet, who denied it. Strangely, I couldn't differentiate whether he was lying or telling the truth."

Does that mean he doesn't believe me? No! Emmet practically admitted to me that he had hit her and that I should mind my own business! I am about to speak when he places his thumb against my lips, his fingers curling under my chin, making my core clench.

"Let me finish." I nod slowly, very aware of his finger against my lips. "I then spoke to Jackie, who, unlike Emmet, isn't really good at lying. There is something going on between them, and I will get to the bottom of it. For now, I've removed Emmet from the position of Delta until I look into this properly. I need Jackie to speak before I can do anything, but rest assured, I will not let anyone get away with abuse."

Every word he speaks affects me. He didn't need to explain this to me, yet here he is explaining it all, and I sure as hell appreciate it. I nod. His finger is still on my lips, and when I part them to speak, his finger brushes down my lower lip before he removes his hand, making me swallow. His eyes flash when I lick my lips, and I look down, staring at his neck rather than those piercing eyes.

"I... thanks for letting me know. You didn't need to, and I actually appreciate it," I reply, my throat feeling far too dry, and it suddenly feels too hot in here.

"I also want to apologise," he murmurs, frowning deeply. Apologise? I look up sharply as he stands straight and steps back.

"For?" I ask.

"For overreacting when I found out you spent time with Corrado. Not only did I hurt you, but I abused my position as someone who is stronger-"

"Oh, please, I did equal damage," I scoff. "I'm just as strong as you." Is he actually apologising? What the hell has he eaten? Wait, is he drunk or something? Something is up... this is too suspicious.

"Yeah, sure," he replies in a tone that makes it clear he doesn't think so. I cross my arms now, looking at him defiantly.

"Wanna try me?" I challenge.

"I already did," comes his cocky reply.

Our eyes meet, my eyes widening in surprise and my core knots. Oh, this guy is totally messing with my head.

Losing It
Azura

"I mean in a fight," I mutter. He raises his eyebrow.

"That's what I meant," he remarks. Wait, no, he... "Is your mind always in the gutter, or do I simply get to you?" *Of course, you do. You damn annoying Rossi.*

"Don't get so full of yourself," I scoff.

"Am I wrong?"

"If I want my mind to be in the damn gutter, I have every right to keep it there. I don't need anyone's approval," I retort, annoyed when he cages me between the worktop once more.

"Even if it involves me?"

"Yes, because it's my mind. So, whether I imagine you naked, or in a pair of neon pink boxers, that's my mind, my choice."

"Oh? So, if I imagine you naked, that's totally okay?"

"Why? Do you?" I challenge.

He doesn't reply, his eyes trailing over me before they slowly flick up to meet mine, and I know I have gotten my answer. I see him swallow, his eyes darkening when they skim to my lips. My entire body is reacting to his closeness. Even with the bond that is hanging on by only a thread, only in need of a few words from me to break completely, I can still feel the intense pull that comes with it...

"You broke up with Nikki," I blurt out. *Wow, nice going, Azura.* His eyes snap to mine, and I feel him tense slightly. He suddenly moves back and turns his back on me.

"That's none of your concern." His voice is hard, and I feel a pang of pain wash through me. So does he blame me for that? "I came here to apologise and that's what I'll do." His voice is low as he turns back toward me, his gaze falling to my neck. "I'm sorry for marking you, and for rejecting you. I never should have done either." Those words cut like a knife, but I do my best to hide the emotions that are threatening to drown me.

"Both?" I ask, raising an eyebrow. His eyes meet mine and he nods.

"Yeah, both. I was clouded by my anger, and I was fighting myself, and so I'm fucking sorry for fucking up your life with what I did. I've already begun working on tracking down this ex of yours and once I have... you can return home."

"Got it." I feel as if I have been thrown into a pool of icy water. "So, since you regret it all, I guess you regret fucking me, too," I spit, feeling my anger rising.

"No. Why should I regret that?"

His arrogance makes my anger flare. Who the fuck does he think he is? I scoff, closing the gap between us and shoving him. My heart is thundering, and my head is beginning to squeeze as pressure begins building. I am losing control of my anger.

"Why not? Because that didn't have any fucking consequences?" I ask icily, glaring up at him. *If only you fucking knew.* I want a reaction; I want him to lose his shit so I can lose mine.

"Calm down," his icy-calm reply comes.

"Don't! Don't tell me to calm down. Do you know how I felt after being fucked, marked, and then rejected? My wolf is still weakened! I don't feel her as strongly as I used to! I was in so much pain that I fainted, and you left me! I gave you everything, yet you were okay to fuck me even though you had a woman, making me feel even worse!" He isn't reacting, not even stopping me from attacking him. I continue to shove him, wanting to see him stumble. "Do you know how I felt when I had to beg someone to give me a phone so I could call my brother? Do you know how it felt to see the rage in his eyes and begging him not to fucking find you because of who you are?" His eyes flash but he says nothing.

"If you really regret marking me, then go mark someone else so I can have this off me!" I scream, shoving him. "At least let me live my fucking life without having this scar as a fucking reminder of you!"

Needing a way to unleash my anger, I extract my claws, ready to plunge them into my own neck and rip off his mark, but before I can even dig my claws into myself, he has grabbed my hand, closing his large hand over mine, and turns me. Pulling my back against his chest, his other arm tightens around my waist as I thrash around, my heart thundering.

"Hush..." His voice is low, and even as I struggle against him, he refuses to let me go.

"Don't tell me to calm down!" I hiss, trying to elbow him, but, unlike Emmet, he is far stronger.

"Listen to me, little she-wolf. I only meant I didn't regret the rest of that night because it was fucking perfect. But marking you... like you said, I ruined your life, and I know I did. I fucking did and I regret the rejection because of the pain I put you through. I'm sorry, I'm fucking sorry. I want to be a better person than them, but I fucked up, too. I'm no better. This has nothing to do with you."

I still in his arms. You're wrong; it has everything to do with me. Nothing can break my spirit, but I am teetering on the edge of despair. I don't know what I want, but earlier when I knew he had broken up with Nikki, I had subconsciously held out hope.

"It has everything to do with me because of who I am, right?" I say quietly. His face is so close to mine, pressed against the side of my head, and I feel broken. He remains silent for a moment. "You regret rejecting me because of the pain but you still wouldn't accept me, correct?"

He stays silent and I have my answer. I sigh, pulling free from his hold. This time he lets go of me and I turn, looking up at him blankly.

"Just leave, Leo. Your apology... it isn't enough. Give me back my life, take this pain away, and remove this mark from my neck. Otherwise, you can fucking go to hell." My voice is calm, yet it is laced with venom.

He doesn't speak, and I can't read his emotions. His gaze dips to my neck for a second. Our eyes meet before he turns away without another word. He leaves the apartment. The door shuts behind him with a small snap that seems to ring in the empty apartment. I turn away, gripping the worktop, my heart thundering as I try to control my emotions. Regretted marking me... *Dickface.*

I walk over to the sofa and sit down slowly. It is my own fault for even allowing myself to lose control of my emotions. I don't know how long it takes for me to calm down, but it is dark outside. I stay sitting there glaring at the table. I unlock the phone he has given me, my hand shaking with uncontrollable rage as I find Dante's number.

Me: I want the necklace.

He comes online immediately, and I stare at the phone, my heart raging. I see the message change to 'read' but instead of replying, his call is incoming. I answer, raising the phone to my ear.

"I want the necklace," I repeat, my voice sounding menacing.

"Okay, My Temperamental Miracle." *I'm no fucking miracle.* "You are. You sure are one of a kind," he teases in his deep, husky voice.

"Don't try to get in my head, Dante. I'm not in the mood."

"I'm not getting in your head, I can't read minds. I just know what you would say."

"I'm angry, Dante. So angry," I reply quietly.

"I know."

"Don't use that shit on me. I want to rip his mark off my neck, I want to leave from here, and I want to-"

"I know but don't act in anger, Azura. We often say things that may not be perceived the way we want them to be. Look deeper." I close my eyes.

"You understand me, right, Dante? It hurts. He makes me want to fucking give up," I whisper, tucking my legs up under my chin.

"Since when can anyone make the Westwood Devil do anything?"

"Easy for you to say," I mutter.

"You've got this. Besides he can't be so bad if he can get under your skin like that."

"He's irritating and damn annoying. Arrogant and so... well, let's just say a typical Rossi." I am feeling calmer talking to someone.

"Well, we are pretty irresistible." I roll my eyes, and a pleasant silence falls between us.

"So still not seeing anything about your future mate?" I ask. He lets out a throaty chuckle.

"I don't know if I have one. You know how my wolf and I are. I don't know if the same rules apply."

"I don't think the Goddess would deprive her favorite demigod of a mate," I say softly. I feel sorry for Dante. He holds so much on his shoulders. He often knows things to come, and I wonder how much pain and sadness he has foreseen.

"Well, as long as she doesn't turn out as terrifying as you, I'm all good," he teases.

"So funny." I smile though. "Thanks for ringing, Dante. I needed it."

"Any time. I'll always be there for you."

"Hey, I'm older, okay? You mean to say I'll be there for you."

"Nope, I meant exactly what I said. Now, go be a good girl and watch some TV or have a bubble bath. Whatever you girls do to calm down." A bubble bath does sound good...

"Yeah, well, we aren't men who go hitting things when angry." Didn't I just do that? He lets out a small, knowing chuckle.

"Whatever you say."

I thank him before ending the call and decide to have a bath and text the girls. I just need to calm down.

Two hours later, I am so much more relaxed. The tub has a heating system, and the water never goes cold. I have some music on, and I feel much more at ease. I even had a good chat with Sky and Kat; sadly Song didn't answer, so it was just us three.

Wanting to feel good about myself, I pull on a pretty lingerie set. Honestly, I need to thank whoever chose this stuff, but the memory that it is paid for by Leo leaves a sour taste in my mouth, so I push the thought aside.

I am just moisturising my legs when I'm sure I hear something. I tilt my head, lowering the music. There, I hear it again.

"Leo?" I ask, grabbing the bathrobe that I had tossed on the floor earlier. I put it on, leaving the bedroom only to see none other than Emmet standing there, looking beyond pissed. His aura is swirling around him, and unmasked rage contorts his face.

"So, you went and fucking snitched, and because of your fucking misconception, Leo suspended me from my position as Delta until further notice," he growls. In a flash, he is in front of me, grabbing my throat as he slams me against the wall. "Oh, and guess what? Leo's gone with his kid. He won't be home for a while. Who are you going to run to now?"

A Blinding Awakening

Leo

We are sitting in the cinema, watching a kid's movie, but I can tell Corrado isn't enjoying it as much as he is enjoying watching me with a huge smile on his face. I feel fucking bad that I am gone so often that he is regularly left without even seeing me on some days. "Not enjoying the movie?" I ask, looking down at him. He shakes his head.

"No, I love it! I'm loving the movie because Daddy came with me." He smiles, and I lean down, cupping the back of his head and placing a kiss on his forehead.

"Me, too. It may be boring, but I like that we get this time, you know?" I remark, adjusting his mini popcorn tray in his lap.

"Thank you, Daddy."

I give him a wink before glancing at my phone. Azura hasn't left her room, which I am relieved about, but I can't get what happened earlier out of my fucking mind. She is still hurting from all the shit I did to her but she didn't get what I had meant. I regretted marking her because of my limited time... I know Jackie has told me that Kiara could probably heal me, but I am unable to put aside my ego and ask them for anything. I don't need their help just for Marcel and all of them to remind me that I fucking owe them.

A couple of young women slide into the seats next to me, whispering and giggling irritatingly. They had been seated elsewhere before they left not long ago. The entire room is pretty empty, and I am certain they didn't pay for the seats they have now fucking taken. Corrado's eyes turn toward them before he looks at me, frowning slightly.

"He's so fit."

"Damn, and who's the kid with him?"

"Let me sit next to him," they are whispering quietly, but obviously, it is fucking loud in my ears. Irritating as fuck. I don't spare them even a glance while watching the screen, despite half my attention being on Corrado.

"Hey, cutie," one of the women waves at him, leaning closer. Corrado raises his eyebrows, looking at me and then at the women again.

"My Daddy has a girlfriend," he declares, and I almost smirk. He has realised pretty young that women try to talk to him to get to me, and he never stands for it.

"Um, sure. What's your name?" I am tempted to speak up, but watching my kid deal with them is far more entertaining.

"I don't tell strangers my name. Sorry. Daddy, let's go home. Azura is waiting for you." My eyebrow shoots up. Azura? Doesn't he mean Nikki?

"The movie?"

"It's boring, and I don't like those girls," he whispers loudly. I sure as fuck hope the women feel fucking humiliated, and I stand up.

"Let's go, kid." I lift him up, walking out the other way. "So, why did you say Azura and not Nikki?" I ask, taking my phone out.

"You and Nikki broke up, so now we get to keep Azura as your new girlfriend." My eyebrow shoots up, and I wonder if this kid is going to be a playboy growing up.

"Isn't that moving too fast? Nikki just left."

"No, Daddy, because you and Nikki argue about more than football for many days now. So, now we keep Azura forever," he declares as we leave the viewing room. Wow... and I thought I did a good job in keeping that shit hidden.

"She isn't an item that we can just keep."

"Why?"

I place him on the ground as we both walk side by side. I look at him to tell him that you can't just own people, but the adorable look on his face stops me. This kid is the damn cutest kid on the fucking planet, and he is mine.

"Because she's a little scary."

"Azura isn't scary, Daddy! You aren't scared of anything!" he giggles. *I am. Of losing you. Leaving you.*

I take my phone out and look at it again. I fucking feel uneasy again, and after last time, I'm not feeling good about her being there alone. Although I can see Jax is there on the steps, clearly alert as his head is turned downwards towards the lower floor. He is using a scent disguiser, and I know even Emmet won't notice him there unless he uses the stairs, so all should be okay.

"Kiddo, shall we get a takeaway and get home? Maybe we can eat it with Azura?"

"Oh, yes! Let's all eat together. Then, you make Azura happy, and we bring her home," he replies as we leave the place.

"Perfect," I reply distractedly as I walk over to one of the takeout shops near the cinema.

I place our order distractedly as I mull over Emmet's reaction when I told him that he's been suspended until further notice.

"It was her, wasn't it?" he asked, barely able to keep his hatred at bay. I raised an eyebrow.

"Whether it was her or someone else, I will follow protocol because we stand for what's right. As future Alpha and Delta, it's our fucking duty to be an example for our people. These are just the rules that we all need to follow."

"You spoke to Jackie, I'm sure she clearly told you we are totally fucking fine," he spat.

"Calm the fuck down, Emmet. Friend or not, I'm not going to break the rules for you," I warned, my eyes flashing.

"You are going to believe a fucking Elite? One who has fucking reaped discord since she's got here? Tell me, who is her fucking mate that ain't accepting her?"

"Jax," I lied, knowing this meant I would have to tell Jax the truth, but he'd keep the secret.

"Jax Adams? And you really want one of your strongest men mated to an Elite?" He looked disgusted.

"I've never stopped anyone from going to an Elite pack or vice versa before if they find their mate. She's been marked, what do you want me to do? Just send her back? The one who marked her needs to fix this shit… somehow."

"Who cares what happens to a fucking Elite?" he spat. I frowned.

"She wasn't one of the ones who caused us any harm. She was a child when all that shit went down. There's no difference between us if we hurt those who are fucking innocent, Emmet. This has nothing to do with her but the fact that you hurt Jackie. Whether it was a one-off or not, it is a fucking crime. Marcel will be the final judge."

"We both know that Marcel is simply Alpha by title, Leo, you are the real one in charge. This is all in your hands." Our eyes met, and I stepped closer.

"Yeah, maybe it is, and if so, then my decision still stands. Until I'm satisfied, you will not step into the Delta title again."

"I'm your best friend, Leo."

"And like I've said a thousand times, I will never let the rules slide – even for someone I consider my brother," I growled menacingly, my aura rolling off me. He was forced to submit and looked down.

"You need me close to Marcel to make sure that he doesn't get wind of what else you do, Leo." Is that a threat?

"I fear no one. What I do is for my pack, and if anyone double-crosses me, then they will fucking pay. Remember that." I ended the conversation, storming out.

"Here's your order. Can I get you anything else?" the woman behind the counter asks.

"No," I reply, taking out my card and paying.

"Thank you," Corrado says, picking up the bags with ease.

"You are most welcome." She flashes him a smile before I pick up the drinks, and we head out to the car park. I help Corrado in and strap him in.

"Seatbelts on," he says, making sure it is strapped in. "Daddy, I'll hold the drinks so they don't spill."

"You sure?" I am sure we may just have more spillage.

He nods confidently, and I pass them to him, placing the bags on the seat next to him, and get into the car. Putting my own seatbelt on, something that I do when Corrado is with me, I start the car. I can feel him watching and see the happy smile on his face.

"We will watch another movie with Azura," he declares. "I think we should ask her to come to our apartment."

"Inviting girls home already?"

"Yes, girls we like." He nods. I smirk as I put some clean music on before we drive out.

I text Jax, frowning, as I switch the view on the cameras again. We aren't that far from the pack grounds, but it is fucking crazy how on edge I feel. Emmet has a temper, and I fucking wish I had moved her upstairs to my apartment or to Marcel's mansion. The screen lights up with Jax's reply, and click on it.

'Nothing to worry about here, Alpha.'

I leave the camera on my LCD screen before calling Eric.

"Hello, Alpha."

"Keep an eye on Emmet. He was pretty pissed when I suspended him as Delta."

"You suspended him?" He sounds shocked.

"No, the fucking tooth fairy did. I just told you I fucking did," I mutter, making sure to keep my voice down.

"Ah, sorry, yes, of course."

"Keep an eye on him." I end the call, finally within mind-linking range of the pack.

No one has gone to Azura's room, and my eyes are fixed on the cameras on the screen so I really need to chill out. That unease inside me is fucking growing like the last time she had gotten hurt.

I tilt my head, frowning as I watch Jax on the stairs away from the floor, but he is standing on alert in exactly the same position he was moments ago. Is the camera frozen? Or is he really not moving?

Jax.

No reply. I park, grabbing Corrado from the back. He passes me the drinks and grabs the food.

"Come on," I murmur, carrying him through to my underground cave.

No one has entered or left Azura's room. She'll be fine. Chill the fuck out, Leo.

But I fucking can't.

"I can walk, Daddy." He smiles, clearly happy with being carried again.

"I know, kiddo." I give him a faint smile, heading straight for the lift up to my office.

Winona, come to my apartment immediately and watch Corrado.

Yes, Alpha. She only lives a few floors down.

"Wait here. I'll bring Azura," I tell him, placing him down in the open living space.

"Okay!" he says happily as he begins taking the food out of the bag. "I'll set the table."

Jax.

Nothing.

I leave the room, and instantly the faint smell that lingers makes me cover my nose with my sleeve. A sleeping drug…

I break into a run just as my phone buzzes. I look at it; Azura's door has been opened. I can't hear anything. The door shuts just as I reach the top of the stairs, spotting Jax slumped on the ground. A fire of rage rushes through me, and my eyes blaze as I run down the stairs, my feet barely touching the steps. I skipped most of them, rushing to her door. No matter how calm I am trying to be, the storm raging inside of me refuses to calm down. I am fucking going crazy at just the thought of something happening to her.

Emmet's scent lingers outside, and I open her door quietly just in case I am fucking overreacting, only to be met with the sound of Emmet's voice.

"…gone with his kid. He won't be home for a while. Who are you going to run to now?"

"I don't need to fucking run because I can deal with you myself," Azura replies icily.

I turn the bend only to see he has her pinned against the wall near the bedroom door, his hand around her neck, whilst she has her arms in front of her stomach defensively. Neither has seen me yet.

How dare he touch her?

"I know your secret," he whispers menacingly. Her eyes flash with fear, something I'm not used to seeing in them.

I am trying to contain the white-hot anger that is festering within me. I have never felt so angry in my fucking life. The urge to shift and rip him apart is taking over. My heart is beating violently, my claws out, and it is then that Azura's eyes snap up, finally noticing me. A wave of relief fills her eyes. *I'm here.*

"Let her go," I hiss, advancing towards him. He freezes, letting go of her as if touching her suddenly burnt him. His heart thuds as she lets out a shaky breath.

I need someone to come to Emmet's floor and apprehend him before I kill him, I growl through the link. I am fucking shaking, ready to kill him. He turns to me, his face pale, his eyes blazing with rage and fear.

"Leo..."

"How dare you?" I growl. "You have fucking doomed yourself."

Jackie... try to think of her...

It is futile; I have lost my grip on reality, and my self-control is slipping. All I can see is the blood dripping down her neck. The sound of the lift opening and footsteps approaching reaches my ears, but my only focus is on the bastard in front of me. Emmet swears, running a hand through his hair.

"I'm your friend, Leo."

"I don't care. You crossed a line that you never should have," I growl, advancing towards him.

"Fuck it... if I'm going down..." In a flash, he spins around, aiming a clean-cut roundhouse kick straight at her stomach.

My eyes blaze in pure anger. I am behind him in a flash, just as Azura screams as she is thrown to the ground, clutching her stomach. My growl of rage rings in the air. I grab Emmet, punching him in the face, feeling something break. I don't fucking care. I slam him into the wall behind him, damaging the wall with the impact.

"What the fuck, Leo?" he groans in pain.

"You touched what's mine," I growl viciously, digging my claws into his neck as I bring my knee up, connecting with his stomach. I feel something break as he howls in pain. His eyes widen, and pure fear flits through him as he looks at Azura on the floor with realisation dawning on him.

"She's…"

"Emmet! Leo!" Eric shouts.

I want to kill him, but at the same time, worry is seeping through me. Why isn't she getting up?

"We've got him," Ace's calm voice comes, pulling me away.

"Lock him up in an isolated cell with no one allowed to see him," I thunder, striding over to where Azura is on the floor, whimpering in pain. Her gown is slipping off her shoulder, but she doesn't seem to care as she sits there clutching her stomach. "Are you okay?" I ask quietly.

I never should have left her.

I grip her elbows, ready to help her to her feet when she whimpers in pain.

"It hurts… no… no…"

I look down at her, frowning. Did she break a rib?

"Let's get you checked out," I whisper, about to lift her when I see blood seeping down her thighs. Where is she hurt? Did I fucking get here too late? She looks up at me, her silver eyes filled with tears.

"My baby can't die."

My eyes widen in shock, and I stare into her eyes, my head spinning as her words echo in my mind. Baby…

I look at her clutching her stomach, and suddenly my entire fucking world comes crashing down around me.

She is carrying our child.

Goddess, what have I done?

Refusing to Fail
Leo

"Your baby won't die. Not on my fucking watch," I promise her, my mind racing as I try to think of the best course of action.

She is looking at me with her eyes flickering from silver to blue, her heart thundering as she clutches her stomach. Her lips part, but she is unable to put two words together. I know my medical shit. Although werewolves can take a hell of a lot more than a human, the trauma of his kick could have damaged the placenta.

"You are going to be okay," I murmur, lifting her carefully into my arms. Her heart is racing, her entire body shaking, and I have never fucking seen her look so vulnerable. *You fucking will be ok.*

I need our top gynaecologist ready to check on a patient with blunt force trauma to her abdomen, I say through the link, the urgency in my voice crystal clear. I run from the apartment to the lift. **Winona, I need you to go down through my office to my underground quarters. Just go through my office, I'll open the entrance for you now. Go down via the lift. In the main room, there's a drawer with the number 78X0**

on it on the left side. The second compartment in the fridge contains a box of syringes. I need you to bring them to the hospital right now!

Yes, Alpha!

I have never let anyone down there, and I just fucking hope she finds it. I quickly unlock the office passageway from my watch. My heart is thundering as I look at the woman in my arms. She is frozen in shock, her hands shaking as she clutches her stomach, her eyes fixed on her bloody thighs. She can't lose this baby; something tells me she could lose the world but not this child. It will destroy her.

The lift opens, and I run to the exit.

Dad! Dad, I need you to get Kiara here right now. Her sister needs her. My voice breaks as fear envelops me. I promised her that her baby wouldn't die... I am fucking going to keep that promise.

Leo, what's going on? What's happened to Azura? Dad's panicked voice comes through the link.

Call Kiara now, I repeat, my voice strained with urgency. **She's going to lose this baby otherwise!**

Baby... what... okay, on it!

Winona hurry!

I'm on my way! Her breathless reply comes.

We are ready for the patient. Room 3C, second floor, Alpha.

My heart is fucking thundering in my ears as I run to the hospital. My feet skid on the tiled floor as I enter before running to the stairs, taking her to the room that is ready for her.

"Place her down!" Doctor Donna orders as she steps forward.

I do, slowly. She is unmoving, but the tears are now streaming down her cheeks. She needs all the strength she can get. What should I fucking do?

"I'm going to do an internal examination."

"Check her levels."

"She's lost a lot of blood."

I need to do something. *Think, Leo...*

"I, Leo Rossi, take back my rejection and accept Azura Rayne Westwood as my mate and Luna," I say quietly, staring at the woman on the bed. My wolf's approval fills my head, and a ripple of gasps fills the room.

Azura's eyes snap to mine as the bond comes to life from the edge it had been teetering on for so long. I feel it strengthen once more as that powerful pull between us returns. If she marks me, it will reinforce her abilities but I am dying...

She is strong enough to survive without me. After the story Dad had told me about her mom and her own birth, I know losing this child would be far worse.

I step closer and kneel down by the bed.

"Mark me, Azura. It may give you the strength you need to heal." I hope so. I fucking need this to work for her. She looks at me as if trying to comprehend what I am saying.

"There's damage to her placenta... she might miscarry..."

Their voices as they whisper amongst themselves are like screams in my head. Azura also seems to have heard them. Her head snaps to mine, the fiery determination of a woman who refuses to give up returns in her eyes, and she gives me a slow nod.

I stand up before lifting her head from the cushions, perching next to her on the narrow hospital bed. With my other hand, I pull my shirt back, allowing her access to my tattooed neck. *Please be okay.*

"What..." Her voice is hoarse.

"Do it." I look into her eyes for a second before she moves closer.

"For our baby," she whispers before sinking her teeth into my neck.

Pleasure erupts through me as I feel the sizzling intensity of the bond erupt inside me like an inferno, and then that powerful tug that sends an explosion of fireworks through me. Her lips brush my neck, and if the situation wasn't so complicated, this would have been entirely different. Our bond is completed. My aura surges around me, and I feel my power growing. I just hope hers does, too.

I can feel her storm of emotions through the bond. The fear for her child. The self-blame that she should have been able to prevent that kick. Disappointment in herself.

She retracts her teeth, her tongue brushing the mark fleetingly before she drops back onto the pillows just as Winona runs through the door.

"Here!" She holds out the box to me, and I take it from her, flipping it open. I am met with a blast of freezing cold air.

"Give me a needle," I order.

"What is that, Alpha?" Donna asks, passing me a wrapped needle after a moment.

"Something I've been working on. It should speed up the process of healing." My aim to try to find a cure. It isn't perfect, but what I have noticed is that it heals external wounds, just not long-term injuries. I'm not sure how well it will work on her, but from my testing, I truly hope it does the job.

"There's no such thing..." one of them murmurs as I take the syringe and attach a needle to it. I ignore them, looking at the woman on the bed. Even in pain, she is the most beautiful thing on the planet.

"Trust me," I tell Azura.

I'm not a healer; I wasn't strong enough to fucking prevent this, but...

I move her gown slightly. One of the doctors has already thrown a sheet over her legs and begun carrying out her internal examination. *Please fucking be okay.*

I force my walls up, knowing she doesn't need any extra stress right now. All I can give her is my reassurance and strength, which I let flow through the bond despite the fear I am fucking trying to hide.

She doesn't even fight or react, her hands on her stomach as I place the needle on the side of her stomach and inject her with the formula I have created. Scarlett Westwood was the research specimen behind this. After the battle a decade ago, I had taken some of her blood for research out of interest, trying to see the scientific build-up of her cells. Right now, I hope the product of that research works more than ever...

If I could, I'd exchange my life for this baby's life.

Come on...

I slide the needle out when the syringe is empty, feeling lost. I have done what I can, and it is obvious that the doctors can do nothing to prevent a miscarriage. I place my hand on hers on top of her stomach, seeing Winona slip out of the room silently. I have given her everything I can, but it isn't enough. I'm not enough... fuck, I never was.

A haunting memory from long ago returns. Just like Mom, she was pregnant when Endora began doing tests on her. She wanted to make the baby into a wendigo before birth, thinking it would be more powerful... creatures created by Endora's sick mind and magic. I know Dad never knew about that pregnancy, and I didn't plan on telling him, knowing it would just cause him more pain.

I tried... I always fucking tried, but it was never enough.

I look down at the woman on the bed. Her eyes are closed as the doctor checks the baby's heartbeat. I know only a few minutes have passed, but it feels like hours.

"Alpha, the heartbeat of the foetus is getting stronger, and she's stopped bleeding," Donna's shocked voice comes. Both Azura and I look up sharply as Donna gives some orders.

"I'll do a scan, but I think the Luna is okay."

The Luna.

Our eyes snap to one another, her heart racing as she clutches her stomach. It doesn't take long for them to get a sonography machine in and set up. She places some gel on Azura's lower stomach, and I force myself to remove my hand.

"It's going to be okay," I say quietly, seeing the tension on her face. **He'll fucking pay.**

Her eyes snap to mine, but she doesn't say anything, nodding slowly.

"Perfect... Alpha, that serum... I think it worked... we will keep assessing her to see that things don't take a downward turn." Donna turns the screen so both Azura and I can see it.

"Make sure you do," I order.

I don't know what to feel... an unexplainable feeling washes through me as I look at the curled-up baby and the powerful blimp of its heartbeat. My pup... thank fuck! I let out a breath as a wave of relief floods the room. I look back at the woman on the bed. Our eyes lock, and she opens her mouth to say something, but before she can, the door bursts open.

In come two women. Kiara Westwood and a cousin of mine, Raihana Somers, sister of Rayhan Rossi.

"Zu!" Kiara whispers as she places her hands on Azura's shoulder, her purple aura swirling around her.

"Kia..." Azura whimpers, grabbing onto her sister's elbows.

"I'm here..."

I remove my hand from where it had been resting on her hip and stand up. Her sister is here to save her. Dad and Alejandro are in the hallway. I can hear them talking. I really don't want to see Alejandro...

As much as I fucking want to stay here, I'm not needed anymore. I head to the door, only for Kiara to speak.

"Leo, wait." I stop two steps away from the door and turn.

"What is it?" I ask emotionlessly. She hugs her sister tightly before she moves back, cupping her face.

"She doesn't need me. She's already healed. Whatever you did, she's perfect." I close my eyes in pure fucking relief. I didn't let our pup die... fuck, at least I managed to save one person.

"Good," I reply emotionlessly. Not waiting for a reply, I exit the room.

The two brothers stop talking when I step out. It has been about a decade since I have seen him. Since the day I told them that they were too fucking late with their apologies. Sure, they came to the pack and apologised, even cured those who had lasting damage from Endora's abuse, but it had been too late. They could cure physical pain but what about the mental pain? Alejandro looks me over as if he is fucking seeing me for the first time. Well, yeah, in a decade...

"Never knew I was such a fucking role model," he smirks. I raise an eyebrow. We look nothing alike.

"You are far from one. Excuse me." I am about to walk off when he blocks my path. My eyes flash as I glare at him menacingly. "Do not fucking cross me. You are here for her, not me."

"I would be here for you, too, if you fucking let us. It's been years, Leo. How have you been?" I look into his onyx-black eyes. He has aged... his once fully black hair is now salt and pepper. We are almost the same height.

"I was better when I didn't have to see your face," I reply.

"Shame, you're just going to have to deal with it. I'm here now, on your invitation, and I don't plan to leave right away," Alejandro counters, looking around as if he has just been fucking given something he has been deprived of. I had made sure they were not to step into this pack ever again but I was the one who called them.

"Then don't. Just stay out of my fucking way." I push past him. I don't have fucking time for this. There are a lot of things I need to deal with.

Leo. Marcel's voice comes through the link.

What do you want? I ask without turning back to him.

Don't leave when your Luna is in there.

She isn't mine, I reply, ignoring the pang of pain that crushes me inside.

You are only fooling yourself...

I ignore him, walking away. She'll be okay. She has her family.

I step out into the fresh air, lighting a cigarette as I exhale, staring up at the sky. Fuck, she is okay. I lean against the wall, propping my foot against it and resting my head back. The relief is unexplainable. However, with it comes a tidal wave of guilt. She had been pregnant when I had manhandled her... what difference is there between me and that bastard? I sigh heavily, taking a long drag on my cigarette.

Winona, where is Corrado?

I'm sorry, Alpha, I left him, but I'm almost back there.

Okay.

Is... is she okay?

Yeah, she is. They both are.

I need to deal with Emmet but I need to do that when I am calmer because right now, all I fucking want to do is kill him.

These Emotions
Azura

verything is a blur...
    Fear, horror, panic.
Leo.

I don't know how, but I want him to fix this. He seems to be the type to always know what to do.

I was always strong and didn't need anyone, but it's weird that he gives me a sense of strength and safety.

When he took back his rejection, I felt my wolf come to life like a cool wave washing over me. Then when he told me to mark him, I knew it was for this baby, and that's all that mattered to me. Our baby deserves to live.

The strength I felt was immediate. The pain in my stomach had subsided, and then whatever he had injected into me seemed to work. I had felt a similar sensation to how it felt when Kiara healed me in the past. A strong surge of coolness washed over me.

He looked guilty. The worry in his eyes so raw and intense that I didn't know what to say. The way his hand rested protectively on top of mine on my stomach...

I was about to say something when Kiara had come, but when she tried to heal me nothing changed, and when she spoke, I understood why. Leo saved our baby by himself.

The sheer relief I feel is unexplainable. My baby is safe. *Thank you, Goddess. Thank you, Leo.*

He had turned away, simply saying 'good' in that cold, emotionless voice of his. That cold exterior had returned with full force. I now look at Kiara and Raihana.

"How are you here?" I ask them.

"Your mate got Uncle to call Kia, and, well, I was the teleporter here." Raihana smiles, her brown eyes warm. Kiara nods as she caresses my hair.

"Leo called you to this pack?" I ask, uncertain of what to think.

"Excuse us." The doctor smiles politely, and all four women present leave the room.

"He did." Kiara smiles. "For you."

My heart skips a beat, but I remain silent. I feel as if I'm not in my body, as if I am looking down on all of this. The most important thing is that my baby is okay. Our baby.

"He sure has changed. I've not seen him in years. He's lost his pretty boy looks," Raihana remarks, making Kia smile.

"It has been ten years since we saw him," she says sadly.

Ten years... yet he called them for me. Well, for our baby. He did this for our baby, not me, and that's okay, because at least I now know that although he hates me, he cares for our pup.

There is a knock on the door, and I adjust my gown before the door opens, and there stands Marcel and Alejandro.

"Hey there," Alejandro greets me. He cups the back of my head and kisses my forehead.

"How are you feeling, Azura?" Marcel asks. I feel a little guilty that he didn't know I was pregnant with his grandchild.

"I'm okay," I reply.

"And so is the baby," Raihana adds as Marcel gives her a hug.

"I'm glad to hear that," he says quietly.

They make small talk, but I am unable to focus. The weight of the situation is heavy on my shoulders. We have marked one another to save our baby but...

what about us as a couple? It isn't enough. It just... isn't. He doesn't want me but now that he knows I am carrying his child, will that change his mind? I don't want that. I don't want that to be the reason. I just don't.

"Are you okay?" Kiara asks, running her fingers through my hair.

"Yeah."

I have my hand on my stomach under the sheet, feeling relieved. Seeing our little baby on that screen again and Leo's reaction, it was a moment that I don't think I'll ever forget. I am a mess.

"Well, it's late. I think we should all head back to mine. You haven't come here in years, and it would be an honour to have you here. Azura, I think you are better off at mine, too." Marcel smiles gently at me, and I nod.

"Sounds like a good plan. I think I'll spend the night with my sister whilst you two catch up," Kiara states, smiling at the men.

"Ah, sounds like a plan," Marcel chuckles. Although Alejandro doesn't seem too keen on the idea, he simply nods, his eyes on his mate.

"I'm going to head back. Thank you for the offer, though, but I haven't even brought my clothes or anything," Raihana says with a toss of her long dark hair. Marcel chuckles.

"Ah, of course, how can I forget that you need your essentials? However, thank you for coming in time."

"Obviously I do, I have a reputation to uphold. Also, there's no need to thank me. We weren't really needed, but I'm actually glad to have popped down to see that ass of a Rossi after years." She shakes her head before smiling at me. "Get him on a leash, girl. You've got it in you to get him in line." She winks at me as Kiara chuckles.

"Thank you, Raihana." I smile slightly, and she gives me a nod before she chants a spell. A wave of power fills the room before she vanishes.

Being the eldest granddaughter of Endora, she was the one to inherit that magic. Witchcraft is passed down from eldest daughter to eldest daughter. Endora herself never had a daughter, so it went to her first granddaughter. She is a powerful witch and the Luna of a pack as well.

"I need to clean up a little," I say. My legs are covered in blood, and I feel sticky.

"Yeah, sure, but I think the fucking question is, how the fuck did you end up in hospital to begin with?" Alejandro asks. I freeze mid-way from pushing my blanket off and look at them as all three turn to me. Marcel frowns deeply.

"The Delta of this pack attacked her. That's all I was told by my Beta, who has him in a cell until Leo deals with him."

"Leo, not you?" Alejandro asks, taking out a cigarette.

"Baby... not in the hospital," Kiara reminds him softly.

I get off the bed, the blood that coats my legs a reminder of what almost happened. Emmet...

"Fuck," he grumbles, shoving the pack back in his pocket.

"Yes, Leo. He is the one that deals with everything."

"Yet you refuse to fucking give him the title. I told you to do it, I don't care about the consequences. I'd like to see what exactly he does," Alejandro tells his brother as he goes over to the box that Leo had left.

"I know..."

"What the fuck is this?" Alejandro asks.

"That's what he gave me to heal," I answer before entering the adjoining bathroom, wishing I had something else but this tiny gown to wear.

I don't know how to feel. Emmet had known about my pregnancy which meant Jackie had told him. He had tried to hurt my baby on purpose. I won't forgive him for that and I want to know what Leo is planning to do about it.

It is much later into the night. I have showered and changed into some clothes that someone had brought from my apartment for me. I only have a little dinner, not feeling up to it after everything that had happened. We talked to Mama earlier, although we didn't mention what had happened, not wanting them to worry. I told Kia to fill her in when she was alone, without Dad around.

I am now lying in bed in one of the bedrooms of Marcel's mansion with Kia curled up next to me. She is fast asleep, her hand resting on my stomach protectively. It is past midnight, but I am unable to sleep. I feel so restless. Emmet's final words ring in my head,

"If I'm going down..."

How sick is he to target an unborn child? And let's not forget that now Leo knows about this baby.

"Can't sleep?" I turn my head, looking into Kiara's gorgeous eyes. I sigh heavily, staring back at the ceiling.

"No."

"Want to share?"

"Well, I was thinking about Emmet. How could he target an unborn child? You know, Kia, he reminds me of him. He was beating his mate, and she was hiding it from everyone. She even denied it! He got angry because I told Leo about it."

Kiara sighs as she props herself up on her elbow. "Mm... so, it reminded you of him. You know, abusers try to justify their actions one way or another. I just hope this Jackie is strong enough to break away." Unlike Indigo...

"Yeah... I hope so, too. I wonder what Leo will do."

"You two have marked one another; maybe you could ask him?" she suggests gently. I had told her that earlier, but she also knows it is still complicated.

"Not today... I don't even want to face him right now," I whisper.

"What is it, Zu?" she asks softly. I sit up slowly and stare at the bedding, shaking my head slowly. How do I explain everything I am feeling?

"At least I know he'll be a good dad," I say, shrugging. She smiles.

"Oh? Have you seen him around kids?" I tilt my head.

"Don't you know that he has a five-year-old son? Corrado?" I ask curiously. No, she doesn't. The surprise on her face answers that.

"Oh... from an omega or..." She closes her eyes, shaking her head. "I'm sorry, I-"

"I don't even know who his mama is, but it doesn't matter. He's adorable." She seems relieved, but I can see she wants to ask me something. "Shoot." She smiles slightly before becoming serious.

"Did it... remind you of Atlas?"

Atlas, my half-brother... a sour taste fills my mouth. I realise why she'd say that. I am being biased, maybe, but Corrado is not born from an affair, or I at least hope Leo was faithful to the mother at the time, and he hadn't been dating anyone else while with her.

"It's different."

"He's a good person Zu..." she whispers, and I simply frown.

"I'm surprised Marcel never mentioned it," I say instead, changing the topic.

"No, he didn't. I'll ask him tomorrow but then again, he hasn't said much about this pack, respecting Leo's wishes. Marcel is just stuck in the middle, wanting this to work," she sighs before smiling gently. "Let's not worry about that for now. Leo cares for you. If he didn't, he wouldn't have called for me."

"Or he cares for his pup," I suggest. I am happy that he does, don't get me wrong but at the same time, I don't think us as a couple will work. He already told me he regretted marking me.

"Talk to him," Kiara encourages softly, almost as if she knows what I am thinking. I nod, not sure if I will, as I turn my back to her.

"Yeah..." I say, closing my eyes. She runs her fingers through my hair tenderly, and I appreciate her not pushing the topic.

I am blessed to have so many who love me but doesn't Leo realise he does, too? I saw the way he became distant when Kia and Raihana had entered. The way he just wanted to leave...

With Kia's comforting touch, sleep soon overcomes me, and I welcome it.

I am staring at something intently through maybe a crack or bars. I'm not sure...

I am terrified. I don't know why, but I am. A shriek of agony reaches my ears, and I begin looking around frantically.

"Please stop! Don't hurt her!" A young boy's voice leaves my lips as my entire body shakes with anger, frustration, and fear. I begin running, climbing over what looks like some rocks, and stare down into the dimly lit room. The sight before me makes my blood run cold.

There on the floor in a five-pointed star, surrounded by symbols written in what looks a lot like blood, lies a woman. She is pinned to the floor with four daggers, one embedded through her wrists and two through her ankles. This is dark magic... I can feel it.

My eyes blur as I take a shuddering breath, and I wipe them in irritation. Pain and agony are clear on her face as a dark, smoky shadow swirls around her. Everywhere it touches her, it slices viciously into her skin.

"Please stop! Don't hurt her!" The strangled sob leaves me.

Where am I? What is this?

"Shut him up before I kill him, too," a woman's voice hisses ominously, and it is then that I see her. Her back is to me. She is wearing a long black dress, her hair is halfway down her back, and she has her hands raised. She begins chanting, and the room seems to become darker. There is an immense evil around her, one that is beginning to grow around the woman on the floor, a woman with brown hair and ashy skin.

Skin that is littered with scars, burns, and bruises.

"Yes."

Marcel? It sounds like him, but it is a voice void of emotion.

"No! Dad, save Mom!" I seem to scream again, and it is then that I realise what this is.

A memory. Not just any memory, but one that belongs to Leo. I am in Leo's head.

My heart is pounding as Marcel approaches, pulling open the barred door and grabbing me by the collar.

"You need to learn to control yourself, boy," he growls.

"Dad! Please help her!" he begs. Marcel shakes his head, his eyes blank as he drops me, or should I say, Leo, onto the ground.

"Lock him up," he growls.

"Please! Help Mom!" Leo's scream breaks into a sob, and then something strikes the back of his head. Jarring pain seems to split my head open, and my eyes snap open.

My heart is pounding violently as I look around. I am back in the bedroom at Marcel's mansion.

That woman was Endora. The one on the ground with daggers in her wrists and ankles was Leo's mom. I feel sick. What had Leo been through and seen as a child...

I sit up, staring at the clock on the wall, unseeing, with only one thought in my mind. *What else is Leo going through?* The fact that that memory or nightmare came to me means Leo is still having nightmares of his past. I pull my legs up, tucking them against my chest and wrapping my arms around them. No matter what I do to calm my erratic heart, I am unable to, feeling tenfold more restless.

Suddenly the restlessness seems to ease, and I realise that it had been Leo's feelings. It is hard to differentiate between my emotions and his. But he must have put his walls up just now.

Leo?

What is it? his reply comes after a moment.

Can we meet? I need to talk to you, I say quietly. I don't know why I said it, but the emotions I just felt were intense. I need to see that he is okay. Silence follows, and just when I think he won't reply, he does.

I'll be there in ten.

Okay.

I slip out of bed, unsure of what I will say when I meet him, but I don't think I am going to be able to sleep anyway. I guess here goes nothing.

Battle of Wills
Azura

I look in the mirror ten times before convincing myself that the shorts and a sports bra are totally okay to go out in. I put on Kiara's strappy black heels, not wanting to rummage in the bag that had been retrieved from my apartment in case Kia got disturbed. Damn, I love this woman's heel collection. Last year I had liked a pair of snakeskin knee-high boots of hers, and she had told me I could keep them. Selfless as always. After zipping them up, I make my way to the door just as I see my phone screen light up. I am sure it is from Sky, she is the only one up at this time, but I'm not going to cross the room when I have just reached the door. I'll get back to her later.

I slip out of the room silently, making my way down the dimly lit hallway, tip-toeing down the stairs. I can see the light in the lounge is still on. Are Marcel and Al still awake? Okay... I don't want them to hear me leaving. Wait, Al has, like, supersonic hearing; he'll know either way, and I have nothing to hide. Right? Right.

I still open the door super quietly and slip out, only to catch sight of the glowing tip of Leo's cigarette. He is standing in the shadows across the huge front lawn, leaning against a tree to the side. His eyes are fixed on me, and when I walk towards him, I feel very conscious of the fact that my tiny shorts barely cover my ass. Maybe I should have come out barefoot. I don't think the heels help.

What am I going to talk to him about? Why did I even ask if we could meet?

His eyes are no longer on my face but rather skimming over my legs. A look of hunger flashes in his eyes before he looks away smoothly. My heart thunders, and the moment his scent hits me full force, I want to close my eyes and inhale it.

"Were you awake?" I ask.

Dumb question. Obviously he was because there was no block or force preventing me when I mind-linked him.

"Yeah." At least he didn't mock me.

He is wearing a pair of sweatpants and a t-shirt that clings to his body, emphasising his every ridge and groove. I force myself to stop staring and look into his piercing blue eyes.

"What did you want to talk about?" he asks. His voice is so ice-cold that I'm taken aback. He means business. Okay...

"What happens from here? Like, what Emmet did. I know you suspended him, but he-"

"Is in prison awaiting trial. I was a witness to what happened to you, and Jackie will talk." His voice is murderous, and the way he says 'will talk' makes a shiver run down my spine.

"So, you believe that he did beat her?"

"I believed you before, but now he has several more crimes added to that fucking list. Don't worry, Emmet will not be getting away with this. Although I won't kill him, I will make sure he can never hurt anyone ever again."

"Great."

I run my fingers through my hair.

A silence falls between us, and the nightmare returns to me. I wonder if he had been dreaming about it. It isn't really my place to ask, but I won't deny that I'm tempted to.

"Why didn't you tell me?" he asks quietly. I know what he means. About the baby. I look him square in the eye, frowning.

"Why should I have? You left me, remember? Rejected me, too."

"If I knew you were pregnant, I would have made sure-"

"Of what? That the baby is okay? I was taking perfect care of it. Heck, if it wasn't for this baby, I wouldn't have even agreed to stay in this pack of yours," I cut in, sounding colder than I wanted to. "I never thought your Delta would have attacked me in your presence. I let my guard down." My anger fades, and I place my hand on my stomach, making Leo's gaze dip down to it. Something in his eyes softens, and I can tell he wants to say something.

"I didn't think he would either. I'm glad you're both okay."

Both.

My heart skips a beat, but, yeah... I need to be okay for the baby, right?

"Thank you for saving our pup and for calling Kia. I know you never wanted to have them here."

"Yeah. I didn't," he replies, his eyes hardening once again. I am hurt somewhat, but that memory of his keeps replaying in my mind. There is more to Leo than meets the eye. But I shouldn't care, right? I hate how the moment he is in my presence, my senses become clouded.

"I had a nightmare just before I mind-linked you," I say hesitantly.

He tenses, his cigarette to his lips, but he doesn't take a puff, as if waiting for what I am about to say. His heart is racing, and I know now that I have started, I need to end this.

"I saw what she was doing to your mother. How you were begging your father-"

"Don't." His eyes blaze as he looks up at me sharply. His anger is raging off him.

"Leo... does your father know what you've witnessed and been through?" His silence gives me the answer I really wished wasn't true. "You need to let it out. You need to tell him, or talk to someone, anyone. I mean, have you talked to anyone about your childhood? We learned about Endora at the Academy, her heinous crimes against the wolves in her hold, but even from what my family was told, there was no mention of you. Does anyone know what you have been through and witnessed, Leo?"

Silence. He is a greater mystery than I had thought.

"Leo? I'll take that as a no."

"I'm not having this conversation with you."

"Well, you are because what I saw-"

"Don't try to fucking get into my head," he hisses, tossing the cigarette to the ground and crushing it under his foot.

"It's obvious you don't want to talk about it, but you really need to-"

"No, I fucking don't. So, as I said, stay the fuck out of my head," he growls. My eyes flash, and I step closer, glaring up at him. Even with these heels, I am much shorter than him.

"Listen to me, Azura, what you saw better stay the fuck between us," he threatens.

"Oh? Or what? What will you do?" I challenge, knowing that this baby is my ultimate shield from Leo. His hands are clenched, and on any other occasion, he would have grabbed my chin or neck by now. He doesn't reply, simply glaring back at me.

"I'm warning you... tell anyone about that dream and I will fucking do the same about your ex."

I feel as if I have been slapped. The icy cold look in his eyes tells me he would do it, too. My heart thuds as I realise he is blackmailing me. Just like Judah. I don't know why it just... it leaves a sour taste in my mouth.

"Wow! I never thought you'd go so low."

"Then don't fucking try me," he shoots back arrogantly.

"I told you that in confidence. You were the one who wanted to know and wanted me to stay, remember? I was going to tell Alejandro. Actually, since he's here, how about I just go and tell him? I don't fucking need you. And since they are here, I'll go back with them to their pack. Yeah, maybe that's better. I'm fucking done." I turn, ready to storm inside, when Leo grabs my arm, pulling me back. I gasp when he yanks me close, glaring down at me. An intense wave of sparks rushes through me, sending a delicious jolt to my core.

"Calm the fuck down," he growls.

"No, why should I! You can get pissed whenever the fuck you want, but I can't?" I growl, trying to break free, only for him to turn us and push me up against the tree. He lets go of me, but before I can even push him away, he cages me between his arms, his legs trapping mine. What the fuck is this guy made of? No matter how much I struggle he refuses to let me go. Instead, he simply watches me.

"Keep struggling. I'm not complaining about the view," he growls threateningly and I freeze, realising his gaze is on my breasts.

"Stop perving," I growl.

"Stop struggling," he counters.

My heart is thundering as our eyes meet, trying not to pay attention to the way his chest is almost touching mine or the way his strong thighs have mine wedged between his.

"You can't stop me," I hiss.

"Don't challenge me because I don't like to lose."

His piercing eyes flash, and my heart skips a beat at how close he is. It is suddenly hard to breathe, and a part of me wants to act up to see what he would actually do, whilst another part of me is trying to remember what we were discussing. This tension between us... this closeness...

His eyes dip to my lips and he licks his own. His ball piercing glints under the moonlight and the intense urge to play with his tongue tempts me. *Fuck, he has such good lips.*

Focus girl.

I can hear your thoughts. His animalistic voice comes through the link and into my haze. I slam up my walls trying to come back to reality.

"Don't deviate from the topic. You expect me to share my problems, but you can't share your own?" I ask quietly. He remains silent, his steel blue eyes looking into mine. "Not even with your friends?" *Talk to me, Leo.*

"Look deeper..."

Dante's words return to me, and I look intently at the man before me. Leo has so much more to him than one would think. So many have things to say about him, at the Academy especially. He is known to be ruthless and cold-hearted. The Rogue Alpha... that is the name they call him. Some who love Alejandro so deeply even go as far as saying they hate him because he doesn't accept the way of the King and his Council, but how could he accept it when he didn't grow up the way those who make comments had? People are so blinded that they judged others without even listening or trying to learn the full story.

"There is no one that I trust in this world."

Those words squeeze my heart even though he speaks like he doesn't care.

I know that he doesn't want me because of who I am but he wants this child. I also know he is physically attracted to me, just as I am to him.

The choice of the path ahead is in my hands...

The Path Ahead
Azura

Do I keep away from him? Let him deal with Judah, and leave? Allow him to see his child and somehow live without him? Or do I selfishly fight for him? Do I try to get through to him? Because whether he likes it or not, his nightmares are now mine, too...

"When he loves... he loves deeply..."

Marcel's words are true. I know they are because I've seen the love he has for his son, the love and fear he had when I almost miscarried. Even though he hates who I am, he still looked out for me and still cared to an extent, no matter how much he denies it.

What should I do?

A sharp wind blows, whipping my hair in front of our faces, and I close my eyes. The screams from his nightmare return to me, and my eyes snap open. *I will always be there for those who need me.*

He reaches over, brushing my hair back, tingles skimming the surface of my skin at his touch. As he brushes the strands back, our eyes meet, and I try to focus on my words.

"Well... whether you like it or not, your dreams are now mine. Your nightmares, too. So whether you tell me or not, I'll find out everything unless you plan to never sleep again. So maybe I can be that person you can talk to, since there's not much you can do about it," I say, glad my voice comes out clear and confident. His icy eyes flash.

"Then the question is can you handle it? Or will those nightmares drive you insane?" he asks challengingly.

My heart is pounding, and when I shift positions, I freeze, feeling his hard shaft against my hip. Goddess... *Do not look down, Azura. Do not!* Well, it is clear he can't focus on anything but his dick when he is this close. Seems like this sexy Alpha sure has it bad, even if it is just sexual. I smirk as I look up at him, realising that right now I am the one holding power. Reaching up, I flick a strand of his chocolate locks that flopped onto his forehead.

"I'm already insane, if you've forgotten." I think I see a faint smirk on his lips, but I'm not sure if I imagined it.

"I'd appreciate it if whatever you saw, you kept it to yourself," he says quietly.

"As long as you promise to tell me everything yourself then." His brows furrow and I raise my eyebrow. "What's it going to be, Little Alpha?" He narrows his eyes, gripping my chin in his fingers.

"Don't antagonise me or-"

"Or what?" I challenge softly. My core clenches, and I feel him throb against my hip. *Fuck...* My heart is racing, and he is the one to break eye contact first.

"Fine. Just keep your fucking gob shut." I roll my eyes as he suddenly lets go and turns his back on me.

"Deal," I reply, staring at his back. "So later, in the morning, you'll tell me?"

"Fine. Also... Corrado was hoping to have dinner with you. If you could come by later..."

"Won't you bring him to Marcel's? I didn't know they didn't know about him, I mentioned him to Kia." He mutters a curse.

"They don't need to know my business," he growls.

"Leo... I know you don't like Alejandro, but at least bring Corrado." I step in front of him, trying to ignore the obvious hard-on that he is sporting.

"We are not having this conversation," he growls. His voice is firm and harsh. Maybe I really am pushing it.

"Fine. I'll come down for dinner tonight. Make sure there's plenty of food."

"Sure," he says, surprising me. His gaze flickers down to my stomach for a moment before he turns and walks away.

I sigh, watching him vanish into the darkness before I try to head back inside, realising I had shut the door, and now it is locked. *Oh, great...*

I knock lightly, hoping someone hears, and that not everyone gets disturbed.

Anyone but Al, anyone but-

The door opens to reveal none other than Alejandro, a cigarette in his hands and a smirk on his lips.

"You owe me fifty," he remarks. I raise an eyebrow as Marcel appears behind him.

"What for?" I ask suspiciously.

"Marcel here thought his son was going to take you home. I told him there's no fucking chance he's going to get off his high fucking horse." I raise an eyebrow, looking between them.

"So you two were peeping out the window like two creeps? No offence, Marcel."

He chuckles, "None taken. Actually, that was Alejandro, who had heard you leave. I assure you we weren't watching."

"Good. Not that anything happened," I state, my stomach fluttering. *Yeah, aside from him having me pressed up against the tree...*

"Yeah, that's why you're carrying his pup," Alejandro remarks. I narrow my eyes.

"You're one to talk. Remember Kia with Dante? Leo is far more like you than either of you will ever admit," I declare, stalking to the stairs.

"So, you admit that he does remind you of me."

"Eww, no."

"Is that an insult to me or the fucker?"

I don't respond to him, smiling faintly as I run up the rest of the steps to the bedroom I am sharing with Kia. I feel lighter and, somehow, I am looking forward to tomorrow. I enter the room, shutting the door behind me, remove the heels, and slip back into bed. I reach for my phone, remembering the text from earlier. I am surprised to see it isn't from Sky but from Song. She is always asleep by twelve at the latest. I hope everything is okay with her. I unlock the phone and click on the message.

> **Song:** Hey girl, how are you holding up? I miss talking to you, so thought I'd drop a message to let you know.

I tilt my head and quickly send a reply.

> **Me:** I'm great, a lot has happened, but I'll fill you girls in tomorrow. Thanks for checking in on me. Love you.

> **Song:** Ok, I'll be looking forward to it.

I place the phone down, my mind drifting to Leo and what happened outside, when I suddenly stiffen and turn back to my phone. Song always replies with, 'Love you too, Hun.'

I pick up the phone, an ominous thought creeping into my mind as I stare at the last message. She is online...

I press call, letting the phone ring as I hold it to my ear. No answer.

"The number you have called is unavailable..." I hang up only to see her typing.

> **Song:** Sorry Hun, just got into bed, so tired. I'll text you tomorrow. Love you.

I let out a sigh of relief and shake my head. Fuck, I am getting too paranoid.

I place the phone down, feeling exhausted after that super long night, and let sleep overcome me once more.

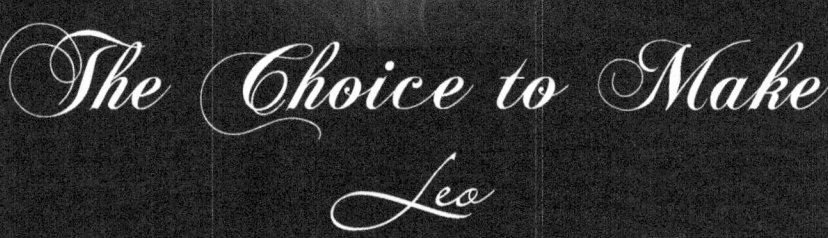

The Choice to Make
Leo

It's the following day, and after crushing Corrado's heart last night, I feel fucking awful. He had been asleep on the sofa when I returned, the uneaten food still on the table. He had gone to sleep hungry.

So, the first thing I do this morning is promise him that tonight we are going to cook together because Azura is going to come over. That cheered him up, and I am going to fucking make sure nothing fucks it up this time around. I leave him with Winona; they will go buy the list of groceries I had sent to her.

I am currently in my office at headquarters, waiting for Jackie. Last night I told Eric to make sure she stayed in her apartment until she was called for. Emmet is in a cell which stops him from linking anyone, and before I talk to him, it is Jackie I need to deal with first. The knock on the door makes me look up before it opens to reveal Eric, Nikki, and Jackie. Jackie's eyes are bloodshot, and it is obvious she has cried a lot. Eric looks sympathetic, but I already had a word with him regarding Emmet. He had been there when shit went down anyway, and he knew what Emmet's temper was like. The two had never seen eye-to-eye often enough.

"Did I ask for an entourage to accompany her?" I ask.

"She's in a state, Leo," Nikki says, her eyes shadowing when they fall to the mark on my neck.

Even with the tattoos on my neck, her mark isn't hidden away. I won't deny that I examined it closely. It is a heart of fire in two shades; half is silver and blue whilst the other is navy and black. It may look like a heart created from flames, but if you look closer, you can see that it is, in fact, two wolf heads nuzzling together with fur made of fire.

Hurt flashes in Nikki's eyes before she looks away, placing her arm around her sister.

"I'll wait outside," Eric says, giving a small nod. I wait for the door to shut as both sisters take the seats opposite me.

Is it true that Azura is pregnant with your child? Nikki's voice comes through the link. My eyes flash as I look at her.

You know the answer to that already.

Wow. Her voice is bitter and irritated. If Jackie wasn't here, I would have fucking snapped, but I don't want to stress her out even more.

We did nothing wrong. She is my mate. My fucking mistake was not ending it with you that day I got back. For that, I'm sorry, alright? So let's end this shit now. We are over, I reply icily. **I don't want to have this conversation with you again, so move the fuck on.** Her eyes glisten, and what fucking irks me is that her sister is in a state, and she is far more concerned about me.

Leo, you have ignored every message that-

"Leave," I command. My eyes are enough of a warning, and she simply shakes her head before standing up and storming out. Once the door snaps shut behind her, I stand up and walk around the desk, leaning against it next to Jackie. "I know this is all hard, and although you are probably fucking confused about the entire situation, I need you to be honest," I say, leaning closer. My hands thread together in front of me as I rest my elbows on my thighs. She looks up at me, her eyes filled with glittering tears.

"I'm so sorry, I didn't know he'd try to hurt her. If I knew you were her mate, I would have told you about the baby," she sobs, her face filled with guilt before she breaks into tears. I frown, not expecting that.

"You knew about the baby?" I ask. She nods.

"She asked me to keep it quiet because you knew who her mate was and that you might tell him, and he wasn't a good person. When I found out she was mated in this pack, I understood it. I'm so sorry."

"Don't apologise, you kept her word." Wait... did Emmet know? My heart thumps, remembering Emmet's words. *"I know your secret."* "Jackie. Did you tell Emmet?" Her guilt-filled eyes meet mine, and she nods.

"I never thought he'd hurt her, especially since he knew..." she whispers.

My eyes blaze as white-hot pain lashes through me.

He kicked her in the stomach.

He intentionally targeted our pup.

"Do you know where he hurt her?" I ask her, my voice shaking slightly as I do my best to contain the searing rage that is rushing through me. "He kicked her in the fucking stomach." My voice is dangerous and menacing, and her face pales. She shakes her head, clamping her hands over her mouth.

"No... he, no... it's my fault, I shouldn't have-"

"No. It's his fucking fault, and he will pay for it. Emmet will not be pardoned for his fucking crimes." A sob leaves her as she crumbles in front of me, a woman who has been broken by her mate and his actions.

"What have I done... Emmet... why did he do this? Leo, what if you let him go? Don't let him stay in the pack. Exile him, and-"

"Do I look like a fool to you? If you set a criminal free, he will come back for revenge. This wasn't an accident or a crime committed by misjudgement, but one he carried out intentionally. Emmet not only abused you, but he also tried to harm an unborn pup and a pregnant woman. It doesn't matter if she is the rightful Luna of this pack or the fact that it was my child he tried to hurt. They are crimes that I'm not going to forgive, whether they were against an alpha or an omega, and he will be punished." My voice is cold, but despite my calmness, there is no fucking way I am going to pardon him. When an enemy walks free, they are a danger just waiting to happen. Emmet will stay in prison for life, or at least the next thirty years before I decide what to do with him... or... someone else does...

"Will you kill him?" she asks in a hoarse whisper.

"I want to. I want to rip him limb from fucking limb for what he did. Don't forget, Jackie, he was like a brother to me. But I won't do that because it would cause your downfall if I did," I reply quietly.

"He hurt a baby." She is crying again, rocking in her seat. I move away from the desk, and crouch down in front of her.

"Jackie." I take hold of her arms, hating seeing her like this. "Tell me. How long has he been hurting you? Please don't lie." She doesn't remove her hands from her face as she continues to sob, her pain and anguish clear.

"It was on and off... maybe it started a year after we were mated. It was just a shove or slap here and there, but then it became more frequent," she whispers, her voice breaking. So, for a few fucking years...

"And not once did you think to tell me or Nikki?"

"He was your friend, and I love him." She looks torn.

"Friend or not, I wouldn't side with someone because of who they are. I would have sided with the truth." *Yet despite Azura just being a young woman, you straight up rejected her because of who her parents are.* I sure am a fucking hypocrite.

"I'm sorry I said that Azura lied that day. I owe her an apology for that and for spilling her secret. I'm so sorry."

"The question is, what will you do now? Emmet will be tried in front of the pack, and he will be fucking imprisoned, rest assured. But now it's on you. Will you stay as the mate of an abuser, someone who tried to kill an unborn child, mated yet apart, or will you let him go and build your life once more?" I ask softly. I know she is in pain, but she needs to make the decision.

"It's not that easy. You mean rejecting him, right? The pain of rejection after marking is devastating," she whispers brokenly. Gone is the smiling woman who always cares for others. I just wish that she could smile genuinely, not a fake mask whilst suffering inside. "Rejection is terrifying," she whispers.

I know how painful rejection is... and I hate that I fucking put Azura through that, but what now? Do I somehow find someone to break the bond, so she can live when I die? I force my attention back to the woman in front of me.

"I know it is. It will hurt, but with time those injuries will heal. He is an abuser, Jackie. You deserve better," I say quietly, giving her arm a gentle squeeze. "Whatever you decide, I won't judge you, but he will remain in prison for his crimes. The rest is up to you." She nods brokenly. It isn't going to be an easy decision, but it is up to her now.

"Whatever I decide, will it affect anything else?" she asks, quietly wiping her cheeks only for more tears to fall.

The Choice to Make

"Only for yourself," I reply. She nods, and we fall silent. I stand up, leaning against my desk, and light a cigarette.

"Leo, the Queen is here... can you ask her for help?" she asks hesitantly. My eyes flash, and I frown.

"No, and I don't fucking want you mentioning that shit again."

I've made sure to avoid Kiara, knowing she can fucking sense when someone is in pain. I need them gone from here. I have already talked to Marcel, saying they need to leave. I don't want them overstaying their fucking welcome. She doesn't reply, simply nodding.

"Can I have a week? To decide?" she asks, fiddling with her fingers. I nod.

"I haven't talked to him yet, either, so I don't fucking kill him in the process. I need to cool down first." She looks at me sadly and nods.

"I'm sorry that he betrayed you, too. I know you trusted him."

"That's life, people come and go. You can't trust anyone. Not even those who you may consider your own."

"Not always. Please don't let Emmet's betrayal remove you further from those who love you," she pleads gently, almost fearful. I don't reply, my face an emotionless mask.

"One week then... if you want to speak to him before that, you can let me know. No one is to see him without my permission, and that includes you," I say dismissively, not wanting to delve into my own matters.

"Okay," she replies quietly, getting up and walking to the door.

"If you need to talk, I'm here, and there are many in this pack who will willingly lend an ear. Don't bottle that shit up inside."

"You, too." She forces a smile, although I know she is ready to break into tears again.

The door shuts behind her, and I smoke my cigarette, lost in thought. I'm not ready to talk to Emmet yet. I had visited the confinement centre earlier, but I didn't go into his cell. He had been sitting on the bed, hands cupped behind his head, unmoving. But I wasn't ready. Not yet... I need to calm down first. I spoke to Jax last night, and it was fucking obvious he hadn't even realised when the drug had taken effect. Only Emmet would have the answer to what his aim was.

He wasn't meant to know Jax was there watching over Azura, but he had known he was there and drugged him. So, I want to know why he had targeted him. Was it because he hadn't wanted anyone watching or because I had lied that he was Azura's mate? Either way, I'll fucking find out when I go to see him.

I glance at the time. I had been notified that a car had come to pick up Alejandro and Kiara and that they would most likely leave soon. Good.

I have a meeting to attend regarding the buyers of the shipment, too. Plus, I have done some more research on this fucking Judah. I return to my underground cave and begin dealing with what I have to. Once this entire shipment is sold, I will have enough funding for all the pack pups.

Enough for them to be settled and live the life I want for them. I spend the next few hours trying to find more details on Judah. I have already sent Dan to see what he can find. I am going to get to the bottom of this shit, one step at a time.

It's now evening, and although the day has been fucking long, I can't deny that there is something about the coming night that I am looking forward to. For starters, the look on Corrado's face when I return on time as he stands there in an apron and chef's hat that he must have picked up today... That is enough to make me smile.

Winona has everything washed and set out for me, and, from what I can tell, the place has been cleaned. Not to mention it smells of something citrus and deep.

I get to work cooking and giving Corrado small jobs, knowing I don't have much time. Winona sets the dishes before she leaves us to it. I hadn't really given Azura a time, and so I mind-link her telling her to be here for dinner at seven. She replies promptly, and now I fucking feel as if I am running out of time.

"So, Daddy, what have you cooked for Azura?"

"For us," I state.

"Yes, and for Azura." Does he have to keep saying 'for Azura?' I give up arguing with the kid and add the diced peppers to the pan.

"Spicy rice, grilled tandoori chicken, chips, and chilli cheese bites."

"Daddy, you didn't cook the cheese bites."

"No, but you love them and I'm still popping them in the air fryer. That counts as fuc- cooking." He giggles and nods, knowing I almost swore.

"Okay! I hope Azura likes it, Daddy... what if she doesn't?" He stares at the food, and I raise an eyebrow.

"I thought you liked the food I cook."

"I do, but what if Azura doesn't?"

"And who cares? I'm sure she'll eat whatever considering she can't even cook," I smirk.

"Oh, yes. Azura can't cook... so she will like Daddy's food." Yeah, she fucking will.

I leave the chicken on the griddle pan and tell Corrado to take the drinks from the fridge to the table. That will keep him busy long enough for me to get changed into something else. I leave the lounge and go to my bedroom. I enter the bathroom to wash my face before I take out some black jeans and a black t-shirt. The bedding has been changed in here, too. Running my fingers through my hair, I return to the lounge only to see Corrado fixing his shirt. He turns and gives me a megawatt smile.

"Do I look okay, Daddy?"

"You look great," I reply as his eyes examine me.

He frowns.

"Why is Daddy not wearing something nice?"

"I've been working all day, kiddo. I like what I'm wearing."

"It's not a dinner outfit. Daddy, you look like a bad boy. Azura likes people who look smart!"

Nah, she likes me just the way I fucking am.

"Well, the main thing is you look cute and smart, and this dinner is for you, right?" His smile returns with full force, and he nods.

"Oh, yes!"

I take the chicken off the grill and place it onto the bed of salad before covering the platter and checking the chips. The doorbell rings, and I stiffen. Just the thought of being around her is extremely appealing, yet fucking confusing.

Corrado runs to the door, waiting for me to open it. I cross the room and open the door. Her scent fills my senses, and I can't stop myself from looking her over. She is wearing a cropped, duck egg, off-shoulder knit top with a black denim skirt paired with over-the-knee heeled boots. The subtle touch of make-up only emphasizes her gorgeous features. She is dressed to kill, and with her looking as sexy as hell, I know this is going to be one fucking hard dinner.

"Hey, boys." She smiles before crouching down and passing Corrado the gift bag that I hadn't even noticed she was carrying.

"Hey, Azura! Oh, thank you!" Corrado replies, peering into the bag before giving her a hug.

"You are most welcome!" She stands up slowly, her gaze turning to me, and it is fucking obvious that she likes me in whatever. I almost smirk when she can't stop herself from running her eyes over me appreciatively. "Not going to invite me in?" she asks, her voice sounding dangerously seductive.

Our eyes lock before I step back slightly, giving her enough space to brush past me. The dangerous sparks of the bond surge through me at the light touch before she follows Corrado into the apartment. I shut the door, my eyes on her ass, as she saunters over to Corrado, who is already giving her a tour of the place. Damn, those legs are fucking fine... *Well, this sure is going to be ten fucking times harder than I thought.*

A Sizzling Dinner
Azura

Corrado is thrilled to see me and is showing me the entire apartment. The delicious smell of food is making me lick my lips, or is that his scent? I'm not sure... either way, the place smells divine.

Kiara and Alejandro had left after lunch and although I'll miss them, I'm glad I at least got to see them for a short while. Kiara's parting words were to take care of myself, and the baby, along with a not-so-subtle comment about talking to Leo and trying harder. In what way? Well, I know what she wants and hopes for. *Think before acting, Zu.*

Marcel had asked if I wished to stay at the mansion, but I had politely declined, deciding to return to the apartment beneath Leo's. The short conversation I'd had with him now replays in my mind,

EARLIER THAT DAY...

"Thank you for everything," I said, looking at Marcel. We had just walked Al and Kia to the pack borders.

"I'm afraid I didn't do enough, but I can assure you that Emmet will be punished for what he tried to do. I know my son, and I know he has a level head on his shoulders most of the time." We walked alongside each other as we made our way back.

"I know..." I said, placing my hand on my stomach. Leo would protect this pup.

"I am happy that I'm going to be a grandfather again." He smiled, and I smiled back.

"Yes, I just fear that this one might just be a little monster brewing with parents like us." I wanted to say like Leo, but I knew I was psycho, too. Marcel let out a chuckle.

"Well, kids aren't always like their parents; Leo is nothing like me or his mother for that matter." His smile faded to a softer, tender one, and I knew he was remembering her. "Petra was a very caring woman with a good heart, strong yet gentle at the same time." A frown creased his brow, and he sighed.

"Are you okay?" I asked hesitantly.

"Of course. Just my time with her and the memories are so vague... fleeting even because I don't remember much. She died when Leo was still rather young..."

The memory of Leo's dream had returned to me, and I wondered how much Marcel knew, or didn't know. Doesn't he have a right to know?

"And this is Daddy's room!" Corrado's excited voice brings me out of my reverie.

"Corrado." Leo's voice comes with a subtle warning.

I skim the room. There was no sign of a woman living there. I guess Nikki really did move out. I glance at the bed and can't deny that a pang of jealousy and pain rushes through me at the thought of them both in that bed. I might be pregnant with his pup but I have never slept with him. Not that I wanted to. Although, I don't think I would be able to sleep if he was in my bed.

Urgh, focus, Azura. Now I really sound like a hormonal pregnant woman.

"Okay, Azura, let's go have dinner. Daddy worked very hard!" He takes my hand, tugging me to the table, and I follow.

I can feel Leo's eyes on me. I had literally gone through everything before selecting this skirt, and I would be lying if I didn't admit that I had chosen this skirt on purpose. I know that Leo has a thing for my legs, and it's pretty satisfying knowing I have that hold on him. I really don't know what I want, or what the future holds, but it's kind of fun to see him struggle to control himself. I also won't deny the fact that I enjoy his attention.

I look at him as he places a platter of grilled chicken on the table, along with a bowl of chips. There is a platter of rice and some nuggets, too. Goddess, the food looks so damn good.

"Daddy cooked," Corrado declares, and I smile.

"Your daddy is pretty good at a lot of things, right?" I ask, ruffling his hair.

"Oh, yes. Daddy is good at everything."

He nods, and I make the mistake of looking at Leo, who is placing a wooden tray containing four sauces on the table. Why is seeing him in this setting so crazily hot? I know Raven finds Liam cooking hot, but I never got it. I just felt like, *yay I am going to get food in front of me...* but then Leo...

His eyes snap up to mine and my heart skips a beat. I'm sure I have the block up... right?

I almost hear the purr of approval from my wolf under his intense gaze. A man looking at me with pure hunger. *Eat me, please.*

No, don't. Go away bad thoughts!

"I never knew you were a good host," I tease, pushing the thoughts of him shirtless out of my head. Corrado pats the seat next to him, and I slide into the chair.

"I'm not," Leo replies coldly, sitting down.

"Well, this meal speaks otherwise, or am I just lucky?" I have to take a picture.

"Yes, Daddy only cooks for Azura and me," Corrado agrees as I quickly take my phone out.

"That is very nice of your daddy," I say, snapping a picture of the table. I almost get Leo in it, and I'm not going to complain if I do, but then he sits back, tilting his head as if he knows what's running through my mind.

Don't worry, I didn't want you in the picture, I say, putting my phone aside. He raises an eyebrow.

I didn't say anything.

"I know that look," I say out loud.

"Do you now?" he counters. I would say more, but I can see the huge smile on the little gorgeous chipmunk's face next to me.

"What would you like to eat Corrado?" I ask instead.

"Chips and nuggets!"

"Chips and nuggets it is!"

I place both on his plate before adding two nuggets and a handful of chips to my plate before helping myself to the rice and two pieces of chicken. Yes, I can eat, and I will eat a lot! I only eat less when I have to cook. Leo begins adding food to his plate last, that same arrogant look on his face.

"So, Corrado, I heard you wanted to eat with me?" I smile down at him, taking a bite of my food. I'll be damned. This chicken and rice is to die for. Damn, the guys got skills, and not only in the bedroom. He nods, swallowing his mouthful.

"I did, but it was Daddy's idea," Corrado continues with a suspiciously innocent look on his face. "He wanted to eat with you, too."

"I didn't," Leo adds, frowning at me. Oh, I can't let such a good chance to tease him pass me by.

"Aww, are you sure, Weo?" I coo teasingly. A flicker of something crosses his eyes as Corrado and I giggle.

"Weo! Daddy's name sounds funny!"

"When I was little, I couldn't say the R and L sounds sometimes, unlike you. So, Leo would have been Weo, you would be Cowado." I smile, remembering I was pretty old when my speech became fluent. There were even a few people who found the way I talked irritating, but no two children were alike. I remember when I finally got a grasp on the letters, I didn't want to use them out of stubbornness. Besides, Liam fell for everything as long as I spoke like that.

"It's cuter than how you speak now," Leo remarks, snapping me from my thoughts.

"Want me to call you Wittle Weo?" I ask with a devilish smirk.

"No thanks unless you want me to call you Lola." Lola?

"Lola is a pretty name, and so is Weo!" Corrado adds.

"Who is Lola?" I ask suspiciously, narrowing my eyes and watching him eat a forkful of chicken and rice. I am so damn jealous of that fork right now...

"Figure it out," he smirks.

"I plan to," I reply, annoyed with that dumb smirk on Wittle Willied Weo's face. Okay, he's far from little but still...

I move my leg, tensing when it brushes against Leo's knee. Our eyes meet, and the intense pull between us only seems to heighten. I slowly move it again, only to knock it against his other leg. I'm sure his legs weren't this close seconds ago.

I raise an eyebrow, moving my legs away as I pick up a drink bottle and pour myself a glass.

"What do you want to drink?" I ask Corrado.

"I will have the apple juice; you should ask Daddy, too." Okay, I think this boy is up to something. Even Leo is frowning at him, but I'm not going to break a kid's heart.

"Tell me, Wittle Weo, what drink would you like?" I ask sweetly, earning a glare from him.

"I can help myself," he replies, icily biting the metal cap off a bottle of J2O and taking a swig.

"Daddy, we have to be nice to Azura. She's our guest."

"Yes, Wittle Weo, you got to be nice to your guests," I repeat.

Keep calling me that and I fucking swear I will remind you how far from little I am. His growl comes through the link, sending pleasure to my core. My entire body wants exactly that and maybe a part of my mind, too...

Well, I don't remember. Guess there was nothing to remember, I reply haughtily as we continue eating. The image of his dick is still clear in my mind.

Oh, fuck. My entire body is a mess of nerves, and that dangerous desire that is pooling between my legs is growing.

Damn it, Azura, focus.

I do my best to focus on Corrado after that, and when dinner is over, both Leo and I get up at the same time to clear the table. Leo is about to say something, but I cut in,

"I'll do it. You cooked," I say when our hands brush, and his gaze rakes over me.

"Fine, you can put that sexy ass to use."

We both freeze, and I can almost see the annoyance on his face at himself for letting that comment slip.

Nice to know you think it's sexy, I remark, brushing past him, my bare shoulder brushing his arm.

Don't push it.

This wasn't meant to be going like this… and how the hell are we flirting when there is a kid watching us with such intensity that you can't miss him.

"I'll help!" Corrado offers as he stands up, about to take the drinks to the fridge.

"Let me wipe your hands first," Leo says, taking a hand wipe and crouching beside his son.

I watch them, feeling my chest tighten at the faint smile on Leo's face, the adoration on Corrado's, and the way Leo wipes his face, too. He is a good dad…

I look away quickly, washing the dishes. My own dad was perfect, the best dad anyone could wish for, and I want my baby to have that.

Once the table is wiped, Leo takes out a platter of dessert shots.

"Daddy didn't make these," Corrado announces, "I chose them from the shop all by myself. Winnie let me."

"Yeah, I can tell," Leo remarks as we look at all the colourful desserts.

"They look yummy," I say as Corrado runs to get spoons.

"What drink do you want? Hot chocolate, coffee, or anything?" Leo asks when our eyes meet.

"Milk," I say, smirking as something else milky white came to mind.

"Is your mind always in the gutter?"

"I didn't say anything," I retort, my gaze dipping to the front of those jeans that hug his perfect legs. He steps closer, about to reach for me when Corrado's little figure stops, observing us intently.

"You didn't need to; your eyes speak loud enough," he replies, turning to Corrado. "You got the spoons?"

"Yes, I did," he says, pretending to yawn. "I'm so tired, too."

"Oh yeah?" Leo asks sceptically. "You wanted Azura here, and now you're ready for bed?"

"Yes! I want Azura to put me to bed, please? And then you can put Daddy to bed, too!" I can't help but burst out laughing at that.

A Sizzling Dinner | 247

"Corrado..." Leo warns him.

"But, Daddy, we had a plan," he whispers, motioning for Leo to crouch down. Leo sits down, lifting him onto his lap.

"There was no plan, that was just you being you. Now, which one do you want?" Leo asks, placing him down on the seat beside him.

"I want this one."

While Corrado helps himself to what looks like a strawberry mousse, Leo walks over to the kitchen to make himself a drink. Leo switches the coffee machine on before grabbing two glasses and a bottle of milk from the fridge.

"Thanks," I say, crossing my legs as I help myself to a custard and cake shot with lots of sprinkles on it.

He pours two glasses of milk. Is it just me or is seeing a tatted hunk with his biceps on show doing something so casual, and still looking so damn sexy, a huge turn-on? His eyes meet mine as he slides the glass closer.

"Thanks, for the meal, too, it was really tasty. I'm pretty impressed," I admit, eating a second spoonful of custard.

"I would say anytime, but I really don't want you to make this into a habit," he replies arrogantly as he walks over to finish making his hot drink.

"Make it a habit!" Corrado adds happily.

"Yeah, and just think, when you're feeding me, it's not only me you're actually feeding," I remind him when he returns and takes a seat next to Corrado.

"Yes, Daddy, Azura can't cook, she needs you to cook!" Leo is now frowning.

"I don't cook daily, Corrado, but yeah, you actually can't cook, so what are you eating?"

"What do you mean?"

"Meaning are you getting the nutrition you need?" Is he really going to grill me on that?

The baby takes what it needs from the mother, so you don't need to worry, your baby will be fine, I say through the link.

Yeah, but you need to keep yourself fed and strong too or have you forgotten that part?

I'm fine. Winona has been giving me food, and I make really good sandwiches.

Yeah, I've heard of your sandwich-making skills, he replies mockingly. I frown.

Don't mock me, I might just make a sandwich out of you, I threaten and then block him out, simply enjoying the dessert.

"Can Azura mind-link Daddy now? Does that mean you joined our pack?" Corrado asks innocently. This kid sure is smart. I look at Leo, deciding it's best if he answered this one.

"It's a little complicated, kiddo. Now, how about you finish your dessert?" He looks at us curiously before nodding.

"Okay, Daddy."

Leo doesn't have any dessert, simply drinking his coffee. We fall into a comfortable silence, and I look at them both, wondering what the story behind Corrado's birth is. Where is his mama?

"I'll go brush my teeth and put my pyjamas on now, I'm so sleepy! Azura, I will call you when I'm ready," Corrado declares, finishing off his milk and supporting a cute milky moustache. That part emphasising how tired he is makes it clear he isn't tired.

"Okay! Call me." I give him the thumbs up before he gives Leo a big hug and runs off.

"He never wants to sleep usually," Leo remarks.

"He's a good kid," I reply quietly as he disappears into his bedroom. Leo nods.

"He is, although I don't really get to spend as much time with him as I want."

"I guess he gets that, considering you are practically running this pack."

"Yeah," Leo says, placing his cup down.

"Was he okay that Nikki's gone?" I ask, feeling a sliver of guilt rush through me. Leo looks at me and shakes his head slightly.

"Yeah, he didn't really care. They weren't really close, which I guess is for the better."

"I can't believe that. He's really social and lovable."

"Towards you, and that's why he thinks I should keep you," Leo replies, frowning as he emphasises the word 'keep'. I smirk, leaning forward.

"Not jealous, are you, that he has taken a liking to me so soon?" I tease.

"Not at all," he replies. Our eyes meet, and I can't stop myself from asking the question that burns in my mind.

A Sizzling Dinner | 249

"Where is his mama?" His eyes flash before he looks away. *Shit, I shouldn't have asked*

"I'm sorry, if you don't want to talk about-"

"It's not that... I've just never told anyone the truth about that," he speaks very quietly.

"Want to share? You already know my secrets," I say, sitting forward.

His gaze dips to my cleavage, and he leans forward, taking hold of my chin. My breath hitches at his touch, and he runs his thumb across my bottom lip, sending sparks rushing through me. The urge to bite down on his thumb is intense.

"Maybe I will, but right now... someone's watching us with a little too much attention," he whispers huskily. My eyes widen and I jerk away, only to see the shadow of the little minion down the hall.

"I'll go to put him to bed," I say, standing up. "Then I want to know that story."

"Fine."

He leans back. This time when I walk away, I don't mind taking it a little slower, giving him a good view of my behind in this mini skirt. *A little extra sway in my hips wouldn't harm anyone.* I can't wait to know what the story behind Corrado's mama is, and I hope it helps me understand Leo a little more.

I smile when I see Corrado scrambling into bed and almost laugh. Oh, he is such a mini-me.

"Oh, hello, Azura. I was just going to call you," he lies innocently.

"Oh, I'm sure you were. Now, how about a bedtime story?"

Something I've Never Shared
Leo

I agreed... I don't know why I fucking did. I just know that she won't betray my trust or mention it to others. She might be crazy, but she's my type of crazy, and one I know won't do anything to hurt anyone on purpose, in serious matters anyway. I mean, I wouldn't put it past her to try to slit my throat in my sleep if I pissed her off, but at the same time, I know the type of things she'd keep quiet. I know if she knew about the fact that I'm dying, she would try to do shit even if it meant breaking a promise, but something like Corrado's truth... *that* she wouldn't tell anyone.

Even Marcel doesn't know, and regardless of that truth, it changes nothing. I clear the table off, taking a bottle of whiskey and two glasses to the lounge area. As a werewolf, I know drinking does nothing to a pregnant woman, so a glass or two won't fucking hurt.

Why does this feel too intimate?

I sigh, remembering the vague memory from long ago. *"Thank you, Weo"* back at Alejandro's wedding... her shoe had slipped off, and I remember slipping it on for her. I remember thinking she was cute. Who would have thought the confused little she-wolf would turn out to be mine?

I look at the bottle in my hand, considering putting it away, only for the sound of a door shutting to reach my ears, followed by the sound of her heels on the floor, making me look up. She comes into view, stretching her arms and making her top ride up slightly, showing off a little more skin. Damn, she looks so fucking good.

Her eyes meet mine, and she seems to become more serious as she lowers them slowly. I am fucking forgetting my own rules. All I can see is her.

I was right. We should never be in a room alone together.

"Whiskey? Hmm, maybe Corrado was right; it wasn't just him who wanted to spend time with me," she smirks as she comes over before sitting on the sofa and crossing those sexy legs of hers. I pour two glasses, giving her an emotionless look.

"Don't kid yourself. I just need a drink if I'm going to spend another couple of hours with you," I mock arrogantly. She raises an eyebrow challengingly.

"And here I was under the impression that you were super smart. I never knew whiskey could help take the edge off anything for a werewolf. If this was absinthe, I'd get it," she counters.

Am I fucking losing my brain cells? She isn't fucking wrong but I blame her. She is the one who fucks with my head.

"It'll keep me occupied," I reply, sitting down. I make sure to leave a gap between us and try not to stare at her sexy legs.

She reaches for the whiskey glass, and my gaze falls to the tattoo on her wrist — the word 'Strength'. It is as sexy as the rest of her. What I like best is that she doesn't need to try to capture my attention. Just like at the club, even with the strippers swinging on those poles, it was her who had caught my attention before I even knew who the fuck she was.

"Occupied by what? You aren't scared to be around me all alone, right?" She looks at me with those big eyes of hers, and I know that she is fucking aware of the effect she has on me... just the way I have an effect on her.

"Careful there, little she-wolf. You don't want to play with fire," I warn, picking up my own glass and sitting back. I know she fucking loves to play with fire. I look away, downing half my glass as she sips on hers slowly.

"So, tell me about Corrado's mama," she says softly, turning so she is facing me, one of her legs now hooked behind the other. Corrado's mother... it is obvious what she is thinking.

"There isn't really much to tell... it doesn't change anything." She doesn't respond, and I frown deeply, remembering the past. "I was in Germany, making allies and building relationships regarding work, when I tracked down and found my mother's pack, or at least what remained of it. She had actually come to England to study, ended up meeting Dad, and her family never heard from her again. She was an alpha's daughter. They had come to look for her, but they assumed she was dead, feeling the pack-link break. Her parents and brother were killed years ago when their pack was destroyed. Her nephew, Stefan Herrmann, a cousin of mine, was the one I ended up finding, but they were living like humans. There were only a handful of them left. His father had made an enemy of a neighbouring pack, and unlike here, where Alejandro does keep the rest of the packs under control, it was a fucking mess over there. This enemy of theirs had murdered the rest of the pack, and he told me he wouldn't stop until they were all dead." I down the rest of the glass, remembering that time. Once again, I failed...

"I told him I'd help deal with the bastard, and they were welcome to come to England and join our pack or at least reside here until they were safe. He agreed as his mate was pregnant, too."

I look at her, and it is obvious she wasn't expecting this. What did she think, that I had gotten some random woman pregnant? I was fucking careful. Well, I was until it came to her. My gaze dips to her stomach. It still feels fucking surreal that she is pregnant.

"I was getting the necessary preparations made for their travel. The men and I would track down Karl, but then Stefan rang and told me that Adele had gone into labour. The phone was suddenly cut off, and I knew something was wrong. I got back there just in time to witness that bastard killing them all. He didn't even spare the children." I still remember the dead bodies but it was nothing new. I was used to seeing the dead...

I'm glad she's silent because now that I had fucking started this, I want to just say it at once.

"I got there just in time to see him kill Stefan. Adele was curled up on the floor, losing so much blood. I still remember the numerous stab wounds they sported. It wasn't just any blade, but a Jagdkommando tri-dagger, a weapon that's fucking difficult to heal from due to its fucking shape. I killed him, but I was too late to save them. I was about to leave the scene, the fire was spreading, but then I heard a heartbeat."

"Corrado…" she whispers. I nod, remembering how I had run to Adele, rolling her onto her back to see the bundle in her arms, still connected to her by the umbilical cord.

"She had just given birth to their son, and he killed them. She had been covering his mouth to keep him silent, but I'm sure if I hadn't killed Karl, he would have killed the baby, too. So, I brought him back, named him, and told everyone he was mine. He is mine, and that's how it will always be. I don't want him to ever think otherwise because, as far as I'm concerned, he was always meant to be mine."

My eyes flash dangerously as our eyes meet. I know she won't tell anyone, but I can see that she wasn't expecting that. Her shock and sadness are clear through the bond.

"He is yours," she says, placing her hand on my thigh and giving it a squeeze, sending a wave of calmness and pleasure through me. "And I think your decision is perfect. Maybe when he's an adult, and if you never wanted to tell him, that's okay, but I don't think he needs to know as a child. Sometimes I wish I had never known about Indigo and Fred. I don't get my parents' love for her. I know it's nasty of me, and Corrado's situation is different, but all Corrado needs is you, and he loves you. You are an amazing father, and I'm sure you'll be an amazing father to this one, too."

I look at her, my emotions a storm, and see the sadness in her eyes. I never expected her to say that. Sure, her dad was a fucking idiot, but what about her biological mom?

"I don't want anyone to know. I trust you will keep it a secret," I say quietly.

"One hundred percent. You don't need to worry about that. There's more of a chance for me to rip your dick off than spill your secrets. I mean, I didn't even tell anyone about your dick piercings…" She pulls a face and shuts up.

"Got it," I smirk, and silence settles between us. I swallow, pouring another glass of whiskey for myself and down it at once. "So, you got some issues with your past, too, huh, and I don't mean your fucking ex." She sighs heavily and stares at her hand, removing it from my thigh. I wish she hadn't.

"Yeah... I guess so. Maybe it's selfish of me, but I always felt like everyone loved her. Sure, maybe they did, but to me, I feel like she only cared for Fred, not me. Like she didn't really care if I died as long as she had him." The pain and bitterness are clear in her voice. "Mama and Dad love her; they always try to talk about her and incorporate her into things. I hate that. I don't like her. I wish I could tell them that. They are my parents, not her. She was far more worried about her mate. I'm glad Alejandro sent him away to his death. I bet if he was alive, I'd be dead, too." I frown slightly. I can tell she hasn't told anyone about this.

"You need to tell your parents that. Otherwise, it's just going to keep on eating you up inside," I say, placing my glass down. She raises an eyebrow.

"You're pretty good at giving advice. Do you ever take it yourself?"

"I'm too smart to take advice. I know when I'm being an ass or stubborn, but I'm a hypocrite like that, and I don't really fucking care," I reply arrogantly. I see her bite her lip, and I almost smirk. She sure loves a dickhead.

"Still," she says, resting her elbow on the back of the sofa as she looks at me. Does she realise that her top is just about covering her boobs? Any higher, and I'll be able to see her underboobs. Not that I'd mind...

"Talk to them. It's the only way they will get it, and I'm fucking certain they will respect your wishes. Elijah and Scarlett are not unreasonable people."

"Yet you dislike them." I frown.

"I dislike all packs who grew up differently than mine."

"Yet did you know that Mama went through a lot of abuse at the hands of her father? She was so young, and he realised she healed fast, so she became his punching bag, or should I say target for torture. I don't know the extent, but she suffered a lot. You know, Leo, look around. There are many people who could probably relate to you."

"Yeah probably... I just..."

I just what? Why does letting it go suddenly feel like it would be easier? I'm tired of the bitterness, the hatred, the distrust... I know what my issue is, and I don't want to risk it. She moves closer, running her fingers through her hair.

"Leo... I understand that what happened was wrong, but Rayhan regrets what happened. I know it's not okay and that the damage done will never be reversed, but holding onto that hatred... is it helping?" she asks, her leg brushing mine. I tilt my head, looking at her for a second before staring ahead, refusing to answer. "What are you afraid of?" she whispers, making me tense. A wave of coldness rushes through me, and I frown, reality hitting me hard.

I opened up too much.

"Nothing. I'm afraid of nothing," I growl coldly, only for her to place her hand on my shoulder, refusing to allow me to move away.

"You just proved that you are by denying it." I turn my glare on her.

"Don't push it," I warn, standing up and turning my back on her. I had gotten too relaxed. What the fuck am I doing?

I walk to the window, staring out at the glittering lights of the pack below. Her scent is fucking intoxicating, clouding my judgement, and I am beginning to regret even telling her about Corrado. That was a secret I should have taken to my fucking grave, but it is too late. I have already told her.

You Don't Know the Pain

Leo

"Leo..."

She walks over to me, and the moment she touches my back, sending a rush of sparks through me, I feel a wave of calmness wash over me. The fucking bond.

"I didn't mean it in a bad way. You know, growing up, everyone called me a freak because I was born with the help of magic, so they found the word fitting. There were even a few people in the pack who refused to acknowledge me because of it. Heck, some still do. As I got older, I stopped telling my family because I didn't want to always cause them trouble." She sighs, and I do my best to remain calm. Flaring anger rushes through me, and I wonder if that is why she is so cheerful because, inside, she is dealing with a lot. "I know you always say I'm the daughter of an Elite. Although my life is nowhere as harrowing as I'm sure yours has been, I just wanted to let you know that things aren't always what they seem." She moves in front of me, her hand running along my waist before she places it on my chest. "It's okay to be afraid. I sometimes am... like right now. I don't know how this will work... with this baby... us... what will we tell our child? Why aren't we together?" She places her hand on her stomach, and that intense urge to touch it once more tempts me, but I don't.

"We'll figure it out," I say quietly. We will. I will figure it out for all of you...

I saw the vulnerability in her eyes when she told me about her situation. Tonight feels like a snippet of the life that maybe we could have. Her, Corrado, our unborn pup... She'll be the mother Corrado will love. Even if she isn't what I would have expected, somehow, she has won him over, the perfect balance of wild, cheeky, and mature. I reach up, brushing her silky locks back. Her eyes flutter shut for a second as my fingers graze her skin ever so lightly. These sparks. What are they? So unexplainable...

She leans into my touch, her head tilting up slightly, and that intense tension returns. I want her.

Yeah, maybe we will," she responds quietly.

We fall silent, but I don't remove my hand from her hair, my thumb caressing her jaw. I know what I am afraid of, but I'll never speak it out loud. I am fucking afraid of us letting our guards down once more only to be cast aside like always.

"Your nightmares," she whispers, her heart thundering as she tries to focus. I frown. For a moment, I thought she had forgotten. I sigh, looking down into her eyes which are watching me intently.

"After suffering under Endora, watching her torture and experiment on everyone, it was pretty normal. When I was five, she began to sense that I was stronger than Marcel was as a child, and so, she began experimenting on me, too. But whatever she was trying to attain wasn't happening. Her magic never really worked on me as it did with Marcel and the others. I was just someone she never wanted to lose, yet someone she hated. I was only a pup who wouldn't be able to do any damage to her anyway, for the time being, but I saw it all. The beatings, the torture, the dark magic... her sacrificing our own kind... her feeding the scraps of our people to our own, creating the wendigos... it was sick. No one would hear me because those who had a chance to do something, well, they were under her control or too scared to rebel. I was just a fool to think that there was good in this world." I turn away, wishing I had a cigarette right now.

"There is good in this world," she replies.

"Is there? Those who I thought were our heroes, our saviours, were allowed to storm into this pack and cause more suffering. I get the reasons, I fucking do. I know the pain when one's mate is hurt, but then I realised violence is dealt with more violence. Is there a difference between good and evil when those views and beliefs become distorted and justifiable when it suits us?" Flashes of the past cross my mind, and I push them away.

Delsanra Silver... that night when Alejandro and Kiara had broken in, I had seen her struggling to free herself, and so I had secretly unlocked the cell and cleared the escape route for her. She never knew I had helped her back then, and I made sure no one saw me, but I had wanted to help her because she didn't deserve the torture either. Sure, when I snuck her food, I'd get punished if I was caught, but it was okay as long as I did the right thing. Right? I don't really know. Right and wrong are blurred into one...

"The cherry on top is that it was her mate who did this. She was someone who, while a fucking child, I tried to protect, although I was weaker at the time. I treated all those in those caverns as my people, including her. I wanted to protect them all. I was seven, and I was burying the bodies of our dead with my bare hands. Endora would come for me, or Dad would take me to her. She'd tie me up, and all I remember is the excruciating pain that she inflicted on me. I would wake up bleeding after blacking out on the floor, and I would just get up and get back to my sorry life." I am unable to hide the pain and bitterness from my voice. "Do you know how it felt to drag the dead body of my mother to try to bury her? A body that I couldn't even recognise after her transformation into a wendigo?"

She reaches up, cupping my face. Her heart is pounding, and her eyes are full of anger and pain. I am unable to stop myself from grabbing hold of her waist. My own emotions are a fucking storm. I have never told anyone that shit.

"I'm so damn sorry that you had to go through that... you've always helped. You were even part of the battle against the Djinn a decade ago. You had a hand in saving Rayhan's mother-"

"Don't go getting any fucking ideas. I did that because no child deserves to be without his or her parents. I did it because it was the right fucking thing to do, not because of the bastard," I reply icily. "Rafael Rossi... I want to believe that if he knew, he wouldn't have let Rayhan do what he did. I did what I did because it just felt right."

"It shows that you have a good heart just like Marcel said," she murmurs quietly.

No, it just shows that no matter what I do, it's never enough. Selene sees everything, right? Are our deeds worth nothing?

"Endora was a monster who deserved so much worse than she got. You suffered too much, and what hurts is no one knows exactly what you suffered at her hands. You told me to speak to my parents, and I think you need to do the same but regardless of that, do you know what I see? I see an incredible human before me. A true leader, one with compassion, strength, and justice. Hell, I can't believe I'm saying this. Did you put something in the whiskey?"

"You had a few sips. I never knew you were so easy to manipulate," I reply mockingly.

"Oh, I'm not, but jokes aside, you are a good person, Leo, and I'm lucky that you are the father of my child. He or she will be lucky to have you."

I fucking wasn't expecting her to say that. Not after the shit I have put her through.

Lucky... will that child be lucky?

"What Rayhan did was wrong, and he regrets it, Leo... Give them one more chance to prove that they mean it. You don't need to be chums with them but maybe putting it behind you will help you move on and look to the future." What future?

"How many chances do I give? When someone betrays you that deeply, there's no way to forgive that," I reply, coldly glancing down into her dazzling silver eyes.

"There is if you truly try."

"Could you do it? Forgive Indigo? You even refuse to meet your half-brother, right? When he was just an innocent part of this entire fucked up situation?" She looks down, her eyes widening with surprise before looking up at me defiantly.

"Are you challenging me?"

"Maybe I'm just trying to show you reason," I reply huskily.

"Then how about this? Let's make a deal. I'll talk to him... and you, you talk to Rayhan." I frown deeply at the spark of challenge in her eyes.

"Not enough. Talking to your half-brother who didn't do shit isn't enough." She raises her eyebrow, her nails digging into my neck. What the fuck is with this girl and violence?

"Fine. I'll visit her grave. I will speak my mind, and I will tell my parents how I feel about Indigo and you, you tell Marcel how hard you had it. It's not fair on you to keep this inside. I think only when we are able to let it all out can we truly move on from it all," she retorts, glaring at me.

"If you weren't pregnant, I'd fucking teach you a lesson. You're fucking violent," I growl, gripping her wrists and yanking her hands away from where she has drawn blood. I pull her hands against my chest, glaring down at her.

"Don't change the subject, Leo. Are you really a scaredy cat?" she taunts. "You are annoying me!"

"I know what you're fucking trying to do, but forgiving isn't that easy," I shoot back, gripping her hips and yanking her close. She gasps as her chest slams against me, and she grabs my shoulders out of reflex. Her heart starts pounding, and my dick throbs at the feel of her against me.

"It isn't... but I've forgiven you for what you did to me. I'm dealing with the fact that you're only being nice to me because of this pup! I'm trying, and all I'm saying to you is to try as well." I frown as I stare down at her. Try...

"You're wrong. I haven't treated you a certain way because of our pup," I shoot back icily, my gaze flickering to her lips. "Even though you're the daughter of an Elite-"

"You do know I'm not a Westwood by blood?" she asks, her eyes flashing with an emotion I can't read.

"Blood doesn't make family, Azura, bonds do. To me, you are and always will be the daughter of Elijah and Scarlett Westwood, and even then, I don't hate you."

"Their daughter..." A soft smile crosses her lips, and she seems to relax. "Isn't it funny that although you hate them, hearing you say that you consider me their daughter really makes me happy?"

"You really are a psycho." I murmur, "Your mood changes like the fucking British weather."

"Yeah, I'm a little crazy, but you don't seem to mind it," she replies, her hands running up my shoulders, and I tense, every nerve in my body reacting to her touch.

"No, I fucking don't, but don't go getting so fucking cocky. We both know you fucking like me, too."

"Too?" she asks softly.

Our hearts are pounding as one, and I didn't even realise I had wrapped my arms around her waist, caressing her bare skin. She bites her lip despite the defiant spark in her eyes.

"I'm not sure if being attracted to someone ridiculously hot counts as liking someone or if it is just an attraction," she adds. I turn us, pushing her against the window as I lean against her, my hard cock pressing against her lower stomach.

"Fair point. Then, since it's only an attraction, I don't think there's any harm in giving in to that for one night," I find myself growling huskily.

I want her. I need her. No, I fucking crave her.

I am expecting her to push me away or deny it, but when she runs her hand up my neck, her eyes darkening with a sexy hunger, I know this is about to be one heck of a night. The consequences? Yeah, there are going to be many but I want this.

"Hmm? On one condition," she whispers in my ear seductively; her arousal scents the air as my wolf's hunger only grows stronger, mixing with hers, and I'm ready to lose all control.

"What's that?" I reply huskily, brushing my nose along her jaw before burying my head in her neck. Fuck, does she smell like heaven and sin.

"Do we have a deal?"

I know what she means; the deal to handle our issues. A taste of her body in return feels like the perfect exchange. Right now, she could ask for the fucking world, and I'd give it to her. All I want is to strip her naked, fuck her senseless, and eat her out until we are forced to stop.

"You have a deal, and Schurke Wolf never breaks his promises," I whisper, running my tongue over the mark that adorns her neck, making her sigh softly.

"Good to know." I bite down on her neck, making her gasp. "Oh, fuck!" she moans, and I know, deal or no deal, she is mine tonight.

Passion and Confusion
Azura

The moment he bites down on my neck, I'm gone, lost in the unimaginable pleasure that only he can give me. I turn my head, giving him better access to the crook of my neck. A low growl of approval leaves him, and I shiver in delight when his tongue runs along my neck once more. *Oh, fuck...*

He sucks on my neck hard, making my entire body explode with need and pleasure. I turn in his arms only for his hand to run over my stomach, the other brushing my hair back as he continues to pepper my neck with rough, sensual kisses. His dick is hard in his pants, pressing against me.

Damn, I want our clothes gone.

Goddess... I wish I could stay in his arms forever. I feel protected. I lean into him, relishing his touch. Every touch, every caress. From the brush of his hair against my cheek, or the way his heart is beating in his chest against my back, or the way his lips feel against my shoulder... it is perfection. I don't know what we are or if this is really happening, but I am going to enjoy every moment of it. I don't care about the deal we have made or how daunting it will be to live up to it when the time comes. Because at this moment, one more night with Leo sounds euphoric. Fuck, I want this. This fire, this passion, this heat.

His hand slips under my top, and I pull away slightly, gripping his wrist as he squeezes my boob, making me whimper. *Fuck, yes.*

I tilt my head up to him. Our eyes meet, and his other hand wraps around my neck. He leans in to kiss me, but I turn my head away, gasping as he twists my nipple. His lips graze the corner of my lips, making my breath hitch. I sigh, pressing myself back against him.

"Fuck you're a tease," his whispered growl comes. I elbow him lightly.

"Oh, am I?" Twisting in his arms, I turn and try to pin him against the window, only for him to look down at me arrogantly, a smirk on that sexy face of his.

"Getting a little overconfident, aren't you?" He pulls me closer by the wrist, burying his head in my neck. My heart pounds violently when he sucks hard.

"Not in a rush, are you?" I counter breathlessly as I pull away.

"Only as much as you are. Your arousal smells fucking good," he murmurs, his hand tightening around my neck as he runs his tongue over his lips. I stick my tongue out, leaning closer. His eyes blaze as he caresses it with his own pierced tongue. *Oh, fuck, this feels good. I want that tongue on every inch of my body.*

It fucking will be. I'm not resting tonight until I've fucked and tasted every inch of this sexy body of yours. All you have to do is be a good girl and spread those legs for me.

Oh, yeah.

The heat between us as our eyes lock, our tongues sensually grazing against each other, is out of this world. *Oh, Goddess.*

There is just something incredibly sexy about this, the storm of his emotions as he fights to control himself, the way he is moving slowly as if wanting to savour the way I taste and the carnal hunger in those eyes.

Fuck... he growls through the link.

Another jolt of pleasure rushes to my core as his hand lets go of my neck and twists into my hair, yanking me closer as he sucks on my tongue, his lips meeting mine in a rough, intoxicating kiss. Sparks fly, and the only thing I can think of is the way his lips feel against mine. My panties are probably soaked, and I can smell my arousal in the air as he devours me hungrily.

Oh, fuck... that's it.

He is such a damn good kisser. My entire body feels like it might just give way. I moan against his lips, feeling him throb against me. The power of the bond and those crazy hot sparks rush through me like a violent storm, a storm created by the pent-up emotions that we had both fought against for what feels like too damn long. This kiss... no words can describe it.

My arms wrap tightly around his neck as he grips the side of my face and the back of my neck, kissing me harder. The taste of his mouth and his plush soft lips are so fucking good. Damn...

I moan against his lips, reaching down, wanting more. I grab the hem of his shirt and pull it off, breaking away from his lips reluctantly to get it over his head. My stomach knots as he allows me to remove it, my eyes raking over his perfect body, and I run my fingers down his chest, letting my nails dig into his skin, leaving scratches in my wake. His eyes flash, and something tells me he likes that. Oh, I could devour him. I can't wait to have his dick inside me once more. He is a damn sex god. Every inch of his body is perfect and so fucking enticing.

He tosses the shirt to the floor, his muscles flexing as I run my hand up his traps, grazing the back of his neck. For a moment, our eyes meet once more, and time seems to stand still, his steely blue filled with so many emotions. So intense... I can't breathe... I-

"Fuck, you're beautiful," he whispers seductively. Those words make my pussy clench. The way he is looking at me... I believe them.

Suddenly, he lifts me up, his hands on my ass as his lips come crashing against mine in a bruising kiss. He begins walking towards his room, and my heart thunders. Flashes from the night of his rejection return to me with a vengeance. The suffocating pain of his rejection as I tried to speak but couldn't. The memory of me crumbled on that floor as I wished he didn't leave. Trying to beg him to stay... the pain of my wolf's heartbreak as she howled in agony. I hadn't been able to breathe... I-

"Azura! Azura, look at me."

I gasp as his hands cup my face, snapping me from my thoughts, and I realise we are in his room, and I am sitting on his lap on the bed. My arms are still around his neck, but I had spaced. My heart is pounding violently as I look around, trying to gather my thoughts.

"Baby Girl, look at me."

I stare into his eyes, wondering if he sensed my thoughts, and my stomach sinks when I see the storm of guilt in his eyes. He had felt it... all my emotions.

I slam my walls up, but it is too damn late. I look away, hating feeling so vulnerable. Sure, I had told him how I had felt, but I had never expected him to feel it.

"I just... I was... I just-" He presses his thumb against my lips, shaking his head.

"I didn't realise how hard the rejection was. I hurt you so fucking much. I fucking talk about being a better person, but the consequence of my actions-"

His phone rings, startling both of us, and I quickly get off his lap, feeling so out of place as I back away from him. I can't place the emotion in his eyes as he watches me, but I am unable to get rid of the memory of that night. I turn my back on him the moment he stands up and answers his phone.

"Alpha. Tracer 7 is on the move, and they are not travelling any of their usual routes." I don't recognise the man on the other side of the phone as Leo moves past me. Grabbing his laptop, he sits down, flipping it open.

"On it. Are you following?"

"No, I'm staying at a distance."

"You got your phone with you?" he asks me. I nod. "Can you grab it?"

"I'll go get it."

Hurrying out to the lounge, I feel confused, realising what we had almost done. The chemistry between us is crazy, but even in that haze of lust and want, the rejection has left me feeling cold. I can feel my wolf's pain in my head, the fact that she didn't get to be near her mate and I realise that unless she heals, I can't move on from that pain either. I can sense her whimpering in the corner of my mind. I haven't felt her presence this strongly since before the rejection. She is getting stronger, but she is in so much pain. I miss her. I want her to return to her full strength.

I grab my phone, staring at the screen blankly for a moment. I have a few texts, but I haven't opened them. I carry it back to the bedroom and unlock it. Leo is sitting there shirtless, laptop in his lap, his phone placed next to him, and he is still on call.

"Text your friend Song. Just ask her what she's up to," he says, glancing up as he runs his fingers through his hair. If it wasn't for what he had just said,

I would have gotten distracted by his body. My stomach sinks as I stare at him before looking down at my phone.

"What's happened?"

"Don't stress it, just text her," he replies. I nod. My eyes fall to his hard manhood before our eyes meet once more, and I realise I have messed it all up. A strange tension has settled between us, and he has his walls fully back up and is once more the cold Leo.

I try to focus as I open Song's messages, realising she hasn't really inputted anything on the group chat, but she has sent two private messages.

> **Song: Hey, Azura, do you think we can video call when you have a moment alone?**
>
> **Song: Azura, you there?**

Song is not impatient.

"Has he got her?" I ask quietly. "That doesn't sound like her."

I hold the phone out to Leo, who takes it from me, frowning deeply. He begins texting, and I sit down next to him, making sure to leave a small gap as I lean over to see what he is typing.

> **Me: Sure, I can call in a few minutes. Just let me make sure I'm alone. I'll call you.**
>
> **Song: Great.**

"What is going on, Leo?" I ask, looking at the laptop. It is a map with a flashing blue blimp moving pretty fast.

"I have been tracking Skyla, Kataleya, and Song just in case he tried something to hurt them. I sent one of my trusted men to keep an eye on Song due to her being the ideal option to target and it seems Judah may have done just that. Her phone is moving at an incredible pace, and she hasn't made any calls in the last few days, only texted and most of those were to you." Leo frowns. My heart thunders as I stare at the screen.

"If he has Song, he will hurt her," I whisper, my heart thundering with anger and fear, anger at Judah and fear for Song.

I need to save her.

"Calm down. Answer the call like normal. I'm hoping he shows his face, it will help. I'm tracking them. We will find them, don't worry." His voice is serious and cold once more, and I simply nod. He takes my phone, pressing just a few buttons. My screen blinks before he passes it back to me. His eyes meet mine as I stare at the phone, feeling a little shaken. "Azura?"

"What?" I reply. He seems to hesitate for a second, muting the phone that is next to him.

"You got this. As for the deal, we'll consider it done. I won't back out of the promise I made you," he says quietly, looking away. My heart clenches, feeling a mix of emotions, and I nod, not knowing what to say. So instead, I sit back against the headboard making sure it looks like I am alone. I take a deep breath, inhaling his scent to calm myself. *You got this, Azura.*

Leo stands up, turning the light up so the room is flooded with a warm light before sitting on the floor with his laptop in front of him.

"Just remain calm. Whatever you see on your screen, I will see on mine. Don't look away from the screen, and make sure he does not realise you are not alone, okay?"

I nod, my heart thumping at the phone in front of me. Taking a deep breath, I call Song, placing a huge smile on my face. *Please be okay...*

The phone is answered only for me to be looking at a blank screen.

"Hey, girl." I smile.

"H-hey, Azura," Song's voice comes. My heart sinks as I realise that is far from her normal voice. It sounds strained.

"Why can't I see you?" I ask, smiling slightly, although my nerves are a mess. Suddenly, the phone tilts and I realise it is some outdoor woody place.

Suddenly, Song comes into view. My eyes widen, my heart pounding as I stare at her bruised face. There is something tied around her neck, and a hand is yanking at her short hair, but it is the fear and concern in her eyes as she tries to shake her head slightly that gets to me. She is worried about me when she is the one held hostage.

"Song..." My stomach sinks as I feel as if a bucket of icy water has been thrown at me.

Keep talking, Leo commands through the link.

Okay.

"Azura, don-" Her head is suddenly yanked backwards before a fist connects with her face, making her grunt in pain.

"Song!" My heart thunders with rage, but it is the face that appears on the screen that is the final cherry on top to ruin the evening for me. His hazel eyes are filled with dull darkness and that ever-remaining anger as he looks me over.

"Well, well, well... it's good to see you again, little pet. Now, how about we stop playing hide and seek and you come to me before I cut this pretty little witch into bite-size cubes and feed her to the fucking wolves."

"Judah," I growl.

"Azura," he smirks coldly. *You are fucking dead.* "I'll be waiting for you. Be a good little obedient bitch and leave that pack without telling that Alpha," he hisses menacingly.

Ask him why.

"Why? Are you scared of him?" I ask coldly. His smirk becomes even sicker as he leans forward.

"Don't try me, or shall I start chopping?" he threatens.

Agree to meet him. Leo guides me with such calmness that I realise he is sending it through the link to calm me.

"Fine. Don't hurt her, I'll come to you."

At least we now have a face, Leo's voice comes. It is strange, but despite the tension between us, I feel safe hearing his voice in my head.

"Good. Keep your phone close. I will tell you exactly where to go. Make sure you're alone, and don't plan anything funny. We have a deal, and unless you want these videos on the net, you will come to me."

"Leave that pack tonight, Azura. Your first destination is that little cavern we used to meet at."

"Fine. I'll leave as soon as I can without anyone noticing," I reply.

"I'll see you soon... don't take too long, or we might be enjoying a little witchy Song for dinner tonight. Sounds..." he trails off, his eyes darkening with rage when they fall on my neck. "Are you sleeping with him?" he hisses so menacingly that I almost flinch.

"No," I growl.

"Good, because you're mine," he spits before the call ends.

No, I'm fucking not.

I toss the phone onto the bed, leaning back as I run my hands through my hair. Fuck, he has Song! I punch the bed, my gaze falling on Leo. He is working on his computer, but it is the blazing anger that is rolling off of him that catches my attention. I don't know how I didn't notice it; it is almost suffocating.

"Leo?" I call, and then I realise why he is so pissed. He had received those videos, too, and although he hadn't clicked on them, looking at my phone, I can see that two of the videos he had sent clearly show me. Naked.

I feel sick at the fact that he has those. I hated how he would antagonise me until I felt like I had to prove that I could do anything.

Leo stands up and places his phone near his ear.

"I want the team to close in but keep hidden. This fucker won't be getting away. Make sure nothing happens to the girl." He hangs up, slipping his phone into his pocket, and turns to me. "He's not getting away. Not this time. Let's move. I'm going to fucking kill him."

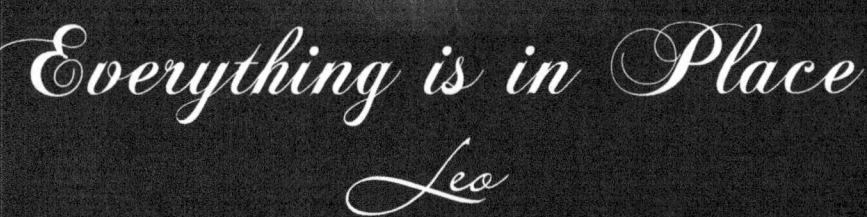

Everything is in Place
Leo

It shook me when she had unknowingly let her barrier down. The sheer level of desperation, fear, pain, and agony when I had rejected her and then walked away from her hit me hard. So fucking hard.

I have not felt such an intense level of pain since I was a child, but knowing these are her feelings makes it a thousand fucking times harder.

She had been unable to breathe as she clutched at her neck, trying to survive the violent pain that had torn through her. It fucking killed me to see things from her eyes, making me hate the fact that I did that to her. Seeing her crumble to the floor as she watched me walk away was fucking ruthless.

I had broken her and weakened her wolf right after taking everything from he. I had done the very same thing Rayhan had. I promised her something, only to rip it away from her the very next. The heartbreak, the fear, and the sadness as she realised what happened consumes me with guilt. The vulnerability as she realised that she wasn't wanted, wondering what she had done wrong. Nothing. She had fucking done nothing wrong.

I had blamed her for something that was not even linked to her, and nothing I do can turn back time.

She is so fucking strong, but inside that tough shell, and behind that 'devil don't care' attitude, is a vulnerability that has been hammered into her all her life and I... I fucking hurt her.

Fuck. How do I process that? How do I forgive myself when I refuse to believe Rayhan deserves forgiveness? Everyone says, if you make a mistake and acknowledge it, you deserve forgiveness and a second chance, but if I can't forgive Rayhan, then I can't suddenly just change my tune to make myself feel better. I promised her I'd talk to Rayhan, and I will, but it doesn't mean that I'll forgive myself for that brutal rejection. There are some things that are just not forgivable, and what I did is one of those.

I've had my walls up since then, not knowing how to process it all. Once we get off the call, I first have her take an x-ray to make sure he has no tracer on her; luckily, it is all clear. I give her a small pair of stud earrings with a tracker in one and a camera with a microphone in the other. Calling Winona to keep an eye on Corrado, I grab a jacket with a hood and change into some black sweatpants before heading down to my cave with Azura.

"Here." I hold out a bulletproof body suit, something that I have worked on myself. The material feels similar to a diving outfit, more flexible and easier to wear than bullet-proof vests. She looks at the full black suit and raises an eyebrow.

"What is this?"

"Wear it underneath your clothes. It's bulletproof. I don't want to take any chances."

"First, you tell me to get some baggy clothes, now this?" she asks, taking it and raising an eyebrow.

"Yeah, because the baggier your clothes, the more you can hide," I reply with a pointed look as I look down at her. *I love her in that skirt.*

She crosses her legs, making my eyes flash, and I look up only to realise she is trying not to smirk.

"You were saying?" she teases.

"You already fucking heard me. Go change." She smirks, turning and strutting off.

I want to see that ass naked, and as much as I want to bury my cock in her, I know it is a fucking dream that won't come true. She looks over her shoulder at me, almost as if she knows where I am looking, but she is no longer smirking. A glimmer of confusion flashes in her eyes before she enters the room and shuts the door.

Walking over to the far wall, I access a built-in touch screen. After my thumbprint and a spoken password in voice recognition, it opens to reveal a room full of weapons that I have created and improved. Judah is fucking dead.

I cross the room and unlock one of the lockers on the far wall to take out a box of bullets. They are lethal. Although I am still working on perfecting the formula of the poison that I have created, it will still do the job perfectly. These bullets are meant to kill instantly, and although I have never tried them, I am certain they'll work. The only thing left to perfect is to make sure that the substance does not remain in the body once it has shut down. I am about to grab a few items for Azura when I freeze and look down sharply. *Killed instantly...*

My heart races as I mind-link. **Dan, the body we had found with Azura Westwood, despite the distress it was in, did the post-mortem say anything else? You said he seemed to have died instantly, correct?**

Yes.

And there was no trace of any poisons?

I'm afraid not, Alpha.

I'm going to send you some files. See if you can trace the three substances listed from his body using the correct methods to bring them out.

Sure thing.

I had gotten him to run some tests on what had been used to kill him. I am not planning on taking any risks – not when it comes to her, but there has been nothing to help. Even the database doesn't seem to recognise him. I don't know how right I am, but if my hunch is anything to go by, then this shit might just be more fucked up than I ever thought. I'll ask how and who later. For now, I have a bastard to find and kill.

I grab a few items before exiting the weapon room, letting the door slide shut and once again blend with the rest of the wall. I have just sent the files over to Dan when Azura comes out, dressed in black pants, a polo neck top that covers the suit, and a leather jacket, her hair in a ponytail. As always, she looks sexy as hell.

"One of my men, Li Sheng, will be in a taxi. He'll appear human thanks to a scent disguiser. He will take you to the first location. Do not converse in any way that will feel suspicious. I don't trust this guy or if he has a way to listen in on stuff," I say, quietly stepping closer. She nods. I don't want to involve her like this or even use her as a decoy, but it is the only way to get closer to him. "I'm not going to be far behind... rest assured, we will find your friend Song. I do think we should tell Alejandro the basics, just so he can keep an eye on his daughters. I will be the one dealing with Judah, but just in case," I say quietly. She looks up at me defiantly, back to her usual self, but that intense snippet of her memory still doesn't leave me.

"Then you can tell him. Why should I?" she states. I frown.

"You're fucking annoying," I say coldly, "but fine, I'll do that."

"Just..." She frowns, and I raise an eyebrow.

"I won't give away anything else. I'm not fucking stupid."

"Perfect then. I wish I could hear this conversation," she replies airily with a toss of her hair. I'm sure you fucking would. I pass her the few items I had gotten for her, quickly telling her how to use them if she needs to.

"I'll be right behind you, and we have the mind-link, so don't worry, alright?"

"I'm not worrying," she replies, rolling her eyes.

You are... you're just hiding it as you always do.

"Good then," I reply arrogantly, stepping closer to her. She looks defiantly into my eyes, that frown still on her gorgeous face. I grip the side of her face and neck, becoming serious. "I will not let anything happen to you and our pup." Her eyes soften, confusion settling in them, but I don't give her a chance to say anything more. Leaning down, I press my lips against her forehead. It feels intimate but the urge to reassure her is real. I move back slowly, looking down at her. "As for those videos, don't worry about them. Now that I have a copy, I'll have them blocked from the net. When the same content goes up, it will be flagged, and I will make sure they are pulled down. We got this."

"Thanks," she replies.

Our eyes meet, and when her gaze dips to my lips, I smoothly step back, motioning her to leave.

She's leaving the pack. Keep tracking, I will be leaving in a few.

Operation Lunar on the move, Ace's voice comes.

Ace, I warn.

Hey, I didn't say Luna, he replies.

Operation Selene? Shane suggests.

Operation Fated, Ace adds.

Quit it. Get moving and focus. Jin is following her, and Li Sheng is already waiting for her.

Okay, we're on it, Ace's reply comes.

I get into one of the cars that I use when I want to keep a low profile and hook up my phone to my headpiece before driving out. Here goes nothing.

"Call Alejandro," I say clearly.

"Calling Alejandro," the computer's voice follows. I wait, half of me wishing he doesn't pick up at all.

"Alejandro," he answers.

"Yeah, I fucking know. I'm the one who called you," I reply icily. Silence.

"Leo?" He does his best, but he is unable to hide the shock in his voice.

"No, it's the King of England," I reply sarcastically. Well, depends on what aspect. I hold far more power than Alejandro knows.

"Fucker." So, he isn't going to ask why I called, but I don't like the emotion in his voice. I need to get this over with.

"I called for a reason."

"I would fucking assume so."

"Don't ask me any questions, but I would suggest you have someone watching your daughters at the Academy."

"Why?" he asks sharply, but even the coldness in it can't disguise his worry.

"Just trust me. There's someone who has made Azura and her friends a target. I will make sure Azura is safe but watch your girls."

"So, you called in concern for your sisters?" he asks tauntingly. Why the fuck does he have to be so fucking antagonising?

"I don't consider them my sisters," I reply coldly. My mind flits to Kataleya, remembering the shit she had suffered when she was a kid. I felt bad for her. No child deserved that. "Just keep an eye on them."

"Understood. Thanks, and before you hang up, I just wanna say it's good to hear your fucking voice." I don't reply, hanging up as I stare ahead.

Alejandro... it is weird how years of hatred and anger are beginning to ease up. Almost as if I am looking at things from their point of view.

I put my foot down on the accelerator, my mind on Azura. I click on her camera, seeing her hailing a taxi. Perfect. That is Li Sheng.

I got her, his voice comes through the mind-link.

Great.

Years ago, when I had told Alejandro how I felt, he had gotten Rayhan and me into a room together to talk shit out. They both got my point, but it had felt too late. I felt like I had been trying to be heard for years, but no one fucking cared.

I remember them asking if they could come to the pack and apologise, but I was the one who said no to them. They still did after I had left. Kiara had healed those who had suffered, and Rayhan had apologized – to those who were willing to see him anyway. But I always held that hatred within me, always trying to control it as it continued to fester inside of me. My priorities are changing though, and I don't have control over them.

Because of her. Or is it because of what I did to her? Azura...

Marcel and many others said I'd get it when I found my mate. Imagine your mate being tortured and abused how Delsanra was. The anger I feel towards Judah, but what will I do? Will I find all his friends and allies in blind rage who had a hand?

Yes.

But if it was someone forced to do something just like Azura had been forced to kill someone, would I punish her? Just like I'm sure Alejandro and the others won't blame her for being blackmailed into doing something because they knew who she was. But me? I won't blame Azura. Even when I refused to accept her or want her, I still saw her as a victim. Even putting Azura in the same context as Delsanra, I know my answer.

No, I wouldn't. It just doesn't feel humanely right, especially punishing those who have been forced to commit those crimes. No, what he did was wrong. So fucking wrong. But I have given her my word that I'll talk to Rayhan, and I know I'll have to deal with that shit at some point or another.

An hour has passed, and I have kept far back but within linking range when Azura sends another message.

He wants me to meet him at a motel on the outskirts of the city, Motel Slumber. It's off Silver Crescent Lane, down by the fuel station. He said to travel on foot.

Okay, just head there. I'm not that far behind, and neither are my men.

Got it. Thanks.

Stop thanking me.

Hmm, well, I'm such a sweet, good girl with manners, I can't help but thank you. Her voice is mocking, and I smirk slightly, pulling my hood up as I drive slower. I'll get out soon, too.

You? A good girl? From what angle?

You haven't seen 'The Face'.

The Face?

My innocent puppy dog look.

I don't think, with a face like that, you can ever look innocent... It is far too fucking sexy. *Especially since all I can think of are your lips around my cock as you look up at me with eyes full of lust...*

I'll show it to you later. Later... I can't help but smirk. She is confident that we'll deal with this shit, and we definitely will.

Looking forward to it, I reply. That same silence falls between us. We both want to say something, but just like me, I don't think she knows where to start.

I give a few orders to the others, thinking a motel is a pretty ideal place for the plan that I have in mind. My phone flashes on, and I click on it to see that it is Dan.

"Hey, Alpha. Was rechecking and comparing the data a little deeper, but I can't make sense of it or what exactly you want me to look for. I think there is a connection between what you sent me earlier. It's fucking weird, but there's something." I frown.

"Send me the file over, I'll take a look."

"Got it."

I hang up, frowning deeply. I know whatever had been used killed him almost instantly, and what irks me is that I have created something pretty similar, but that is not something I have released into the world, and the plan is to keep them for emergencies within the pack. There are only to be used as a last resort. I don't know why, but I feel fucking uneasy.

Everything is in Place | 277

Seeing the incoming email, I glance at the road for a second before picking up my phone and opening the email. My eyes scan the report. My heart thunders as traces of three substances stand out, their names glaring at me, making me simply stare at the email. This...

I put the phone down, running my fingers through my hair before I pull my gun out of my jacket pocket. Is it a coincidence that it is the exact fucking same as I use in the poisoned bullets I have been working on? And, if so, how is it fucking possible?

I scan the sheet carefully; it is almost the exact same build-up that I had put together, but I hadn't tol- wait...

I suddenly feel cold, my gut twisting as I realise when I first began working on these bullets, I had mentioned the concept to one other person. A person who is pretty smart, too. Someone I had trusted enough, but clearly someone I didn't really know as well as I thought I did. *Fuck.*

My hands tighten on the steering wheel, my eyes blazing as one name screams alarm bells in my head. *Emmet.*

He's here, Azura's strained voice comes.

Stay calm, I'm right there with you, I reply, pushing the thoughts away. I'll deal with that shit later, but for now, my girl needs me. I park up and get out of the car, breaking into a jog.

There must have been a reason he has chosen this place, but whatever the reason, I won't let him get away, not this time.

Is everything in place? I ask my men through the link.

Oh yeah, Jax's growl answers. I smirk slightly.

Perfect.

A Showdown
Azura

I haven't even gotten to the entrance to the motel when the phone beeps, and I look down at it. Judah. I feel sick, and my heart is thumping before I even click on it.

I hate being around him. I hate how whenever he is near, something always goes wrong. I just wish he was gone from my life for good, or better yet, I wish I had never fucking met him.

I look down at my phone, frowning at the message.

> Unknown caller: I want you to take out any weapons you are carrying and toss them in that trash bin. Then make your way around the back and up onto the rooftop. Leave the phone there, too. Don't play smart. I'm watching you, my pet.

He's here, I tell Leo through the link, trying to sound as normal as possible. I hate him with a passion. I am glad Leo is near; I feel a little at ease.

Stay calm, I'm right there with you. His voice is powerful, calm, and confident, which equates to sexy as hell.

That sick feeling only grows with each step as I take out the dagger that Leo had given me. He had also given me a few other items that don't really look like weapons but would give me some protection, although he was sure I wouldn't need them.

What is with you and all these gadgets? Are you Batman? I ask through the link as I toss the phone and dagger into the trash.

A billionaire with a troubled past and smart as fuck? Kinda fits, but no, because I'm not a hero, he says. *You're becoming mine…*

Well then, Leo Rossi, are you a villain? I ask, almost cursing myself for sounding a tad too flirty.

Do you need to label me, Azura Rayne Westwood?

Maybe?

Then I'm just someone doing what I need to do. Call it whatever the fuck you want. I don't need to be a hero or a villain. I'm just something in between.

I spot the rusty metal steps and look at them. They lead all the way up. I begin walking up them slowly, trying not to smile at his tone. A sharp wind blows, and I scan my surroundings.

Well, I think Batman fits, but then, he doesn't have a sexy butt. So maybe you can be Buttman or Sexy Butt? I cackle, trying not to laugh out loud.

Very amusing… now focus. Where are you headed?

He wants me to make my way up to the rooftop.

And you didn't tell me that? Be careful, and do not antagonise him.

Understood, I reply, keeping my face blank just in case he is watching me.

The stairs creak and clang under my feet as I continue slowly upwards. The noise feels too loud in the silence. An occasional car driving past can be heard, or a street cat. I am extra aware, trying to listen out for anything; even the rustling of the leaves in the trees feels loud. My mind turns to other things. Is Song with him? Is she safe?

I am near the top when Leo's voice comes again.

I can see you, and I have the camera connected. Don't try anything reckless, okay?

Okay. I'm not a reckless person.

Sure you aren't, comes his sarcastic response.

I reach the top and realise that just talking to him had helped the unease that now returns with a vengeance. I scan the area, my heart skipping a beat when I see the slumped body of Song tied up against the railing, her blond and ash hair catching my eyes. My stomach twists sickeningly as I see the bruises and cuts along her entire body.

"Song!" I am about to run over when a shadow falls over me. I turn just in time to see Judah lunge at me. I duck, stepping back. "Stay back," I growl murderously.

Keep your distance, try to stall him, Leo's voice comes, calm and in control.

"Ah, little pet... how I've missed you," Judah says, his voice sinister and dark. He walks slowly as he advances on me like a predator would, but he forgets that I'm not his prey.

"Shame. I didn't miss you," I counter, my eyes flickering to Song. The distance between us is growing as I keep stepping back, making sure I am far from the edge of the building.

"So, that bastard who texted me really thought he could keep you?" he spits venomously. "Your so-called mate?"

"I'm not a fucking pet or animal that anyone can keep. I do what I fucking want. We were done a year ago, Judah. Just get the hell out of my life!"

"We had a deal. You will obey me, and then I will decide if you can go." His eyes flash dangerously.

"I don't care about the deal anymore, Judah, I'm done! Want to release those videos? Go for it," I say icily.

"Don't push me, freak, because I fucking will." His eyes darken as he advances on me, his face contorted in rage. How did I ever find him handsome? How did I ever even kiss him? Just the thought makes me sick.

"Fuck off."

Relax, Leo's voice comes, calm and in control.

Don't tell me to calm down, I growl back.

You are only going to anger him. Trust me. Think with a level head.

"I would be very careful if I were you," Judah growls, and he is in front of me in a flash. I tense, staying alert, ready to protect my baby if I have to.

A Showdown | 281

"Fine. You wanted me, you got me. What do you want with me?" I ask coldly, trying to control the anger that I want to unleash, and I know if I wasn't pregnant, I would have. He is within reach now, and although I feel stronger since both Leo and I have marked one another, I don't want to risk anything. Especially when I know what he is capable of.

"I want so much but the question is, have you really removed all your weapons? Strip for me just how you used to." I frown, my anger flaring through me as his eyes rake over me, making my skin crawl. "Let's see that body of yours again. Watching those videos just isn't enough, you know?" Judah continues.

I suddenly feel such an intense wave of anger it makes me gasp and step back. These... these emotions aren't mine.

Fucking bastard, Leo's venomous growl comes.

My heart is pounding as Judah takes out his gun, cocking it and pointing it at me.

"Strip, you bitch, before I fucking blow your brains out," he hisses.

I'm right here, Leo's trembling growl of pure rage assures me.

I remove my jacket slowly, knowing I have the bodysuit on anyway. It is then that I see a black shadow behind Judah. Leo.

"And I will fucking blow your brains out if you ever talk to her like that again," he hisses venomously, his steely eyes full of rage, as he holds the barrel of his gun against Judah's forehead.

Then, everything moves too fast. Judah turns, raising his gun just as Leo kicks Judah's wrist. I hear something snap, and the gun goes flying, a shot going off. Judah growls in rage, his dark aura swirling around him. My heart is in my throat as the smell of blood fills the air. I see Judah lunge at Leo, and both men fall to the floor in a scuffle. Leo is stronger and definitely more agile, but Judah seems to be fast. Too fast... His movements look strange, almost inhuman. Well, we aren't human, but the angles his body move at look abnormal.

They are a blur as both exchange powerful hits. I run toward Song, only for Judah to yank me away as he escapes from Leo. I hiss when his hand wraps around my throat in choke hold. I elbow him, slamming my foot up behind me straight in his crotch.

"Bitch!" He yanks me back, and just when I feel my arm being violently pulled behind me, Leo is in front of us. "I have-"

Judah is cut off when Leo shoots him at point blank rage. He dodges instantly, forced to let go of me. Leo pulls me against him, his arm snaking around my waist possessively. My heart pounds as I look up at him. Even in this dangerous moment, my core clenches as I look up at him. His eyes are cold and deadly. Yup, I love a bad boy. Especially this one. And those piercings, that I never knew I had an interest in, are now something I love. His hand squeezes my waist gently, reassuring me before he moves me behind him.

"You just signed your death warrant," Leo hisses, glaring at Judah, who has narrowly dodged the bullet. I come back to reality, looking around before rushing over to Song.

"Song!" I whisper as she looks at me through her bruised, puffy eyes. "How dare he-"

"I'm all good," she says, trying to smile the moment I remove her mouth gag. "I'd help, but he has poisoned me."

"Seriously, girl, stop thinking about helping," I whisper, beginning to work on the ropes around her legs. I hear footsteps and turn to see several of Judah's boys approaching, guns in hand. Some I remember...

"Not so fast boys," a deep voice warns, and both Song and I turn to see four men. I grip the ropes and extract my claws to slash through them before pulling her to her feet.

There are four of them, all dangerously handsome, well built, and dressed in black, but they ooze power. One of them breaks away as Judah's men rush at them, but before I can pay attention to what is happening, I feel a searing pain in my chest. I double over, and it takes me a moment to realise it isn't my own.

"Azura!"

"Leo!"

I turn, panic and fear for Leo consuming me, to see Leo is still standing, whilst Judah is clearly losing. Leo's aura is incredible; I can see the sheer level of it whipping around him like a violent storm. He really is a Rossi. His power is incredible. It feels like waves of power are rolling off of him. Things seem to be moving in slow motion. I see Leo draw his gun, cocking it and aiming it at Judah, who is scrambling to his feet, bloody and raging with anger, but it is nothing compared to the anger that I can feel within me from Leo, despite how composed and in control he looks.

Why am I in pain?

"Azura..." Song murmurs, her arm now supporting me. I can't breathe. What is happening?

"I have a million fucking questions, but everyone knows the sooner you kill the bad guy the better. Before I finish you off, I have one question, where did you get those bullets?" Leo growls, slamming him to the ground, his foot on Judah's chest. Judah simply lets out a choked laugh.

"Wouldn't you want to know? I'm not telling you anything," he spits back, grunting when Leo places more force on his chest with his foot. "You fucking alpha!"

"If that's how you want to play, fine. I'll get my answers one way or another. See you in hell," Leo says, his voice void of all emotion.

He pulls the trigger before my very eyes, shooting him square in the forehead. Judah's gaze snaps to mine as Leo empties his gun, making sure every last bullet impales Judah's chest. His eyes are filled with something, but he doesn't speak, and I am in too much pain to. His body jerks with every shot, and I have to look away.

"He's dead," one of Leo's men says calmly to Leo.

"Yeah, Jax, I can fucking see that," Leo growls back, but it is clear the anger he feels is not gone. Is this really it? The end of Judah? I am shocked he didn't escape. It feels surreal.

"Is he really dead?" I ask hoarsely as I exchange looks with Song. "I'm shocked he didn't try to escape."

"I think he is, Hun," she replies, giving me a small smile.

"He's dead. I had an electric voltage barrier placed around this motel; if he tried to leave, he would have been fucking fried," Leo replies icily. He has some cuts and bruises but nothing major... then why am I hurting?

"Like a toasted barbeque. Shall we bring the body back to the pack?" One of his men asks.

"Yes," Leo replies, crouching down to check if he really is dead. "He's gone."

I let out a breath I never knew I was holding. He is gone.

"Come on, ladies, let's get you both somewhere safe," Jax says, his green eyes calculating as he looks us both over. "Luna?"

I can't answer, the discomfort in my chest growing.

"Shit. Did she get hurt?" The one in the taxi, Li Sheng, comes hurrying over.

What is happening? I press a hand to my upper abdomen as I lose my balance. Both men reach for me quickly, but it is Leo who catches me. The intense sparks and his scent cocoon me. This is my safe place.

"I... I don't know what's happening... it hurts," I whisper, my vision darkening. "Song."

"We got your bubblegum friend," Jax's voice promises, and I think I hear a huff from Song, but I'm not sure.

The warmth of Leo's body and the sparks that dance along my skin feel relaxing, despite the pain. He lifts me bridal-style, but he is panicking... why?

"Fuck. Azura!" I hear him curse as my vision darkens. What... why am I... wait...

Leo... Leo... are you hurt? I manage to murmur through the link as I clutch his shirt, forcing myself to look up at him through my lashes.

A glimmer of guilt fills his eyes before I lose consciousness, and my world turns dark.

Letting Her Misunderstand

Leo

"So, that's him?" Song asks Azura quietly.

"Yup."

"Okay, Azura, he's so-"

"Don't. I bet his big ears are listening in," Azura mutters.

I am outside the hospital room whilst they talk inside quietly, but yeah, I can still hear and see them with the door slightly ajar. Azura is sitting next to her friend with her arms around her. We had gotten back pretty fast. I had Azura with me, and I knew instantly why she had felt that pain. In the fight, I had overexerted myself, and she had felt it. Luckily, she had regained consciousness pretty quickly before we even got back to the pack grounds. Since then, she has been watching me intently, almost calculatingly. I have to fucking make sure that doesn't happen again, for her sake.

But then what about overall? The bottom line is I'm fucking dying, and that pain will only increase as the days and weeks pass by.

The doctor has checked her over, and she is fine. As for her friend, she has been tended to and is in good care, although she'll be hospitalised for a few days. My injections aren't really ideal to use on a human. However, I recommended they give her a very diluted dose to see if it helps. If it doesn't help, it doesn't, but just trying the small amount holds no harm.

"So, what are you going to do now?" Jax asks, hands in his pocket as he stands across from me.

"Regarding?" I ask, walking away from the hospital room and down the corridor.

"Regarding our Luna and her friend?"

"Song Daquin is welcome to stay until she's healed," I reply shortly.

"And the Luna?"

"Stop calling her that," I mutter.

"Until she joins the pack?" Jax persists. Why the fuck is he so pushy?

He is the only one I will be seen around the pack with. Not everyone knows how close I am to The Six, and I prefer it that way. We'll occasionally go for drinks on a night out, but lately, everything has just felt so fucking busy.

I don't fucking know, I reply, ignoring the two nurses who are giggling and staring at us. Why are most women so fucking annoying?

Can I say for once Schurke Wolf doesn't have the answer? Jax's reply comes as we step out into the dark. I take out a cigarette and light it, not replying to him and instead taking a long drag.

Did you place the body where I asked? I ask the others through the link.

Yeah, treat it as if he's alive, Ace's voice answers.

I'm not going to take risks, I reply, frowning deeply. The link is open so all seven of us can converse.

What are you worried about? Jin asks quietly. I frown, my mind wandering back to the drive home as I stared at the stars in the sky.

I slowed down, feeling as if I was missing something as I turned a sharp corner. I didn't feel at ease, and it wasn't Azura.

Shane, Li Sheng, change of plan. Do not bring the body inside the pack. Keep him in the underground cells at location twelve.

Roger, *Shane said instantly.*

Understood, *Li Sheng's reply followed.*

Why? *Jin asked.*

Just do it. I don't want that... thing inside this pack. He isn't a werewolf; I know that much. Besides, those bullets were made to kill werewolves instantly and he survived after multiple shots. I know he's dead, but... just keep him the fuck locked up until I run his prints and do some tests. Then we'll dispose of the body.

Seeing the way he moved, even after I shot him point blank with a bullet that should have killed him immediately, didn't go unnoticed. He was still able to move. So what's the guarantee that the other bullets worked?

I looked over at Azura, who was asleep, her chest rising and falling, and ran my knuckles down her jaw. I'm not going to take any chances.

It was too easy. I've seen Azura fight Emmet. She's good, yet she didn't stand a chance against Judah. So how did he go down so easily? I say.

Because Schurke Wolf beat his ass? Ace offers.

Isn't Sera wanting you home? I counter.

Always, but she'll be fine. She knows I'm working. Either way, I guess it's better to be safe. Shall we just burn him and get that shit over with?

Burning isn't always the answer, especially if Leo doesn't think he's a werewolf, Dan reminds him.

And the tests he wants to run, Shane adds.

We'll figure out what he is. Dan, I want you to begin running some tests, but keep him bound, and I want at least four of you there with him, I order.

I think you are being too paranoid, Leo, Jax adds thoughtfully.

Nah. You can never fucking be too careful. Think smart. I frown.

Like you always do? Ace's cocky voice asks. I know he means the entire situation with Azura, but that shit is totally different. I know I will have to talk to her sooner or later, and I can't avoid her forever.

The way that bastard had talked to her had made my blood boil. I hated the bastard with everything I fucking had.

He's under surveillance, and we have six men watching him. You can relax. If we see or think anything is out of the ordinary, I will alert you, Li Sheng says. Currently, he is watching him as I wanted one of The Six to constantly be on alert. That location is close enough to be within linking range.

Good. I'll come to check on him tonight if I get time. I need to go pay a visit to Emmet, too. Think we all need to get some rest for now. Jax, are the preparations for the drugs to be traded with the buyers ready?

Yes. Regarding that, I meant to tell you that Web is one of the buyers. He went through another, but it's definitely him. Do you want me to cancel it?

I frown. I had killed his son because he tried to double cross me. Why would he do business with me, even if the drugs are sought after? He definitely has a reason, and I am certain that it is to get revenge.

No. Let him be. We'll keep an eye on him, I reply.

Johann Weber, also known as the Web, is a forty-nine-year-old mobster, one who I hate fucking dealing with. That is the type I fucking want dead. His son, who I had killed, was worse than his old man if that is even fucking possible. A rapist and a sick bastard. Although I put his death down to Johann Weber trying to double-cross me, I got rid of him because he was sick. There are things I can look past, but someone like Harry Weber didn't deserve to fucking live.

Did you send the money to the orphanages, I ask?

Yup, 50k donated to each orphanage in the county by an anonymous benefactor, Jax replies as he walks beside me.

Good.

You're a good person, Leo, you just need to let it all go. Just ease up and remember you deserve some of that happiness, too. I get that you want others to be better off but I mean, not everyone cares about humans as you do.

Human, werewolf, or whatever, those are still children. Even fifty thousand won't make a dent in the support they need.

You're doing enough, Leo.

Am I?

Turn in for the night. I'm going to-

"Leo!"

We both stop and I take a drag on my cigarette as I spot Azura running over, her breasts bouncing and looking damn fine.

"Excuse me," Jax smirks slightly before walking off. So much for avoiding her.

She watches Jax walk off before her gaze returns to me. She is wearing the same outfit as earlier, although she had removed the bulletproof suit before the doctor had done her checks.

"Why didn't you get checked?" she asks, almost accusingly.

"Because I'm fucking fine," I reply, blowing out the smoke slowly. She frowns slightly, looking me over as if expecting to see an injury. She meets my gaze, observing me intently, but I remain emotionless until she shakes her head, looking uncertain.

"Good…"

"You should get some rest," I tell her, glad she didn't push it. I turn away, ready to leave. I know I can't keep denying or ignoring the situation and that soon, I will need to figure this shit out for her, Corrado, and our unborn pup.

"Why are you avoiding me?" she asks, grabbing my arm.

"I'm not." She raises an eyebrow.

"I'm not stupid, Leo," she growls. "Is it because of what happened when we were making out?"

"No," I lie coldly. It is partially; her memory… "Besides, it was a fucking mistake."

"Yeah, everything when it comes to me is a fucking mistake for you, isn't it?" she hisses coldly.

I know my words have hurt her, and although I didn't fucking mean it in the way she's taking it, I don't have the fucking courage to tell her why it is a mistake. Maybe her hating me will work better for her. I am someone who is always fucking in control, but when it comes to her… I am a fucking mess.

"Think whatever the fuck you want. Regarding the deal I made with you, how do you want to do it? Let's get it over and done with soon." A flicker of hurt flashes in her eyes as she searches my cold ones.

"Then what?" she asks sharply. "Are you trying to get rid of me?"

"Why? Do you want to stay?" I shoot back coldly. Her eyes flash, and she glares at me.

"No, why would I want to stay with a dumb twat like you? Yeah, let's get the deal over with then." I know she is speaking in anger, but is it wrong that pissing her off is pretty amusing?

"I'd rather be dumb than look like a fish."

"Excuse me?" Her eyes narrow dangerously.

"Have you seen the movie *Shark Tale*? You look like Lola with those lips." She pauses for a moment before her eyes flash silver.

"You love these lips," she growls, glaring at me.

"Wrong," I reply arrogantly. *I love those lips.*

"Fuck off, Leo. I don't know why you're being a dick but carry on. Thanks for dealing with Judah. Once we've both fulfilled our halves of the deal, we will go our separate ways," she says. I feel the flash of hurt and anger through the bond before she slams her walls up completely.

"Perfect," I reply. My gaze dips to her lips before I look away. Maybe it is for the fucking best. I don't want her getting attached.

We look at each other, and I guess there is one fucking thing we have in common. We are both stubborn-as-fuck. Her chest is heaving as she glares at me icily.

"I'll speak to Marcel in the morning, and in the coming days, I'll arrange for Alejandro to call that bastard to his pack, and I'll do that shit. While we're there, you can talk to your brother."

"You sure are in a rush to get rid of me," she says bitterly. No, I just don't have much time.

Our eyes meet, and it is fucking suffocating. All I want is to pull her close and fix this shit, but we can't always have what we want.

"You are always welcome to this pack." *Even when I'm gone.*

"Welcome to visit... thanks," she says sarcastically, her eyes meeting mine. "You are a total dickface."

She turns and is about to storm off when she stops. Turning back, she steps closer, grabbing hold of my jacket. Our eyes meet and her heart skips a beat, the intense pull making me struggle to control myself. Just when I thought she might yank me down and kiss me, she punches me in the stomach. Fucking hard. I clench my jaw, refusing to give her the satisfaction. She packs quite the fucking punch. I glare at her.

"You are so fucking violent," I growl.

"I am going to find a staple gun before I leave," she mutters before storming off, making me raise my eyebrow. I can't help but smirk as I massage my stomach. It hurts more than it should have. Fuck, I am getting weaker.

Nice ass, I taunt.

Fuck off. *I might just do that, whilst picturing you in my head.*

The moment she enters the hospital, I look up at the sky. I know Jackie always pushed me to see Kiara. Parts of my body have already begun shutting down, and if it wasn't for the medication and shit I am using, I would be long dead. I have left it too late, and now when there may be a part of me that wants to live on, even if it means putting aside my ego, deep down, I don't think Kiara can heal me. She won't be able to fix this, I know I am past that point. She is only able to heal something that is damaged, not completely gone, just as she can't regenerate limbs.

I take my phone out, staring down at a number I've always had but never rang, but I don't think even he can fix this shit. I just need to get everything I need doing, done before my time comes to an end. For everyone.

Hitting Home
Leo

I get a few hours of sleep in before going for a light run, making sure not to overexert myself, especially since I do not want Azura to feel my pain. I return home, shower, and dress before dealing with a little paperwork that I am falling behind on.

It isn't long after that Corrado wakes up, and I stop working to spend a little time with him. We are now seated opposite one another with a breakfast prepared by Rosaline in front of us. Corrado eats silently, a deep frown on his face.

The first thing he did when he ran out of his bedroom was ask where Azura is, not hiding the fact that he had expected her to be here. Seriously, this kid. He then become serious, frowning and watching me like a father would their disobedient pup.

"What did you do, Daddy?" he asks suddenly, placing his spoon down. I raise an eyebrow while drinking my coffee.

"What did I do?"

"Why isn't Azura here? Did you make her angry?" he asks, looking at me with concern and suspicion.

I sigh, "Maybe?"

"Daddy! I thought when I woke up Azura would be here, too, wearing your shirt!"

"Wearing my shirt?"

"Yes. It means you are going to share everything with her!" He looks at me questioningly, and I place my mug down. Yeah, wherever this kid is getting his information is pretty questionable. I should have a word with Winona. "Daddy! We can't lose Azura." His eyes are now full of worry.

"Hey, kiddo, listen. Things aren't always as easy-"

"So, you will still try harder?" His hopeful look makes me frown slightly. I look at him seriously.

"Corrado, why do you like her? I was with Nikki for two years and you were never this attached, although she had been living with us for over a year as well. So, why are you so attached to Azura?" I ask. He shrugs, looking down at his plate.

"I don't know, Daddy. I like Azura, and when she spends time with me, she doesn't go on her phone or look bored. She's happy to play with me and talk to me. Nikki was only happy when Daddy was there..." he mumbles.

My heart fucking clenches, and I can't stop myself from moving closer to him, taking his face in my hands as I crouch in front of him. I feel fucking guilty. He may be young, but, like all kids, he has good intuition. He picks up on things that you would never think he would.

"I'm sorry Nikki made you feel like that. Why didn't you ever tell me?"

"It's okay, Daddy, she made you happy. I just... Azura is special and... I think Daddy likes Azura a whole wide world more than Daddy liked Nikki," he says, stretching his arms wide as he smiles brightly. I smile slightly.

"Oh yeah?"

"Yes, Daddy. When you look at Azura you look happy."

"I'm happy all the time." He shakes his head.

"No, Daddy, I mean when you are with Azura, it's the same happy like when we are alone. You are different."

I don't reply, wrapping my arms around him tightly as I pull him down from his chair, his small arms wrapping around my waist. If I leave him, who will he have? And what about our unborn pup? I want to meet him or her, too. What will the pup look like? Azura? Me? Maybe a mix?

For them, do I ask Kiara? Who knows, maybe she can delay the process to buy me some time?

"Daddy, I love you the most," he whispers.

"I love you the most, too, kid," I reply quietly. For them, I fucking need to do something.

"But I am okay if Daddy also loves Azura, too." Love... I chuckle, moving back and ruffling his hair.

"You really are something, kid."

"I am Corrado Herrmann Rossi!"

Rossi... I frown slightly but say nothing. Many of my businesses are under Herrmann, but deep down, I still feel my name is Rossi, and as Alpha, being tied to the name you believe in is the only fucking thing that works, even if I fucking hate it. So, it fucking stuck, no matter how much I began to despise it,

"You sure are." I stand up, giving him another faint smile. If he wants to be called Rossi, he sure as fuck can be. He is, and always will be, my son, regardless of anything else.

It is a while later, and I have dropped Corrado off at Marcel's, telling him I'll be popping down later once I have dealt with some shit. He had been happy to have him and clearly thrilled that I was going to pop down later, even going so far as to ask me to eat dinner there tonight. I had agreed, much to Corrado's excitement before I left.

I am now making my way to Emmet's cell. He is sitting there on the bed, unmoving; I observe him through the cameras for a bit before I turn and walk to one of the questioning rooms, ordering the guards to bring him out. I don't even fucking know how this conversation is going to go. I have grown up alongside him, and the fact that he did that. Just the memory of him kicking Azura makes my blood fucking boil.

He is brought in and pushed into the seat opposite me.

I can handle him. Wait outside, I tell the two men, my gaze on Emmet, who is simply staring at me. His eyes are heavy with emotion and probably the effect of the silver in the cell.

"You finally came to see me. I won't say I'm not hurt. I thought we were brothers."

"Are you really playing the sympathy card? You kicked a pregnant woman in the stomach when you knew she was carrying a pup," I growl coldly, taking out a cigarette to keep my hands from strangling him. I light it as I watch him, trying to remain calm.

"An Elite, remember?" Emmet replies, his eyes watching me calculatingly. "So, she turned out to be your mate, but she's still one of them." My eyes flash as I slam the free one down on the table between us.

"What the actual fuck? Are you for fucking real? You tried to kill an unborn pup and obviously have no fucking remorse," I spit venomously.

"That's the mate bond talking, Leo, not you." I stand up, my aura raging around me as I lean over the table and grab him by the collar of his shirt.

"No. Trust me, it's not, because I'm doing my fucking best to try not to remember that it was my mate who you fucking hurt or the fact that that is my kid you tried to kill. Because if I go by that, I would have fucking killed you already," I hiss, tightening my hold on him. He simply smirks and shakes his head.

"Nah, you wouldn't... because of Jackie," he replies cockily.

"I don't even fucking know how we were friends," I shoot back, coldly slamming him back in his seat. "Besides, Jackie admitted to the fact that you hurt her. You will be tried, Emmet, before the pack. And yeah, maybe I won't fucking kill you, but you will live a life worse than death. A life in confinement." He frowns, and I sit down again. "Tell me, Emmet. Aside from beating and abusing your mate, trying to harm a pregnant she-wolf, and assaulting your Alpha's child and rightful Luna, is there anything else you want to tell me?" I ask, my eyes locked with his. There is nothing there. Just like when I first asked him about what Azura had said, he was smooth as could be. Who knows how many times he has lied to me?

"Alpha-to-be," he says after a moment, a faint mocking smirk on his face. "Right?" Low blow, considering he's the one person I ever expressed my feelings about that to. I smirk arrogantly, taking a long drag on my cigarette.

"The thing is, whether I hold that title or not, I'm still an alpha. Not because of my position but because an alpha's duty is to protect, and that is what I'm doing. Title or not, I'm still the fucking Alpha." With those words,

I lean over, yanking him forward by the collar as I glare at him. Although I can't do real damage, I can still hurt him to an extent where Jackie won't feel the pain, just like a ruthless round of training. "Now tell me who you gave the formula of my 0395s to. Only you knew about them. So, want to tell me exactly how I came across someone else with the exact same fucking bullets?" I ask coldly, my eyes locked with his. His heart rate changes.

Bingo.

It seems like he wasn't prepared for that question. The confidence on his face falters before he looks away, running a hand through his hair.

"I don't know what you're talking about," he denies, his eyes flitting around the room before he looks back at me.

"Oh, you fucking do. So either you tell me, or you are forced to answer me," I threaten dangerously.

"So, you'll do what every other Rossi does and compel everyone to speak the truth?" he spits venomously.

"If I have to, I will."

"You really are more like them than I thought." His voice is filled with resentment, and I wonder if this is my fault. Did I instil this hatred in him? Nah... we both thought similarly enough.

"Then I guess I am, and there's fuck all either of us can do about it. This is about what's fucking right and wrong, and you, what you did, was worse than what Rayhan Rossi did," I hiss.

"So, you will just forget the years of friendship and trust over a few mistakes?"

"Mistakes? What you did wasn't a one-off, but we're going off fucking topic. The thing is, I think you're forgetting that I was able to cut off my own blood. What makes you think I won't do the same to you? There's a limit to forgiveness, Emmet, and you're way past that. Now tell me, who did you give my formula to, knowing full fucking well the damage they can do in the wrong hands?" I ask, letting my command roll into my voice. Although I am not the official Alpha, my command is still strong enough. He frowns deeply, clenching his jaw. "I'll count down from three. Speak, or I'll fucking make you speak," I growl.

"There's nothing to tell! I told no one!"

"Lie." My eyes blaze as I stand up, tossing the cigarette aside and slamming my hands on the table. He flinches, his eyes flashing with irritation towards himself for letting his fear show. "We have been friends long enough. You should know that I don't forgive. One last time. Who did you sell the make-up of those bullets to?" Under my command, he lowers his head. "Answer me!" I shout.

"I didn't give anyone it! I made them!"

"Then who the fuck did you sell them to?"

"Web!"

We stare at one another, and to say I am fucking shocked is an understatement. I don't know what to think. Of all people, someone like him with those bullets...

"Say what?" His heart is thundering, and he knows he is done for.

"I needed the cash."

"You had me. If you needed cash, I would have given you anything you asked for! How many did you sell?" My heart is thundering with fear at the thought of those bullets out there in the hands of men who are far from good. Fuck, what have I done? He stays silent, his own heart racing.

Drugs and weapons are an entirely different situation. The world is full of them, and if one supplier isn't giving them, another would. Weapons and drugs exist, but those bullets... they should never have seen the light of fucking day.

"How. Many?" My voice is a menacing animalistic growl, my heart thundering as I try to control myself.

"Fifty thousand."

Our eyes meet, and all I can hear is the thumping of our hearts. Fifty thousand.

"When?"

He refuses to answer, and I let out a menacing growl. In a flash, I am by his side. Lifting him from his seat, I throw him across the room with full force. He grunts when he hits the wall, crumbling to the floor before he gets up quickly. I grab his shirt, slamming him into the wall.

"One last fucking time. When?"

"Th-the first batch of five hundred was about eighteen months ago and then..." I tighten my hold around his neck, and he begins turning purple. "The, the total number, it was a few months ago!" His face is full of anger, hating the fact that I used the Alpha command on him.

I let go of him, my heart thundering. Fifty thousand... shit... shit... shit!

I need to talk to Web. I need to get to the bottom of this and get them all back. If he is the one Judah is getting his supplies from, then I need to know what more he knows. This also means there could be supernatural beings out there who know of these bullets. A threat to all...

Fuck!

My mind is reeling as I remember the whispers and rumours of strange deaths. Stuff that sounded pretty normal that I didn't even fucking bother too much with, not knowing that maybe, just fucking maybe, they were caused by my own creation. The young boy we had found with Azura was probably an innocent victim, too.

I stand there, my mind a violent storm of emotions. I feel a dull pain in my back, but it is nothing compared to the pain within. I vaguely notice four guards running in as I simply stand there, pulling Emmet away and out of the room as he shouts things I don't fucking hear. Is someone calling me? I don't know. I don't care...

Fuck, indirectly I am now responsible for the lives of many. So many more than he ever was. I look down at my shaking hands, my vision blurring. The blood of thousands taints these hands.

What have I done?

Speaking the Truth
Leo

Two hours have passed, and I am working with Ace, Jax, Dan, and Li Sheng. There is so much I fucking need to deal with, and although it feels like everything is fucking spiralling out of control, I will fix it.

Emmet had grabbed the chair when I was distracted by the sheer shock of his revelation. He had slammed it into my back with such force that the leg ripped through my clothes and back, but I was far too wrapped up in my thoughts to realise what had happened until he was dragged away to his cell, and my men had begun to worry over me. The dull ache remains in my back, but it is healing quickly enough. I have had it cleaned and bandaged by one of the guards, not wanting to waste time by going down to the hospital.

"Alright, I need to get going. Start the preparations. Ace, you need to get to Web. Dan, check Emmet's laptop and office. See if you can find any bank statements or if he has any accounts that we don't know of or in any other names. Li Sheng, have Emmet's apartment searched. I'll let Jackie know in advance, so hold up until I give you the order. Jax, try to find out exactly where he created these bullets. I want to know where he got the funding to create that much without me even fucking realising," I order, frowning as I snap my laptop shut. "Get ready to execute both options."

"Are you sure these are the only options?" Jax asks, frowning slightly. I had told the five of them about the bullets, having no other option but to bring in all the force I can and execute their retrieval.

"If Plan A fails, then yeah, this is the only way, but let's focus on Plan A first. Send our buyer to him, offer him whatever he wants, but I want all of those bullets back at any price."

"This is going to cost us a lot." Ace frowns.

"It doesn't matter, I'm not going to risk those bullets out there. If he refuses or doesn't have answers, then we'll do this via Plan B. Have everything prepared for that, too. I need to have a word with Marcel, but I'll be available via the mind-link throughout. Tonight, I'll meet you all at Kingdom of Sin." I stand up when Ace sits forward, sighing.

"What if you ask Alejandro Rossi for assistance?" he says quietly. I frown. Maybe I need to. I know I can deal with this shit myself, but the more manpower, the faster the job gets done.

"I need to talk to him anyway. I'll see what happens. I'm still going to deal with this myself." I turn and leave the office.

Mind-linking Jackie, I ask her to come to the large oak tree that isn't far from Marcel's mansion and isn't too far from the hospital either. I have already been given a change of clothes after Emmet's attack so I am going to head straight to Marcel's after meeting Jackie. It is already late in the afternoon; work has taken fucking longer than I expected it to.

Eric, have you been keeping an eye on Azura?

Yes, I have. She went to Alpha Marcel's around lunch, and she hasn't left the mansion since then. She has been on my mind, and although I know I fucking hurt her last night, there is nothing I plan to do about it. I don't want her getting attached.

Okay, thanks. I'm headed over there myself, I'll take over watching her.

Anytime, Alpha.

Marcel probably invited her over for dinner, too... why am I not fucking surprised.

"Leo." I turn to see Jackie hurrying over.

"Hey," I greet. Her eyes search mine before she looks me over, and I know she is assessing me.

"You need to take it easy," she says quietly, glancing around.

"I'm fine. I called you because of something I learned about Emmet." Her face falls, and I switch to mind-linking.

He stole a formula of mine and has sold a pretty large number to someone dangerous. I need to have a search of your apartment take place just to see if we can find out any more details. I'm really sorry it's come to this, but it's got to be done. You could move out for a night or two, just until we've covered the entire place. She looks down brokenly and shakes her head.

"You can go ahead and search."

"Thanks. Is there anything you can think of that could help? Any property he may have had that you know of, or anywhere he could have possibly had the facility to mass produce something?"

"No, there's..." She frowns, and her heart thuds faster as she looks up at me sharply. "There isn't anywhere I know, but he would often be gone for hours at a time. And most often, it was when you weren't around. Maybe I'm just being paranoid-"

"No, I don't think you're being paranoid. Thanks for sharing that. If you do remember anything else, let me know, alright?" She nods, and I give her shoulder a squeeze. "You aren't alone," I say quietly. She brushes her tears away as she tries not to cry.

"Yeah. I know... I... I heard from one of the boys at the hospital that Emmet attacked you today." I don't reply. I can't deny it, but at the same time, I don't want her to feel guilty for it. "I've... made my decision," she says, twisting her shirt sleeve in her hand. I look at her sharply as she struggles to keep her tears at bay. I hook my thumbs into the pockets of my pants, waiting for her to speak. Deep down, I want her to reject him, but I know it isn't an easy option. "I'll... I'm ready to reject him," she says quietly. "Will you accompany me when I do it?" Her words fill me with relief. With their bond broken, it will be far easier for her to move on and for me to deal with him.

"Sure, I will. I know it's not easy, but you got this. Things will be rough, but after a while, it will become easier. This isn't the end, and who knows what the future might hold?" She looks up at me and nods slowly.

"Thanks..."

"Let me know when you want to do it, and we'll go to see him." She nods before we go our separate ways

I really hope she can move on from Emmet and rebuild her life. Mates... they are said to be a blessing, but at the same time, I feel like they are also a curse. You can't live without them and if something happens to one, the other will suffer, too.

I enter the mansion, hearing laughter, and silently make my way to the back lounge. The door is slightly ajar, and I stay silent, seeing Marcel sitting on the sofa whilst Corrado and Azura are painting. Corrado is a mess with paint on his face and clothes, whilst Azura is in a slightly better state with a huge piece of paper on the table as they both finger-paint on the shared paper.

She is wearing skinny jeans with a baggy top as she shows Corrado something. Her eyes sparkle, and the smile on her face is genuine as she speaks, but I am far too lost in how fucking good she looks to care about what she is saying.

"Oh, I get it!" Corrado adds, imitating what she is showing him.

"That looks like fun," Marcel chuckles. I step back, unable to face her after how I hurt her last night.

Let's talk, I say to Marcel through the link, walking away towards the front of the mansion. Noticing the boxes that are in the hallway, and the extra staff around, I raise an eyebrow, but I'm not really bothered with what is going on and take a seat, taking out a cigarette. I don't fucking know how I am going to do this, but I need to get this shit over with.

Good luck. I freeze, frowning slightly as Azura's voice comes into my head.

I don't need luck, I reply coldly.

You sure do, now shut up. You got this, her curt reply comes.

Always so fucking charming, aren't you?

Yeah, well, I don't do charming when it comes to Little Alpha Dickface, her clipped reply comes. I raise an eyebrow. Just then Marcel enters the room, shutting the door behind him.

I'll deal with you later.

Can't wait, comes her sarcastic reply.

"Everything okay, Leo?" he asks, concerned as he takes a seat on the sofa opposite.

"Yeah, there is just something I want to tell you," I say, smoking my cigarette. I sit forward, resting my elbows on my knees.

"Go for it," he replies, clearly unsure of what to make of it. Yeah, maybe I need luck or some shit.

Just tell him everything you experienced... how you had to go through so much, and although you dealt with it, it didn't mean it was easy or fair on you. You suffered, Leo, and it is time to tell him that. No matter how hard it is on him. Her voice is soothing and calm.

Yeah, I know the damn deal, I reply. I won't admit it, but I am fucking grateful for her words. I kinda don't know where to start.

"What's with the stuff in the hallway?" I ask, trying to stall.

"Oh, well, that's for tonight," he smirks, running his fingers through his hair.

"What's happening tonight?"

"Ah, well, it's just a little dinner for Azura. We haven't really welcomed her into this pack since she got here, and there is something else..." He doesn't want to talk about it, and I frown but don't bother questioning him.

"Whatever. What I want to talk about is the past."

"The past?" He frowns, becoming serious.

"About the caves, the life of hell that we lived down there. You were one of the luckiest because you were entirely under her control but what about the rest of us who had to live and deal with the nightmares of that past?"

"Leo..."

"I don't want to fucking sound like I'm whining, but my hatred of everything stems from back then. We went through hell down there."

"I know, Leo, and I wish I could have done more... you were somewhat immune to her compulsion, and-"

"Yeah, I was, so I witnessed it all. You just standing there blankly whilst she tortured Mom. You know, Dad, she was expecting when she died? Endora not only killed Mom but your unborn child. And I was the one who was forced to stand there and watch it all. Unable to fucking do anything." None of this is coming out like it was meant to. I just sound like someone being petty-as-fuck about an unchangeable past. What purpose will telling him bring? He can't change the past. It is done.

I look at him. He has turned ashen. He stares at me while his heart is thundering. I can see the toll my words are having on him, and he stands up, clearly shaken.

"Why... why didn't you tell me she was pregnant? I mean even after..."

"Why should I have? It would have only hurt you, right?" I reply, now standing up and turning my back on him, no longer able to handle the look on his face.

"But you kept it inside... suffered all by yourself..."

"Yeah, because I could handle it. Do you know how it felt having to watch you do whatever Endora wanted? And what fucking hurts the most is when you were given your free will back, you allowed Rayhan to come here and once again hurt our people. I get it, they weren't all good, but you just stood there just like you always did. Doing nothing," I say, hating how my voice is fucking strained and my emotions are showing in it.

"Leo... I failed you, your mother, and..."

I close my eyes, hating that, despite his flaws, I am causing him pain. I get it... we all make mistakes... I get that Marcel's hands were tied, too.

"No, but you failed my trust. You always say you won't hand over the Alpha title because you fear what I'll do if I am Alpha, but are you really a better alpha than me? I mean, you were never able to protect this pack. Nor your mate... nor your children." I hate hurting him. It fucking hurts me too, but I feel lighter getting it off my chest.

"No, Leo, I was just worried that you wanted to break away from Alejandro's Coun-"

"I'm already running this pack the way I want but, once again, you keep on putting others first!" I snap, turning and glaring at him, my eyes a magnetic steely blue, my aura filling the room.

"No, Leo, I want to give you the-"

"What? The Alpha title?" I ask. He nods.

"Yes, you are ready-"

"No," I cut in, raising my finger. "Nah, the only reason you want to pass me that title is because Azura's here, right? Not because you have faith in me but because of her, right?" My anger is raging around me.

"Leo... no, I just, you misunderstood me. You were always so cold and heartless and-"

"Yeah, I sure am, you sure know your own son. I told you what I needed to, so I'm fucking done," I say, turning to leave the room when he blocks my path.

"Not until you hear me out," he says firmly, his eyes flashing. I don't speak, my eyes cold as I wait for him to just say whatever the fuck he wants. I want this conversation to be over and done with here. "Leo, I love you, and I know you feel that I chose them over you, but I didn't. I love my family, but you are my son. How can I not love you?" His voice is thick with pain as he looks at me with such emotion that I am forced to look away. "I didn't want you to do anything wrong, but know I alone am the one who has withheld that title from you. Alejandro keeps telling me to pass it on to you. Rayhan did, too, the last time I met him, saying you are capable. They care for you, Leo, as do I. Azura or no Azura you deserve this title. As your father, no one will be happier when you become Alpha than I will be. To see you take the title that belongs to you, to come into that position that you have worked on for so long."

"Yeah, well, it's too fucking late. You can keep it," I shoot back coldly. "I didn't come here to beg for that fucking title." *I'm fucking dying anyway.*

"Leo, let's put aside our differences." *There's too many... and no time.*

"It's a little too late for that," I reply, quietly brushing past him. He grabs my arm, stopping me with incredible strength. I am still stronger, and if I want, I can pull away.

"Leo. Don't do this. Please," he says quietly, his eyes full of emotions. "I'm begging you for forgiveness for not being the father and Alpha you needed. I'm sorry. Forgive me, son." It is too late... but then life is short. "I will hand that title over to you, not because of anyone, but because you deserve it. You suffered so much, and the fact that I didn't know... I'm sorry. I wish I could turn back time, take your pain, and make it my own. I wish I had been able to protect you from the truth. No son should have to protect his father like that... yet you did." I look away, refusing to answer. Refusing to give in to the pain and emotions inside of me. "At least I know my son cares for me." I look at him sharply.

"I always fucking did. You were just too blind to see it," I say quietly, pulling free from his hold and heading to the door. I have just opened it when he speaks.

"Then, one last time, forgive this old man of yours, son. Please." His voice is breaking my resolve, and I am about to refuse him when I stop in my tracks, seeing Azura and Corrado standing there, a few meters from the door, covered in paint, but both have their eyes on me.

Forgive him, Leo. Everyone deserves a chance, Azura says softly as Corrado watches me, his eyes glistening with unshed tears of confusion. **Let it go, Blue-Eyes.**

Our eyes meet, and I know the choice is mine, forgive Marcel and move on… or continue with my bitterness, and let it eat me up until I die. I look down at my own son before my gaze flickers to her stomach. If I made a mistake, I'd want my children to forgive me.

I have made mistakes too, just like Marcel, like Rayhan… Do I want forgiveness?

I exhale before taking a long drag of my cigarette. I look back at Azura, her gorgeous eyes baring into mine. I need the strength to do this. Almost as if understanding, she walks over to me, and, uncaring about the paint on her hands, she places them on my chest, sending intense sparks coursing through me and making Corrado gasp, but we are both too consumed in one another's gaze to realise. It is almost as if she is giving me strength. Her scent soothes me, and the urge to pull her close and bury my nose in her neck tempts me, but I should stay away from her.

Don't be so stubborn. Her voice through the link makes me come back to reality. **Forgive him, Leo.** I pull away, blowing out slowly, my mind made up.

Family
Azura

I sense his struggle and know I have to do something, even if he was a total asshole to me last night. I mean, he has protected me from Judah and gotten rid of him.

Don't be so stubborn. Forgive him, Leo, I say softly.

I want to do more. I want to cup his face and tell him he isn't alone, but I can't bring myself to do so when he doesn't want me, and so I simply try to comfort him silently through the bond. He exhales sharply, taking another drag of his cigarette before he turns back to his father, his tattooed hand closing around my wrist just when I am about to remove it, not letting me move away.

"It's in the past; you don't need my forgiveness. I just needed it off my chest," Leo says curtly, acting as arrogant as ever, but it is obvious that Marcel's words had gotten to him.

"Thank you, son. I'm glad you told me," Marcel says quietly, approaching us. The father and son look at one another, and I slowly tug my hand free. This is their moment.

Corrado's eyes, which were glued to Leo's grip on my hand, now flick to mine. Curiosity, happiness, and still a bit of confusion linger in those vibrant hazel eyes.

"I really am sorry, Leo, and it just shows that I was wrong... wrong to think of you like that, when I should have known you wouldn't harm anyone innocent," Marcel apologises, placing his hands on his son's shoulders. I smile down at Corrado, stepping back and giving his hand a squeeze.

"Yeah, you should have, because if I wanted, we both know that I could have finished Rayhan years ago," he says. His voice is equally icy as it is quiet, so Corrado doesn't hear. I admire him. Even when his emotions are so intense, he is able to keep himself in check around his son.

"I know what he did was complicated, but he has apologised, Leo. You will be happier if you let it go." If Marcel knew he was planning on talking to him, I know he'd be proud of him. Truly proud.

"Yeah, well, let's not get ahead of ourselves," Leo replies coldly. Marcel smiles slightly and nods.

"Yes, you're right. I lost my mate and a child I never knew of, but I'm so grateful that I still have you. You are my greatest blessing," he says quietly, his voice thick with emotions. Goddess, it is too damn emotional! Marcel steps closer to Leo and embraces him. Leo stiffens almost as if he is not used to it. "If you have truly forgiven me, I wish you would try to bring yourself to call me Dad again," he says so quietly that I only just caught it.

Urgh, I'm going to blame the pregnancy hormones, this is not meant to be emotional! How the hell is Leo so stiff and cool? I know both are hurting and it makes my heart ache to witness this. Life really is short, and looking at Marcel now, I realise in a way, he really is alone. No mate, and his own son has pushed him away. Even if he does have other family, it isn't the same.

Damn it, hug him.

Slowly, Leo raises his arms, embracing his father, and I smile down at Corrado, who is watching with wide eyes. I am sure even he realised his father isn't very close to Marcel. I hope that changes going forward.

"I have never seen Daddy hug Grandad," he says in a loud whisper.

Marcel chuckles as Leo moves back. He is as stoic as ever, but when our eyes meet, he is unable to hide the fact that they are full of emotions. I know it wasn't easy for him, but I truly am proud of him.

"Come on over here, son." Marcel motions him over, his arm still around Leo's shoulders as Leo simply takes a drag on the cigarette he is still holding.

"Group hug!" Corrado exclaims, running over to them.

"Yes, you, too, Azura." Marcel smiles. My eyes widen slightly, not expecting that.

"I don't think-"

"Come on, Azura, we are having a family hug!" Corrado says, turning and beckoning me over.

"Family hug…" I place my hand on my stomach for a second, feeling Leo's eyes on me, before I walk over to them as Marcel lifts Corrado into his arms.

"Yes, Azura is family, isn't she?" he asks Corrado as I stop a little away, feeling awkward. Leo's scent doesn't help matters either.

With Marcel's hands busy, does he expect me to hug Sexy Alpha Dickface? No, I'm so not going to do that. I'm still going to get that staple gun and execute my revenge…

"Yes, she is. We are going to keep her," Corrado whispers into Marcel's ear, making my eyebrow shoot up. He lets out a laugh before nodding.

"Yes, I like the idea." Leo frowns.

"Are we done yet?" he asks coldly.

"Oh no, Daddy, we have to have a group hug!" Corrado reminds him, holding his arm out to me.

At the same moment, Leo reaches out, his arm snaking around my waist as he pulls me close

My heart pounds, the electrifying sparks of the bond dizzying. Our eyes meet for a moment, and I can hear his heart deceive him. So close, yet so far away… I place my hand on his shoulder, placing my other hand on Marcel's back. Forcing my gaze away from Leo's, I rest my head against Corrado's. He giggles, resting his hand on top of mine.

"I love you, Azura!" My heart thunders as I look up into that innocent face of his.

"I love you, too," I whisper. Reaching up, I kiss his nose and smile at him. Somehow this little gem has made a special space inside of my heart. There are just too many emotions inside of me.

Deep down, past that stubborn ass exterior of mine, is it wrong that I want this? Want Leo. Want to have Corrado in my life? Want Marcel to get to see his next grandchild grow up around him, too?

My breath hitches when I feel Leo's fingers caress the side of my stomach. My heart pounds as I turn my eyes hesitantly to his. Those icy blues that I love so much stare back into mine with such intensity that I almost forget to breathe.

"I'll put them..." We all turn to see Winona standing there holding some dress bags, freezing in her tracks as she realises the room isn't empty. "I'm so sorry," she says quickly, looking flustered, as Leo moves back first.

"Not at all," Marcel says, smiling slightly. "We were just having a moment, and I appreciate all the help. You didn't have to do any of this." He walks over to her, and she smiles slightly, nodding.

"Thank you, Alpha," she replies, looking down at the bags.

"I'll take them," Marcel offers. "We all need a change of clothes anyway."

I watch curiously, wondering what those clothes are for. Marcel's words make me realise I have put paint on Leo, and Corrado has put some in my hair and all over Marcel.

"Ah, this one is yours," Marcel says, passing one of the bags back to her. Winona looks at him, surprised.

"Alpha, I can't accept this." She turns to Leo for help, looking confused.

"You are as much part of this family as the rest of us. You have taken care of my grandson, and that alone is enough. Since it's of your choosing, you can't really refuse," Marcel says firmly.

"Alpha." She looks at Leo, who simply raises an eyebrow.

"I don't know what sh- is going on, but you agreed to help him," he says, smoking his cigarette, smoothly stopping himself from swearing.

"And that should be enough of an answer to show you can't refuse. Alpha's orders," Marcel says dismissively. Winona stares down at the dress, her cheeks burning as she tries her best to protest.

"I didn't realise it was for me..." she mumbles.

"You will look great in it," Marcel says confidently, making her blush deeper and become even more flustered. "Now, pass this one to Rosaline for me?" he adds, not even realising the flustered mess he has left the poor woman in as he passes her another bag. Well, even I have to admit Marcel is some fine wine, what woman wouldn't get hot and bothered? I smirk, finding it rather amusing. She nods, looking at me for help, and although I kind of get what is going on, I'm not going to side with her when I feel she sure as hell deserves that dress.

"So, what are these dresses for?" I ask, going over.

"The party tonight," Marcel explains, smirking slightly.

"Party?" Leo asks sharply.

"Oh yeah, a party! Me and Grandad planned it! It's for Azura!" Corrado gushes. "I want you to look pretty in that dress, Winnie! You helped us, too!"

"Did she now?" Leo remarks, his voice sounding deep and rough, as Winona lowers her head apologetically. I can't help but smirk.

"What's wrong? Never been to a party before?" I taunt him.

"Only the ones I need to," he shoots back.

"Well, you need to come to this one," Marcel adds.

"It's for Azura. I don't need to. I agreed to come to dinner. Not to a party." Corrado turns, his smile vanishing as he stares at Leo.

"Daddy..."

"You won't come, Weo?" I ask, turning to him and giving him the best innocent face that I can muster. I so hope it works. *Please do not be immune like Mama!*

He looks at me as I stare back doe-eyed, my lips set in a downwards pout. His eyes flash as he narrows them.

That doesn't fucking work on me, his arrogant voice comes through the link. Damnit.

Oh? That's okay, because although I'm never enough for you, I seem to be enough for your body, I taunt, my innocent expression replaced by a seductive one. I slowly run my tongue along my lips, smirking when he swallows, his gaze dipping to my lips. His nostrils flare and his eyes flash. **See?** I turn my back on him before he can even reply. One point to me!

"Winona, show Azura to one of the rooms upstairs so she can get ready, too. We don't have long, and I know women take pretty long."

"Right away, Alpha." Winona smiles before she takes my dress bag from Marcel and motions for me to follow.

I don't bother looking back at Leo, feeling his gaze burn into me before I leave the room. I'm not sure why Marcel is throwing this dinner party, and although I had made it clear to him earlier that Leo wants nothing to do with me, he doesn't seem to get it. Well, there is nothing I can do about that, I guess. I will just enjoy all the delicious food tonight and not think about anything else.

Winona instantly forces me to go shower, saying I have paint all over, which I do. Alone in the shower, my mind drifts to everything else that is going on. Judah is gone, Song is safe, although she is still recovering in the hospital. I feel light, relieved, and content. He will never be able to bother me again. I feel relieved that he is gone. Everything will be okay now, right?

I guess after the visit to Alejandro's pack, I will return home... which means before I leave, I will need to ask Leo what he wants to do regarding the baby. Will he want to set up a day every week or month that he wants to see him or her? Then again, he's a busy man.

What should I do? I mean even though he doesn't want me in his life, I want him in this child's life. When I was younger, I always used to say that once you mess with the devil, there's no escape but it is obvious that if I want him, I am going to have to be the one to break down those walls. Do I want him?

He can go fuck himself. Ass.

I sigh, running my hand over my stomach. I can feel the slight curve to my stomach now. If it hasn't already gotten out by now, I guess it will any day now.

I step out of the shower, drying my hair with a towel before I wrap it around myself and enter the bedroom. My face lights up when I see Song sitting on the bed as both she and Winona stop talking and turn to look at me.

"Song!" I rush over, pouncing on her and crushing her in a hug.

"Hey, ow, ow..."

"Shit, sorry, I forgot you're hurt!" I quickly get off her, only for Winona to chuckle.

"Well, I'll leave you two to it. Alpha Marcel needs me downstairs. Someone will pop in to do your hair and make-up soon," she says with a small smile.

"My hair and make-up?" I ask. She pauses at the door and looks over her shoulder at me.

"Of course. Alpha Marcel insisted that you have everything you need."

The door shuts and I look at Song, planting my hands on my hips.

"What were you two discussing?"

"I don't know, but check the dress out..." She tilts her head towards the bed next to her, and my gaze falls on the top dress bag.

Unzipping it, I stare at the stunning dress that is inside. Somehow this doesn't feel like just any ordinary dinner party. Hmm, what is Marcel planning? He and Corrado, together thrown in with Winona, mean trouble. And although the Westwood Devil can handle trouble, I'm not so sure about a cherub, an angel, and an alpha with a wish. *Goddess, these three really are trying to get Leo and me together.*

I tilt my head, an idea popping into my head. Well, even if they are just hoping for something that will never happen, I can't throw out the chance to torture Leo. I mean sure, I am not as hot as Nikki, but thanks to the mate bond, he is attracted to me.

"Oh, you're up to something," Song replies, smiling slightly.

"Hmm, maybe..."

"Tell me what's going through that naughty brain of yours."

"I'm just thinking I might take a note out of Mama's book, and show Little Alpha exactly how a Westwood woman rocks the colour red."

Tonight, I plan to be the devil in red, and I will make the most of the mate bond to mess with him.

Oh, Little Weo, you are so damn screwed.

A Call
Leo

She played me fucking dirty and left. But despite the fucking beast she awoke within me, it was her words that really got to me. *Although I'm not enough for you...* If I wasn't half as stubborn as I fucking am, I would have told her the truth; that that shit ain't true, but, that's all there fucking is to it.

I feel lighter getting that over with, and it reminds me of the past when I at least had my father. It's just a shame it's too late for all of that to be back. Right? I am delaying. I know I am far past the stage of Kiara being able to help me, but I don't think I want to hear it. Even if I already know the truth.

I push the thought away thinking back to the moment between Azura and Corrado. Corrado has only ever said 'I love you' to three people before now: Dad, Winona, and me. It hit hard; he has taken to her. I don't need any more fucking signs that she is meant for me.

That hatred I felt... even the word Elites... it all seems so fucking far in the past.

I walk to the bottom of the garden of the mansion and pull out my phone. *Time to ring Alejandro.* I smoke my cigarette while looking down at my phone.

Although I don't want to hear his cocky comebacks right now, I can't delay it. I find his number and hit call. He answers after a few rings.

"Leo." His voice is level, yet it is obvious he is happy to get this damn call.

"Alejandro," I reply.

"I'm getting lucky with all the calls. How are you?" *Not so fucking good.*

"Perfect."

"Good to hear. How's your son, or should I say, my grandson?" I frown, obviously that wasn't going to stay a secret forever.

"Stop acting like I consider you anything close to a father," I reply icily, refusing to answer his question. "I called for a reason."

"You always fucking do." *Just get it over with, Leo.*

"Arrange a meeting at your pack with the Alpha of the Black Storm Pack. I need to speak to him," I say coldly. There is a pause before I hear the sound of a cigarette being lit.

"With Rayhan… is everything okay?" he asks, concern now evident in his voice.

"Perfectly," I reply.

"So, you're ready to talk to him." I do not want him thinking this shit is from me.

"I made a deal with Azura that we will both do what we don't want to. She'll talk to her brother, Atlas Kamdon, in return." He lets out a low chuckle.

"You two are fucking perfect together if, in that short time, you both have gotten each other to do the two things both your families have been trying to get you to do for years. I'm fucking impressed." Yeah, she got me to agree to shit I refused to for years. I know that, somehow. Even when I kept her at arm's length…

"It is a deal, nothing to be so fucking impressed about."

"Oh, yeah? Well, it fucking worked. I'll get that meeting sorted. How soon are you looking?"

"How soon can he fucking do it? I'm sure he's either fucking too busy with his hair or some other weird shit, like his singing."

"Got to give it to him, he can sing, and that video that went fucking viral years back was courtesy of Skyla, who wanted him to be her popstar cousin. He's quite a popular search on BlueXZ. I'm surprised you didn't have it pulled down since you're the owner of it."

I hate him, and I made sure to keep an eye on all news I could get, but I wasn't going to waste my time pulling him from the fucking net. After all, I'm the one who fucking created the search engine BlueXZ. It is accessible only to the supernatural, and something that is now beginning to be used across the continent. Alejandro knows I was the creator of it, I know that from Marcel since he used to always fucking share whatever shit I was up to. Years back, when I first created it, I had been surprised that Alejandro had verified it as safe, although he had never commented on it to me, but it is now something used frequently. I have a team that is ever-growing to expand BlueXZ. The Sangue Pack just isn't enough, but I always refuse to branch out to other packs.

"I don't have time to bother with the likes of him." Until now anyway, since I'm fucking trying to set a meeting between us.

"Fair enough. That was a smart move. If you ever want to expand, let me know. There are plenty of people who would love to work for such a company."

"Hmm."

"You know, Azura hasn't had the easiest life, Leo." I frown, and although I want to tell him to fuck off, I also want to hear what he has to say. "She may have been raised in one of the most powerful packs in the country, but due to her birth, she has had a lot of negativity from many. Even at the Academy, she was classed as the troubled child, and has been suspended several times for getting into fights. She's a good kid, and she has a good heart with a tough fucking exterior, but don't let it fucking fool you. Don't hurt her. You already did that by rejecting her after marking her. I'm fucking surprised she's able to stay strong after that. It's going to take time for her and her wolf to heal, but just don't fucking hurt her again. At least remember that she's carrying your pup." I know that and I know the extent of what my rejection did to her.

"Yeah, I know. Text me the date, and we'll be there."

"One hundred fucking percent. Bring your pup. I want to see him," he replies, not pushing me.

I don't reply and hang up. I don't want to take Corrado because, although he is an alpha pup, Stefan was nowhere near as strong as me. I don't want anyone to ever fucking question his birth.

I slip my phone into my pocket as I finish smoking my cigarette. I guess I'll go get ready for this thing, and I can't wait to see what exactly she is wearing because, according to Corrado, she is going to look 'so so so so pretty'. Heck, she could be covered in garbage, and I'd still think she looked fucking gorgeous. I'll always remember the first time she caught my eye; it was before the bond snapped into place and something about that always felt perfect.

I hide my smirk, making my way back inside.

It is two hours later, and I have changed into a black pair of pants and a white shirt with my sleeves pushed up and a few buttons left open. I look in the mirror applying some cologne before I begin styling my hair. Not sure why the fuck I am putting in the effort, but I look good.

I can hear the music being played outside; whoever is in charge of it isn't doing so badly. The current song reminds me of Azura and me. I pause for a moment, the words resonating in my head.

"... Smoking just to forget life... We might just be dancing... dancing to forget..."

Suddenly the night doesn't seem so bad. To spend it with my family, with her. Who knows if the chance will come again? Although I wonder what exactly Marcel has planned, it won't stop me from at least relaxing a little.

Alejandro had replied saying he had scheduled the meeting for the day after tomorrow, but we are welcome to come earlier. Now that a date is fucking set, I'm not looking forward to it.

I have just put my shoes on, deciding to deal with some emails one of the boys have sent me on my phone, when there is a knock on the door.

"I'm coming in!" Corrado says, turning the handle and running inside without waiting for a reply. I raise an eyebrow as he stands there, hands on hips, looking me over.

"You look good, kid," I say. He is dressed in black jeans, a white blazer, and a red shirt.

"Yes, Daddy, but I need to check if you look good, too! I saw Azura. She looks so beautiful," he says dramatically before glancing towards the door as if someone might hear him.

"Oh, yeah?" I ask, fucking hating that my heart has to race. What the fuck am I? A damn teen?

"Yes, Daddy, but I can't tell you what she's wearing. It's a surprise, so come on! We need to go down before Azura comes down!" he says, pulling at my arm.

I stand up, not knowing if I should tell him that she is expecting. I know he'll find out sooner or later, I just don't want him to hear it from someone else. How would I explain it to him? Life could be so damn complicated and yeah, I fucking know half of it is my own fucking ego that's making it harder. Too bad I ain't fucking changing.

I leave the room, allowing Corrado to think he is pulling me along. His little legs run to keep up with my stride as we make our way downstairs.

A Devil in Red
Leo

The entire mansion is abuzz. I have never fucking seen it so alive. Marcel doesn't really host parties, and those that do take place are usually in the pack hall.

"Leo, Corrado, ah, you are both ready," Marcel says, coming over, wearing a pair of beige pants and a black shirt.

"Care to share what exactly this party is for?"

"For Azura!" Corrado adds.

"Yeah... I get that," I say, tugging his cheek before looking at Marcel seriously, mind-linking him.

But the reason? She's not a part of this pack, and neither are we... a couple.

No, seems not, or not officially, but she is still carrying your child. A part of this pack's future, he replies through the link.

The pack knows that.

Exactly, and so we are celebrating that, Marcel says with a small smirk just as we hear the sound of heels running over.

"Alpha Marcel, I have the last of them. Sorry I'm late," Winona's breathless voice comes.

We both turn to see Winona holding a small box. She is wearing a one-sleeved fitted ruched black dress that reaches just below her knees, with her hair curled. She looks incredibly different than she usually does, and for a moment I don't recognise her. Sure, her make-up is light, but I have never seen her in black since she always wears neutral colours, and she is always without make-up.

"Oh, wow, Winnie! You look so beautiful," Corrado compliments her, making her blush.

"Thank you, Corrado," she says, smiling gently at him before turning to Marcel, who seems to be even more surprised than me.

"Yes, you do… wow, I didn't even recognise you. See, I told you you'd look great, although you exceeded even my expectations," he murmurs, looking her over, which only makes her shy away. I raise an eyebrow, clearing my throat as I cough lightly, placing my fist in front of my mouth.

Marcel looks at me sharply before shaking his head and looking down at the box she is holding. "Thanks," he says before Winona hurries away. "Ah… yes, I need to go put this away." He frowns slightly, shaking his head, and walks off.

What the fuck was that? Corrado giggles before he runs out to the back garden. That was fucking weird. *I need a drink.* I look around, ready to head out to the back garden, when her scent suddenly hits me. Intoxicating, alluring, and so fucking seductive. *Fuck.*

I know if I turn, I am only going to fucking make it harder for myself.

Just turn. She looks incredible, Jax's voice comes, and I glance back to see him walking down the hall towards me, dressed in navy pants and a white shirt.

I glance towards the steps, freezing when my eyes fall on her as my breath catches in my throat. My heart races in my chest, my eyes flashing as they trail over her, drinking up her appearance hungrily, from those red-soled black heels up her sexy legs that are glistening with a gold shimmer. She wears a two-toned, blood-red satin dress that is ruched from the middle, accentuating her killer curves. Her hand runs down her hip almost as if smoothening her dress or emphasising how fucking hot she looks. She wears a few rings, and her nails are painted the same shade as her dress. The neckline of her dress dips, showing off her sexy cleavage and every inch of her skin glistens just like her legs. Her breasts rise and fall, making me want to ravage her right now. I look up at her face, and if I wasn't fucking gone before...

Her black hair is curled, falling over her one eye. Her make-up is sultry and dark, and those matte red lips are begging to be devoured. Our eyes meet, ice blue against bright blue, her heart pounding. No one else matters or exists as they all fade away. It is just the two of us; we are being pulled together by this fucking intense chemistry between us.

She doesn't look like heaven because she is far too fucking hot for heaven to ever be able to handle. Only hell could handle this level of heat, temptation, and sin that she is exuding. She is the fucking epitome of sexiness, and I am ready to bend the knee if it means I can have her until my last breath...

She reaches the bottom, and although I see her eyes run over me and hear her erratic heartbeat, she doesn't speak even a word to me and instead turns to Jax.

"Hi."

"Hey, you look incredible. You both do," Jax says to them both as Azura raises her hand, running her fingers through her curled locks. My eyes fall on her back, and I realise she is wearing a gold upper armband that looks fucking hot.

"Thanks," Song says with a smile.

"Aww, thank you, Jax," Azura adds, her voice holding a hint of seduction.

So, she is going to play like that? With my own fucking men? Irritation seeps through me, and the urge to hide her from the fucking world tempts me. *I don't fucking think so.* I am about to speak when the sounds of footsteps reach my ears. The front door opens, and three familiar scents fill my nose, one of them only making my irritation heighten.

Azura looks behind me, her eyes shadowing before she looks away.

"Hey, guys," Eric greets us, and I turn to see him with both Jackie and Nikki. Jackie is dressed in a simple dress, whilst Nikki has obviously tried her hardest. She is now watching me, her heart racing.

Like what I'm wearing? she asks suggestively through the link. I frown, about to reply, when Jackie walks over to Azura.

"Azura, can I have a word?" she whispers just as Azura is turning to leave with Song.

"Sure," Azura agrees, drawing my attention back to her. *Fuck, does she have to look so fucking good?* They walk to the side, my eyes on Azura's ass. *Damn, I fucking need to get laid.*

"I'm sorry. I'm sorry for everything he did to you. Forgive me?" Jackie whispers. She is speaking silently, but I can hear her still despite the music. Azura tilts her head, her glossy locks just itching to be played with.

"You didn't do anything wrong. It's fine," she says, smiling gently. "It's really okay. Please don't worry."

"Thank you," Jackie replies as both women embrace.

"Stay strong," Azura whispers just as a sudden wave of heat washes over me, but it vanishes as soon as it comes.

"I won't forgive him. I will reject him," Jackie whispers, her voice breaking.

"Rejections won't break us. We will come out of this stronger," Azura replies as she moves back.

"Thanks," Jackie says, smiling at her. I frown, wondering what had happened to me moments earlier.

"Come on, let's go outside," Azura tells Jackie, motioning Song over. She doesn't spare any of us a further glance as she leaves, hand-in-hand with Song, her other hand on Jackie's back.

"Wow, the Luna is angry with me?" Eric asks quietly.

"She isn't the Luna, Eric," Nikki says sharply.

"She bears our Alpha's mark, so she is," he replies firmly. For someone who was always welcoming, he seems a little hostile towards her, not that I fucking care. Either something is in the fucking air, or my senses are on overdrive.

I turn, leading the way out back, not wanting to spend an extra minute in Nikki's presence. She really fucking doesn't get the damn fucking hint.

You know, I'm glad you dumped her, although it took you two years, Jax remarks through the link.

Yeah, and just so we're clear, stay away from Azura. She's mine, I growl back. I frown in shock at my words as my eyes meet Jax's, who simply smirks. What the actual fuck is going on with my mood?

My eyes find her, her scent reaching my nose, and I inhale deeply, watching her talking to Winona and Corrado. Is it just me, or is it too fucking hot out here?

"Leo-" Nikki's hand touches my shoulder, and, in a flash, I grab it, ripping it off me.

"I have been fucking patient with you, so before I have you thrown out of here, get the fuck away from me," I growl.

Silence seems to fall over the garden of people, and I can feel all eyes on me, but I don't really fucking care. The hatred that is coursing through me feels stronger than ever. Nikki's eyes fill with tears as she tries to tug free.

"You're hurting me, Leo."

"Then don't fucking touch me," I reply venomously, letting go of her.

I turn away only for my eyes to meet with Azura's. She is frowning slightly as she watches me with concern, her eyes a blinding silver. The predatorial growl of my wolf fills my head as I look at her. I need her; no. I fucking want her.

My mind feels murky.

Claim her so the world fucking knows she is mine.

Suddenly, time that had seemed to slow down returns to normal, and the rush of sound surrounding me returns. Chattering, laughing, and music...

"Leo?" Jax asks quietly, now concerned. I glance at him, frowning before motioning a member of staff over and taking a glass of wine from the tray.

"Since we're at a party, drink up," I say casually, downing my glass in one. My eyes once again find Azura.

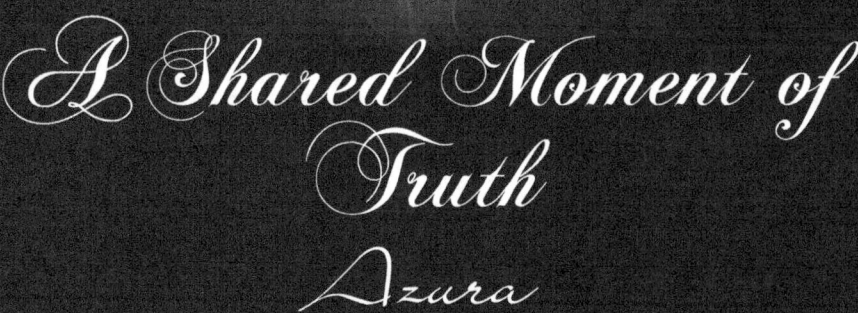

A Shared Moment of Truth
Azura

It is so hard having to pretend that he has no effect on me when all I want is to be in his arms. My entire body reacts to just his presence being near. I feel giddy, and even breathing becomes difficult. The way that he looked at me had made my core clench in desire, but Nikki's presence had been a pretty good slap in the face. I was thankfully able to keep control of myself and give him the cold shoulder.

I walk into the garden, gulping in a desperately needed mouthful of air. I need something to drink.

Jackie excuses herself, so Song and I make our way over to the drinks bar, both of us grabbing a non-alcoholic drink.

"So, was that her?" Song asks softly.

"Yup, that was her," I reply, downing my drink and sighing.

"I can't believe she's in red," Song murmurs, trying to keep her voice down.

"Hmm, I guess it was purely coincidental," I reply. Song frowns.

"I don't like her, and something tells me it really wasn't coincidental."

"Yeah, me neither," I mutter.

Just then, I feel an intense wave of power and turn sharply to see Leo holding Nikki's wrist. Even a fool can see there is nothing casual or intimate about it. Leo is exuding rage.

"I have been fucking patient with you, so before I have you thrown out of here, get the fuck away from me," he growls, making everyone go quiet. My heart thunders as Nikki looks near tears. Harsh, but she kind of deserves it.

"You're hurting me, Leo." *Then get the fucking hint that he doesn't want you.* Seriously, this woman...

"Then don't fucking touch me," Leo hisses, letting go of her.

He turns suddenly, his eyes meeting mine. Once again, he is consuming me, those steely magnetic eyes burning into mine. My heart pounds as he looks at me with such power, almost as if he is devouring me from where he stands.

"Leo?" Jax calls him. He looks away, and the intense connection breaks. I turn, too, my heart thumping.

"What was that?" Song asks curiously. "I've seen mated couples, but that... damn. You two really have crazy chemistry, and that sexual ten-" She stops when I give her a pointed look. I don't know what to say. Even my head doesn't feel right.

"It's probably the hatred," I reply, frowning slightly. She rolls her eyes with a knowing smile.

"You are stubborn, and I think so is he... he is, after all, a Rossi," she muses, glancing around.

I can tell people are more tentative towards her, with her being a witch. Some want to approach me, but because of her, they are not coming closer. This pack is a lot more isolated than the rest. Magic isn't always accepted, but I am glad no one is giving her hateful looks.

I can feel Leo's eyes on me, but I don't turn back, not wanting to be caught up in him again.

"Oh, wow, Azura, I like your lipstick," Corrado compliments as he runs over. He had spent the last hour watching me get ready and complimenting my dress, but I hadn't put any lipstick on at that point.

"Thank you! Oh, we're both wearing red, we should get a picture," I suggest, smiling down at the gorgeous little cherub.

"Yes, we should," he agrees just as Marcel comes over, smiling slightly.

"You ladies look beautiful. Welcome to our pack, Song. I hope your stay is going well," Marcel says, offering her a handshake.

"Thanks for allowing me to stay, Alpha Marcel. Yes, it's going great, thanks," Song replies, taking the offered hand.

"Any friend of Azura's is welcome here," he says, turning to me. "My, you remind me of your mother right now." I smile. I don't need to ask him if he meant Mama or Indigo. We all know who the queen of red is.

"Thank you. Winona really does have an eye for clothes," I say, brushing my hand along the fabric.

I was pleasantly surprised to find that she was the one who had purchased the clothes that Leo had gotten for me. Despite her wearing neutrals and plain clothes, she has an eye for this stuff. I mean, some of that lingerie was pretty sexy. I would never have guessed she was the one who had purchased it. Even seeing her in that black dress that Marcel had ordered, for a woman of her size and shape, it had complimented her slender frame so beautifully. In return, Song and I had made sure she wore some make-up to go with it, and right now, I wonder how the hell Leo hadn't chosen her for his girlfriend over Nikki. Winona is gorgeous inside and out, and I can tell she is getting a lot of attention as she walks around, making sure everything is in order. She is even the perfect mother to Corrado.

"She does indeed," Marcel agrees, smiling down at Corrado as he almost touches his hair, but Corrado ducks.

"Not the hair, Grandad, I styled it," he says, smoothing his fringe.

"Sorry, son, my mistake. Do forgive me." Marcel grins as he turns to look over towards Leo. "Well, I think I should make a toast before we get this party on its way."

"Thank you, Marcel, for tonight. You really didn't have to do this," I say.

"It's nothing at all," he replies as Corrado observes Song.

"Who are you, miss?" he asks innocently.

"I'm Song, a friend of Azura's," she says, crouching down. "What's your name?"

"I'm Corrado Herrmann Rossi," he says proudly, puffing out his chest. Song laughs.

"Oh, that's an impressive name!" she compliments.

"Yes, it is," Corrado agrees.

"Can I have everyone's attention?"

I turn to see Marcel standing next to Leo, who now has an alcoholic drink in his right hand and a cigarette between two fingers of the same hand. He turns towards Marcel, as always oozing sex appeal, power, and arrogance. Damn, he looks so good tonight. Hell, when does he ever not? Why was he created so perfectly? I force my eyes away as everyone becomes quieter, giving their Alpha their full attention.

"As everyone knows, I called this party on short notice, and I appreciate everyone who dropped everything to attend. The guest of honour for this evening is Azura Westwood. It's an immense pleasure to have her here, amongst us. As you all may already know, she is holding a very important part of this pack." Marcel speaks clearly. At his last sentence, I see Leo look at him sharply, his gaze snapping to Corrado as Marcel continues smoothly. It is clear he isn't about to just drop the bomb on Corrado. Leo needs to just calm down. Idiot.

"Tonight, we drink and celebrate in their name. I do have another announcement; however, as it is not part of this celebration, I will save it for the end of the evening. Thank you, and enjoy the evening, ladies and gentlemen," Marcel finishes, raising his glass.

Everyone claps, and I can feel many eyes on me. I can hear the whispers as well. But surprisingly, there aren't any negative ones, aside from a few emphasising me being a Westwood. Most are just compliments on my looks and how amazing I look. *See, Leo? Your pack thinks I'm pretty decent.*

"Can I offer you ladies a drink?" Jax asks, coming over with a smirk on his lips. Instantly, I feel Leo's attention on me, and I smile slightly.

"Thank you," I say with a toss of my hair, taking a glass as Song thanks him and takes the other.

"The décor looks good," Jax remarks.

"It does, doesn't it?" I agree.

"It goes perfectly with the colour of Azura's dress," Song says.

"Only nowhere near as beautiful," Jax says with a wink. Oh, he is doing it on purpose, and I am certainly not complaining. "Want to dance?" he asks as I sip the wine.

"Jax," Leo's menacing voice comes. Jax smirks.

"Maybe later, my lady in red," he says lightly before turning and walking over to Leo. So, what is he going to do? Growl at any man who comes near me? I am about to say something to Song when Eric and Jackie come over.

"Congratulations on that news," Eric says, smiling as he glances at my stomach and gives me an exaggerated wink. I smile back and, reaching over, pat his face.

"You look extremely handsome, Eric, but my fingers are itching to work on that beard of yours," I say with a smirk. I'm sure behind that beard of his, he has a handsome face. Bless his soul; some men suit beards, but in Eric's case, I am sure a trim would do him much good.

"Thanks, Lun-Azura," he says sheepishly, smoothly moving away from my touch. I give him a dangerously sweet smile. Maybe I'll focus on Jax instead. He seems to not be as scared of Leo as Eric.

"Oh, Brody!" Corrado calls, running after another child and leaving the four of us alone. Jackie stifles a yawn, massaging her temples.

"If you want, I know a spell or two for getting good sleep," Song offers.

"I'm okay, thanks though," Jackie replies, smiling gently, although it doesn't reach her eyes, which are full of pain. Earlier inside, I had just wanted to get away from Nikki, but now I want to speak to her.

"Mind if Jackie and I leave you for a bit?" I ask the other two.

"Not at all, I'll keep your friend occupied," Eric replies with a grin.

"Yeah, take your time," Song says before turning to Eric. "Want to dance?"

"Me? Sure," Eric says with a shrug. "Not that I've danced much..."

"Don't worry, I'll lead," Song replies with a laugh. I smile slightly and look at Jackie, who looks concerned.

"Is everything okay?"

"Yeah, come on," I say, feeling Leo's eyes searing into my back.

We walk together through the crowds, although I have to stop a few times as people introduce themselves and compliment me. A few even ask about the baby.

I see Song begin dancing, her grey dress with silver sequined flowers sparkling under the fairy lights above. Although Eric said he couldn't dance, he is doing pretty well.

When we are finally on the other side of the garden near the pool, which looks pretty with red petals and floating LED candles, we take a seat on one of the benches as an upbeat song begins playing. Even though we are in a secluded area, we can still hear it clearly. The rustle of the leaves in the trees and the whisper of the wind can be heard too.

"Don't be scared. The only person who should be worried around me is Leo," I say with a small smirk. "I didn't say it inside, but, you know, if you ever want to talk about anything, I'm here."

"Thanks, and I'm not scared! Just more... just disappointed. I feel like I really did fail you. You know, I didn't even tell Nikki about the baby, but with Emmet, sometimes we just tell our mate things we usually wouldn't. I never thought he'd tell anyone, but yeah, he didn't. He just did way worse." Her voice is pained and bitter. "I can't believe he'd ever hurt a child, but he did. He did." She runs her hands down her face. I place my hand on her knee.

"I get that. It's just the way the bond is. Sometimes I wonder why the Goddess makes some pairings, like, did she make a mistake?" I murmur, looking up at the faint moon that is beginning to get brighter. Like mine. Why did she pair us?

Hitting a Nerve
Azura

"Yeah, I get what you mean. Before Emmet, I had a boyfriend. In fact, I never liked Emmet back then. He just... we just clashed. Our mentalities were different, although both of us were friends with Leo. That was until the bond... and it's so strong... it consumes you. And I know a bond with an alpha is even more intense. Anyway, when the bond snapped into place, everything changed. My boyfriend and I broke up. Although I knew it really affected him, it was the obvious thing to do when you find your mate, and he didn't make it harder for me. Soon I found myself falling for Emmet. Then, when I was completely smitten, deeply in love, that's when it all began. I'm sorry I lied to you and in front of Eric, too. I just, I just didn't know what else to do." She hugs herself, staring at the water in the pool. "I'm going to reject him. I know it's going to be hard, but I'm going to do it. I should have done it ages ago when he first began hurting me to vent his anger."

I look at her, my heart pounding. I never wanted another Indigo to suffer, and seeing the strength in Jackie makes me proud.

"You know... my biological mother was a victim of abuse, too, at the hands of her mate. When I realised what Emmet did that night, I lost it. I felt like I was seeing her in you. Her mate ultimately led to her death. She was said to be a feisty, confident young woman, yet years of living with an abuser wore her down until she was just a shell of the woman she once was," I say quietly.

"And seeing that situation between Emmet and me triggered you. I don't blame you, and I'm grateful that you at least stood up for me. You did the right thing, even when I asked you not to," she murmurs. She stiffens and turns to me sharply before taking a furtive glance around.

"Are you okay?" I ask, concerned. She nods, taking hold of my wrist.

"I just... I think it's time I did the same. Break a promise for the better. After all, you are the sister of Kiara Rossi, the Queen." Her voice is barely above a whisper. I frown, looking at her, wondering what she is about to say when we hear the sound of a thud.

"... care!"

Nikki?

We both stand up and look towards the back of the garden. What is she doing here?

"That was an order, which you should have followed," Winona's gentle yet firm voice follows.

"I don't follow your rules. You are just an omega who works for Leo! Remember that, scumbag!" Nikki yells, her voice filled with irritation and disdain. Jackie gasps, and I feel my own anger rising. Alejandro had abolished the rank system years back, and it is obvious from Jackie's gasp that it is something that isn't meant to be happening here either.

Where are they? I scan the garden and spot a flash of red from beside the small cabin. Nikki...

"I know I'm an omega, but Alpha Marcel gave me a job to do, and I made it clear that the dress code was anything but red, and you knew why. Is this why you called me here?" Winona asks.

"Really?" Nikki scoffs.

It is obvious that against someone like Winona, Nikki isn't going to back off, and it is clear neither did Jackie as she hurries towards the sound of their talk.

"Yes," Winona says quietly.

"I don't really, like, care. If I want to wear red, I can. Besides, I look better. Leo is mine, not that skank he knocked up."

"That is our Luna!" Winona's shocked voice comes.

"Nikki!" Jackie exclaims at the same time, just as the two women come into view. Nikki, who is standing there with a bottle in her hand and her arms folded, gives me a dirty look.

"Oh, look who it is: the skank herself," she spits.

I raise an eyebrow, quickly looking Winona over. She looks visibly upset, and I don't miss the mark on her shoulder. My eyes flash dangerously. Nail marks... my gaze snaps back to her.

"Let's make this clear, once and for all," I say calmly, walking over to the shorter woman in red. She looks back at me defiantly, and my eyes blaze silver.

"You aren't anyone important here," Nikki says, tossing her hair. "You saw Leo, right? I mean, no matter what I do, he still has a soft spot for me."

"Do not do this, Nikki. Please," Jackie pleads as she hurries over to the distraught Winona.

"You know, if you want to play bitch mode, I'm more than happy to entertain you," I say, crossing my arms. "First of all, I'm the mate, so whether we're together or not, I have priority over you. Secondly, stop calling me a skank, or any other name, before I rip every last hair off your head because I swear on the Goddess, piss me off, and I will order a few kilos of superglue and dunk it on your head, so don't test me," I warn, my voice calm and sinister. I am right in front of her now. Our eyes lock as she tries to challenge me.

"Whatever." *Yeah, that's all you got?*

"You know, I tried to stay away from Leo when I found out he had you by his side. So, really, do explain how I'm the skank. He dumped you. Your issue is with him, not me. Remember that."

"You can't talk to me like that, he doesn't even want you. Weirdo," she retorts, just as I am about to turn away. *Oh, bitch, you did not...*

"Oh, yeah?" I snap now, turning back to her. "Why can't I? And do not fucking call me names!"

"If Leo saw your true colours-"

"Bitch, please, I don't sugarcoat shit for anyone. Do you think Leo doesn't know the real me? I'm not you, acting all sweet and shit in front of him. I'm always the real me! I'm damn pissed at how you treated Winona and those marks on her shoulder... something tells me Leo will be more fucking pissed at the fact that you hurt her than about me offending you," I growl.

"Let's leave. I don't want the night spoiled for you." Winona tries to calm me down, discreetly trying to cover her shoulder with her hair. I reach over, taking hold of her wrist and trying to calm my own emotions at the same time. They had worked hard on this evening; she is right, I shouldn't spoil it.

"Yeah, walk off. Just remember, even after finding you, Leo chose me. He came right back and straight into my bed. The sex was still as good as ever. I mean, not once did he seem to remember you... ouch," she taunts in her sing-song voice, making me stop dead in my tracks. She hit a sore spot, and she knows it as she lets out a laugh.

"Azura..." I hear Jackie's voice, but I am far too pissed to care.

I turn, letting go of Winona, ready to slap that bitch. I storm over to her, raising my hand just as her eyes widen, realisation hitting her, but before my hand connects, a tattooed one grabs hold of my wrist, stopping me in my tracks. Intense sparks course through me, but they don't drown out the pang of pain that squeezes my heart.

He is protecting her.

"Stop," he commands, his voice emotionless and cold. A small smirk crosses Nikki's face as I turn my gaze to Leo.

"You two really are perfect for one another," I say bitterly, and with that, I rip free from Leo's hold. No one, and I mean no one, can tell me to stop.

My heart is thundering as I look at Nikki's arrogant smirk. I turn away, and, as expected, I see her relax a little. In a flash, I spin around and punch her straight in the nose. A sickening crunch tells me I have broken something. She yelps in pain, stumbling back. The blood spurting from her nose is pleasantly satisfying.

Leo's eyes flash, widening in surprise as he looks at me. I look back at him, my heart thumping violently.

"You really can go to hell, Leo. I fucking hate you," I spit.

"Azura, listen to me." I am about to turn away but stop and look back up at him.

"Just shut up. I'm done. I'm fucking done with you," I say quietly, stepping closer.

His eyes flicker with emotions, but before he can speak, I raise my knee, aiming right where the sun doesn't shine, and knee him hard. He growls as he staggers back, his eyes blazing a steel blue before he doubles over from the pain.

"I hope those piercing just got buried right in, or better, ripped off!" I hiss, before shoving him hard and storming past both Jackie and Winona.

I am done. I am fucking done.

"Azura!"

I ignore Leo, speeding up. I want out. I want to be gone from here right now.

"Azura, fuck, at least listen!" Leo's growl comes as I walk past the bench, but before I can get any further, he grabs my arm, spinning me into his arms. Why the fuck is he so strong?

"Let go of me!" I hiss, ready to rip him apart if he doesn't let me go, but instead, his other arm tightens around me as I struggle against him.

"Not until you listen. Can you fucking stop acting fucking crazy?" he growls.

"I am! Okay? I'm fucking crazy, so just let me fucking go!" I shout, digging my nails into his chest, but it doesn't seem to bother him.

"Azura, fuck! You're fucking misunderstand-"

"No. No, I'm not because she's right. You rejected me and came back to her," I say, my chest clenching. "Let go of me."

"Not until you listen."

Our eyes are locked, our hearts racing, and even in my anger, I can feel his body moulded against mine so perfectly... yet not for me.

"There's nothing to hear. You already made it clear the other night."

"That's different. This situation with Nikki is-"

"The very fucking same, so unhand me before I rip your dick off," I growl, my eyes blazing.

"No. What are you going to do?" he challenges equally stubbornly.

With all the force I can muster, I hook my leg around his ankle and yank. At the same time, I pull back, shoving him towards the pool. His gorgeous ice blue eyes fly open as he goes toppling backwards, but before my smirk can cross my lips, his hand shoots out, grabbing my arm as he pulls me straight into the water with him.

These Choices of Ours
Azura

I gasp when we hit the water with a huge splash, drenching us both. Leo's arm snakes around my waist. He even has the damn audacity to place his hand on my ass for a fleeting moment, a moment that makes my entire body tingle with pleasure. I hate that.

I try to yank away, clawing at his chest. These nails are sure coming in use! I don't get far, though. He grabs my wrists, twisting them behind my back and against my waist, holding them there with one hand as he presses me against himself. His white shirt is practically see-through, sticking to his skin and making my core clench at how damn good he looks soaking wet.

"Behave," he commands, his steel blue eyes boring into mine.

My heart is thumping as I continue to struggle, but it does nothing but make my core throb. I can feel his dick rubbing against me, and despite how my entire body feels hot and the way our hearts are pounding, I refuse to calm down.

"Fuck, let me go!" I hiss, my own eyes flashing.

"Not unless you calm the fuck down. I seriously won't let go. Fuck, just listen," he growls, his free hand taking hold of my chin. My heart thumps loudly, my anger only rising.

Where have the others gone? I scan the area. Weren't they just here?

"If you're looking for Winona or Jackie, they left on my command. It's just the two of us," he says huskily, forcing my chin up and making me look at him. Strands of his wet, brown locks tickle my forehead as his words sink in.

"Shame. Now, how about I excuse myself so you and your bitch of an ex can take a swim in here?" I hiss, twisting my hand until I feel his wrist and digging my nails into his skin. He frowns, and I'm not sure if it is because of my words or the pain, but frankly, I don't give a shit.

"Do you have to resort to violence and anger every fucking time?" he growls.

"And if I do? What's it to you?" I snap, wriggling in his hold. His nose brushes mine, and my breath hitches, making me tense. We are too close.

I can see behind his anger and cold exterior the carnal hunger he is trying to hide. I can feel him hardening against me, and I pray that my own arousal doesn't reach his nose.

"Fine. Struggle as much as you want. I just won't let go until you're done," he says, running his tongue along his lips. That piercing...

I swallow hard, glaring at him. I need him to let me go. For more reasons than just my anger.

"I think I broke your girlfriend's nose. Why don't you go check up on her?" He frowns.

"She isn't my girlfriend."

"Oh, but you just had to protect her when she deserved that fucking slap," I growl, whipping my head to the side, trying to get my hair off my face. He runs his fingers through my hair and brushes it all back slowly, almost as if enjoying it. I hate the way my body wants to relax into him, the way I relish the sparks. I can feel his hard dick against my lower stomach, and that same intense heat seems to settle between us.

"Yeah, she did, but that's not how lunas behave." My eyes flash, and my chest squeezes.

"I'm no luna, remember? So, I'll behave however the fuck I want. Let go of me, or I swear, I'll claw your eyes out," I hiss. He suddenly lets go of my wrists, but just when I am about to pull away, his arm snakes around my waist firmly.

"Go ahead. Even if you do, I won't let you go until you have fucking listened to me," he growls, his voice low and husky.

My heart thunders as I massage my wrists, wanting to attack him. But when he is letting me, it doesn't seem so tempting anymore. Instead, I reach up, running my fingers through the long hair on top of his head and twist my fingers in it painfully, yanking his head back. He doesn't even flinch, simply looking down at me, that chiselled jaw set in an arrogant pout.

"I don't mind pain. Carry the fuck on," he remarks, looking down at me with those gorgeous eyes. *Fuck, stop looking so good.*

"What do you want to say? Hurry up before I mess up that pretty face of yours."

He smirks, "If you wanted to, you would have already done it. Right, beautiful?"

"Don't play me." His words sting. *Don't call me that when I'm nothing to you.* His smirk fades, his eyes looking into mine almost as if searching for something.

"I didn't mean to," he replies quietly, his gaze dipping down to my boobs. My dress is soaking, and it is clinging to me even more than before. That's all it is to him. The pull of the damn mate bond.

"I've decided after we go to Alejandro's pack, I won't come back here," I tell him quietly, looking up into his eyes, our faces only inches apart. Surprise flashes in his eyes as he searches mine. His heart thuds, and I wish I could read his mind, but his walls are up. His scent is like a dream... it makes me giddy, and I feel safe and free.

"The day after tomorrow then. Alejandro's set up the meeting between Rayhan and me," he says quietly. So soon...

I swallow and nod slowly. Maybe it is for the best.

"Cool. The sooner the better." *Won't you stop me? Do you want me in your life or not Leo?*

"Yeah... I guess." *Guess not.*

"What did you want to tell me Leo?" He seems to hesitate, and I realise his grip on me has eased.

Pull away, Azura.

I don't. I can't. Is this the last time he'll hold me? I let go of his gorgeous chocolate locks, slowly running my hand down the back of his head, paying attention to the sparks that run through my fingertips. This feeling... it is magical.

For a moment, his eyes close, almost as if he is enjoying my touch, but I doubt that. He sighs, opening his eyes, and a few strands of his hair flop sexily in front of his face.

"Nikki, she means nothing to me. What she said is a lie. After I met you and rejected you, it was hard trying to act like everything was normal. We did get intimate a few times, but once you taste something so fucking incredible, nothing else feels good enough. You keep saying that you aren't good enough for me, but you actually caught my eye at that club before the mate bond even snapped into place. It's not every day you see a woman just saunter into a strip club alone, looking so fucking fine. Anyway, the only reason I rejected you was because of my anger at the Elite, even though Elijah and Scarlett Westwood have never done anything wrong, they are still related to the Rossis through Kiara. I just... it wasn't you. I marked you because despite it all, I fucking wanted that... but, yeah..."

My heart is thundering, a storm of emotions inside of me, but I don't get it. Why now when I am brave enough to leave? He can't keep playing me again and again.

"Why tell me this now?" I ask quietly. Why? Why confuse me when it's obvious you hate me? He frowns, looking down, only for his gaze to dip to my breasts. "My face is up here, you old perv," I growl, trying not to let the pain of his constant rejection hurt. A ghost of a smirk lingers on his face as he looks at me arrogantly.

"You can't stop me from looking wherever I want. I just told you because I don't want you to fucking misunderstand because of Nikki." He becomes serious once more. "So, since you're leaving... want to tell Corrado tomorrow about the baby?" *You really won't stop me from leaving...*

"Sure," I reply, trying to ignore the pain inside, and I keep my walls up. "What do you want to do about this baby? Do you want to, like, visit? I mean, I want him or her to know their father. Weekly, monthly, or holidays even?" Why is this so painful? Even with his arms around me, holding me firmly as if he never wants to let go, we are talking about splitting up. He looks down before looking back into my eyes, but this time the look in his eyes is regret.

"It doesn't really matter."

Wow. I nod, trying to fight my emotions as I slowly pull away. His words hurt. He doesn't even want to be a part of this baby's life...

"Okay, whatever," I say, wading through the water to the edge of the pool. I am about to pull myself out when his arm snakes around me from behind, and his hand rests on my stomach.

"Even if I'm not around, I'll make sure you and our baby are taken care of," he says quietly, caressing my stomach gently. These emotions... these tingles... I tense when his lips brush my shoulder, his hand slipping my strap that had slid down, back up. I scoff, glad he can't see my tear-filled eyes.

"Yeah, I'm sure you would, but don't bother. The Westwoods don't need your charity. No one needs a father who isn't there for them. Maybe it'll be easier just to tell my baby that you're dead," I say coldly, pushing his hands away from me. His heart is thudding, but I don't care if my words fucking hurt him. I want them to hurt him just the way he hurt me.

He doesn't reply, and I place my hands on the edge. I am ready to pull myself out when his hands grip my waist, lifting me out. I don't look back as I get to my feet, walking away with whatever confidence I can muster, not once looking back.

Goodbye, Leo. Just tomorrow night, and we will be going our separate ways...

I return to the party, feeling so many eyes on me. Well, I can't blame them; I am dripping wet. Song runs over the moment she sees me.

"Zu!" She stops, whispering a spell, and I feel an intense cold surround me, and then a tingle before I look down. My dress is completely dry, but my hair is still soaking and completely straight once more. "Come on, I can quickly fix your make-up before dinner is served, and we can get your hair dried. I wish I had some of my crystals..." she says, smiling gently, almost as if she knows what I am feeling. Only the strongest of witches can do many spells without crystals, herbs, and engravings. Those at the level of Delsanra Diana Rossi, Raihana Somers, and the high witches of the Coven.

I nod, not arguing, as I allow her to lead me away.

She has begun working on my hair, and I don't speak. I don't say anything. Just her silent comfort is enough. After she has fixed my make-up, we return to the garden. Nikki is nowhere in sight, and I really don't want to see her anyway.

Marcel calls me over to sit with him, but I refuse to be anywhere near Leo for any longer than necessary. I am relieved that Marcel doesn't push it when I decline. I force myself to eat, and I do my best not to even look at Leo. He has changed out of his wet clothes and is now in a pair of jeans and a grey shirt. Corrado is sitting at Leo's table, and I can hear him asking why I'm not there. I'll miss him too. Will he ever get a chance to play with his sibling?

Eric, Jackie, and a few other pack members are at our table, but I can barely focus on anything, whilst Song keeps them occupied enough for no one to bother with me.

I learned from Song that Jax had left shortly after Nikki, and she wasn't sure about anything else. Well, I sure hope that Marcel does something about it because I'm not so sure Leo would. Okay, maybe he would since he did put his best friend into prison, but still. I will make sure Winona gets justice. No one should have to suffer at the hands of another like that. I plan to fill him in on what happened after the evening is over.

Raj, the Beta, comes over to congratulate me on the baby just as dinner is finished. He has his mate, Kesha, and his seven-year-old daughter, Katrina, with him.

"I really am pleasantly surprised to learn who you are, so once again I would like to welcome you to the pack," he says. I shake hands with both him and his mate whilst smiling at their daughter, who seems to be an innocent soul. Then again, never trust kids. She shies away, hiding behind her mama. I give her a wave before turning back to Raj.

"Thank you, you were polite and welcoming even then," I reply simply. It isn't like I am here for long anyway. Once they move away, Song gives me a small smile.

"You okay? Wait, dumb question," she murmurs, shaking her head.

"I'm fine," I reply, my eyes looking around the garden at the pack members. Somehow, I feel comfortable here. I have gotten used to all of them. A life that isn't meant for me. I exhale slowly, placing my hand on my stomach.

Give me the strength to remain strong. I am a fighter, not someone who succumbs to another.

"Zu..." I turn to her, my eyes flashing silver with a surge of strength and confidence.

"I'm fine, Song. Stop stressing. I may not have a crown, but I'm a fucking queen, and I sure as hell can handle anything that comes my way," I reply, frowning deeply, my eyes blazing. I am, and I am not going to let anyone break me. She smiles.

"That's the Westwood Devil I know."

I give her a smirk just as Marcel stands up. Winona hurries over to him, passing him a box before Marcel takes it and turns to everyone.

"Azura." I turn my attention to him as his eyes find me, and he smiles. "I just want to say thank you for being here with us tonight, and gracing us with your presence-"

"Yes, thank you, Azura!" Corrado adds. "We love having you here!" Several people chuckle as Marcel lifts his grandson into his arms.

"I've loved being here, too," I reply, trying not to get emotional. I will have to break his heart, too. I can see Leo sitting there like the arrogant jerk he is from the corner of my eyes.

"Then stay forever, okay? You won't even have to cook," Corrado offers, smiling brightly. *Sorry, baby, I can't promise that.*

Marcel's smile falters, almost as if he can read my expression. I force a smile, but the moment he returns it with a sad one of his own, I know he knows. Knows that I'm not going to stay...

"Thank you for everything," he says quietly. Our eyes meet, and I don't reply, breaking eye contact. He looks down at the box Winona has brought and opens it with one hand, placing Corrado down as the little boy peers into the box.

"Ooo," he says dramatically, only piquing everyone's curiosity.

"I know everyone probably doesn't want to hear me rambling on and on, but there is one final thing I want to share with you all. Something important. My real reign as Alpha started roughly nineteen years ago when we were freed from the reign of terror inflicted upon us, by one whose name I won't mention tonight. Nineteen years later, this pack has thrived. Despite everything we went through, we are now a normal pack with everything we could have hoped for. I'm sixty now; damn, I'm getting old."

"Not that old, Alpha! You still look amazing!" One of the middle-aged she-wolves yells, whilst everyone agrees, making Marcel smirk slightly.

"Thank you." Yeah, like I said, fine wine.

"He is so handsome," Song whispers, making me smile slightly as I nod in agreement.

"Well, I still think I want to just sit back and just spend time with my grandchildren now and so, tonight, I will pass that title to my son, Leo-" He stops, his gaze turning to Leo, who is looking at him sharply. They are conversing through the link.

"Daddy will be Alpha!" Corrado says excitedly.

Yet, I don't feel good. Despite the excitement that is rippling through the garden, something between the look of coldness in Leo's eyes and the confusion in Marcel's, tells me things aren't going as planned.

"Now I know why there's a special knife," Corrado adds. My heart thumps as Leo stands up.

"Leo..." Marcel begins, unable to hide the sadness and hurt in his voice.

"I don't need the title to be Alpha. I no longer fucking want it. Keep it," he says coldly before he turns and walks away, leaving a shocked silence in his wake.

A Disappointing Failure
Marcel

The evening that I hoped would go well has gone downhill. Both Leo and Azura had returned soaked from what was obviously a dip in the pool, but, with it, their moods had gone down. Not once did they even talk after that, obviously avoiding one another.

I am now ready to make the announcement to pass Leo the position of Alpha, a title he deserves, and one I wish I had given him years ago.

"Well, I still think I want to just sit back and just spend time with my grandchildren now and so, tonight, I will pass that title to my son, Leo-"

Stop. What the fuck do you think you're doing? Leo's voice is harsh as he speaks through the link, his eyes flashing when our eyes meet.

Giving you something I should have years ago, I replied through the link.

It's too fucking late to fix that shit. I told you I fucking forgive you, but I don't want it. Don't do this.

"Daddy will be Alpha!" Corrado's voice comes, but Leo's words have shaken me. "Now I know why there's a special knife."

Leo, you deserve this.

I said I fucking don't want it, he replies venomously, and I am taken aback. Leo stands up, his demeanour cold and hostile.

"Leo..." I don't know what to say. This isn't how tonight was meant to end.

"I don't need the title to be Alpha. I no longer fucking want it. Keep it," he says coldly, staring me dead in the eyes before he turns and walks away, leaving complete silence behind.

I don't know what to say, unable to ignore the pain I feel. I can feel all those pairs of eyes on me as I slowly sit down again. The hope I felt that maybe things could be better has just come to an abrupt end. Raj is making conversation, and he soon manages to replace the shocked silence with the hum of chatter.

"Grandad... why did Daddy say no?" Corrado asks.

"I'm not sure, son," I reply, patting his back as Winona comes over.

"Come on, Corrado, do you want to go to the dessert table?" she asks him. I glance at her, grateful that she has come over, and she gives me a small smile.

He'll come around, Alpha, she says through the link as she helps Corrado down from his seat.

I hope so, I reply before they both walk away.

The night has ended in disappointment, and the plan that had sounded great this morning, ended up a total failure. Everyone has slowly retreated, and I don't miss the sympathy in the eyes of many. After all, Leo had rejected the title outright.

I sigh heavily, running my hand through my hair. I have gone wrong somewhere. The silence feels loud, just like it always does in this huge house. Even though I know Corrado is now fast asleep in Leo's old room upstairs, he had been upset and confused after Leo walked out. Although Azura, Winona, and Song had tried to cheer him up, it is obvious Azura herself isn't completely here. In the end, Winona had taken him away to turn in for the night. Song and Azura will be staying the night here, too. Neither refused when I suggested the idea. The sound of someone walking in the hallway comes occasionally as the staff are clearing the garden and house up.

I am now in the kitchen, making myself a cup of coffee. I feel far more tired than I should. It feels like I am losing it all.

Hope. I had let myself hope, and even that has been ripped away from me. I truly feel like I have only ever had a few years with Leo. Under Endora's reign, it was all a blank, and what I remember is a hazy blur. The snippets I remember are tense, and I just remember a child who always held a fire in his eyes. As he got older, from the age of six, he began pulling his weight and acting far older than he was. When I first created this pack, we had become closer and I hoped he got the childhood he had been deprived of, but that all changed once Rayhan had come here.

Now just when I thought I'd get him back, I lost the chance. Even if he said he has forgiven me, I wonder if it is just because he really just doesn't care anymore. I tried to reach him several times through the link after he left, but he has his block up.

I frown, realising the coffee machine isn't working. Great. The sound of footsteps and Winona's light, citrus scent reaches my nose. She always smells refreshing. I don't turn as she enters; I had asked her to come to see me when she was finished putting Corrado to bed. Azura's words before she had retreated to bed aren't forgotten.

"I know it's not my place, but a member of your pack was disrespecting Winona today. And although I think I broke her damn nose, I don't think Leo will be holding her accountable for her actions, so I hope you do. Winona's shoulder has scratches, too."

I frown as I push the button a few more times. Why isn't this stupid thing working? I shake it, cursing internally, before a pale, slender arm reaches out and switches the socket on. Right...

"It was switched off, Alpha," Winona says, smiling politely. "You asked for me?"

I look down at her. She is still in that black dress, and it is easy to forget that she is the same Winona I know. I look away smoothly, watching the coffee machine for a second before turning back to her and nodding. Crossing my arms, I lean against the worktop.

"Yes, I did. Azura mentioned something that happened earlier, regarding someone disrespecting you," I begin. Instantly, she rubs her arm, looking away for a second.

"It's sorted, Alpha. Azura defended me, and it really wasn't much."

"I will be the judge of that. Tell me exactly what happened," I command lightly. My gaze falls to her bare shoulder, and, reaching over, I brush her hair back, feeling her tense at my touch. My eyes take in the faint marks of nails left behind. She heals slowly, after all.

Winona is one of Leo's additions to the pack. He had found her when he was twenty. He had come home, visiting England due to setting up some business or other, and he had found her being bullied at a human orphanage. She had come of age and was being forced to leave, although she had nowhere to go. Along with having nowhere to go, she couldn't shift. She wasn't a rogue, but she also had no idea what pack she was from. With nowhere to go and living in fear, Leo had dropped her here with the pack before leaving once again. Although one would think she is an omega, I'm not so sure. Due to the fact that she can't shift, I think people simply assume that. Besides that, the rank system is long abolished.

"It was my fault. I asked Nikki why she wore red when I made it clear the Lu- Azura was going to wear red," she says, tugging on the sleeve of her dress, avoiding looking me square in the eye.

"Nikki." I frown. I was surprised to see her show up, and it was obvious she had been there to cause problems. I feel disappointed in her.

"Will you explain exactly what happened earlier?" I ask, taking the coffee mug and passing it to her. "Take a seat."

She looks down at the mug, her eyes full of worry, but when she sees me making myself a second mug, I am sure she understands that I am not going to take no for an answer.

"*...and then Alpha* Leo told us to clear the area..." she finishes after spending the last fifteen minutes telling me exactly what had happened. I sit back, frowning as I look at her. She looks almost disappointed in herself. I shake my head, exhaling.

"That is... I wasn't expecting that from Nikki. I will make sure she is confronted about this myself." She nods and sips her coffee. Watching her, I realise she is forcing herself to drink it.

"You don't like coffee," I state. She freezes, looking up at me sharply.

"I, uh..."

"You could have refused, Winona," I say. Reaching over, I take the cup from her, placing it aside. Her heart is racing.

"I'm sorry, I just, I'm a tea person." I raise an eyebrow.

"Well, I'll remember for next time."

"Next time?" she asks, startled.

I smirk, "Am I that bad company?"

"Not at all, Alpha! I just... I'm sure you have many others you can have coffee with," she says quickly.

"Yeah, I guess but then, not even my son wishes to be around me, it seems," I say quietly, looking down at my hands. The faint scars that run up my hands and arms catch my attention for a second. They are mere lines now, scars that left no memory, yet the internal scars are the ones that Leo is suffering from.

"I'm sorry, Alpha. I'm sure one day he will come around. Please don't blame yourself," she says quietly, giving me a small smile that lights up her pretty face.

It is weird; tonight, it is almost as if I am seeing her for the first time. Those large brown eyes, her angelic features. It is strange how I have looked at her countless times but never really seen her.

She blushes under my gaze, and I hide a smirk, rather amused.

"It's late. Stay the night."

She freezes, her eyes widening, her face flushing, and if that isn't enough, her heart starts thundering loudly, and I almost chuckle. As much as I want to tease her, it isn't really appropriate.

"I'm sure Corrado will be happy to have you here when he wakes up, especially since his father just left. He is clearly upset over it all."

"Yes... did we make a mistake tonight?" she asks, the flash of guilt in her eyes making me feel disappointed for her, too.

"I honestly don't think we did anything wrong, but both are far too stubborn. Leo isn't helping matters either. We did what we could, even if it didn't work out the way we wanted. We did it with good intentions, and that's the important thing. Thank you, Winona, for all your help," I say with a small smile. Yeah, I do think I have messed up, but I am not going to allow her to blame herself. I just hope that Leo really does realise what he is doing before it is too late.

A Mama
Azura

It's the following day, and after a restless night, I have gotten dressed in blue jeggings and an oversized white top. Leo has just popped over, saying it is time to talk to Corrado. There is something different about him, but I can't pinpoint what it is. He is wearing a white tank top and grey sweats. His hair is a sexy mess, and it is obvious he has been running his hand through it a lot, and he looks a bit pale. But there is something else; did he even get any sleep?

He first takes Corrado to the garden, and I see him crouching in front of him and, from what I can make out he's apologising for last night. Corrado stands with his arms crossed, looking displeased, before hugging him and smiling. Children really are so innocent.

They come in soon after, and Leo looks at me.
"Shall we?"
"Sure," I say, turning away from him and allowing him to lead the way.
"It's so fucking hot," Leo mutters as the three of us head to the lounge.

Have you even planned what we'll say? I ask him through the link. I really don't want to do this, but I know for Corrado, I will. At least he is letting Corrado know that he will be a big brother, despite not really seeming to care about seeing this baby again.

No.

I frown slightly but say nothing, not knowing how this is going to play out. I shut the door behind us, the airy room making the sounds of our heartbeats sound even louder. I don't respond as I cross my arms, and Leo sits down, making Corrado stand in front of him.

"Daddy, why are you so serious?" he asks worriedly.

"There's something that I need to tell you."

You or we? Leo looks at me, and I stare back emotionlessly. If he wants help, he will have to ask for it.

We. It feels like an eternity. The pain and intensity of his gaze make me look away first.

"There's something that the both of us want to share but I need you to understand, okay?"

"Okay, Daddy," he says, looking up at me. "Did you and Azura make up?"

"Make up?" Leo raises an eyebrow.

"Because last night you argued," he states. I feel awful. So, even this kid picked up on the fact something is wrong.

Nice going, I say icily. Leo doesn't respond.

"This is about something else."

"Oh..." He is clearly disappointed, and I can't help but go and sit next to Leo for Corrado, but I make sure there is a gap between us.

"Azura is having a baby," Leo says hesitantly. For once, Mr. Smartass obviously doesn't know how to go about this.

"Ooo," Corrado says, turning and staring at my stomach. "But, Azura, your belly isn't big... where is the baby?"

"It's still little yet," I reply with an amused smile. He really is such a cutie. I see Leo massaging his neck as Corrado's face falls.

"Where's the baby's daddy?" he asks before looking at Leo worriedly. He steps closer to him. "Can we still keep her? Please, Daddy, you can be Azura's baby's daddy, and I will be a good big brother! We will take care of her!" he whispers. This is going to hurt him; do we need to do this?

A Mama | 351

"Corrado, it's... no, we can't." Leo places his hands on his shoulders. Corrado's face falls, and he looks absolutely devastated. Leo glances at me – a silent request to help. If it didn't involve this cherub, he could have gone to hell.

"Come here," I say, smiling gently at the child and forcing myself not to let my emotions show. I reach for him, and Corrado shuffles towards me, looking confused.

You really don't know how to do this shit, I shoot through the link. Heck, even I don't know what to do.

"Corrado, this baby is your daddy's which means you *are* going to be a big brother," I begin, realising that no matter what angle we do this from, it is going to hurt him.

"I'm going to be a big brother!" he gasps, his eyes widening before they sparkle with excitement. "Daddy! I'm going to have a baby brother or sister!" he exclaims, looking at his dad excitedly.

"Yes, you are, kid," Leo replies, smiling faintly at him as he ruffles his hair.

"So Azura and the baby can come live with us. The baby can share my room!"

Yeah, explain shit to him now.

Our eyes meet before he looks at Corrado, but when I think he'll be able to explain it, he simply looks away, frowning.

"Corrado." I reach for him once more, and he looks up at me with even more adoration than before.

"Yes, Azura?"

"I won't be staying here; I'll be returning to my own pack but I promise you I will send you lots of videos and pictures. And we can video-call and visit. I promise," I explain, my heart breaking as I watch the little boy crumple before me. His excitement is dissipating, and it is replaced by sheer sadness, his eyes glistening with tears that begin welling up in his eyes fast.

"Why?" he whispers, raising his fisted hands to his eyes as he begins crying. "Doesn't Azura want to be my mommy, too? I promise to be good. Does Azura not love me? I won't ask for anything, Azura, I promise I'll be a good boy." I can't stop my own tears from streaming down my cheeks as I drop to my knees in front of him and hug him.

"No, baby, it's not you. I promise I love you so, so, so much," I whisper, my voice breaking.

"Then why won't you be my mommy, Azura?" he sobs.

"Corrado... enough. Come on," Leo's voice comes, thick with emotion, as he pulls Corrado from my arms even when I don't want to let go of him.

"But, Daddy..."

"That's an adult decision, Corrado. Azura is leaving tomorrow," he says quietly before he stands up, lifting his son into his arms and walking away. He pauses at the door and glances back at me; the look of regret is clear in his eyes. I can hear Corrado's sobs as he asks what he did wrong.

"We have to go to Azura, please, Daddy. Don't let Azura go. Don't let our baby go away. I be a good big brother, Daddy. I promise..."

Corrado's words break my heart, and they are the only thing that I can focus on as I kneel there, silently crying my heart out. *"Doesn't Azura want to be my mommy, too?"*

I clamp my hands over my mouth to stifle my sobs. I can't breathe properly; the pain is almost suffocating me.

Of course I want to be your mommy. I would have been the happiest person in the world, as would this baby, to have you in our lives.

Then why don't you fight for what you want, Azura?

I freeze, staring at the floor in front of me, suddenly feeling cold at my own question. Why don't I fight?

Because it just hurts too much...

Maybe I'm not as strong as I always thought I was. Since when do I cry over something?

Fight for what you want.

I run my hand through my hair, my mind a whirlwind of thoughts. Leo is giving me whiplash... but... when I stormed off last night, he came after me. Maybe he just needs some time. It is like at the same time he is telling me that he wants me, then he pushes me away. Why?

Maybe there is more to it, but it is hard for me to think past my anger.

Look harder... Not everything is as it appears...

Dante's words return to me, and I know that whatever he says always means something. *Look harder...*

Am I missing something? Is there a reason for Leo's hot and cold attitude? Goddess! What should I do?

"Corrado!" Leo's voice comes, and I hear the front door slam shut. I stand up, rushing to the window, only to see Corrado running down the lawn as fast as he can, and I frown, my heart breaking for his little soul. Even when Leo picks him up with his little fists pummelling his shoulder, I am still unable to let it slide.

Fuck this, for Corrado and this little one. I suddenly feel as if I have been hit with clarity. I know what I need to do, even if it isn't going to be the easiest. I run from the room and out into the front garden.

"Corrado!" I shout, running over to them. He turns, looking at me with his tear-stained face.

"Azura..." I hold my arms out to him, ignoring the spark that rushes through me when my arm brushes Leo as he holds his arms out to me.

"It's okay, kiddo. You can keep me. I will be your mama if you want me to because I really do want to be your mama, too," I whisper, hugging him tightly. I hear Leo's heart race and sense his intense gaze upon me, but I ignore him as Corrado hugs me tightly, his tears soaking my shoulder.

"Promise, Azura?"

"I promise."

I promise on everything I have. I don't care what Leo thinks or what I feel.

I don't know how, but if it means making a child happy, a child who I am lucky enough to want me to be their mama, then I will sacrifice my own ego for him because no child should feel unwanted, especially by those they love.

The Beginning of a Haze
Leo

I stand there, looking down at her as she claims my son as her own. A thousand emotions course through me. She didn't accept him for me, but because she wanted to. Fuck, why is this so fucking intense?

"*I really do want to be your mama, too...*"

Her words shake me. No, she didn't come running out of that house for me, but for him. Her eyes do not once find me as she wipes those tears from Corrado's face. She is still young, wild and temperamental, but she has a heart of fucking gold, and he is lucky to have her.

She hugs him tightly, and, at that moment, I selfishly wish I could enjoy the fucking time I have left but I don't want her to get attached to me unless I can fucking make it. Then again, I think she already has. There is no denying what we feel for one another. I really need to find a solution... a solution to living.

I step away from them, feeling another wave of heat rush through me. I don't know what the fuck is wrong, but I need to get checked out.

I cast one last look at the duo. This right here is my fucking world. All three of them.

Live for them... But I am not a god, and I don't have the power to restore life.

Jackie, I don't really feel great. Mind if you can do a check over? I ask through the link.

Right away. Her voice is full of worry as I cast a final look at Azura and Corrado before I walk away.

I'm on my way, I reply through the link.

Twenty minutes later, Jackie looks up from the monitor.

"It's just, I don't really know why you feel like that. There's no huge change from the last time. I mean, your organs are failing, but there's nothing majorly different," she muses worriedly.

"I don't know, I just feel really hot, and everything seems fucking heightened. Restless. Even my wolf seems to have spurts of rage and... hunger?" Explaining this is fucking weird, and last night I had a dream where I was fucking Azura. Yeah, not the first but it sure as fuck woke me up this morning with such a fucking hard-on that I had to jerk off to the thought of her in the fucking shower. But I am not going to fucking tell her any of that shit. She frowns slightly.

"That's strange." She looks me over as if trying to find the answer. "Anything that seems to make it worse? Overexerting yourself? Or any certain time of day?" I frown.

"Not really."

"I'll try to see what I can find. Right now, nothing is coming to mind. Your temperature is normal, and there doesn't seem to be anything unusual."

"Hmm, maybe it's nothing."

"I doubt it's nothing. I'll run some further tests on your blood," she says, her eyes shadowing as she looks up at me. "You need to ask for help, Leo."

"Let's be serious, Jackie. Kiara can't regenerate something that is fucking dead. These artificial replacements aren't cutting it; I failed," I say, leaning forward to take a look at the results.

"Leo, you did well, but maybe if she could cure the poison that is the cause, at least then-"

"Then what? I keep trying to use some shit that isn't working; heck, I'm not even able to fucking shift without having to replace all that shit."

"Does Azura know?" she whispers hesitantly. I look down at my hands.

"What do I tell her? That I'm dying?"

"Maybe she can help," she replies worriedly. "You are going to Alpha Alejandro's pack tomorrow. There must be something. They have powerful witches; this damage was done by a witch. Perhaps it's a witch who can help? Don't give up hope, Leo." I don't want to. I don't want to give up, but is it wrong to try to prepare for the inevitable?

"They can do nothing."

I've left the hospital and gone for a light run to clear my mind.

I'll talk to Kiara, but I know the answer already. I also know I need to tell Azura, especially since Kiara will probably fucking tell her. Then there is the fact that she has refused to leave. I didn't expect her to do that, to agree to Corrado's request. Last night, after Nikki was a right-out bitch, I panicked when Azura stormed off. It had proven to me that no matter how much I fucking act like I can live without her, I want her. The intense urge to fucking stop her and tell her that she's the only fucking one I crave had overcome me, but then I back peddled before it got deeper. Yeah, I know I am fucking hurting her again and again.

Fuck it all. I frown as I slow down, covered with a layer of sweat after an hour of running. My hair flops in front of my forehead as I light a cigarette. My mind ponders over the future as I make my way around to the back of the apartment block and lean against the wall to smoke. Should I put her down as legal guardian to Corrado after me? At least I know he'll be okay.

Last night I commanded Jax to go after Nikki and deal with her since I didn't fucking want to see her again. Then I put my block up so no one could fucking contact me. I can't deny that I feel guilty about how I handled the Alpha title shit last night. I ordered Jax to suspend her position on the training regimen. She is to move out of my apartment block, and her personal allowance as a member of this pack will be cut down. Plus she will do one hundred hours of community work at the daycare since I know she doesn't really like kids. Lastly, she is to apologise to both Azura and Winona.

Jax?

Here.

Did you handle it? I ask.

Yeah, she's been moved to the far block, so she shouldn't be around your apartment any longer. Eric did have a firm word with her, too. Alpha Marcel had a word with her this morning as well. I let him know of the punishment you decided, and he said to have her do an extra fifty hours of cleaning around the training areas, Jax replies, clearly finding it amusing.

Good. Make sure she apologises to Winona in Dad's presence. He doesn't reply, and I frown.

Jax?

Yeah, yeah, I'm listening, I just... nothing. I'll make sure the Alpha is there. What about Azura? I frown, wondering what the fuck his problem is.

Bring her down before we leave for Alejandro's pack tomorrow. I'll make sure she does so in front of me, I reply coldly.

I heard what she had said, and although I don't want to give her the fucking time of day, I am not going to let it slide. I don't trust her not to play up in front of anyone else. She insulted Azura, and that is something I need to fucking make sure never happens again.

I like you defending our rightful Luna. It suits you.

Yeah, whatever. Did anyone check Emmet's office and apartment?

Yeah, Ace has some stuff that he'll go through.

Keep on it. I need answers, I say, feeling suddenly suffocated as I pull my top off and toss it to the ground.

Got it.

I toss the cigarette on the ground as I end the link, once again feeling the same weird energy that enveloped me yesterday.

Jin, any update on tracking down the bullets?

Making progress. Li Sheng is on one right now. I will keep you updated.

Okay.

Fuck, what is wrong with me? I clutch my head, feeling the surge of my wolf's restlessness inside of me. Why is it like he wants to take over? I can't afford to shift right now.

I slump against the wall, taking deep breaths, suddenly feeling fucking hungry for sex. Can't fucking blame me. It's been far too fucking long.

"Leo?" The voice is distant, yet it still seems to ring in my head. I can hear the rushing of blood in my veins and my wolf's hunger growing. A she-wolf...

A hand touches my arm, fucking burning me, and I let out a menacing growl.

"Leo!" My blazing eyes snap open only to see Nikki standing there looking concerned.

"Leave," I growl, feeling something inside snap. My canines elongate, and my eyes rake over Nikki, my heart pounding as the urge to fuck consumes me. Nah, that shit ain't me.

"Leo?" she says seductively, almost as if she knows what is going through my mind.

"Leave," I growl, feeling myself harden.

I suddenly realise exactly what is happening, something that is fucking rare, but it is definitely pointing in that direction, and it fucking makes sense, too.

Shit. Azura. I want Azura.

The menacing growl of my wolf fills my head, and my eyes blaze as she grabs my arm once more.

"Babe..." Her hand on my arm sends shots of pleasure south, and I know I need to get away.

"Back off," I thunder, my Alpha command rolling through my voice as I shove her hand off me.

Suddenly, a seductive blossomy scent fills my nose, making my eyes flash. It holds hints of jasmine, tuberose, rangoon, and something so intoxicating, yet there is only one name I can give it: *Azura*. This is the scent I fucking crave.

Azura is nearby. The image of her under me as I fuck her flashes through my mind, and I sniff the air. *Find her.*

I make to leave when Nikki blocks my path.

"Leo, what's wrong?" she murmurs, running her hands over my shoulder. A part of me just wants to fuck her, and a larger part wants me to find Azura.

The Beginning of a Haze | 359

"Don't touch me..." I growl, trying to move away, but it feels like my body is resisting.

"Leo-"

"Didn't he just tell you not to touch him?" Fuck! That is the voice that I want to hear, screaming my name as I fuck her hard.

Suddenly, Nikki is pushed away from me, and I lean against the wall, my eyes on Azura. Everything from those fucking plump lush lips of hers to those breasts is driving me crazy. Her top is loose, but it drapes over her breasts so fucking teasingly. She shouldn't be here because all I fucking want to do was rip her clothes off... and ravage her.

"This is between us. You're not his woman," Nikki retorts.

"No, maybe not, but I'm his baby mama, and as long as I bear his mark with no rejection, I hold way more importance than an ex, and unless you want a few more bones broken, I'd leave if I were you," Azura growls as she comes over, moving me away from Nikki.

The moment her hand touches my arm, I suck in a breath. A wave of coolness and pleasure rushes through me, and I feel myself throb. Oh, fuck.

"Leave, Nikki, or I swear I will fucking kick you out of this damn pack, or worse, toss you in fucking prison," I growl menacingly. I don't even look at her, my eyes on the sexy doll in front of me. I hear Nikki run off, but it only excites me, knowing I have this blue-eyed devil alone.

"Leo, what the hell is wrong with you?" Azura's voice asks, and I look into those gorgeous eyes.

"I'd leave if I were you," I growl huskily. I still grab hold of her hand despite my words, raising it to my lips. Fuck, I want her. I press my lips against her hand, inhaling her scent slowly.

"Leo..." Her eyes widen, and I yank her close, pressing her up against the wall. "No, what's up with you? You're acting weird," she whispers breathlessly. *Oh, yeah, keep talking in that tone.* Her words make me smirk slightly.

"Baby mama, huh? I prefer the term, `Sexy Mama'," I murmur, my gaze dipping to her lips as I lock my arms around her waist. Those lips aren't only fucking gorgeous but felt so damn good when they were wrapped around my cock. I throb as white-hot pleasure spreads through me.

"Leo, you're acting damn weird. Wait, did she drug you?" She sounds aghast, but all I want is to taste her. "Leo!" She digs her nails into my shoulders, making my eyes flash in approval.

"No, but if I were you, I'd leave because what I feel right now won't end well if you stay. I'm in haze, Azura. I'm sure you know what the fuck I'm talking about."

"Haze?" She seems to be thinking hard, and when her eyes widen with realisation, she stares at my mark, her heart thundering, "I marked you and we didn't..." I wrap my hand around her neck, squeezing slightly as I crush her body between the wall and my body, so she can feel exactly how hard I am. "Oh, fuck," she moans, her grip on my arm tightening.

"Exactly, so unless you want me to pin you against this very fucking wall and fuck you like a whore, I'd leave," I warn huskily. Her eyes flash, her cheeks take on a faint pink hue, and the scent of her arousal fills my nose. Fuck...

Everything is fucking heightened. It is too much, from the way her body feels against mine to the way she is touching my shoulders. I can feel her hardened nipples through her shirt and bra grazing against my chest. I want her so fucking much.

"What are you going to do..." She swallows, and I let my walls down, allowing her to see exactly what I fucking want to do to her. Her cheeks darken, and she bites her lip as she looks at me with eyes that are full of obvious lust. Her heaving chest only drives me crazier.

"Unless you run, little she-wolf, I will devour you," I growl, letting go of her neck and slipping my hands under her top, stroking her smooth skin. Sparks erupt through me, and she tenses, sighing softly at my touch, her body reacting to the skin-to-skin contact.

"I think you forgot I'm not afraid of the big bad wolf," she replies seductively as I wrap a hand around her neck, pinning her against the wall once more.

We aren't together... I can't let her get attached.

Through the lust and haze, I see her frown slightly, and I struggle to raise my walls once again.

"You're a little too late to think about that," she replies as I lean closer, my nose brushing against hers. "Unless you want to spend the next few days like this, I suggest you give in. No strings attached?"

The Beginning of a Haze

We are already tied in every fucking way. Deep down, I know that if I do this, it is going to make things a shit load worse but I want to taste her, even if it is for the last time. Will she pull away? Will she back out just like she had last time? I should talk to her, but...

Damn, I know that if I do, it is going to be fucking hard to pretend it is just one fucking night...

Who cares, right? I'll fuck that pussy until she's left dripping cum for fucking days.

The questions and thoughts that swirl in my mind are suddenly pushed to the back, overridden by the lust and hunger I feel for her. There is only one way to find out what the outcome of this will be and that is to stop thinking and enjoy the fuck out of her. We'll ask the questions later.

I run my tongue over her lips slowly, making her sigh in pleasure, her body arching as she presses herself against me. She tastes tantalising.

I throb hard against her. Just when I think I am feeling a little more in control, suddenly, a surge of intense heat rushes through me, making my skin burn, and I groan. Her tongue flicks out, running along her lips before I caress it with my own, making her whimper in pleasure.

You just lost your chance to leave, I growl through the link.

I already gave that chance up, she moans back as our tongues play with each other's sensually.

All of the self-control I have fucking snaps, and my lips come crashing down against hers in one fucking hot kiss that sends explosive fireworks through me.

Fuck it all, I'm taking her.

All I Want

Leo

O ur hands are all over one another, and the way her touch feels... fuck, I missed it. My entire body reacts to her as fire does to oil, exploding with fucking pleasure.

I groan as I plunge my tongue into her mouth, tasting every fucking inch. She is an addiction, and I could just kiss her for fucking ever, but there is far more I want to do to her. I break away from her lips, kissing her along her jaw and neck hungrily.

"Leo... let's... fuck!" She gasps when I suck hard on her mark, that gasp changing into a lustful moan as her hand runs over my cock. I lean into her touch. *Oh, yeah...*

As much as I fucking want to fuck her here against this wall, I am not about to take her out here. Not this time...

"Let's get out of here," I murmur, raking my hands down her back before I grab her ass and lift her up.

"Good idea," she whispers, kissing my neck sensually as she wraps her legs around my waist, her arms around my neck, and her hand running through my hair. Fuck, that feels so good.

Even through the hunger and lust, I am trying to cherish this fucking moment, not wanting it to ever end. I carry her down the back of the apartment block to my separate, personal entrance and scan my thumb. The door slides open, and we step inside. My lips find hers once again as I pin her up against the wall of the lift, letting go of her and cupping her face and neck, deepening our kiss. Her heart is pounding as she kisses me back with equal passion, fighting for control, control I am not going to relinquish. I am about to reach for the up button, but I hesitate. I don't want to take her where she isn't the first woman to go. I don't want anything negative to come to her mind so I hit the down button. I'll take her to my cave, where only the two of us have ever been.

She growls when I win our battle of dominance, and I kiss her harder, sucking hard on her tongue. The growl instantly turns into a little mewl of pleasure.

That's my little she-wolf, I murmur huskily through the link. I am rewarded with a whimper as she clings to my shoulders.

The doors open, and I carry her through to the bedroom, one hand on her ass, the other opening the door before I kick it shut behind me. I walk over to the bed just as she breaks away from my lips, gasping for air. I take the chance to reach down, pulling her oversized top off and tossing it to the ground, my eyes drinking up the side view before me.

She is fucking gorgeous. Her firm breasts are squeezed into that light pink bra. Through the skimpy lace, I can see her hardened nipples. Fuck, I love that shade, a perfect match to her lip colour.

My eyes flash as I grab them, bending down and taking one in my mouth. She grips my shoulder, arching her back as she presses her stomach against me, moaning in bliss.

"Fuck, Leo..."

I place her on the bed, leaning over her as I litter her breasts with kisses, pulling down the straps of her bra and peeling it off her boobs. I let them spring free, my dick throbbing hard at the sight of her firm round tits. The things I fucking want to do with these...

My eyes flick to her blazing silver ones, and reaching up, I kiss her slowly. Despite wanting to fucking ravish her, I want to cherish the fucking moment, too.

Her hands lock around my neck as she kisses me back, our lips once more fighting for control. She tries to flip us, but I keep her pinned down.

You're such a fucking tease, I murmur through the link as I lace her hands with mine and pin them to the bed by her side.

I won't go down without a fight, her breathless reply comes as she runs her tongue over my lips before I capture it in my mouth.

I'm okay to fight with you as long as you're ready to get down and dirty afterwards, I growl back, nibbling on her bottom lip.

Her eyes flutter as she moans in ecstasy before she uses all her strength to roll us over. I smirk, allowing her. I like the fact that she doesn't just obey. She has the spark to keep up with me and my shit.

She looks down at me victoriously, kissing me once more as another wave of heat courses through me. Fuck...

She cups my face, looking into my eyes; her touch is soothing as she claims my lips in a kiss. I kiss her back roughly, hungry for more. My wolf surfaces, my eyes flashing as I reach behind her to unhook her bra, but instead, I rip it off before tossing it aside and grabbing her breasts once more. I yank her close as I suck on one of her nipples.

"Fuck, baby, that's it," she whimpers in approval, cupping her breast as I suck on her nipple hard before tugging on it between my teeth. She bites her lip as she sighs softly. Her other hand tightens on my shoulder as her fingers graze my neck.

I bite down, and she gasps, her eyes fluttering open as she looks down at me, her eyes full of lust. I smirk slightly, holding her gaze as I tug on her nipple slowly before releasing it. Her heart is pounding as I lick the hardened bud teasingly. Her lips part as I switch to the other breast, slowly licking and flicking it.

Like that Baby Girl? I ask, throbbing hard as I squeeze her breasts.

I do... fuck, she responds as I reach up and kiss her lips once more.

Sitting up, I push her back onto the bed. Getting on my knees, I straddle her thighs as I admire her sexy figure beneath me. My hands hook into the band of her jeggings. I slide them down her hips, my gaze lingering on her stomach for a moment. I place sensual kisses down her stomach, making her sigh softly as I pause, placing a tender kiss on the centre. *Hey, little one...* Her heartbeat picks up, and I wonder if she realises the change. I smoothly continue kissing her down to the band of her pants.

The scent of her arousal makes me growl. Another wave of heat rushes through me, and my claws come out, ripping through the fabric of her jeggings as I yank them off, leaving her in only a tiny pink thong. *Oh, yeah...*

"You really are the sexiest fucking she-wolf I've ever seen," I murmur, forcing myself to stay in control. My wolf's hunger is growing, and I am fighting to keep him at bay.

I look into her eyes for a moment before leaning over her and grabbing her throat as I kiss her bruisingly, pulling her up onto my lap. I run my hands down her back before dropping back onto the pillows. I tap her ass, yanking her thong up between her ass cheeks and admiring the way the fabric strains against her pussy. I can't fucking wait to bury myself in that pussy. Grabbing her hips, I lift her up to my shoulders.

"On my face, beautiful," I command, running my tongue along her inner thigh, licking up her juices that have trickled out of her dripping pussy. Sweet and tantalising. Fuck.

She gasps as I push aside her thong and lick her between her slits. She is already fucking wet, the taste of her juices making me want to fuck her right now. Every lick makes her whimper in pleasure.

Another wave hits me, and I can feel my claws elongating, my heart thundering as my wolf fights to come forward, wanting to fucking devour her as I had promised to do... and I fucking will.

"Oh, fuck, Leo, that's it!" she moans, her hands braced on the wall above us, her legs parted as she grinds against my face.

My eyes are blazing, my aura is surging around us, and my claws are digging into her thighs. The way she tastes makes pleasure rush through me, and I plunge my tongue deeper. I feel my tongue changing into that of my wolf's, growing longer, burying further into her. She groans in pleasure, her head tilted back, her back arching as she rolls her hips against my face. I have never experienced this before, but the feeling of having my tongue buried deep within her, is fucking intense and so fucking good.

"Leo... Goddess!"

I am fighting for control, on the brink of shifting as I fuck her harder with my tongue. Somehow, that balance between wolf and man is in my hands, and I relish that power and the way this fucking feels, that control that has me on edge. Fuck, if I could taste her so deeply every fucking night I would...

"Oh, fuck, baby," she whimpers.

Delivering a sharp slap to her ass, I squeeze her ass cheeks, playing with her thong. My nose is rubbing against her clit as I tongue-fuck her, lost in her. Her scent, her taste, her touch, her very presence.

I fucking love her.

My heart thunders as I realise what I have just thought, but it isn't a lie. Everything about this woman is perfection. I don't want another day or night without her.

"Leo! I'm coming," she moans.

Then come for me. Let me see you squirt those juices like a good little girl, I growl, plunging my tongue deeper into her. There is no better sound than hearing her illicit moans as she calls my name in the throes of passion.

"That's it! Keep going! Oh, fuck, Leo, right there... fuck!"

I can feel her sides clamping around my tongue. Her juices leak out of her as she lets out a scream that is cut off mid-way from the intense pleasure that she is in. Her entire body tenses as her orgasm rips through her. I don't stop until she has ridden it out. Wave after wave hits her as I carry on my assault of her pussy until she is left a shaking mess.

"Fuck... Leo..." she whimpers as I slip my tongue out, pushing my wolf back and licking my lips.

Her entire body is convulsing from the orgasm, and with it, her walls come crumbling down, letting me feel the full force of her emotions. Her love, her desire, her pain, her vulnerability, and her insecurities. I can feel her emotions at the back of her lust-hazed mind, how she feels she is inferior to Nikki, that she isn't good enough for me, how I don't want her...

Despite the hunger that is consuming me to fuck her senseless, I know I need to tell her that she is way fucking more than she is thinking before I do. After how I ended our first time, I'm not going to leave space for regrets this time. Even if it is our last fucking time together, I want the memory to stay with her forever.

I slowly lift her off my face, her body still shaking from the orgasm. Her plump lips, sore from the kissing, are parted as she breathes heavily. Her black silk hair falls in front of her face. I sit up, wrapping my arms around her.

"You are way fucking more than her... more than good enough for me... are you fucking crazy to think otherwise?" I whisper huskily, kissing her neck over the mark that adorns her neck. My words have her heart pounding violently.

"I thought we already agreed that I'm kinda crazy, and a total psycho?" she replies breathlessly, moving back. She yanks my sweatpants and boxers down together, her eyes flickering silver when she admires my cock, licking her lips. *Fuck, Azura.*

The hunger to fuck her is getting stronger, and I force myself back, looking into those gorgeous blue eyes.

"Well, then you should know that you really are the only one I fucking want. As for being a psycho..." I reply, yanking her thong down.

She slides it off before I grip her hips, lifting her onto my lap once more. She bites her lip, her breasts looking so fucking good as she reaches down, wrapping her hand around my dick and guiding it to her entrance. I suck in a breath when the head rubs against her clit. The sparks of the bond ripple through me, stronger than ever.

Fuck! Focus...

I looked up at her, my eyes flashing a magnetic steely blue.

"You're my crazy psycho, and I really wouldn't change anything about you. You're perfect, Azura, just the way you fucking are."

Her heart thunders, her eyes filled with emotions I can't read, but I don't give her a chance to reply. With those words leaving my lips, I slam into her, burying myself deep into her. She cries out, gasping for breath as she tries to adjust to my size. I let out a breathy chuckle, feeling a coolness wash over me as pleasure rushes through me.

"What's wrong, little she-wolf? Can't take it?" I tease, massaging her hips. My gaze dips to her pussy with that thin Brazilian strip. She looks as hot as the first time, if not more... and with my cock stretching her like that, she looks even fucking sexier.

"Oh, I can fucking take it perfectly," she whispers back, twisting her hand into my hair as she tilts my head up, looking into my icy eyes, one's that I know hold a thousand fucking emotions.

"Yeah?" I reply, running my tongue along her lips until she slips her tongue out, and I flick hers sensually before sucking on it for a moment. I throb inside of her, my senses screaming at me to fuck her till we drop.

"Yes," she replies, and with that one word, she begins riding my cock like a fucking pro.

I let go of all my restraints as I began meeting her thrusts, fucking her harder than ever.

Pushing Boundaries
Azura

He sits up, wrapping his strong arms around me.

"You are way fucking more than her… more than good enough for me… are you fucking crazy to think otherwise?" he murmurs huskily, kissing my mark sensually. Despite these crazy sparks, it is his words that have my heart beating erratically.

"I thought we already agreed that I'm kinda crazy and a total psycho?" I reply, unable to stop myself from sounding so breathless.

I don't know what to think. From the moment I saw him pushing Nikki away, the way his eyes had found me and softened, I was unable to stay away.

Look harder… push further… It is the same thing. I just need to break down those barriers of his, but I wasn't expecting these words.

My heart is pounding, and the whimper of my wolf's excitement and happiness is obvious. She, too, has forgiven our mate.

I move back on my knees in front of him and slip my fingers into the band of his sweatpants and boxers. I tug them down, my gaze raking over those sexy abs, the perfect groove of his V.

My eyes flash silver when his large cock comes into view. I lick my lips, my throat suddenly feeling dry. My pussy clenches as I take in those piercings, how hard it is, the tip wet with precum. Just the thought of having him inside of me again is making me feel all hot and a thousand times hornier.

I can feel his burning gaze on me, and I look up meeting his sexy eyes. Oh, fuck, he is all mine.

"Well, then you should know that you really are the only one I fucking want. As for being a psycho…" he begins, reaching over.

He skims his hands down my hips and tugs my thong down. I climb out of them, and he grabs me by the hips, lifting me into his lap. I bite my lip as I reach down, wrapping my hand around his cock and biting back a moan as I run my hand along the shaft. Fuck, I can't even wrap my hand around it.

He hisses when I guide it closer, letting it rub against my clit. Oh, fuck.

His eyes meet mine, and they flash a magnetic steely blue.

"You're my crazy psycho, and I really wouldn't change anything about you. You're perfect, Azura, just the way you fucking are," he finishes quietly.

My heart thunders. Something inside of me that I have never ever felt before comes over me just as he slams into me, making me cry out as he stretches me out. I gasp, trying to breathe and adjust to him. Fuck, he is huge! He lets out a sexy breathy chuckle, his eyes on me.

"What's wrong, little she-wolf? Can't take it?" he teases, massaging my hips.

"Oh, I can fucking take it perfectly," I shoot back, twisting my hand into his hair.

"Yeah?" he replies, running his tongue along my lips. Yanking his head up, I stare into his icy eyes. There are so many emotions in them. Why do I feel like he won't leave me this time? How the hell am I so confident about it? I stick my tongue out, letting him flick it sensually before he sucks on it, making me sigh softly. This feels so good.

"Yes," I reply, wanting to feel him fuck me hard.

I grip his shoulders and begin riding his cock, falling into the perfect rhythm. He grabs my hips harder as he meets my thrusts with his own rough ones, making me cry out. Each thrust knocks the breath from me, sending jolts of pleasure through me as he fucks me harder and faster. I can feel his piercings rubbing against my walls, only adding to the intense pleasure that consumes me.

"Oh, fuck, Leo..." I whimper. I can't comprehend anything but this feeling, this pleasure that he is inflicting on me.

He lets go of my hips and grabs my bouncing tits instead. I lean back, bracing my hands on his thighs as he fondles my breasts, licking and sucking on my extra-sensitive nipples. This is really happening. I feel so many emotions right now.

When he yanks me closer, flipping me onto the bed, I can't help but smile slightly as he pins my hands to the bed, kissing me once again, a sizzling kiss that makes me whimper against his lips.

"Fuck, Leo," I moan when he breaks away. Gripping my knees, he pins them to the bed and fucks me harder.

I can feel the pressure hitting my spine as he fucks me fast and rough. I am screaming, but I'm not able to stop. My orgasm is building, and I can tell he is getting closer, too.

I look at him through my lashes. He looks so damn sexy with that hair falling in front of his forehead, that look of lust and something else in his eyes, making my heart pound with so many emotions of my own. He is looking at me as if I really am the only woman in the world.

"Fuck..." he groans, his eyes flashing, "You're fucking perfect."

His lips come down on mine, but as much as I want to kiss him back, I am unable to. The pleasure is so great that I am gasping for air. His movements become jerkier, my orgasm on the brink as I teeter on the edge. Fuck...

My eyes fly open as intense pleasure courses through me. My orgasm rips through me like a tidal wave.

"Leo," I groan, my back arching as he comes inside of me. I sigh as he finishes with a few sharp thrusts, my vision full of white dots. My entire body shudders from my orgasm. It is intense. Wave after wave of pleasure consumes me as I lie there unable to move.

"Fuck..."

He groans sexily as he slides out of me, making me flinch as I am reminded of his size once more, despite him not being as hard as before. My heart thunders as I lie there in a daze, a part of me is wondering if he'll get up and leave just as he had the first time...

When he rolls off me, for a moment, my heart squeezes, but the moment doesn't last long as his arm slides under my head, the other wrapping around my waist, and he pulls me into his chest. I cuddle into him, overcome with emotions. This is real.

I place my hand on his chest, feeling his heart beating under my fingertips. His body isn't as hot as it was earlier. He is still warm yet not burning up, and he feels at ease. He buries his head in my hair, inhaling deeply.

My body feels light. Those orgasms were fucking intense, and that trick with his tongue... damn. It had just ruined a normal tongue going down on me.

Should I speak? Will it ruin the moment? I bite my lip when I feel him hardening against my lower stomach.

"So... that was a nice tongue trick," I say, looking up at him, only for our eyes to meet.

"Yeah? I never realised I could do that shit," he replies, making my heart skip a beat under his gaze. Guess that means I am the first one to have that treatment. *Damn... this really is real...* "Shall I assume you liked it?" he smirks slightly.

Oh, fuck... keep at that, Blue-Eyes, and I will want you buried between my thighs once again.

I wouldn't mind that, his husky reply comes, and I instantly realise I have somehow let my walls down. I slam them up, my heart thundering, only for him to smirk.

"You are prying in my mind." I frown.

"Nah, you were just expressing your emotions openly." He shrugs, his hand running over my ass. Is that why he stayed in bed?

I raise my leg, cupping it around his hip, making his eyes flash as he cups my ass cheek, squeezing hard. *That's it, baby...* I sigh softly as he begins stroking and squeezing my ass, his gaze locked with mine.

"And in case you start thinking it's your thoughts that got me to stay in bed, it isn't," he says, his voice as arrogant and cold as normal, yet his touch is getting naughtier. His fingers brush my back entrance before they tantalisingly slip into my dripping pussy.

"Good to know," I reply, feeling myself throb again.

Our eyes meet, and I wonder if we will talk.

Well, duh, girl, we will because I sure as hell want to talk some stuff out.

I bite my lip when I realise he is pressing his finger harder against my back passage again. His finger is now coated in cum, making it easier, as I realise what he is doing.

"Tell me, Azura... have you ever had anything up this sexy ass of yours?" he asks quietly, making my eyes widen.

"Why, are you a pro at anal?" I'm sure he can tell that I have never been touched there, and although the idea seems incredibly filthy, it is such a turn-on.

"Nah... but it's a fucking first I want and I plan to fuck you in every fucking entrance of yours tonight," he replies, making my core throb.

"Then I guess I'm all yours, but first... I want a taste," I say, pulling out of his arms and making him sit up.

I look over his sexy, tatted body. He really is a work of art. I push him down again as I go lower until I am level with his cock. I wrap my hands around it before running them over it. He swears as I look up at his pleasure-filled face before I stick my tongue out and run my tongue over his tip. He tenses at my touch before I begin licking him from hilt to tip, taking extra time to run my tongue along the centre of his piercings and up along the entire length. He groans quietly, and I lick him slower, wanting this down my throat.

The taste of both of our juices lingers on him, making my stomach flutter. This is so fucking perfect. I wrap my lips around his tip and suck hard.

Oh, fuck...

He hisses as his hand comes down, tangling in my hair as I slowly begin taking more and more of him in my mouth. He props himself up on his other elbow, watching me as he groans in pleasure, my core throbbing, too. I go faster, and soon Leo is fucking my mouth harder, his grip on my hair tight.

"Fuck, beautiful, that's it," he growls in approval.

Like me sucking your cock? I ask, my eyes flashing with hunger.

"Oh, yeah... fuck..."

His head tilts back. The look on his face is so fucking hot, and when he slams his cock down my throat, I take it, relaxing my throat as I breathe through my nose. I suck on him hard as I gag slightly, but he doesn't let up, fucking me harder and faster. My mouth is fully stretched around his dick, and it burns my throat as he slams into me. I moan against him, feeling his body tensing. He is near; his sexy groans make my pussy drip.

I need him to fuck me again. My legs feel like jelly, but I don't care.

"Fuck, Azura," he growls just as he slams himself down my throat to the hilt, choking me for a second, his balls brushing my lower lip.

He swears, and my pussy clenches in desire as he shoots his load into me. He keeps thrusting, and I swallow what I can, trying not to choke on him. My eyes blaze with desire and sting with tears at the intensity of his speed. He suddenly yanks me back and up on top of him. His hand wraps around my neck as his lips come crashing against mine. He kisses me breathlessly, his breathing still hard as I straddle him, his tongue ravishing my mouth before he pulls away, his eyes blazing.

"My turn," he growls, spanking my ass.

I smirk, my entire body shivering with anticipation, my heart pounding as I slowly pull away and turn my back to him. Slowly running my fingers through my hair, I go down on all fours, my ass raised in front of him.

"Fuck me, Alpha."

His eyes blaze before he delivers another sharp tap to my ass, making me moan. He massages my ass for a moment, and I know he probably left a mark. His touch soothes the burning sensation. His fingers plunge into my pussy, rolling around as he coats them with our juices. He squeezes my ass with his other hand before sliding his fingers out.

"Fuck you're all ready for me again," he mutters as he parts my ass, his finger once again pressing against my pucker hole. He reaches over, his hand wrapping around my neck as he pulls me back up against him. "Tell me you want me to finger fuck your ass as I fuck that pussy of yours; we both know the idea fucking entices you," he growls in my ear as I feel his finger penetrate me slightly. I moan; the feeling is different, but... I like it. The excitement in it makes me want to tell him he can do whatever the fuck he wants with me.

Then tell him, girl.

"I want it just as much as you want to give it to me," I whisper hornily.

"I didn't hear you," he taunts.

"Fuck me in my ass and pussy, Leo, or do you want me to find another man?" I taunt. I feel his aura radiate off him as he swears, shoving me forward on the bed, and I smirk.

"I'll teach you exactly who the fuck you belong to and I don't fucking share," he growls, "You're a fucking tease."

"And you love it," I shoot back as his finger keeps getting deeper into me, slow and steady in a circular motion.

"Without a fucking doubt," he whispers before his finger plunges deeper into me, making me gasp. It hurts a little, but the way he is simply curling a finger inside of me is soothing, and just when I relax into it, he slams his cock into my pussy once more, making me cry out as he begins fucking me once again.

I don't know how long it's been. Down here, without a window, there is no sign for me to know whether it is evening or not. We have fucked as if we have been deprived for far too long, and in a way, I guess we have.

Leo's haze finished the moment we fucked the first time, but we didn't stop. Even when we took breaks, he held me. I must have passed out at some point because I don't remember falling asleep.

My eyes flutter open, my heart pounding as I look around the bed, realising Leo is missing. *Leo...* I relax when I hear the water running in the bathroom. The door is partially open. I look down to see the duvet is over my naked body. Did Leo tuck me in? I push it off, getting to my feet only to fall to my knees, yelping at how heavy my legs feel the moment they hit the floor.

"Goddess!" I mutter.

A shadow falls over me as I look up to see Leo standing there, showered and wearing a pair of black sweatpants. His soaking hair looks like a sexy mess.

"Careful," he says, lifting me to my feet.

My heart pounds, remembering how I had collapsed the last time after sex... when he had walked away... but this time, he didn't. Instead, he supports my body, holding me despite the fact that I am a dirty mess right now and he has just showered. I feel like a mess standing in front of him.

"I'm fine," I say, brushing my hair back, only to realise it feels sticky.

We sure behaved like animals... He smirks as if he knows what I am thinking, but I made sure my walls were up. Right?

"I've run you a bath," he says, lifting my naked body bridal style and carrying me to the bathroom.

"I can walk."

"No, you fucking can't," he remarks, looking down at me. I frown and am about to retort when I realise that I do, in fact, feel exhausted, and my pussy is aching.

"That's your fault," I declare when he lowers me into the bath.

"Yeah? Well, what were you expecting? You know I'm not small."

"Far from it... it's still your fault even if I enjoyed it," I murmur, flinching the moment my butt touches the bottom of the tub. He had only fucked me in my ass with that one finger, that one round, saying he'd break me in slowly, but I still feel sore there as well.

"Good, because it won't get any easier," he smirks arrogantly. "I'll go get us some food; I need to say goodnight to Corrado, too, but then I'll be back, alright? There's something I need to talk to you about."

Those words make my stomach sink, and almost as if he realises that, he reaches over and caresses my face.

"Don't sweat it. I won't pull away from you, not this time," he says quietly, easing my mind with that one sentence.

"Good to know. While you're at it, apologise to Corrado for hurting him, too, and bring plenty of food. I'm starving."

"Guess I didn't fill you up enough," he smirks as he leans over, pressing his lips against mine. Sparks ripple through me, his lips brushing mine so slow yet... passionately.

My heart thunders at the intimate gesture, wishing it lasted longer, but he moves back, standing up and walking out. It is crazy how my simply pushing a little has achieved so much. Okay, I have to give half the credit to the haze, too.

I relax back in the bath, wondering what he wants to talk about.

Today has been perfect, and I am sure, regardless of what he wants to talk about, it is going to be okay.

Something I Wasn't Expecting
Azura

I stay in the bath for a while, and when I hear the door open, I know Leo has returned. I get out with my jelly legs and enter the shower. I wash as quickly as I can. The soak in the bath had helped, and I feel lighter.

Through the steamed glass, I see him enter the bathroom, placing something over the heater before he leaves.

I step out after a few minutes, grabbing a towel from the shelf and towelling my hair with it. I reach over, wiping the mist from the glass, and inspect my reflection. My skin is glowing, my lips look even plumper from all that kissing, and I have several marks littering my neck. I bite my lip as memories flash through my mind. I can't stop smiling like a lovesick airhead. I feel good. He wants me. He'd countless times told Nikki to get the hell away from him.

Well, bitch, he's mine now. Try messing with him again, and I will claw your eyes out and toss them into a blender. I smirk at my own thoughts. Down, girl.

I look around, realising he has left me some underwear, a pair of satin pyjama shorts, and cami on the heating rail. Have to admit he is considerate.

After drying my body, I get dressed in the black set and enter the bedroom, trying my best not to walk as if I have tree trunks for legs. The bedding is changed, and the smell of sex is almost gone. He has placed the food bags on the bedside cabinet as he does something on his phone, a frown creasing his brows. He looks up when I enter and puts his phone away. His eyes rake over me. I don't forget how I sat on his face letting him eat my pussy just hours ago. I still feel very conscious of his gaze.

"Come here," he says, making my eyebrow shoot up.

"Why?" I ask suspiciously. He smirks slightly as he stands up and reaches over, taking hold of my wrist and pulling me closer.

"Cause I want to kiss you."

I freeze when his lips meet mine, sending delicious tingles through me, my heart racing. Goddess, when did he get so damn flirty? I kiss him back, my core clenching once more. The ball piercing of his tongue flicks my tongue, and I am unable to stop the moan that escapes me. His arms are wrapped around my waist tightly, and he pulls me against him completely, one hand resting on my ass, the other cupping the side of my face and the back of my neck.

We kiss for a few sizzling moments, our bodies react to each other, and we are getting turned on again. He forces himself away, leaving me breathless. I know if he didn't pull away, I have a feeling we would be going for another couple of rounds. My stomach rumbles, and I pout when he chuckles lightly.

"Let's feed that monster," he says mockingly.

"It's not a monster. I'm the monster," I insist, plopping onto the bed and grabbing the food bags.

"Yeah, I believe that." I give him a narrow-eyed look as I open one of the bags.

"Never knew you could be so considerate," I remark, seeing how they have everything from tissues to disposable cutlery.

"That is Winona's doing," he says, picking up the bottles of drinks and biting the metal caps off. Damn, that looked so hot. "Is there anything I do that doesn't look hot to you?" he remarks arrogantly, making me curse and put my walls up. I really need to work on those.

"Ass. So is Corrado okay?" I ask, not wanting to fuel his ego even more when I had practically begged and complimented him when we made love. *Just great, Azura. Way to boost a guy's ego.* He is still smirking arrogantly, and I am about to stab him with the fork when he speaks.

"He is fine since you said you are staying," he says, his smirk vanishing.

"What's wrong? Regretting this?" I ask, opening the pasta pot and taking a big forkful of the cheesy chicken pasta. Goddess, this tastes so damn good!

"No... I kinda always wanted him to have a mother figure, but it never really happened. He took such a fucking strong liking to you that it didn't make shit easier."

I look down at the pot, taking another forkful as I lean back against the headboard, crossing my legs as Leo unwraps a packet of homemade chunky fries, eating a few. Yup, he really does look sexy no matter what he does.

"You know, I was ready to be just his mama. I know you kept pushing me away, but I didn't want him to feel like he wasn't wanted," I whisper, my grip tight on the pot. "I was ready to stay for him and this one." I place my hand lightly on my stomach. His gaze dips to my stomach, his eyes soften, and I remember the moment he had paused when we made love. He had placed one kiss on my stomach, which was different.

"I know... and for the record, yeah, the first time I rejected you was over your surname, but then there was other shit. That is what I want to talk to you about, actually," he says, surprising me. Is he about to tell me the reason? If it isn't because I am a Westwood, then what? He eats some of the pasta, frowning deeply.

"You know, if you keep frowning like that, you're going to get even more wrinkles on that forehead. Plus, you ain't that young anymore. You don't want to look even older, do you?" He glances up but doesn't say anything, and suddenly, I wonder what it is that he wants to say. I place my pot down, frowning. "Leo, what is it?"

"I haven't mentioned this shit to any one, and I'm just thinking I should have fucking waited for tomorrow rather than drop it on you tonight. Call me fucking selfish, but I'd rather tell you before we go to Alejandro's pack."

Whatever he wants to tell me, he is struggling with it. He is acting as cold as ever, but his hand is clenched in a fist, and his knuckles are white. I am worried, and I realise his cold exterior is a defence mechanism.

"What is it?" I am fighting to keep myself calm, not wanting to think of the worst-case scenarios.

"Years back, Endora did a lot of experiments on me using magic and shit. I was immune to a lot of her magic, especially when it came to compelling me to obey her. It, in turn, only piqued her curiosity. When she tried to get me to obey, it just felt like disobeying an Alpha command. You struggle, but it's possible. She said I was stronger than Dad was at my age, and so the tests began." His voice sounds thicker, and he isn't looking at me as he speaks. I stay silent, waiting for him to continue, knowing it will only make it harder for him if I question him.

"Even after her death, the effects remained, causing permanent damage. And by the time I figured it out, the damage had spread. I know you will say I should have gone to Kiara, but I wasn't going to ask for their help, so I started working on my own shit, trying to find a cure. Yeah, I know, I was fucking stubborn, but I thought I'd be able to do it, and I pretty much failed. The injection I gave you when Emmet hurt you was something I created by trying to imitate the build-up of your mother's cells. But it still wasn't enough. My organs are shutting down, and some already have. It's why I didn't want you to get too close to me because I don't fucking have long left."

My heart is ringing in my ears, my breathing becoming laboured as his words hit me hard. He is dying. The hints have been there... his past comments and my own filled my mind, making my heart clench in pain.

"It doesn't matter..."

"No matter what, I'll make sure you and our pup are taken care of..."

"Maybe it's easier to tell my baby that you're dead..."

I run my hand through my hair as everything seems to make sense. His hot and cold attitude. He has been struggling internally and...

"I know I was fucking selfish, but I didn't really give a shit, I just... I thought I'd be able to find a cure. But I never realised I'd actually fail until a few months ago, and although Jackie told me to go see Kiara, I knew it was too late-"

"You can't say that, not until she tries. There's not only Kiara, but Delsanra and Raihana! Dante, too! Goddess, you are not going to die," I say, my eyes flashing. Getting off the bed, I walk over to him and drop to my knees in front of him. I look up at him, my heart still beating violently as I cup his face. "You can't say it's too late until we have tried everything. Goddess, I want to slap you across the head for being so damn stubborn! Did you ever think to ask anyone for advice or help? It doesn't make you any less of a person! Tomorrow we will ask Kia to help, I'm sure she can! There's nothing that she..."

I trail off, realising there are things she can't heal. Some of his organs have already shut down. My heart is pounding as I freeze, staring up into those icy blue eyes.

Leo really is dying...

I open my mouth to speak, but I have a lump in my throat, and I am unable to string two words together. His arms wrap around my shoulders, and my heart breaks when he presses his forehead against mine, once again, unable to look into my eyes.

"I will try to explore all avenues to live for the three of you. But if anything were to happen to me, and I know I'm swinging this shit at you so suddenly, but will you be willing to let me put you down as Corrado's legal guardian?"

His words shatter me in ways more than his rejection ever had, and I almost crumble before him, but I need to be strong for him.

First of all, you don't need to ask me that. I have taken him as my own, so yes, in my eyes, I'm already his guardian. Secondly, I swear I will find a way to come to the afterlife and drag you back if you die on me! You are not going to die! You are not going to leave our babies... and what about me? I choke out, refusing to give in to the fear and despair that is trying to eat me up. I am Azura Westwood, and I refuse to give up without a damn fight.

Our eyes meet, and I can see the turmoil in his.

"I'm fucking sorry," he says. My eyes flash, refusing to believe this. No, a sorry means giving up. No, just no. For a split second, he looks surprised.

"No. No more apologies. I want you. I just got you. I want this baby to meet its father. You can't leave us, Leo!" The pain I felt when he had fought Judah makes sense now. How much has he suffered all alone? "Who else knows?"

"Only Jackie, since she is the one who first ran some tests on me and realised what was going on. But I made sure she told no one."

"Well, it's time we found an answer together," I say determinedly.

He gives a small nod, but I can tell he holds no hope. I lock my arms around his neck, hugging him tightly. I promise we will find an answer, and if he has given up hope then it is time to do this together. He simply holds me tight; his heart is beating slightly faster than normal, and I just wish I could do more. This is not over. We will find a damn answer.

He lifts me up, and I straddle his lap, hugging him tightly. I don't know how long we remain there, but when I feel him throb against my core, I move back, looking down at him suspiciously.

"You're dying and you're getting turned on?" He smirks, the tension around us lifting.

"I was dying when I was fucking you earlier, too," he replies cockily. "Doesn't seem to be affecting my ability to fuck." His eyes run over me, darkening with desire, and although my core clenches, I roll my eyes, getting off his lap. Shouldn't he be taking it easy?

"I think you're probably exaggerating; you are going to be totally fine. Trust me."

Inside, I am scared of the worst-case scenario, but I'm not going to give up. I was able to be saved from the womb of a dead woman, which is a miracle, so why can't Leo be saved? I won't give up until we have exhausted all our options, and even then, I will keep looking. We begin eating again, and although I have lost my appetite, I refuse to let that revelation ruin these moments. Every moment in life is precious, isn't it?

I have just found Leo. Finally, we've become a couple or something of the sort, and now I might lose him? His refusing the Alpha title makes sense now, too...

Once we have eaten, I clear up the bags, and Leo places them outside before we get ready for bed. My heart is racing as I realise he is going to stay by my side, and, Goddess, when he peels that shirt off, I am ready to spread my legs again if he wants. *Damn, he is so bloody sexy.*

He turns, smirking arrogantly as if he knows what is going through my mind, and comes over to the bed. He gets in, pulling me close and once again that feeling of safety and home cocoons me and I snuggle close, placing a kiss on his chest.

"Guess what I just realised," I muse, now smirking as I look up at him deviously.

"What?" he asks suspiciously. Oh, he has good reason to be suspicious. I inhale his scent, wanting to lick every inch of him.

"Well... now that you're sleeping next to me, it means I can get revenge with ease every time you offend me. I won't even need a voodoo doll to torture you," I say, smiling innocently. He cocks a brow.

"I have no fucking doubt that you'll do that shit, and you do know those damn dolls don't work?"

"Hey, I at least picture they are you and it's satisfying to torture. You know, I made one of you when you hit my head with that ball years ago."

He smirks, "Damn, you really are a psycho."

"Regretting it?" I ask, smirking back.

"Not one fucking bit," he replies before claiming my lips in one hell of a burning kiss.

The Black Storm Alpha
Leo

Morning has arrived, and usually, I'd be out of bed by now but just getting to hold her and watch her sleep is fucking incredible. I can't describe it, but despite all the shit going on, I feel at peace. Is this the power of the mate bond? No wonder people yearn for this.

Letting it go, the stubbornness, and trying to fight my emotions has been exhausting. Acceptance... that feels better.

Last night when her eyes had flashed, for a moment, they looked different, but it was far too fucking fast to see. Maybe I had imagined it.

Her lips are now pressed together in a pout, her chest rising and falling with plenty of cleavage on show. Strands of her hair are falling in front of her face, and, reaching up, I slowly brush them off her face. She moans slightly, rolling onto her back, making me suck in a breath when her leg brushes my cock. I am already rock-hard.

Her top rides up slightly, and I run my hand down her waist. So fucking sexy.

I place my hand on her stomach, hearing her heart skip a beat, and I look up into her eyes which are now open. She sure has gorgeous big eyes.

"When did you wake up?" she asks sleepily.

"Not long ago," I reply, my voice huskier, and begin tracing circles on her stomach. She bites her lip, her body reacting to my touch. Our eyes meet before my gaze flickers to her lips, and she slowly licks them in response.

"Do I need to ask you to kiss me?" she asks, raising an eyebrow and making me smirk slightly.

"I don't mind you begging a little," I murmur, brushing her hair back. I twist it between my fingers and tug her head up slightly. I flip over so I am straddling her.

"Fuck..." she murmurs, biting her lip, and the moment my dick presses against her stomach, she lets out a soft sigh. I lace my hands with hers, claiming her lips in a deep passionate kiss.

Yeah, we ended up fucking all over again. By the time I get to shower, I'm having four different conversations via the mind-link in my fucking head. I wish I didn't have to do this shit right here but I do.

They had tracked some of the buyers, but we are no closer to contacting Web. The dinner party I am hosting in celebration of our new drug deals is coming up, and I told Li Sheng to send him an invitation. To start anew... Sure, I know he won't buy that shit, but I need to get to him. Somehow. He'll come if the incentive is high enough, and so I have decided to say there will be something special up for auction at this dinner. I just need his fucking greed to come into play and cloud his judgement.

Jin has found several bank accounts Emmet had abroad and under different names, two of which are in Jackie's name, and she has no idea about them.

Dan has begun running some tests on Judah's body. He wasn't a werewolf. That has been confirmed.

Then we have Eric, who reported on Emmet acting fucking crazy and playing up in prison, demanding to be let out.

We get dressed before we head up to have breakfast with Corrado. He is already sitting at the table when we step out of my office. The table is laden with a pretty extravagant breakfast, and I hear the door click shut, signalling Winona has slipped out. She really is far slyer than she lets on. The clothes she purchased for Azura said a lot, too. She, Marcel, and Corrado are a trio that should not be together.

But it is Corrado's smile that makes me smile back. He is practically radiating happiness.

"We are going to have breakfast together!" he exclaims, jumping off his seat and running over, straight into Azura's arms. She crouches down, hugging him back tightly.

"Hey, kiddo! Yes, we are, and I'm very, very hungry!" she says as they part, and he quickly wraps his arms around my legs. I lift him up, carrying him to the table.

"I'm so happy, Daddy!" he whispers to me before turning to look at Azura. "See? I told you, Azura Mommy, if you stay, we will have nice food. You won't have to have lumpy sandwiches." I smirk, glancing at her. She pauses, and for a moment, I almost chuckle, thinking she is offended, only to see her looking at him with emotions in her eyes.

"Azura Mommy... I love that," she says, softly ruffling his hair. "But my sandwiches are so good!"

"No, they're not." He giggles as I place him down.

Azura Mommy... I won't say it, but seeing them have that bond is... perfect.

"Yes, they are!"

I sit down, and we're all tucked in. This feels pretty good.

It's now after breakfast, and we are getting ready to leave. Azura's friend, Song, will be coming along, too, and from there, she'll head home.

"So why is he here?" I ask, seeing Corrado carrying a small backpack as he holds Azura's hand.

"Azura Mommy said I can come to visit our family too," he says proudly. She looks at me challengingly, and I simply give her a cold glare. Am I really not going to fucking argue?

I am about to say something, looking at the defiant duo who are staring at me, and I fucking swear they are double of one another with those expressions, but, hearing footsteps, I turn.

"Hey! I'm glad I caught you guys before you leave. I baked some cookies. Definitely have them on the journey," she says, handing the tin to Azura.

"Oh, thanks, Jackie."

"I will miss you."

"Oh, I'll be back." Azura smiles, surprising her, and Jackie suddenly hugs her.

"Thank the Goddess!" Azura smiles.

"Yeah, see, Leo? Everyone likes me but you." She gives me a dirty look.

I do fucking like you. I just didn't want to admit it, I say through the link pointedly. She simply gives me a haughty look.

Well, you have the rest of our lives to make it up to me... she trails off, and I know what came to her mind.

Yeah, guess I'm going to have to figure shit out so I can make it up to you, I say, masking my emotions. Our eyes lock.

We will.

Jackie now turns to me, giving me a small smile. She speaks, drawing me from my thoughts.

"Leo, when you return, I want to reject Emmet," she says quietly, twisting her hands in front of her as she comes over to me. I nod, giving her a one-armed hug. I can sense her fear, feeling her shaking slightly.

"I'm proud of you, Jackie," I say quietly.

"Well... I'm glad. You've always been like that older brother to me, Leo. Thanks. I won't be tied to an abuser and a traitor. I won't stop living either, so you don't either, okay?" I smirk glancing over at Azura and Corrado.

"I tried and failed, but no, I won't give up," I say quietly.

"Good. She makes you happy Leo, and you need someone who is willing to challenge you."

I raise an eyebrow. I am not that fucking stubborn. Who the fuck am I kidding? I fucking am. I hear footsteps approaching and know it's Jax and Nikki before they even come into sight.

"Jax, take Song and Corrado to the car," I command. My mood instantly darkens as I glance at Azura, who is looking at Nikki without even a glimmer of warmth on her face.

"Got it, Alpha. Nice to see you again, Luna." Jax says.

"You, too. You'll be seeing me more often, don't worry," Azura replies. Something tells me that is more directed at Nikki. Jax smirks.

Good going, he says through the link before motioning for Song to follow him. Song takes Corrado's hand, glancing at Azura before following Jax.

"Come on, Corrado, let's go get in the car first!" she exclaims brightly.

"Yes!"

I can feel Nikki trying to mind-link, but I keep her blocked out.

"Are you really going to make me apologise?" she asks me out loud after Jax is out of sight.

I close the gap between Azura and myself, and wrap one arm around her shoulders from behind, resting my chin on top of her head.

"Yeah. You insulted my Luna, and that's not something I'm going to fucking let slide," I say coldly as Azura leans back against me. Nikki stares at me, clearly shocked before she looks at Azura.

"Luna... so, you, like, made up?" she asks almost accusingly.

"Are you dumb, Nikki? Seriously, I'm sure that's clear enough. Get a move on with it, we have to go," Azura replies in a clipped tone. Nikki looks humiliated as she looks at us.

"Now," I growl.

"I'm sorry for what I said," she says it as if it were the hardest fucking thing to say.

"With a little more regret," I warn dangerously.

She looks at me with a hurt expression, but I really don't fucking care. I apologised the first time when I fucking ended it with her, although she knew once we found our fucking mates, it's totally fucking okay for it to be over. I owe her nothing.

"I'm getting bored," Azura yawns. I press my lips to the back of my feisty girl's head. She sure doesn't hold back, but Nikki deserves it.

"I'm sorry... Luna," Nikki says in a softer tone, and when she lowers her gaze in submission, I decide it is near enough the best we are going to fucking get from her.

"Cool. I get that it's not nice when someone comes in, and you lose the man you love, but I won't apologise for it. He was made to be mine, and I plan to keep him... even if he is a stubborn ass. I hope you can find your mate soon, too," Azura says quietly. In her own way, she is offering Nikki an olive branch. That alone shows she is by far the better person.

Nikki doesn't reply, simply nodding.

"You can go," I say coldly. She looks at me before nodding and leaving. A little too calm for my liking...

Eric, keep an eye on Nikki, I command before Azura tilts her head up.

"Shall we get going?" she asks.

"Yeah, let's do this shit."

Our eyes meet, both knowing what is to come. It is time for us both to face our issues head-on. I lean down, kissing her lips softly, not caring if anyone sees us, before we both head to the car.

The Nightwalker Pack, home of the Lycan King, Alejandro Rossi, and his family. It has been a decade since I have entered these pack grounds. There are many changes, and it is obvious it has expanded a lot. We drive through the streets that are no longer dirt paths, despite the trees that surround vast parts of the grounds. The gates to Alejandro's mansion swing open, and I can feel the excitement from Corrado in the back of the car as he stares out through the tinted windows.

Azura's hand rests on top of mine, calming my conflicted emotions. I turn to her, lacing my fingers with hers. Our eyes meet, and she doesn't need to say anything for me to understand. *We got this.*

Marcel had been pretty impressed to hear that we were coming here; it seems Alejandro had told him. He had called earlier on the drive here, and when Azura had said we'd be back soon, he had instantly picked up on the 'we' and did nothing to hide his happiness.

Alejandro has his hand in his pocket, and a young girl with black hair is standing on the steps next to him with her arms crossed. I am certain it is Alessandra; you can see the similarities between her and her father. She would be around ten now, the youngest of Alejandro's four kids.

"Oh, Daddy! Who is that man?" Corrado asks as we park up.

"That's Alejandro Rossi, your grandad's brother," I explain emotionlessly.

"Oh, King Rossi!" Yeah, I am sure Dad told him about that.

"Maybe I shouldn't have come," Song says, staring out as Alejandro approaches.

"Too late for that. Come on, you have seen Alejandro before."

"Yes, and I wanted to run," Song murmurs.

"Hey, don't get doubtful. You wanted to see you-know-who, remember?" Azura whispers with a smirk on her lips. From the corner of my eyes, I see her blush but don't bother thinking much of it as Alejandro opens the passenger door for Azura.

"Hey, Alejandro," Azura says, hugging him as I get out, too.

"Hey, Firework. You okay?" he replies, giving her a squeeze before letting go of her as she nods.

"Perfectly," she replies before she rushes over to Alessandra. "Hey, brat!" She hugs the younger girl, who frowns.

"Don't call me that. You're so loud," she grumbles. Definitely Alejandro's pup.

"Azura!" Kiara's voice comes as she hurries out of the mansion and runs over to her sister, hugging her tightly. Didn't they just fucking see each other not so fucking long ago?

"Kia!" Azura smiles.

My eyes meet Alejandro's as I open the back door for Corrado and Song since the child locks are on.

"Thank you," she says, getting out.

"It's good to see you here," Alejandro says to me, a tiny smirk on his face as he approaches.

"Not so sure it is," I mutter as Corrado climbs out. Alejandro's attention instantly goes to him, and he crouches down in front of him.

"So, this is your pup," he says, observing him with that small smirk.

"Obviously," I retort.

I can feel him pulling back his aura as much as possible, as not to scare Corrado. It is still powerful, and I can tell Corrado looks daunted for a few seconds.

"Hello, King Rossi. I'm Corrado Herrmann Rossi," Corrado introduces himself, puffing out his chest as he holds his hand out to Alejandro.

"Now that's confidence I like," Alejandro says, taking his hand and giving it a shake. "But we don't greet family with a handshake, now do we?" Corrado smiles and shakes his head.

"No, we give them hugs!" he answers.

"So, are you going to give Grandad Al a hug?" Alejandro asks. Corrado looks up at me, his eyes widening.

"Can I?" he whispers as if Alejandro can't hear him.

"Sure," I agree. Not going to fucking stop a kid from doing whatever he wants.

It is fucking weird seeing those two together. I'm not fucking stupid, I can see Alejandro is fucking genuine, but that is a fact I like to ignore. I'm the king of being fucking hypocritical, and I don't really give a shit.

I turn to see Song talking to Kiara and Azura as Alessandra simply stands there frowning, her eyes now fixed on Corrado.

"Corrado, come here! Look, this is my sister, Kiara," Azura calls. Alejandro stands up, lifting Corrado in his arms as he walks around to the women.

"I see you're here. I'm sure the girls will be fucking disappointed that they ain't here," Alejandro says to Song.

"Yeah, nice to be here..." Song says, smiling politely whilst Kiara gushes over how cute Corrado is.

"Aww, you are such a cutie."

"You are very cute, too," Corrado replies, making Kiara laugh.

"I dislike kids," Alessandra grumbles.

"Ain't you one yourself?" I ask.

She gives me a scathing glare before her gaze softens, and she frowns, looking at her palm before she turns and looks at the sky. Weird little pup.

"Leo, how are you?" Kiara asks, drawing my attention away from the girl. I feel Azura's eyes on me as the older woman turns her attention to me.

"Good," I say. The urge to step away from her is almost tempting.

I can almost see her observing me. Her smile falters, but before she can say anything, the mansion doors open once again, and a man steps out dressed in a white shirt and black pants. His Alpha aura is radiating off of him, yet even I know it isn't at its fullest. He runs a hand through his curly black shoulder-length hair that looks more unruly than I remember it from a decade ago. His face looks sharper, too, and you can tell he looks older. He was my age back then.

He comes to a stop when his grey eyes meet mine. A sharp wind blows around us. Suddenly, it feels colder, and it's like it is just the two of us. My own aura is swirling around me, and a storm of emotions rushes through me. A small frown crosses his face, but despite my own hostile hatred towards him, he remains calm.

Ten years have passed since I saw him. Ten years of hating him for everything he had fucking done. Time seems to fucking stand still as our gazes remain locked.

I once vowed I never wanted to see him again, but that vow was broken because right in front of me is none other than the richest Alpha in the country. The man who owns the majority of the Rossi assets and several multi-billionaire companies around the globe. The man that I fucking hate to the core.

Rayhan Rossi, the Alpha of the Black Storm Pack himself.

A Mansion Full of Rossis
Azura

The journey was pleasant, and despite feeling a little nauseous at times, I wouldn't have changed anything about it. Leo's constant touches, the way he caressed my thigh, the way he tilted his head as he drove, giving me the perfect angle of that sexy jaw of his, or the way he looked at me. Well, I couldn't focus on anything else much.

But there is one thing that really got to me. It is the tin of cookies that Jackie had given me. There inside is a small square of paper with the words 'read when alone' on it, tucked under the first layer of cookies. I'm curious, but with Leo being so sharp, I snuck the note into my boot to check later.

Song, the twins, and I had texted a little, too, and both the twins were disappointed that they were at the Academy. As for Song, she's had a die-hard crush on Rayhan for ages. Well, that isn't anything to be surprised about. He is damn handsome, and the majority of the girls at the Academy are smitten with him. Rayhan is much like the Arden twins. All are rich, sexy, and powerful, although those brothers have been abroad for a few years. With Rayhan being here in the country, we hear of him often, and then there is the fact that he is mated. There is just something about wanting something you can't have that is enticing. Sky used to even sell his pictures, which she would take sneakily, for pretty high prices, and the girls would happily buy them, as well as a couple of the boys.

The moment he steps out of the mansion, I hear Song gasp, squeezing my arm. She sure has a strong grip! But it is Leo who has my attention. His entire body tenses and his eyes seem to become far colder than I have ever seen them. His aura is raging around him, and even Corrado looks scared in Alejandro's arms, clearly sensing the tension. I reach out, wrapping my hand over Leo's larger, fisted one, and it feels like something snaps between the cousins, and Leo looks at me.

You got this, I say as he slowly takes my hand, giving it a squeeze. Rayhan walks towards us, glancing at me and giving me a small smile.

"Hey, Azura, it's been a while. How have you been?" he asks, stopping beside Alejandro.

"I've been great. How are you?" I ask, feeling my cheeks heat a little under his gaze. *Dammit, Azura, focus. Yup, he is damn handsome.*

Yeah, fucking focus. Leo's cold voice comes through the link, giving me a pointed look.

I slam my walls up, thinking I do not need Leo to know that I do find his older cousin pretty handsome. Can you blame me? He is absolutely yummy. Okay, Leo is yummier and way sexier, but that does not take away from the model-like god in front of me. *Urgh, focus girl.*

So, my mate had, or shall I say has, a crush on that bastard? Leo, ever the smartass, remarks. Am I that obvious? He isn't looking at me, but I'm not sure if he is annoyed or not. Well, I sure hope not, but I guess if he had a crush on someone I disliked, I wouldn't be happy.

Hey, I liked him when I was like ten. He was my first crush, and it was just a silly little girl's fantasy, I retort. His eyebrow shoots up, his eyes flash steel blue, and I kind of think I made it worse. **Don't blame me, it's the damn Rossi gene. Maybe it was because he looked a lot like my future mate?** I try, putting on my best innocent face. **Wait, are you jealous?** I taunt. His frown deepens, and I realise I really am making it worse.

"Rayhan! This is my friend, Song," I say, pushing Song forward, hoping Leo doesn't push it. She gives me a glare, her face on fire as Rayhan gives her one of his charming smiles.

"Nice to meet you," he replies in his sexy melodic voice, taking her hand and giving it a kiss. Song squeaks, and I can't help but chuckle.

"I don't get what the fuck girls like about him," Alejandro grumbles.

"No kidding," Leo growls as Rayhan smirks and looks down at Corrado. It is obvious he isn't as snarky as the other two alphas.

"Hey, what's your name?"

"Corrado. Corrado Herrmann Rossi," Corrado replies, watching him curiously.

"Nice to meet you, Corrado Herrmann Rossi." Rayhan gives him a wink before turning his attention to Leo. Tension seems to settle between them. "Leo… good to see you," Rayhan says, offering his hand to him.

"Rayhan." Leo's voice is cold as he takes the offered hand. They exchange a shake before Leo lets go pretty fast. I don't miss the small soft smile on Rayhan's face, but he masks it fast before Kiara claps her hands.

"Shall we head inside? I'm sure everyone must be hungry."

"Oh, yes, please. Azura Mommy will be happy with a nice meal," Corrado declares as Alejandro puts him down, and Kiara holds her hand out to him, which he takes happily.

"He sure knows you can't fucking cook," Alejandro snickers, and I pout.

"This kid," I sigh.

Kiara looks at me curiously, and I know it is because of what he called me. Her eyes, which are now poking out at me, say enough. I motion with my eyes that I'll tell her later, and she gives me a small nod, smiling slightly.

We all head inside, and Leo brings up the rear. I feel him hesitate as we cross the threshold, and I slow down, falling into step with him.

You did great, I murmur through the link, slipping my hand into the back pocket of his jeans. He looks down at me.

Hmm… I ain't letting that shit from earlier slide, he says icily, and I cock a brow.

Shall I start looking into your past and at every single woman you ever had a crush on? Bet they all had big asses and big boobs, right? I counter, suddenly feeling very possessive.

Don't really know if I can even class them as 'liked' because it sure as fuck doesn't even make a dent in comparison to what the fuck I feel for you.

Oh, fuck... he sure knows how to make a woman wet. My heart is thundering, and I don't even realise we have stopped until Leo's hands grab my ass and yank me against him.

"Fuck, you're just so damn good with your words," I grumble.

"I'm just fucking honest," he says, and I squeeze his ass as I tilt my head up.

"You know, you're way sexier?" I whisper, trying not to focus on how my body is reacting to him.

Our eyes meet. That sizzling chemistry raging between us makes it hard to breathe, but I don't care, and when he leans down, his tongue flicks out. I caress it with my own, feeling my pussy clench. Oh, fuck. There is just something so damn hot about this.

I slip my hand out of his pocket, wrapping my arms around his neck as Leo captures my tongue in his mouth, kissing me hard. I sigh softly, kissing him back. We are lost in one another until someone clears their throat. I pull away, much to Leo's irritation, as he turns and gives the smirking Alejandro a scathing glare.

"Don't tell me you're lacking that much action that you need to watch the fucking show," Leo says coldly, his hand still around my waist.

"Oh, far from it. I don't call Amore Mio 'Nympho' for nothing. I just never knew you two were fucking together," Alejandro counters cockily.

"Fucking together..." I smirk, knowing he didn't mean that in that way. Both men look at me before Kiara comes out into the hall.

"Come on, guys, have some refreshments before lunch."

"Great," I say, reluctantly pulling away from Leo and sauntering over to Kiara.

I can feel her watching me as we walk side by side, but she says nothing, and for a moment, I wonder what it is, considering she isn't smiling. She looks... concerned. Could it be that she has already sensed Leo's health issues?

A short while later, we are getting ready to have lunch. Kiara has gone to check up on the food that she has prepared, and I really can't wait to eat! She really is one of the best cooks in the world. I would have gone to help her, too, but I don't trust leaving Leo alone here with them. He needs me.

Corrado is playing in the garden with Alessandra. Despite her grumpy personality, she has still given him some colouring books and crayons whilst she sits on the garden steps and reads her book.

The lounge is a little tense, with Leo sitting silently, his exterior ice-cold. Song and I are talking to Alejandro, with Rayhan adding to the conversation here and there. I think by now, he knows that Song is a little jittery around him, but he is as smooth as ever and doesn't make it obvious or put her on the spot. I think he is used to it.

"So, what the fuck were you doing at Leo's pack? This ain't got anything to do with the same shit when you told me to watch the girls, right?" Alejandro asks Leo.

"It's dealt with," Leo replies, frowning slightly.

"Good to know. Not going to share what that shit was about?" Alejandro asks, observing the three of us.

"It's not necessary," Leo counters, his arm going around my shoulders once again. My heart races, and I can feel Alejandro's eyes on us again.

"So, when did you two figure your own shit out?"

"Is that any of your fucking business?" Leo shoots back, raising an eyebrow.

"If I make it my business, it fucking is," Alejandro replies with a cold smirk. Rayhan smiles slightly, clearly amused.

"It's like I'm seeing double," he remarks.

"I totally agree. Right down to the tattoos and all," I snicker, earning a look from Leo.

"We are nothing alike," he growls icily. Alejandro smirks.

"Deny it all the fuck you want," he says, taking out a cigarette pack and offering Leo. It is almost like a test. Refusing it to prove he's not like him but I also know Leo is a stubborn ass and ignores him. I reach over instead, taking one from Alejandro. Leo cocks a brow as I place it between his lips.

"Don't be stubborn," I murmur as Alejandro tosses me the lighter. I catch it and flick it on, bringing it to the edge of the cigarette. Our eyes lock, and my heart thunders at how incredibly smoking hot he looks.

Goddess... I press my thighs together, and Leo smirks slightly, his gaze dipping to my chest for a second before he looks away, taking a long drag of his cigarette. His arm that is around me loosens slightly, and he begins tracing circles on my shoulder teasingly, sending delicious tingles through me.

"As much as I'm enjoying the bonding, we do have a guest present who can't heal from all the second-hand smoking," Rayhan remarks lightly. The patio doors are wide open, but he has a point. Song smiles slightly, and I swear I am not going to let this go. *Oh, girl, I'm teasing you for forever!*

"I'm okay," she says, blushing so much. I just wish Skyla was here to tease her.

"Kiara will heal her," Alejandro offers with a small grin at Song as if that made everything alright. I shake my head.

And that is why Rayhan is swoon-worthy. But I can't deny it is the bad boy with a 'devil-may-care' attitude next to me that turns me on.

Keep looking at me like that, Baby Girl, and I will fuck you until you can't fucking walk, his animalistic growl promises through the link. The idea isn't bad and I suddenly remember Jackie's note.

"Be right back," I say softly, kissing his lips. His hand twists in my hair, and he kisses me back before letting go of me.

You're up to something, he says as I get up, feeling his eyes on me. He somehow makes me feel so damn sexy.

Not really, I lie, leaving the room.

I hurry to the bathroom and take my shoe off, emptying it and picking up the small square piece of paper that falls out. Frowning, I open it and read it.

Leo is unwell. Please get the Queen to try to heal him. Only you can do this.

I stare at the paper, my heart thudding, and I realise this is probably what she had wanted to talk about at the party. She had said something about doing the right thing and breaking promises. Goddess, she is such a good friend who actually cares for Leo.

Now the tin of cookies makes sense. I guess she didn't trust my phone because Leo is so tech-savvy. I reach into my pocket, wanting to call her and thank her, but I realise I have left my phone in the car. I slip the note into my pocket instead and exit the bathroom, walking down the hall slowly. She is going through so much, yet she is still being damn strong. She is Delta material. I pause, mind-linking Leo.

Want me to tell Kia? I ask. Silence follows before he speaks after a few moments.

Fine, but I don't want anyone else to know. His voice is quiet, and he has his emotions masked, so even I don't know what he is feeling.

It's going to be okay, I say, but the fact that he doesn't think Kiara can heal him eats me up. It is scary to know that this may not work, but I refuse to let that thought get me down.

I enter the kitchen to see Kiara sprinkling some flaked chocolate on the trifle bowls whilst Claire, one of her housekeepers, is placing dishes onto a tray to take to the dining room.

"Hey, Claire," I say, smiling at her.

"Hello, little miss. It's lovely to see you again," she replies, giving me a jolly smile before she bustles out of the room with the tray laden with food. She is getting older, but it doesn't deter her from keeping the job.

"The food smells too good," I say, inhaling deeply.

"Thanks. So, you two worked it out?" Kiara asks with a smile and eyes that scream 'details!'

"Yeah..." I say, trying not to blush as I remember last night. "Yesterday, actually."

"Ah, that explains the incredible glow. First, I thought it was just the pregnancy," she teases. I pout.

"Something like that." I walk over to the counter and lean on it opposite her as she places the dessert bowls onto the tray. "I mean, I found out the reason he was refusing me." Her smile fades, replaced with concern, as she watches me. *Goddess, this is hard...* "He's ill, Kia, thanks to Endora. He's dying," I say softly, looking down at the counter, unable to look her in the eyes. My voice sounds far more vulnerable than it is meant to. Her heart skips a beat, and she reaches over, cupping my face. She forces me to look at her.

"We will fix that. He isn't going to die," she says, her voice full of confidence and determination. I nod, unable to tell her that he may not be able to be healed by her. I know if I voice that fear, I'll end up crying.

"He doesn't want everyone to know, so if you could try to heal him when we're alone," I request quietly. She nods, walking around the island and giving me a tight hug.

"Don't give up hope, Zu," she comforts me softly.

I nod, finding comfort in my sister's embrace, when a powerful aura suddenly fills the room, and a deep, husky voice interrupts us.

"Am I intruding?"

I pull away, turn, and stare at the tall, muscular man in the doorway. I was not expecting him to be here. He is just an inch short of seven feet and dressed in a pair of jeans with a black T-shirt and jacket. He has a head full of tight, glossy black curls, an angular jaw, and plump lips. A Rossi through and through. A pair of shades covers his eyes that are a deep red, something he wears the majority of the time, as rarely can anyone bear to look him straight in the eyes. Even with the amulet of concealment around his neck, his aura is exceptionally powerful and intense, different from any other I have ever felt, even making Leo's and Alejandro's pale in comparison. The pull that comes from him offers calmness and strength. There is just something different and otherworldly about the being before me, something that makes you want to lower your head and submit. Something I'll never admit, of course. I mean, I won't bow to that giant shrimp! I'm a full day older! But this is the feeling when you are in the presence of the one and only demi-god himself.

A small smile crosses his lips, and I know behind those shades, he is looking right at me.

"Hey, My Temperamental Miracle."

Talk between Four Alphas
Azura

"Hey! You're here?" I ask, rushing over to him and flinging my arms around his neck. He catches me, lifting me off the floor, and gives me a warm, crushing hug.

"I couldn't miss this reunion now, could I?" He places me back on the floor, and I grin.

"So, you knew," I say, and he smirks slightly, just as Kiara comes over, and Dante wraps his arms around his tiny Mama.

"Maybe. Hey, Mama. How have you been?" he asks, kissing her forehead as he looks down at her.

"Better now that you're here," Kiara replies, caressing his face. He smiles down at her.

"Then I'm glad I'm here."

Ah, he is annoying with his perfect hair, but he is a mama's boy and treats her like a queen. Kiara smiles up at him and gently moves away.

"Well, you're just in time for dinner."

"Perfect," he says, turning to me.

Like always, it feels like he is peering into my soul, even with those shades on. He doesn't say anything and simply smiles before we head to the lounge. I realise it's been ten years since the three cousins will be reuniting. Each of the Rossi brothers has one son, and there is roughly a nine or ten-year age gap between the three.

The moment we enter the lounge, I feel the power of the four alphas hit me at once. It is a lot harder to ignore it when it is this intense, and I can tell even Song feels the same or worse. Damn Rossis... I know all four have it reined in, but they are still so strong.

"So, you're fucking back?" Alejandro asks from where he is relaxing back on the sofa. He stands up and pulls Kiara into his arms, kissing her neck.

"Isn't that obvious?" Dante replies with a small smirk. "I'm not really that easy to miss."

"Dante, it's been a while. How have you been?" Rayhan asks, standing up and meeting his cousin with a brotherly hug, one Dante returns. Rayhan slaps his back before moving back.

"I've been good. How about you? How're Delsanra and the kids?" Dante asks.

Delsanra had been Dante's childhood crush. I didn't blame him, Delsanra is as gorgeous as Rayhan is handsome, and Dante sees her in her demon form, which is said to be incredibly beautiful, all the time.

"They're great. Del's been a bit worried as Si's starting at the Academy soon," Rayhan replies.

Sienna is Rayhan's twelve-year-old daughter. His son, Ahren, is thirteen and already at the Academy.

"Si will be alright. She's still young," Dante replies, turning his attention to Leo. Rayhan frowns slightly, and I know he is analysing Dante's words. It is hard not to; often, he may say something that may mean more. "Leo, this is a pleasant surprise."

"I'm sure it wasn't a fucking surprise to you," Leo replies as he stands up, looking at the taller man, but it is obvious that no matter how cold he acts, he holds nothing against his younger cousin. He only proves my point when he holds his tattooed hand out to him. Dante smiles slightly.

"Can I at least pretend that it is a surprise? Ten years... that's a long wait. Life is short, and every moment should be cherished."

Leo frowns as Dante ignores his offered hand and instead gives him a hug. My eyes meet Leo's over Dante's shoulder, and I give him a small nod before he hugs Dante back. I can't help but smile softly. With Dante here, I feel that things can be sorted between Leo and Rayhan a lot more smoothly. He is the wise old man who will get it done. I am positive!

Leo moves back, and can I just say, my man looks so damn sexy right now? My gaze dips to the bulge in his pants, and I can feel him watching me, my core throbbing. Oh, how I want to take his dick in my mouth all over again.

I like the fucking idea too. Considering there's still a lesson I need to fucking teach you to remind you who the fuck you actually belong to, his growl comes through the link as his eyes find mine.

Yes, please.

His eyes flash, and I walk over to him, wrapping my arms around his neck for a moment and resting my forehead against his shoulder.

I can't wait, I whisper seductively through the link, trying not to react to his dick pressing against me. **I'm proud of you, baby.** He doesn't respond, but his arms wrap around me tightly.

"Song, hey," Dante greets.

"Hi," she replies, giving him a smile and a small wave. Dante turns his attention to the open patio, where Alessandra suddenly looks up.

"Dante!" she exclaims, a huge smile crossing her lips.

Yup, Dante is the only one who can get that pile of grumpiness to smile. They close the gap between them before Dante goes down on one knee, hugging her tightly.

"I missed you," she whispers.

"And I missed my favourite sister, too," he says, ruffling her hair. She plants a kiss on his cheek before she points to the garden.

"That's Leo's son," she tells him, to my surprise, but she doesn't have any issue with conversing with Dante. Dante stands up and walks over to the garden, where Corrado is watching him intently.

"Hey, Corrado," Dante greets.

"You know my name?" Corrado asks curiously.

"Of course I do." Dante smiles, holding his hand out to him. "How would I not know my nephew's name?" I wonder if Dante also knows his truth. Either way, it isn't like he will tell anyone.

Corrado looks at him with his head tilted, and I know he is probably feeling the effect of Dante's aura. Dante smiles faintly, ruffling his hair.

"I'm your dad's cousin."

"Oh, hello! I never knew Daddy had a big family," he says sadly, looking at Leo. His eyes light up, and he smiles when he sees us hugging, forgetting all about his disappointment. I don't blame him, but I promise going forward, this kid of ours is not going to miss out on anything else!

Once they have finished their exchange with one another, we all make our way to the dining room, where the table is already laden with the delicious dishes Kiara has cooked. I am actually incredibly hungry! I tuck Corrado's chair in as he sits between Leo and me, with Song seated opposite me, and, to her luck, she is right opposite Rayhan. I give her a wink before we all tuck in.

Leo

It is later in the day, and I know Kiara wants to get her hands on me. Although she doesn't say anything in front of the rest, I feel her watching me several times. At one point, she places her hand on my shoulder as she chats about something. I have a feeling she is trying to assess the level of my pain, but I move away from her touch fast.

My main issue is the bastard. I don't want him fucking knowing. But I also know the answer I will get from Kiara, and I want to delay it until after I have dealt with Rayhan because Azura will need me when she hears it from Kiara herself, that there is nothing that she can do. But I'm not against searching for further solutions.

The women are spending some time together, and Azura will also go to speak to Atlas later. I asked her if she wanted me to come, as did Kiara and Song, but she was adamant about handling it alone. I guess that fucking makes sense. Who would want a fucking audience? But if she needs me, I'll fucking be there, besides she is fucking awful at keeping her walls up. It is like a constant conversation going on in her head.

I am now walking around the pack grounds with Alejandro, Rayhan, and Dante. I didn't argue when Alejandro suggested it. I could use the fresh air, but I would have preferred having Azura with me. Corrado isn't even fucking bothered when I leave, happily content.

"That shit is all new. We made it around four years ago," Alejandro explains, pointing at the huge training facility before glancing at me. "It's taken from the blueprint and design concept that you created; we integrated the same into the academies."

"Yeah, I can fucking tell," I say. Marcel is fucking annoying at times.

"I did leave you a message to ask if you were okay with me using that shit," Alejandro says as I smoke my fourth fucking cigarette since getting here. Being in their presence is fucking my head up.

"Yeah, I saw it. You can imitate shit, but it just pushed me to improve and create something better without Marcel shoving his nose in my fucking business," I say coldly. "Besides, you were fucking trying to rile me up when you sent emails of the plans for the academies."

"At least that shows you were at least fucking reading my emails," Alejandro smirks victoriously, which I return with an icy glare.

"You have an impressive mind with ideas and concepts that could earn you millions. Have you ever considered starting a business and selling ideas to other packs around the world? Even security systems for humans?" Rayhan suggests. I frown but ignore him. *I'm not ready to talk to you.*

"Hm," I simply grunt.

We fall silent, and my mind goes to the bullets. If anything was to happen to me, then I need someone to clear that shit up.

"There is something that I think perhaps you may want to tell your Council or other packs about. Let's speak somewhere secluded," I say, taking a drag of my cigarette.

Alejandro frowns but nods, changing route and heading to headquarters. This has been changed, too. Alejandro leads the way to his office, his men clearing the path for us. The murmurs of awe follow, and I guess it isn't every fucking day they see four Rossi Alphas together. That, or they are fucking shocked I am here. The moment Dante shuts the door behind us, all three of them look at me as I walk over to the window, looking out at the pack grounds.

"What is it, Leo?" Alejandro asks.

I frown before I begin, "I created a weapon that can kill our kind the moment it penetrates the skin. You don't even need to hit a vital point for these bullets to work." I feel the room tense, but I don't turn to look at them. "It's a weapon that was meant to only be used by my most trusted if we were ever under attack. However, a man I trusted like a brother stole it and mass-produced it, selling it to several cartel and mafia organisations. According to my data, a couple of buyers were also supernatural." I now glance back at them; Dante's face is as passive as ever, whilst the other two are frowning as they listen.

"Are you sure it's that dangerous?" Alejandro asks, his brow furrowed.

"Yeah. There's someone who had some of these bullets, and they sure as fuck worked. These bullets can kill so fast that if you are in wolf form, the body doesn't even revert to human form. Emmet Garrons produced fucking thousands. I've still not fully managed to account for all fifty thousand. I'm trying to track them down, but you may want to let other packs know, just in case any of them come into contact with them."

"There've been two cases that now seem to make sense," Rayhan says quietly. "Uncle, remember I mentioned to you how we were unable to figure out how the rogue that I found near my pack was killed?"

"Yeah, that was a couple of months back. Luckily, there haven't been many stories. So, I'm sure those bullets aren't just fucking flying around, but fifty thousand. That could fucking wipe out most of our kind in the country," Alejandro says seriously.

"Yeah. I know. We've traced down some and are taking them back. I plan to buy the rest back from all the buyers they were sold to by any means," I say coldly. Web will return them to me, or I will be fucking ruining him, and take them by force.

"We'll get on it. If you have a sample, I'm sure some of our trackers can do something to help," Alejandro says as I turn back to them.

"I wasn't expecting you to be so fucking chill about it. Why? Is it because I'm a fucking Rossi? I fucked up, right?" I ask coldly. I know I am trying to instigate them, even if it isn't fucking working. Alejandro sighs.

"No, it wasn't your fucking doing but your Delta's. So, if anyone needs to be punished, it's him," Alejandro says from his seat. Rayhan is sitting opposite him, nodding his head in agreement.

"An alpha is the one who needs to take fucking responsibility for the actions of his people," I say quietly. Dante smiles faintly as he turns to me from where he is leaning against the door.

"And you're doing that by tracking these bullets down. I'll help. The more of us looking, the faster it'll get done. We all make mistakes. Don't blame yourself. We only learn from them," he adds after a moment.

"Agreed." Alejandro nods.

I don't reply, staring out the window. No one had brought up the reason why I had asked for Rayhan to come here, and I know I am going to have to fucking do it myself. I'd rather get it over with soon. I don't want to fucking be in his company for long. I look directly at Rayhan.

"Let's go for a drink. It's time we talk," I say coldly. His eyes meet mine before he gives a nod.

"Sure," he replies quietly.

"I can't wait. Drinks sound fun," Dante adds. "When are we leaving? I know a club not so far from the pack."

"We? You ain't fucking coming." I raise an eyebrow.

"Sure I am. You can't have a boys' night out between brothers without me," he counters.

"We are not brothers. You and your old man need to stop acting like you are my fucking family," I say coldly.

"We are, though. Nothing can change that, and if we can call our pack our family, then why can't I call my own blood, brother?" Dante asks. His voice is calm, but there is a subtle hint of victory in it. Fucking Rossi.

I wonder why he wears those shades. In all the images I have ever seen of him, he has them on. Sure, his eyes are red, but on pack territory, is it necessary? Something tells me there is definitely another fucking reason behind it.

"Well, then, I guess that shit's sorted. You three fuckers head out. I'll make a start on getting a team together to head out and see what we can find on these bullets."

"I'll send you the reports and details," I say, taking my phone out and texting Dan.

"Sounds like tonight is going to be eventful..." Dante murmurs.

"No shit," I mutter.

"So shall we head out in, say, an hour?" he suggests.

"Sounds good," Rayhan says, and I simply nod.

I need a shower and a little time with my girl. Then... then it is time we talk this shit out so I can let it go and move on.

A Punishment
Leo

I am in the shower. The excessive smoking throughout the day made me smell of smoke. I run my hands through my hair, washing the shampoo off.

I'm not looking forward to tonight, and I'm not going to fucking deny that I need to see her without anyone around. I just... yeah, I just fucking need to just hold her for a bit.

I said I'd do this shit, but how the fuck am I going to start that conversation?

The bathroom door opens, and I glance through the steamed glass of the shower. The blurred outline and the scent give her away. She locks the door before pulling her top off. I can see the outline of her black bra, and I throb hard, knowing she is about to join me. I slide open the glass door just as she slides her pants down.

"Hey," she says, her eyes raking over me before she swallows hard the moment she looks at my cock. I am already hardening under her gaze. I wrap my hand around my cock, stroking it slowly as I look at her.

"Hey."

She licks her lips, and I smirk slightly as she steps into the shower, still wearing her lingerie, the water instantly drenching her. I watch the water dripping down her body, my eyes flashing. *Fuck, she is fine.* She runs a hand up my arm, her other hand cupping my balls when I grab her by the chin.

"You've been a bit of a bad girl; I don't think you should get to do whatever the fuck you want," I growl huskily, taking hold of her wrist with the other hand and pushing her up against the wall. She bites her lip, smirking slightly.

"Then what are you going to do? Punish me?" she challenges. I press my body against her, letting go of her chin. I tangle my hand in her hair and yank her head up.

"Not in the way you fucking you think. You're going to get down on your knees, and I'm going to fuck this pretty mouth of yours. Oh, and I assure you I won't be going easy," I reply huskily, my other hand raking down her stomach. Her body reacts to my touch, and a gasp leaves her lips.

"Sounds good to me," she moans breathlessly.

"This is a punishment for thinking of another man, and when I'm done, the only one you will fucking ever think of will be me," I whisper, flicking her mark with my tongue before I move away, and spin her around, pressing her up against the cool wall of the shower.

"I wasn't think- ah!" she cries when I deliver a sharp slap to her ass. "Fuck!"

"Ten should do it, don't you think?" I ask, my eyes blazing as I look at her ass that is sticking out, her hands pressed against the wall.

"I can handle whatever you give me," she says, looking at me challengingly over her shoulder, her silver eyes filled with lust.

"Let's make that twenty, then. Legs apart, Baby Girl," I growl, hooking my finger into her thong and pulling it up between her ass cheeks tightly. I lick my lip, relishing how fucking good her ass looks, swallowing up her underwear. "Time to show you exactly who you belong to," I growl as I spank her ass again. She hisses, and I massage the red patch on it before I do the same to the other cheek.

Ten down, and I am fucking turned on to the point I just want to fuck her hard. She whimpers when I deliver another spank to her raw ass.

"Fuck, Leo..."

"Who do you belong to, beautiful?" I growl, delivering another spank.

She moans, gasping for a moment, and I run my hand over her burning ass. The water from the shower is pouring down on us both.

"You."

"Again," I growl.

"Fuck! You! I belong to you!" she whimpers.

I can smell her arousal, and when I deliver her final slap, I know she is near to release. I caress her ass, making her moan before wrapping my other hand around her neck as I begin massaging her pussy, pulling her back against me.

"Oh, fuck... Goddess..." she moans when I rub her clit with two fingers. I slip my fingers into her pussy, feeling her walls tighten around my fingers.

"Seems like someone enjoyed that punishment a little too much," I growl, pulling my fingers out as I suck on her neck, leaving a mark before tugging her away from the wall and pushing her to her knees.

"Obviously," she smirks.

She tilts her head up for a kiss, but as much as I fucking want to kiss her, this is a punishment, so I push her down to her knees. Instantly. Her hands go to my thighs, and I brush her wet hair from her face as she wraps a hand around my cock, stroking it.

"Admit you like it when I take your cock in my dirty little mouth," she moans hornily, sounding too fucking sinful.

"I sure fucking do," I growl huskily.

Clearly satisfied, she begins licking and sucking on it. Pleasure courses through me, and I am unable to control the groan that leaves my lips. The moment she wraps those lush lips around the tip, I suck in a breath, swearing. My hand tightens in her hair, my other braced on the wall as she begins taking me deeper into her mouth. I begin fucking her harder, thrusting into her mouth roughly, the pressure heightening, and I fuel all my emotions into it, letting it all go.

I am close, and I slam into her harder. The moment I come, releasing into her mouth and letting the intense waves of pleasure rip through me, I pull out – but she wraps her hand around my dick as she continues to suck me off. She grips my thigh, choking for a moment before she gasps, having milked me until the last fucking drop.

"Fuck, baby," I swear, pulling her up. She licks her lips, wiping off the drop of cum that has leaked out as she stands up and locks her arms around my neck.

"See? I can be a good little bad girl. Maybe I'll piss you off a little more often if it means I get to be punished like that," she whispers seductively. I smirk, wrapping my arms around her, about to kiss her when, teasingly, I kiss the corner of her lips instead.

"Shame it was a punishment, though," I whisper huskily, "so, you won't come. Not until tonight." She pulls her head back, looking into my eyes as if checking I am serious, and I smirk arrogantly.

"You're going to leave me hanging?" she asks, shocked. I smirk cockily.

"Guess I am," I say arrogantly, pulling away and tilting my head up, letting the shower water pour over my face. She looks so fucking hot, and although I want to fuck her so badly, I won't.

"Fine, then," she says with a cold glare as I slide the door open. I pause, not expecting that reaction. She reaches behind, unhooking her bra and sliding it off before tossing it at me. I catch it before it hits my face and smirk.

"Seems like you really did have the wrong fucking idea," I mock arrogantly. "Maybe you'll remember it the next time you find a certain bastard hot." She rolls her eyes as she slips her underwear off and kicks them aside.

"Fine. If you won't make me come, I'll do it myself," she challenges me with a smirk as she parts her legs, her finger finding her clit. Fuck... she knows she is fucking me up.

Two of her fingers part those lips of hers, her finger running over her clit, and, to make it fucking worse, the shower water running down her pussy and legs doesn't help matters. Her nipples are hard, her breasts pressed together as she pleasures herself. She looks far too fucking good. *Oh, fuck...* The moment she rests her head back, moaning in pleasure, I am struggling to leave.

"You should leave. I guess I'll just imagine someone else and-"

I growl, cutting her off as my hand tightens around her throat.

"Do not fucking say it," I growl, making her let out a breathy chuckle.

"Then fuck me," she challenges.

I glare at her, unable to deny that her feisty temper is a fucking turn-on. It is fucking different to know there is someone who'll challenge me and doesn't give a shit if I get pissed. I am very aware of her body pressing against my already hardening dick, and my gaze dips to her lips before I claim them in a bruising kiss. Sizzling sparks fly as pleasure erupts through me. Through the bond, I can feel her pleasure and approval.

She moans against my lips, locking her legs around my waist as she kisses me back with force. It is rough, hot, and fucking perfect as we try to dominate each other, licking, sucking, and trying to claim the other completely. The taste of blood fills my mouth, and I have no fucking idea whose it is, and I don't care. Her moans get louder, and I don't care when my own are heard. We kiss each other until I win, sucking hard on her tongue before slipping mine into her mouth, devouring her until she can't breathe and breaks away from me.

So are you going to fuck me or- Fuck!

She gasps when I press her up against the wall and slam into her with one rough thrust. Yeah, she may have fucking won this round, but I don't really care.

Boys' Night Out
Leo

You got this. Azura's words when I leave are in my mind. The fuck in the shower had been fucking hot and did far more than relax me. I feel refreshed, and when she kisses me and tells me I will be okay, it just gives me a whole new level of fucking confidence to get this shit over with.

The only fucking problem is the smirks from Kiara and Alejandro when we come down. I know Alejandro's hearing is good, but I'm not sure if that means through soundproof walls. *Ah, well, he's a fucking prick. I don't give a shit.*

We leave the mansion when Dante motions to his ride, and I raise an eyebrow.

"No, thanks."

I am not going to fucking sit in the back. I walk to my own car, feeling both Rayhan and Dante watching me, and get in, only for Dante to open the back door of the car and get in.

"What the actual fuck?" I growl.

"What? I'm sitting in the back because I'm the youngest. It's fair, right?" he asks, smirking. *And the fucking biggest.* He can't read minds, can he?

That means that the bastard is about to- yeah. He fucking got in.

I cast both men a cold glare before hitting the gas and turning the car violently, speeding towards the gates. Great, now I am in the same fucking car as him.

"This is a nice ride. I like the added tech," Dante remarks.

I don't reply, driving towards the nightclub Dante has chosen, a club that belongs to me, and I know he fucking knows it is mine.

We get to the nightclub at record speed, and I get out, mind-linking my men to stay clear of me. The three of us head inside without even a pass, obviously. The bouncer lowers his head towards me as we enter from a back entrance.

The moment we enter, the music reaches our ears, but I avoid the main club, heading up to the topmost floor via the lift. Rayhan glances at me but says nothing. Dante just has a small smile on his face, still wearing his shades, although it is night. I know werewolves can see in the dark, and I'm sure as fuck he can, even if he isn't exactly a werewolf. I know he is a demi-god or whatever that shit is, but I wonder what exactly his wolf is like. Can he even shift? He doesn't really smell exactly like a werewolf and if he can shift, what does his wolf look like? Well, I don't care how intrigued I am. I hate how I want to know everything. I'll just ask Azura.

"This place looks pretty neat," Rayhan remarks. So he has clocked on that it is mine, too.

"Hm," I reply, not wanting to entertain him.

I lead the way to the VIP lounge on the top floor. There are several men in suits and women in dresses, some just having drinks, others deep in discussions. One of the human managers approaches me. It is obvious he feels intimidated; he is a professional and a strong man for a human, but no one can ignore Dante's aura.

"Hello-"

"We'll be seated out on the balcony. Make sure no one disturbs us," I say, sounding cold and emotionless.

"Of course, sir, but there is a reservation. Someone booked out the entire floor." He lowers his head apologetically. "Shall I cancel?"

"That would have been mine. Dante Rossi," Dante smirks. The manager looks a little uneasy, looking up at him but nods.

"Ah, yes, it was. Then that's perfect," he says before he leads the way, holding the doors to the rooftop sitting area for us.

A human bartender is at the bar. This place is usually reserved for a select few. Music is playing out here, but it is far quieter than inside. I choose a seating area far from the bartender, and a waitress comes over to take our drink orders once we are seated on the leather sofa. I raise my eyebrow when Rayhan chooses a non-alcoholic one. Once she comes back with our drinks and leaves us alone, I can't help but question it.

"Why come to a club if you don't drink?" Rayhan picks up his mocktail and raises an eyebrow.

"You invited me out after so many years, why would I refuse?"

"Hmm," I grunt, downing my glass of whiskey and pouring another.

"The weather's nice," Dante remarks. Weird shit.

"And? As a werewolf or whatever the fuck you are, does the weather even matter?"

"Let me enjoy the small things in life. I'm still human," Dante replies. His head tilts up as he looks at the sky.

"Only you're fucking not," I reply, but I get what he means. Just because he is different doesn't mean he can't live a normal life. In a way, I feel bad for him. It is obvious he is someone who lives far more isolated than the rest of us. Even his own pack members find his presence too much and he's their future Alpha. I guess I can relate to that.

"It is a good night," Rayhan agrees. The tension is growing again, and I know I have to fucking make a start somewhere.

"You just got the two kids, right? Or you got more?" I ask him. He looks at me, almost surprised at my question, before smiling and nodding.

"Yeah, Ahren and Sienna," he replies, taking his phone out and showing me the lock screen. There is Delsanra, her hair as white as it had been since the day it changed. In front of her are his kids. The girl is smiling brightly, whilst the boy has only a hint of a smile on his face.

"They've grown," I say. I haven't seen them since back then.

"They have. Corrado is a lovely kid, too, and clearly has taken a liking to Azura already," he replies. I nod.

"He has."

I remember when I tossed Sienna up in the air years ago to scare Rayhan, only for her to start crying. It had pissed him off, but I get it. Anyone who scared Corrado like that would be fucking dead but Rayhan had kept his shit together better than I would have.

"So, let's cut the small talk," I say, placing my glass down and lighting a cigarette as I look ahead coldly, refusing to look at either. "You know the reason that I fucking hate you all. I still don't think what went down was right. How you went about that shit affected so many innocent lives. I mean, even your mother hated Delsanra, right? We were all raised to hate witches, but because your sister ended up being a hybrid, your family became more accepting, and because she was your mate, otherwise... no one fucking cared. You dealt me a hand of injustice, and I get it. I get that she's your mate, and I don't hold her accountable for any of it because she was a victim, just like us. What you did is not something I'll ever forget, but I'm going to try to let it go. Not just for me, but for Marcel and that fucker of an uncle... and for Rafael... because of all you fucking Rossis, he was different." He really was. A silence falls at the mention of Rafael, and I take a drag on my cigarette before continuing,

"I have a question. When we had that talk after defeating that Djinn years ago, did you even understand the repercussions of your actions?" I ask, now turning to him. He is frowning, a hand to his chin. He sighs heavily and looks at me.

"I did. At the time, all I saw was Delsanra's pain. But when you put it like that, ten years ago, back then, I realised I was wrong. When we visited your pack, I genuinely meant that apology. I should have looked deeper into it; I shouldn't have let myself put Marcel in that position. I messed up, and I get it. I'm sorry, Leo, for causing you pain, too. For breaking the trust that you had in us – in Uncle Al," he says, looking out over the city. "When I saw those memories... when we went into her mind and witnessed everything that she had gone through from Endora to the hunters, it was too much. I realised I had already failed her, and I wanted to somehow fix things. I went about it wrong, and that is a regret I still hold. In all honesty, it was as if I was doing it for myself to make me feel better because she told me to stop. I'm sorry, and

I know you won't ever be able to forgive me fully, but I do hope that we can move past it, although it isn't something small or easy to forget. I wish I could go back and do things differently."

Our eyes meet, and I realise he isn't the same man he was years ago. There is wisdom there and regret. I look away first. It makes me feel better knowing that he regrets it.

"I'm letting it go. Not for you, but for me. We all make mistakes and I'd be an even bigger hypocrite if I didn't admit that I've fucked up, too, and only after did I realise the consequences of my actions. Those bullets I made have killed and will probably kill many more."

"We'll fix it before it gets out of control. I've already got my men to work with Uncle's, too. I have connections in the human world as well. If anything comes to light, I'll let you know."

"Yeah? Great," I reply. I have my own eyes and ears in the underworld, and I will probably be able to track them all down faster, but at least they are on it if something happens to me.

There, it is done.

How do I feel? Lighter. It isn't something I'll forget, but I am willing to move on, and I will.

I did it, I tell Azura through the link.

I'm proud of you, and I, I… I'm going to go see Atlas soon, too. She was going to say something else. I frown but decide not to push it.

Good luck, you'll be fine. If anyone, I think he's the one who needs the good luck, I smirk, drinking my whiskey, almost imagining her pouting.

Hey, I'm not that bad!

You're as bad as they get, I reply huskily.

Yeah? Well, you like it…

The memory of earlier in the shower comes back to me, and, fuck, just the thought is a damn turn-on.

Without a fucking doubt.

She laughs, **See you later. Have fun with your cousins; I'll be having some girl time with my sister until you get back.** That is her way of telling me to talk to these two for longer.

I don't think there's any way I'd find these two fun to hang with but take care of yourself. I'm here if you need to talk.

I know. You're tied to the Westwood devil for life now.

I guess I have fucking sold my soul.

Oh, absolutely.

We end the link, and Rayhan speaks,

"So, you own this club, if I'm correct?"

"Yeah."

"I'm sure he has several businesses under different names," Dante adds. Fucker.

"Maybe."

"You have a fair share in the Rossi Empire, too," Rayhan says, running his hand through his hair.

"I still don't want it. Not because of whatever, but because that empire went to those heights because of your father. So why the fuck would I take that shit?" I ask.

"He made it for us, but it was started by our grandfather. We are the Rossi Legacies, and it belongs to us all," he replies.

"Well, carry on running that shit… if I ever need money, I know where to come," I say, although I have no plan to take his money. I want the conversation done. He may be on the list as one of the richest men in the world, even the humans know who he is, but like I've said before in the shadows, I am king.

"Great," he replies with a smile. "Thank you, Leo, for giving me a chance. I assure you I will not give you any more room for complaints." Yeah, I don't do fucking mush and shit, so I simply give a careless nod.

"And you thought you'd be fucking needed," I mutter, glaring at Dante. He raises an eyebrow.

"The night isn't over," he replies with a small smirk.

What? I am pretty smart, but the way he talks grates on my fucking nerves. What is he going on about?

"So, why do you wear those shades?" I ask, frowning.

"People don't really like looking me in the eye," he replies, and despite the light tone of his voice, I can feel the heaviness in it.

"Or more like we are unable to look into them," Rayhan adds.

"Show me," I say coldly, unable to fucking stop myself from asking.

"Sure, if you want."

He places his glass down, removing his shades. For a moment, his eyes remain lowered, almost as if he is scrutinising his sunglasses in his hands. He has thick lashes, and I kinda get why Azura has issues with his hair, something that crossed her mind at least three fucking times today. That or how she is a whole day fucking older. She is stuck on that weird shit, just as Corrado is stuck on her not being able to cook. They are the perfect duo of weirdos. My weirdos.

He looks up slowly, and I find myself looking into deep red pupils. Instantly, I feel like I can't breathe, and I am being sucked in. My surroundings seem to vanish, and all I can see are those burning orbs. My eyes sting as I try to hold his gaze. My entire head feels like it is going to split open from the intense pressure, and just when I think I can't take anymore, he quickly looks away.

"Sorry. It can get a little intense," he says when I let out a sharp exhale. My heart is thundering, and I realise it had been just a glance. What the actual fuck?

"Yeah, no shit." Rayhan chuckles, and I glare at him.

"Sorry, but if it's any consolation, you did better than most."

"What the fuck is that?" I ask, glancing back at the younger man.

"I wasn't doing anything," he says, picking up his glass again. "It happened when I turned thirteen."

"Is that when you shifted? Like a Lycan, then?" I ask.

"I wouldn't call it a shift..." he says, making me look at him sharply.

"Yeah, definitely not a shift," Rayhan agrees. I look between them, and Dante simply smiles faintly.

"I'll show you sometime."

"Just be ready for another intense experience," Rayhan smirks.

"I wonder why the fuck Selene put a demi-god on Earth," I muse. The distant sounds of a police siren and a car horn blaring far below can be heard, and Rayhan's brows furrow.

"Even I don't know the exact answer to that," Dante murmurs.

We fall silent as a soft wind blows around us, and I suddenly realise that this isn't so fucking bad. Am I actually just relaxing with these two? Well, shit... seems like I am.

"Another round," Rayhan says, motioning to the waitress who stands to the side. She doesn't take long, bringing us a fresh round, and we all reach for our glasses at the same time.

"To the future?" Dante asks, raising his glass of tequila.

"To a better bond," Rayhan adds.

"Whatever," I say, making them both smirk as I begrudgingly clink my glass with theirs before we down them in one go.

Building Bridges
Azura

"Are you sure you're going to be okay?" Song asks me. I nod. Mama had called earlier as well. I know she was surprised that I am actually going to go see Atlas, but I can tell she is happy. When I told her that Leo and I had figured things out, she smiled and said, "That's my girl. Get that man in line." Goddess, she is a queen.

"Yeah, totally. He's just a guy," I say, shrugging.

"Okay, hun, if you're sure," Song replies, giving me a tight hug. I glance at Kiara when I move back.

"You sure his mother isn't going to be around?" I ask, my voice sounding resentful despite not meaning to. Her eyes soften, and she nods.

"He doesn't live with her anymore, and I let him know you were coming." She smiles gently, and I nod.

"Okay," I say, shoving my hands into my pockets as I turn on my heels.

"Are you sure you know the way?"

"Yeah, I'll ask someone if I can't find it," I say before heading for the gates.

It is late, but I know he had work earlier, and if Leo could face Rayhan, then I certainly should be able to face this guy.

I finally get there a good hour later after loitering around the pack and even stopping to get a bottle of wine from one of the shops. I mean, I can't go empty-handed, right? I finally reach his apartment and ring the bell, taking a deep breath and hoping he doesn't answer.

The door opens a little too fast, considering I have just rung it. Was he waiting?

I look up at him. He is tall, over six feet, and he has dirty blond hair and light blue eyes. He is well built, but the first thing that comes to my mind is that he looks a lot like 'him'. I have seen a picture of Fred, my sperm donor. Okay, maybe they aren't that alike, but they have similarities.

"Hey." He speaks softly, almost as if he knows I am ready to run. I press my lips together, frowning deeply.

"Hi," I say, holding the bottle out without looking at him. I see him smile from the corner of his eyes before he steps aside and accepts it.

"Come on in."

I don't want to. I don't want to be here.

I hesitate before balling my fists and stepping inside. *You just spend a little time, then you turn, and you leave.*

The moment I look around, I realise he wasn't just thinking this would be a quick visit. On the coffee table in front of the corner sofa are bowls and plates with pasta, roast potatoes, and enchiladas. The place is clean, and a cinnamon and spice fragrance fills the air.

The door shutting behind me makes me snap out of my thoughts.

"Come on, take a seat and thank you for this," he says, giving me a grin as he raises the bottle. For a moment, he reminds me of Liam.

No. Liam is my brother, Atlas isn't.

I feel a sliver of guilt, knowing he has nothing to do with his parent's decisions. Even Alejandro told me that he was raised without Fred even bothering to visit him at all.

"You're welcome," I say, walking over to the sofa and sitting down gingerly on the edge. He places the bottle down before opening the fridge and getting some juice cartons out.

"Are these okay?" he asks, holding up a mango carton and an orange.

"Yeah, totally," I reply, looking at the oil painting on the wall of a boat sailing.

He comes over, placing the cartons on the table before sitting down. The sofa dips under his weight, but I am grateful he has left a big gap between us.

"Pasta? I did ask Luna Kiara if you were okay with it," he says. His voice is gentle, almost as if not wanting to trigger me. He is making an effort, and I really need to give him a chance. That's what I'm here for...

"So, Kiara was being sneaky, huh? Yes, it's fine. It all looks good. You didn't need to make anything. I mean, I didn't come to eat, I'm not hungry or anything." *Wow, nice, Azura.* "I mean, I'll eat because you made it and went through the effort..." *Really?* Word vomit at its finest. He laughs lightly and nods.

"She did, but I'm grateful for it. You know I've wanted to meet you for a while now. When Alpha Alejandro told me you wanted to see me... I was...I'm grateful."

"I guess I'm glad I'm doing this... kinda..." I trail off, instead just giving him a small smile as he begins plating some food for me.

Ten minutes later, we are both eating, and he makes light conversation. Although I am mainly answering him, he is the one keeping the conversation going and I am finally relaxing a little.

"So, you're mated?" he asks, motioning to my mark. I place my hand over it for a moment, smiling slightly.

"Yeah, to Leo Rossi. Alejandro's nephew."

"Oh... nice." He seems to realise who he is. "Are you happy?" My smile fades, and he shakes his head.

"Shit, sorry, I just meant he treats you well, right? It's just that I know what Fred was like, too. I'm sorry."

I guess I'm not the only one with a blabbering issue. He is looking down, but I can tell he is tense. I reach over, placing a hand on his leg.

"Hey... it's okay. You don't need to worry that I'll get offended. The hardest part was facing you, and I totally aced that," I say lightly before smiling. He looks up, and I am surprised to see the sadness in them.

"I'm sorry, on behalf of both him and my mom, for what happened to your mom and how their actions affected her." Yeah, talking about her does hurt, about Fred, too, but it isn't Atlas's fault. I sit back, picking up my glass, and take a sip.

"I'm going to be honest. I hate the fact that your mom got with him when she knew he had a mate. If she didn't know, it'd be different, but she did. I don't know if it was a full relationship or a one-night thing; either way, I'll never forgive her. But I'm not going to hold you responsible for their actions," I say, thinking it is the right thing to do... just as Leo had done. He looks at me, a slight frown on his forehead as he nods.

"I agree. She didn't do the right thing. Thanks for giving me a chance."

"Can I ask why you even want to know me? I mean, neither of us knew our sperm donor, we weren't raised by him. So, why?"

"I just wanted to have the chance to get to know you. I mean, does it matter if we weren't raised by him? We're still related by blood. You're still my sister, my only sibling." I frown slightly; I get that. Just the way I want this baby to get to know Corrado... to get to spend time with Leo...

"Okay."

"Okay?" He raises an eyebrow.

"I'm ready to at least try to get to know you. Fred's abuse towards Indigo really affected me, but I know it's not your fault and I know it's going to take me time to open up... but I guess what I'm saying is, we can try to be friends." I shrug, stabbing a potato and shoving the full thing into my mouth. Okay, it is a little big, but if I can take Leo's dick, I sure can take a tiny potato. I can see he is trying not to smile.

"Sure, I'd really like that."

Okay, somehow, this is harder than giving Leo a blowjob. I am struggling to break it down. I swallow my potato, feeling it stick in my throat, and he swiftly passes me my glass again. I take it and gulp it down.

"Thanks," I say as I feel the potato going down. "Don't you dare laugh." He grins.

"Alright, I won't."

"Good! Now eat up. This is a lot of food for two."

"Oh, I eat a lot."

"Me too, but I can't cook like you."

"I can imagine that," he jokes, giving me a smile, and I can't help but smile back at him.

I stay for another hour, and we make small talk. Although I'm not ready to welcome him into my inner circle, it is a start. We have exchanged numbers, and he has asked questions about what I do, my birthday, and I tell him I am pregnant. Surprisingly, he isn't hard to talk to, and I ask him a few questions, too. He doesn't want to be a warrior, and I have a feeling it is because of Fred; he is instead a trainer for the younger pups at the pack.

He walks me to the mansion, stopping a few metres away, and watches me enter. I give him a small wave before I take a deep breath and saunter to the door. Only to freeze when Leo's scent hits me. I turn to see him standing in the shadows, leaning against the wall, one foot propped up against the wall, and smoking a cigarette, looking absolutely fuckable. Damn that man is fine meat.

"Leo!" I run down the steps and pounce on him. He catches me with one arm, looking down at me with a raised eyebrow as I tighten my hold around his neck. "Did you miss me?"

"Not really. I was enjoying the peace and quiet without you around," he replies, making me frown.

"What did you just say?" I growl, digging my nails into his neck.

"Fuck, woman, stop with the violence. I said I was enjoying the peac-" I clamp my hand over his mouth.

"I gave you a chance to rectify your mistake and choose your words wisely. Ass."

He pulls away, biting the side of my hand lightly. A knot forms in my stomach as his lips caress my skin, placing a soft kiss before letting go.

"Okay, fine. I'll rephrase," he says, his arms wrapping around me tighter as he leans down and claims my lips in a deep kiss that takes my breath away. *Kiss me forever?*

My heart is pounding as pleasure rushes through me; his lips move against mine so deeply and sensually that I can no longer think of anything else. He moves back after a few moments, and the kiss suddenly feels too short. He smirks sexily when he places me on the floor but refuses to let go of me, and I think I needed it.

"As I was saying, I missed having my psycho circus clown around to entertain me," he snickers, releasing me.

"Oh no, you did not just call me a clown. No, no, no! You are so done for!" I lunge at him, and he dodges, smoothly taking a drag on his cigarette. I try again, but he ducks. "I am going to skin you alive! Or better, I'll make a rug out of your fur! Wait, I need a staple gun!"

He tosses his cigarette to the ground, crushing it under his boot before grabbing my arm as he spins me into his arms, my back hitting his chest.

"What's the staple gun for?"

"To add a few more steps to your damn dick ladder," I growl, trying to bite him.

"You really are my perfectly imperfect little psycho."

To my surprise, he starts laughing. My heart thunders, and I freeze, tilting my head up at the beautiful sound. It is probably the most carefree laugh I have ever heard from him, and it makes me feel so many emotions. He looks years younger, his pearly white teeth only adding to his beautiful smile. He catches me staring, and his laugh fades away as he raises an eyebrow.

"What are you planning?" I shake my head.

"Revenge, my dear mate, will come later, but I was just admiring your laugh; it's beautiful," I reply softly, unable to stop the surge of emotions in my chest. I made sure my walls were up earlier through the mind-link. I had almost been about to express my feelings, but I didn't want to do it over the mind-link.

"Oh, yeah? I might try to laugh a little more often if you end up looking at me like a love-struck little puppy a tad more often," he smirks, squeezing my cheeks. "I'm not sure who has juicier cheeks, you or your son." I glare jokingly at him.

"Hey, I am not looking at you like a puppy!" *But I am lovestruck...* "And of course Corrado!"

"Oh, yeah, you can't be a puppy. You're Lola the fish, right?"

"Oh my god, you ass!" I pull away, smacking his shoulder. He smirks, dodging me as I chase him.

"Hey, for what it's worth, she's one gorgeous fish."

I smirk as I tackle him to the ground. I know he let me because he is not that easy to bring down. My heart skips a beat when he catches me, making sure I don't take any of the impact of the fall. I smirk, straddling him and bunching his shirt in my fists.

"And if I'm Lola, then you're Oscar. You have some damn big lips, too," I say, bending down and kissing him softly.

"Only thing is Oscar was only infatuated with Lola. What I feel for you, is way fucking more than that," he says quietly, his hands slipping under my top, dancing along my skin as he kisses me again.

"Same," I say, thinking this is my moment.

"You were going to-" Leo is cut off when the front door opens, and Alejandro leans against the door frame.

"If you two are fucking done? I don't need you lot getting it on out here. Wasn't earlier enough?" He smirks, making my cheeks burn. *Oh, he's so dead.*

"Kiara! Control your mate!" I growl, jumping off Leo and running at Al.

"Hold up there, kid," Al drawls, still smirking annoyingly and clamping his big hand down on my head.

"Ow, ow! *Ow*!"

I bring my knee up, ready to hit him in the privates, when he steps back, snickering as Leo pulls me into his arms.

"Baby, be nice," Kiara scolds him, coming up behind him.

"I'm always fucking nice, Amore Mio," he says, grabbing her by the back of her neck and kissing her.

"Hey, don't play dirty!" I know he is just trying to distract Kiara! I stick my tongue out at him, leaning into Leo's hold.

"You're fucking immature, you know that?" Leo asks Alejandro when he moves away from Kiara.

"Does it look like I give a shit?" Al counters.

"Clearly fucking not," Leo replies coldly.

"Okay, how about we retreat to Alejandro's office? Corrado is playing with Rayhan and Alessandra," Kiara suggests, and I realise what she means.

Time to try to heal him!

"Yeah, let's," I say, feeling unease settle into me.

Knowing the Answer
Leo

The office is tense, and even Alejandro is dead serious. Any sarcasm is gone as he stands there with his arms crossed, watching me coldly. That is his concentrating expression.

Azura is sitting on the armrest of the chair I am in, and Kiara tells me to remove my shirt. I pull it off and Azura takes it from me, holding it to her chest. I can hear her heart beating violently, although she is trying not to let it get to her.

Kiara takes a deep breath, a frown of concentration crossing her face as she kneels in front of me. Her eyes blaze purple, and for a split second, I am reminded of the flicker I saw in Azura's eyes the other night. Usually, when your wolf comes to the front, if you watch carefully, or in my case, record it and slow down the speed just to observe it, you will see the wolf's eye colour bleed into yours. What just happened with Kiara's is like a flame spreading from the bottom of the iris.

I am brought out of my thoughts when Kiara places her hands on my shoulders. Her frown deepens as she runs her hands down my chest, my flanks, and parts of my stomach as she tries to assess the extent of the damage. I hear her heart skip a beat. I keep my face a mask of indifference as I know what is coming,

She will try and fail, but you know what is going to be fucking hardest? When I'm going to have to act like it's fine and watch the emotion in their eyes...

A coolness begins spreading from her hands, and I feel it wash through me. An edge of the pain seems to lift a little, but I know she isn't succeeding. She doesn't stop, her purple aura wrapping around us both to the extent that Azura is being pushed away, but she refuses to let go of me, her arm firmly around my shoulders. Kiara bites her lip, her forehead now covered with a layer of sweat as she pours everything she has into me.

"What's happening?" Alejandro asks, his voice dark and cold as he looks between us.

Kiara isn't able to reply as she looks into my eyes. A trickle of blood runs from her nose, and her eyes glitter with tears as I feel another strong surge of intense power rush through me, but we both know it is futile. The blood isn't stopping, and even Azura is beginning to worry. Kiara's entire body is tense, her brows furrowed as she gives it her all. She is going to fucking pass out at this rate.

"Stop!" I command sharply, taking hold of her arms and moving her back. She collapses to the floor, and Alejandro is by her side in a flash, scooping her up into his arms. Azura's heart is pounding, and when Kiara looks at me, I know what her next words are going to be.

"I'm sorry, I'm unable to heal you," she whispers, her gaze going to Alejandro, who looks shocked. There it is – the concern, worry, and sadness as he looks at me, but I know as long as I don't look at Azura, I'll be okay.

Her arms tighten around my neck, and trickles of her thoughts and emotions seep into my mind. Her worry and pain. Her fear of losing me, of our children losing me. Her terror of nothing being able to heal me. I can feel her body shaking a little, and despite the fact that it is going to fucking break me, I pull her into my lap, wrapping my arms around her.

The moment our eyes meet, I realise she is fighting herself not to cry, and it fucking hurts. This is the pain I wanted to keep her from. I can't give her the life she wants.

"I was expecting that answer anyway," I tell Kiara and Alejandro, who are obviously conversing through the link from the looks on their faces. Azura shifts, straddling me, and locks her arms around my neck tightly. I close my eyes, inhaling her scent deeply as I caresses her back.

"It ain't fucking over until we have drained every fucking avenue. How long do you have?" Alejandro growls. I lean back slightly, my hands on Azura's ass, making sure my face is still set in the same 'I don't give a fuck' expression.

"A month or two max, if that," I reply coldly.

"And you didn't think to seek out help earlier?" Alejandro frowns. "Does Marcel know?" My irritation rises. I know he is fucking worried, but I don't need to explain shit to him.

"I never fucking realised it was that serious until it was far too fucking late, and it wasn't like I was going to ask the very same people who I didn't want to fucking face for help," I growl, unable to keep my anger at bay.

"We're family, Leo, and-"

"And what? I fucking told you I didn't think it was fucking serious!" I growl, my aura raging around me.

"You shouldn't have taken the fucking chance. You have a son, and what about your father?" Alejandro shoots back, his aura filling the air. I place Azura down and stand up, glaring at the man who stands opposite me. Our Alpha auras rage around us so intensely you can feel it. Blazing red eyes meet magnetic blue.

"I'm not a fucking god that I can see the future. Now end this shit. It's fucking done. Don't make me regret even allowing Kiara to try," I snarl, my eyes flashing.

"This isn't over, Al – relax. I know you're upset," Kiara whispers, cupping his face and forcing him to look at her.

"Fucking hell," I mutter, taking out a packet of cigarettes and taking one between my lips.

"Still, he tried to deal with that shit alone," Alejandro growls, "He may not care for us but I fucking care."

"I know, baby."

Dickhead.

"You don't fucking know me, so don't think you know shit," I growl back.

"Stop it. Both of you," Azura snaps, standing up. When she places her hand on my shoulder as she looks between us, it is clear she is angry as much as she is upset.

"There's no point in ifs and buts. It's happened, and I'm not able to heal him. We need to find a solution," Kiara says quietly.

"Yeah, and he's trying, okay? Despite everything he's been through, he's trying to be a better person, Alejandro! Try to see that. I get that you are upset, but this is hard for him, too," Azura adds, her eyes flashing with pain and frustration. Alejandro's eyes meet hers. A frown on his face.

"Then he better fucking try harder to live," he growls, his eyes flashing once more before he turns and storms out of the room. Kiara looks at Azura and me apologetically.

"He's just hurt. I told him only a little earlier... I hoped I could fix it – he feels he failed you entirely," she whispers, reaching over as she places a hand on both our cheeks before she looks down. "We will find a way. There's Delsanra, Raihana, and maybe Dante might have the answer. We are going to figure this out. Excuse me."

"Thanks for trying," I say when she turns to leave. I don't even look at her, simply smoking my cigarette. She sighs softly, and I see her nod sadly before she leaves.

"We will find a way," Azura murmurs, and I look down at her, wrapping my arm around her shoulders.

"Yeah," I murmur while kissing her forehead softly. She leans into me, and just then there is a light knock on the half-open door.

"Mind if I come in?" Dante asks, entering anyway. Azura turns to him, her heart racing, and I know she is about to ask him for help.

"Give us a minute, beautiful?" I ask quietly. It is obvious Dante wants to talk about something, and I really don't want her to hear any more bad news today.

"Why can't I be here?" she asks. I kiss her lips slowly, and she sighs in frustration. "One minute," she says, frowning.

"Make it five," I reply, smirking slightly. She nods slowly and reluctantly lets go of me. Our eyes meet, and I realise she only agreed because she is about to break.

"Okay," she says, gripping my face as she pulls me down and kisses me hard. I kiss her back, letting the sparks roll through me.

Knowing the Answer | 433

I will try — for her, for our kids, and maybe for the other bastards who throw a hissy fit when shit doesn't go their way.

She pulls away before turning and leaving the room.

"What do you fucking want?" I ask Dante, smoking my cigarette. He smiles slightly, taking a seat in his dad's chair and crossing his ankles on the desk.

"I have a question. Years ago, I swore an oath on Azura that I would grant you a favour whenever you need it. Why didn't you ever call? I owed you; it would have just been a favour owed, nothing more." I raise an eyebrow.

"Don't you usually fucking know everything? You should know the answer to your question," I reply. I'm fucking surprised I never looked deeper into why he had chosen Azura to swear on. The fucker is smart, I'll give him that. He smiles faintly.

"I think people forget I don't know everything. I'm a demi-god, not a god, and even then, even gods are not all-knowing or all-powerful. Even they have weaknesses," he replies.

"Hm."

"So, tell me why you didn't call on that favour?" Great, he's still stuck on that.

"Why would I call on a favour that involved saving someone's life?" I mutter, turning my back on him. A moment's silence follows as I walk over to the window and open it, leaning against the frame as I smoke.

"Rayhan's mother, who you hated at the time."

"Still hate," I growl.

"Sure. But answer the question."

"I have nothing against her, and besides, no one deserves to lose their parents... unless, of course, the parents are fucking twats." He chuckles, and I hear him get up.

"You're really a good person, Leo. If only you knew..." He leans against the other side of the window and looks up at the moon. I wonder what he means, but even if I ask, he won't tell me.

"I should have fucking known something was up when you took an oath on her back then. It was fucking weird since you two argued and fought a lot," I remark.

"Well, I had to play it smart since I didn't know what you might ask for, and I knew you'd never be able to take a wrong oath on her."

"You were a smart little shit."

He smirks, "But if we're talking smarter, it's you. I just know things; you figure them out."

Azura enters the office again, and I glance at the time. She sure didn't waste time; she left exactly five minutes ago. When she comes in front of me, I can see her eyes are red. She has been crying...

I pull her close, wrapping my arms around her and kissing her neck softly. She leans into me, her heart pounding under my touch.

"Well, first of all, Delsanra, Raihana, and even I can't heal you, but..."

Azura is about to react when I tighten my arms around her.

Relax, Sexy Mama, I murmur through the link, seeing Dante's face turned towards the moon.

"But what?" I ask. He looks at us before turning back to the night sky.

"It's just a little clue, but I'm sure you'll figure it out" Clue? He sighs softly before he continues, "When the full moon is at its peak, only in those moments can the Heart of Fire heal all. Find it, and you will live." His words echo in my mind as I try to make sense of it.

"Heart of Fire?" Azura asks, now turning in my arms to look at him with hope ignited in her eyes.

"Leave the thinking to Leo," Dante teases her, making her try to kick him, but he is far enough away that she fails.

"The only Heart of Fire I've come across is..."

Suddenly I think I may have the answer. I don't know how or what will make it happen, but... I think I'm right. I look up at him sharply, my hand going to my neck, when Azura's gaze snaps to it, realisation dawning on her.

"Wait, my mark?" she asks, confused, looking at my neck.

"Like I said, My Temperamental Miracle, leave the thinking to Leo."

"Ass. So, somehow, my mark will help?" She pulls away, turning and looking at me sharply.

"No..." I say slowly, watching Dante, and when the corner of his lips curl upwards, I know I am right. I look into the bright blue eyes of the woman I have come to love without realising. "The Heart of Fire itself..."

"What is that?" She frowns, but my attention is back on Dante, and when his smile grows, I know I have hit the nail on the fucking head.

"You. You're the Heart of Fire," I murmur, my head spinning as I stare at her. I may have found one answer but there are a thousand more questions that take its place.

She looks confused and doubtful, turning to Dante for confirmation. He simply tilts his head and says one word that confirms it all.

"Bingo."

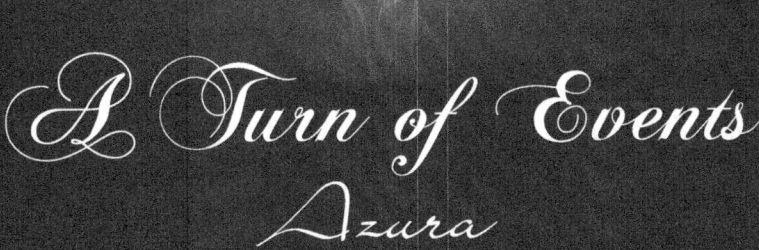

A Turn of Events
Azura

It is the following afternoon, and we are ready to head back home.

Last night when I thought all hope was gone, I realised I'm the answer. Sure, we don't know exactly how it will work, and I know Dante isn't going to tell me the answer, but at least we know the main thing, and we won't let the chance pass by. There are less than two weeks until the next full moon, and we'll figure it out. Or I'm sure Leo will, and I will just stick to Leo and hope for the best.

Last night we didn't sleep much. He held me in his arms, stroking my hair and back. It wasn't sexual, but it was so intimate that the emotions I was feeling were unexplainable. I love him, and as mushy gushy as that is, I do want to tell him. I just need to find the right time.

"Are these all for me?" Corrado asks in awe as Dante finishes loading the trunk with all the toys and clothes that Kiara had gotten for Corrado. The weather is warm, and despite the sun being up, a cool wind is blowing.

"Yes, they are." She smiles as she leans down and gives him a soft kiss on the forehead.

"Thank you so much, Aunty Kia but I don't need so many things. My daddy gets me lots of things," he replies, looking at Leo, who is smoking, as if for approval to accept all the things. I place my hands on my knees, bending over next to him.

"It's okay, kiddo, it's from Aunty Kia. You can keep them all," I whisper, ruffling his hair.

"Aunty? She's his grandma," Alejandro smirks as he comes out of the house with another two boxes.

"She isn't as old as you. Besides, she's my sister, so he can call her Aunty through me. You can stick to being a grandad. I mean, you're old enough to be my grandad," I state, making him grab my head. I know he is going to give it a squeeze, so I duck, swatting his hand away. "You need to treat the Westwood women better," I glower. He always treats Raven, who is one of Kiara's best friends, in the exact same way.

He dumps the boxes in the boot, only for Kiara to catch them in time and place them down gently. Dusting his hands off, he looks at me.

"Oh yeah? You're practically a Rossi now. Remember when you used to go on about hating Rossi men?" I roll my eyes; he's got me there.

"Not really. I mean, I said most men. I'm okay with the Giant Shrimp and Rayhan-" Leo's eyes narrow, and I stick my tongue out at him. "And of course, Leo. Besides, he's totally different from you."

"Is he?" Rayhan asks as Dante scoffs before he hides it fast, earning himself a glare from me. "I don't see much difference," Rayhan adds as he walks down the steps, raising an eyebrow as he looks at me. Folding my arms, I pout slightly.

"You have a point..." Kiara laughs as Corrado looks between Leo and Al. His eyes become wide as saucers.

"Oh, I see it!" Both tattooed men look at him. Alejandro smirks as Leo raises an eyebrow, both speaking at the same time,

"I'm his secret role model."

"We're nothing alike." Leo glares at him. "Like I said, we aren't alike..." Dante simply chuckles, pulling the trunk shut and leaning against it.

"Oh, you two definitely have so much in common. It isn't a bad thing."

"Whatever. Let's get going," Leo says, taking a final drag of his cigarette before getting rid of it. Our eyes meet, and he closes the gap between us as he pulls me into his arms, kissing my neck, clearly not bothered that everyone is watching us. He wants me, and I want him just as much. It's crazy how strong this connection and the hunger for one another is.

"Atlas." Alejandro's voice makes me slowly move away from Leo.

He approaches, holding a bag and smiling slightly. His gaze goes to Leo, who simply watches him coldly, and it is then that a thought occurs to me, one regarding my other brother Liam. *Liam is not going to forgive Leo as easily as the rest have...*

"Hi," Atlas greets. Kiara smiles, brushing her hair back.

"Hello, you came just in time." He scratches the back of his neck.

"Yeah, I'm glad. I wanted to say goodbye." He looks at me, and I nod, gesturing at Leo.

"This is my mate, Leo, and this is our son, Corrado."

He doesn't question anything, simply holding his hand out to Leo, who takes it, giving it a firm shake before he winks at Corrado.

"Hello." Corrado tilted his head.

"Hello. Who are you?"

"I'm a frien-"

"This is one of my brothers. Atlas," I announce, cutting Atlas off.

He looks up at me, surprise clear in his eyes, but I'm not going to lie. I realised I was being unfair; he has done nothing wrong, and the time I spent with him showed he isn't a bad person. He doesn't deserve my hostility. Sure, we aren't close, but who knows, maybe someday? A small half smile crosses his lips, and I smile back before brushing my hair back.

"Oh... so you're my uncle. I have such a big family now. I need to remember everyone's names!" Corrado says thoughtfully. Atlas smiles at him.

"Definitely, but once you get to see everyone more and more, it gets easier."

Corrado nods before I motion Atlas to follow me to the mansion steps. He follows, and I stop on the bottom step, looking at him. Ah, this is better; the step gives me some additional height. The rest can still hear, but I don't really care. At least the Rossi giants aren't surrounding me. Atlas looks down at the bag in his hand.

"I won't keep you for long. This is just a little something for you. I'm sorry, I didn't know you had a son, or I would have made sure to get him something, too," he explains, holding the bag out to me. Accepting it, I smile, and he shoves his hands into his pockets.

"Don't apologise, it's not like I told you. You didn't even need to get me anything, but thanks," I reply with a small smirk. He runs his hand through his hair.

"Thanks... for reaching out to me."

I look down at the bag, then glance at the Rossi men, watching Rayhan and Leo conversing before they shake hands. I smile softly and look at Atlas. We did the right thing.

"I'm glad I did."

He is about to speak when the mansion door opens, and Song steps out, busy texting on her phone. She is so lost in her phone that she doesn't realise there are steps and falls face forward, stumbling as she slips on the stairs.

"Whoa!" I exclaim, making to grab her, only for Atlas to catch hold of her. She snatches hold of his shirt, her heart thundering as she slowly regains her balance, his hands supporting her waist. Atlas slowly lets go of her.

"Easy there." She glances up at him, her eyes widening as she stares up at him. My eyebrow shoots up, and I clear my throat.

"This is Atlas," I introduce. Her eyes widen, and she nods, jumping back, almost stumbling over the bottom step. If Atlas didn't grab hold of her elbow, I am sure she would have been knocked on her ass again.

"Oh, hey!" she says, her cheeks tinged pink. "I mean, thank you!"

It is amusing seeing her so flustered. She waves at him before looking as if she wants to kick herself. *Ah, babe, I'm not going to let this slide. First Rayhan, now Atlas? The girl needs to get laid.* Smirking at my own thoughts, I cross my arms.

Atlas smiles slightly, holding his hand out to her.

"It's nice to meet you..." he trails off, and Song smacks her forehead.

"Oh, yeah, sorry, I haven't introduced myself. I'm Song."

"Nice to meet you," he says as I see Leo getting Corrado into the car.

"Come on, Mommy!"

My heart skips a beat. Last night he called me 'Mommy' without Azura once, and I loved it, but I thought he hadn't realised and had done so by accident.

"Coming!" I call, turning to Atlas and raising the bag. "Thanks for these, and I'll definitely keep in touch." He nods as we look at each other, almost as if waiting for the other to make the first move. Oh, for fuck's sake! Stepping forward, I give him a quick, awkward hug around the shoulders. I am about to move away when he gives me a gentle squeeze. I really am glad we did this.

He lets go of me and gives me another smile.

"Take care of yourself."

"You, too. I'll be fine," I say confidently before Alejandro calls us.

"You three fucking done?" I roll my eyes, and Atlas smiles slightly.

"Coming! Are you desperate to get rid of me?" I question as we walk over.

"Nah, but I just realised you three got some weird shit for names."

"What do you mean? I like my name," Song protests.

"A song, atlas, and a colour," Alejandro smirks.

Maybe I need to staple gun his ass, too. Oh my god, imagine if Alejandro has a pierced dick! Wait, does he? Eww, I don't want to know! Gross, gross!

Yeah, why the fuck are you even thinking about that shit? Leo's voice comes through the link. Shit, these damn walls. I need to really question Selene about the right to privacy.

Hey, don't make me sound like I'm weird, I just have a very advanced overactive imagination. I bet you men think of women's boobs and stuff. I feel a sliver of jealousy at just the thought.

Na, not once have I wondered who has what piercing or what fucking wax they got going on. Unless it comes to you. You're really something else, you know that? I smirk smugly. I have the perfect comeback.

Of course, I am. I'm the Heart of Fire, I cackle, hugging Kiara tightly. **Something totally special.**

I'm going to hear that often, aren't I?

Absolutely.

Once I have said goodbye to the Rossis, I get into the car. Alessandra isn't around, but I met her in the morning before she left. Leo leans over, shutting the door for me and kissing me softly. I kiss him back before he straps me in, and we begin our journey. We will drop Song off at home and then return home.

We dropped Song off over an hour ago and stopped at the service station for McDonald's. It has taken a little longer with an accident on the motorway, but we should be home within the hour.

Home. I smile softly, sitting back in my seat as I finish my fries off. Corrado has fallen asleep in the back after eating. Leo is tracing circles on my thigh, making sparks dance, his eyes on the road.

"Any ideas exactly how I will heal you? Maybe you have to, like, drink my blood." He cocks an eyebrow, smirking, and I know before he even opens that sexy mouth of his, he is going to mock me. I shove a few fries into his mouth. "Don't you dare," I warn. He swallows and is about to reply when his phone rings. He accepts the call as the music lowers.

"Leo, you need to get back here!" Jax's voice is strained. My heart lurches as I wonder what is going on. I have never heard Jax sound so… distraught? Leo's heart is racing, and his entire body looks tense.

"Update." His voice is icy as he slams his foot on the accelerator, speeding up. I am thrown back into my seat as the speed increases super fast. I can hear shouting in the background of the call. Jax takes a shaky breath.

"Three is down."

Suddenly Leo's face pales, and his foot hits the brake, making the car jolt. A horn blares from behind, and we narrowly miss the lorry as Leo pulls us back into our lane, speeding up again. My heart is thundering as Corrado stirs in the back. Three? Who is three?

"Jax, what happened?" I ask.

"Shane… he's dead." His voice barely hides his anguish, making my blood run cold. Turning to Leo, I realise he has just lost another loved one. Leo's eyes are blazing.

"What happened?" The passing cars are a blur as he rushes to get back.

"He and Dan were performing some tests-"

"She's dead… *fuck*!" Ace's voice comes from the background.

"Shit… Leo, get back here. I'll tell you everything then."

"No, tell me, who is Ace talking about?" Leo threatens. His heart is thundering no matter how in control he is acting.

"Jackie. She tried to sedate him, but he… fuck. I'm sorry, Leo, but she's dead."

My heart sinks, horror enveloping me, and my ears ring. Leo's shock and pain begin seeping through the bond, mixing with my own. I know they were close, but the pain I am feeling in my chest is intense. She was dear to him. Like a sister to him.

Tears sting my eyes as memories of them as children flash in my head. Him promising to be there for her always...

My heart bleeds for the man I love. He has just lost two of his closest people in the blink of an eye... just when he has begun mending his broken bonds. She will never know that Leo will be okay. I never got to thank her for caring. She had an entire future in front of her... I wish I had called her last night. Goddess...

I run my shaking fingers through my hair as Leo begins questioning Jax.

"... Details now." His voice is so cold and void of emotions that I almost don't recognise it. How is he able to hide his pain? I feel his walls go up, and once more, he is in alpha-mode.

"Dan and Shane were conducting some tests; we were all fucking there, this shouldn't have happened, but... I don't fuckin-"

"Fuck it, get to the point," Ace's voice comes in a menacing growl, but it is his next words that shake me to the core. "Judah, the dead guy, well, he wasn't fucking dead. He's gone, Leo, and I'll tell you one fucking thing. He ain't no werewolf."

Those words sink in, settling into the pit of my stomach, the sheer weight of what has just happened shocking me to the very core.

Will I ever see the end of Judah, or will he forever torment me? That is until he destroys me completely because he's coming.

He's coming for me.

To be continued...

Read on in <u>Leo Rossi: The Rise of a True Alpha</u> for the conclusion of Leo and Azura's explosive romance.

Enjoy the book?
Support the Author by leaving a review on
Amazon, Goodreads and Goodnovel

SIGN UP FOR MY NEWSLETTER

*Be the first to know about new book releases,
see behind the scenes content and much more:*
http://bit.ly/moonlightmuse

TO LEARN WHERE TO FIND MORE OF MY WORKS

Website: *authormoonlightmuse.com*
Linktree: *Author.Muse*
Instagram: *author.muse*
Facebook: *author.moonlight.muse*

Made in the USA
Las Vegas, NV
07 April 2025

20643071R00267